Theory *of* Remainders

A NOVEL

BY SCOTT DOMINIC CARPENTER

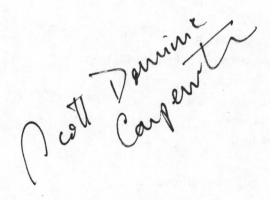

Winter Goose Publishing

Winter Goose Publishing
2701 Del Paso Road, 130-92
Sacramento, CA 95835

www.wintergoosepublishing.com
Contact Information: info@wintergoosepublishing.com

Theory of Remainders

COPYRIGHT © 2013 Scott Dominic Carpenter

Hardback: 978-0-9889049-0-3
Paperback: 978-0-9889049-1-0
Library of Congress Control Number: 2013931120

Cover Art by Winter Goose Publishing
Photograph by Paul Carpenter
Typeset by Michelle Lovi

Published in the United States of America

Other Books By Scott Dominic Carpenter

Fiction

This Jealous Earth: Stories

Nonfiction

Aesthetics of Fraudulence in Nineteenth-Century France: Frauds, Hoaxes and Counterfeits

Reading Lessons

Acts of Fiction

"No mortal can keep a secret"—*Sigmund Freud*

One

The more a patient cried out for his attention, the less Philip Adler was inclined to give it. Right now, for example, he sat slouched in his chair, his back to the desk, his chin resting on his palm, fingertips lost in the nap of his salt-and-pepper beard. He was contemplating the empty stares of three masks mounted on the wall over his couch—an African scowl with its mouth open in a hoot, a sand-colored Japanese Noh face, and a South American fox with a narrow snout.

Below them, hunched at the far end of the sofa, sat a glowering sixteen-year-old girl, her skeletal joints jutting beneath a black T-shirt and black skinny jeans. Even her hair was dyed black, and coal-like mascara ringed her narrowed eyes. Wrenched toward the end table, she held her crossed arms tight against her fists.

When she darted a glance in Philip's direction, he dropped his gaze to the notepad on his thigh and began rounding out a doodle of bulging shapes, which he now enhanced with—why not?—tentacles. He shaded the curves with cross-hatching.

He wasn't insensitive to Melanie Patterson's plight. To the contrary. But if she wished to speak, it had to be because there was something to say. He didn't want her playing to his curiosity. It needed to be about her and not about him.

So far they'd gone thirty minutes without Melanie uttering a word. He'd always considered sessions a bit like chess games where the patient played white—with the obligation of the first move. For now he continued etching thin strokes with his pen. Drawing relaxed him, easing the pressure that formed low in his chest every time he dealt with adolescent girls in his practice.

By the time Melanie broke the silence, he was zeroing in on completion of the artwork.

"You're *not* my fucking father, you know," she sneered into the arm of the sofa.

His pen paused. Her phrase had punched down the clock, and now it was his turn. He let half a minute pass before leaning forward in his seat, arching a bushy eyebrow. "You're right about that," he nodded. "I'm not your father."

Just a pawn. One space. He settled back in his chair. Her move.

Melanie emitted a snort of disdain and twisted even further away, glaring at the end table where a book about lighthouses and an untouched glass of water rested by a sculpture of an African woman. From this angle Philip could see the marks on her rail-thin forearm where she'd been cutting herself.

No, he certainly was not Melanie's father. Oh, he had met Neil Patterson, all right, a conspicuously jocular man who had done all the talking while his round-shouldered wife sat with her purse clutched in her lap. Patterson had stepped up and pumped Philip's hand at the introductions, his eyes thinning while he parsed the doctor's name. Then had come the explanation about his daughter's *issues*, the wink as he complained about *kids today*, the wag of the head over the lack of self-discipline. He and Cindy had done everything for Melanie!

Bluster. The real problem, Philip had understood immediately, was this man, the one falling all over himself to come across as normal, better than normal, indeed, superb in his Brioni suit and Moreschi shoes. And yet there wasn't a chance in hell that this CFO of a newly listed technology firm would kick his feet up on a psychiatrist's couch. It was bad enough having his daughter in treatment. It was the wife who had pushed for it, and only after Melanie's first hospitalization.

Since Philip wouldn't have access to the source of the problem, he worked indirectly with its effect: this troubled girl, clenched with anger and fear, who, after six weeks still didn't know if she could trust him. Until and unless Melanie decided to open up, he wouldn't be able to help her—which he could do precisely because he was not her father. No more than he was anyone else's.

He winced. The knot in his gut was back and the doodling no longer sufficed to soothe him. His eyes wandered over a collection of pre-Columbian vessels—chubby little pottery monsters. Above them hung a pair of paintings that squawked with color. Near the corner, a glass cabinet held terra cotta figurines, after which came the polished stones, three potted plants, the plush drapes.

Usually this office served as a machine for the imagination, but today it felt musty and staid. What drew his eye instead was the window. The office faced north, and down past the highway, beyond the park, the wings of sailboats fluttered on the surface of the Charles River under a blue sky. A motorboat chugged down the middle. People had left their offices early, were getting a head start on the weekend. People for whom free time was a blessing.

Melanie shifted on the couch and dug her foot into the fringe of the Persian rug. Still she didn't speak. That was fine by him. He was an expert at waiting. Besides, time had a different value inside these four walls, and silence wasn't always empty. Some patients needed to build up to speaking, the way you take a running start before a leap. They'd hold out until the very end, delaying until it was almost too late, when any new topic would have to be left for the next session. He called it the Columbo moment—that instant when the patient, one foot out the door, paused, scratched behind his ear, and turned back around. *You know*, he'd say, *there's just one little thing that bothers me . . .*

Melanie grunted with impatience. There was so little flesh on her bones that Philip could make out the fibers of muscle as she tightened her jaw. No doubt he was meant to see this, just as she made sure he noticed every glance at her watch or roll of her eyes. It was quite a performance.

"Are you really going to, like, make me sit here the whole *fucking* time?" she said to the wall.

His move. "That's what we agreed to. Last week you said you'd try."

"That was last week," she shot back.

"Are you saying that something has changed?"

She snorted again and shook her head in disbelief.

He was pretty sure it was a *you-don't-know-the-half-of-it* snort, and he considered telling her as much. "Would you like to talk about it?" he asked instead.

"It's none of your fucking business."

"I'm just trying to help."

She gave a sharp laugh. "Right. Just what my dad would say."

He paused. "Really? What do you mean by that?"

But Melanie had turned away, pulling her legs up onto the couch and putting her head to her knees, her stick fingers buried in her stringy hair.

"Why won't you speak to me, Melanie?"

"Leave me alone," came the muffled cry.

His pieces were in position, and it was time to press. He leaned forward, resting his elbows on his knees. "I'd like to, but your parents are afraid you'll hurt yourself again. Frankly, so am I. Give me something to work with."

She growled.

"Oh, come on," he said.

Now came a thin roar of frustration. She was shaking her fists in the air and glaring at him. "You want something to work with? I'll *give* you something to work with." Her right arm whipped out with surprising speed, and Philip heard a clunk. A flapping mass with gray-white wings careened over his head, smacked into the wall, and collapsed. He swiveled around to examine the corpse. It was the book from the end table.

"How about that," she cried.

"Ah," he nodded. "Now we're getting somewhere." And he meant it. The moment of the transference was crucial.

"Getting somewhere!" Melanie howled. She leapt up on her spindly legs and whirled about. This time it was the water glass in her hand—a heavy-bottomed affair that could do real damage.

Philip was so busy studying the rage in her eyes that he forgot to duck. Luckily she threw like someone who had never pitched a ball in her life, so the glass ended up too far to the right, smashing against the wall between his framed diploma and the clock. He got off easy, catching only a spray of water.

It was good to see her letting loose—this could be productive—but he needed to keep it from getting out of hand. "Now that's enough," he said, deepening his voice.

"Don't tell me what's enough." She turned to arm herself again, but the only weapon left on the end table was the African sculpture of a long-necked woman with prominent breasts. It stood nearly three feet high, and Melanie needed both hands to lift it from the metal rod supporting it.

At this sight, Philip rose to his feet. Usually he tried to downplay his height, but now he stretched to his full six-foot-three, maximizing the illusion of authority. It was time to put his foot down before somebody got hurt. Besides, he liked that sculpture, had spent a long time choosing it.

"Put that down," he ordered.

She glared at him through slitted lids. "No."

"*Now.*"

"*Make me.*"

He took a step forward, but Melanie raised the wooden figure higher, threatening to heave it in his direction. Given how bad her aim was, he wouldn't even have a chance to catch it. Not daring to go forward, he also couldn't retreat. Melanie's eyes shone with triumph, accompanied by a flicker of anxiety. What should he do? If he backed down, she would find herself in charge, which was exactly where she didn't want to be. But if he didn't step back, she'd be compelled to sling this sculpture—a collector's piece, very expensive—at the one person who was trying to help her, which wouldn't do either of them any good. They were in a stalemate. A terribly interesting one, Philip reckoned, but a stalemate nonetheless.

A knock came at the door. At least, that's what it sounded like—though in twenty-five years of consultations, no one had ever interrupted one of Philip's meetings with a patient. Sessions were sacred. He wasn't sure he'd heard right. Perhaps the noise had come from the wall or ceiling, the clanking of a pipe or the clatter of heels upstairs. But Melanie, too, looked toward the office door, confusion in her eyes. The spell had been broken, and he wasn't sure he could conjure it back.

Three sharp raps sounded again, more insistently. The battle of the titans evaporated, and now there were just two people, a girl and a man, Melanie Patterson and Philip Adler, the little one and the tall one, the one with a wooden sculpture and the one without, both feeling a touch ridiculous. They exchanged a look and Philip cracked a smile. A sputter of laughter escaped from Melanie, nearly causing her to drop her weapon.

The knob turned and the door opened a few inches, breaking the seal of the vault. In the crack Philip made out the drawn features of Linda Durrell, whom he and Jonas had recently hired. What could have possessed her to interrupt him now? Was it Melanie's shrieks? The broken glass?

"I'm *terribly* sorry to bother you," came the thin voice as Linda widened the opening. Her eyes slid to the left, taking in Melanie doubled over with laughter, one hand still gripping the neck of the sculpture.

Philip straightened his smile, and while he spoke, Melanie labored to contain herself. "We're fine, Linda," he said. "Our discussion grew a little animated, and Melanie, she . . . she . . . dropped a water glass." He glanced at his patient, whose lips bulged with mirth, trembling like a flooded levee about to give way. She was a beautiful girl, really, when she gave herself half a chance. "Against the wall," he clarified.

Melanie exploded with laughter.

Linda looked at the floor. "It's not that, Dr. Adler," she said. "I'm used to . . ." she hesitated. "What I mean is, I know I shouldn't interrupt your appointments." She fiddled with a pleat in her skirt.

"It's all right," he told her. "No harm done."

"There's a woman on the phone, Dr. Adler."

He squinted. It was an absurd statement. They didn't interrupt sessions every time the phone rang. That was the whole point of having a receptionist.

"Couldn't you take a message?"

"She says it's important."

"Can't Jonas handle it? After all, I'm rather—"

"I'm *really* sorry," Linda said, her face pained, "but she asked for you personally. She . . . she won't talk to anyone else."

He was completely flummoxed. "Right this instant?"

She closed the fingers of both hands into small fists, relaxed them, and closed them again. "You see," she said, "it's . . . your wife, Dr. Adler."

He gaped. While he searched for words, Melanie's snickering petered out.

"Yes sir," Linda nodded with vigor. "That's what she said."

While Linda and Melanie exchanged a glance, Philip pressed his professional smile back in place. "Of course. Thank you, Linda." He turned to Melanie. "Would you excuse me for a moment?"

He crossed the threshold into the beige plainness of the reception area, exposed by glass doors to the fifth-floor lobby. At Linda's desk he reached out for the phone, hesitating at the last instant as if it were too hot to grasp. It was impossible. There was no Mrs. Philip Adler. Hadn't been for—he did the quick calculation—nearly thirteen years.

He picked up the handset and studied it like an unfamiliar object before raising it to his ear.

"Hello?" he said. "Hello?" Then he listened. All at once he stood a bit straighter. "Yes, it's me." Again it was his turn to listen. Now he felt himself sinking, and he braced himself against the desk. The next time he spoke his voice had softened. "*Calme-toi*," he said in heavily accented French. "*Calme-toi*."

A series of beeps jostled Philip from his stupor, the noise coming from the telephone he still clutched, and that had tired of humming its dial tone. He hadn't moved, but was short of breath. How long had he stood there after she hung up?

At the sound of footsteps he turned to see Melanie escape through the glass door of the reception area, her backpack slung over her bony shoulders as she made a break for it, crossing the lobby to the elevator. While waiting for the getaway vehicle, she avoided his gaze. He understood why. She'd seen him on the phone, had witnessed his contraction from a doctor into a man. Her downturned eyes were a sign of embarrassment. For him.

He'd let her go for now. They would line up their pieces next week and start the game afresh.

Meanwhile, the way to his office was blocked by Linda, her eyes wide with questions he didn't want to answer. So he forced a smile and made for the only exit left to him—the door opposite his own. Rapping once, he slipped in as the voice called for him to enter.

What greeted him was the back of Jonas Seeberg's head, curls of dark hair springing chaotically, a bulge of neck showing above the back of the chair. Papers and books cluttered most of the surfaces, including the floor. Jonas sat hunched over a stack of files on his lap, running his fingers over the tabs, flicking through them one by one. "Good grief," he muttered. "It was here a minute ago."

Philip sank onto the leather couch, a manila folder lying on the cushion beside him. After letting Jonas hunt, he reached over, picked the file up, and prodded his partner's arm with it.

The other man swiveled around and stared at the offering. His eyes brightened. "Where'd you find that? Like a needle in a goddamned haystack."

He began to paw through the papers on his desk. "Oh, for Pete's sake. Now I can't find the notes I have to put in there. I'm telling you, Philip, I need a personal assistant. Someone who can—" He halted, sat up straight, and rotated back around in his chair. "Say, what are you doing in here, anyway?"

He shrugged. "I need an excuse?"

"Wasn't that glass I heard breaking in your office a little while ago?"

He swept the question aside with the back of his hand. "You know how it goes. Sometimes you do your best work when things get a touch out of control." He cast about for an appropriate image. "I put us into a controlled skid."

"Sounded like a patch of ice."

Philip pictured Melanie about to lob the sculpture at him. Yes, perhaps things had gone too far. He could admit that. But sometimes you had to take a chance. He checked his watch. Linda would have returned to her desk by now, and probably he could sneak back into his office. He stood. "I'll let you get back to your hunting and gathering."

"That's it?" Jonas said. "You slink in here, find my files for me and then vanish? What is this—*The Elves and the Shoemaker?*" His eyes thinned. "What's going on?"

He shook his head. Nothing was going on. Nothing except that he had a three o'clock coming in, then two more patients after that—all before he could start the day's paperwork. He headed for the door, but with each step he slowed, finally pausing and closing his eyes as he came to a stop.

"Yvonne called," he said.

Jonas leaned back in his chair, absorbing the information. "You don't say?"

"Anne-Madeleine has passed away. Her mother. My mother-in-law."

"Your *ex*-mother-in-law."

Philip ignored the correction. "Not really a surprise, of course, at eighty-two. Still, the news comes as a blow."

Jonas folded his hands over his belly, waiting.

"She didn't need to call, I suppose," Philip continued. "Probably a letter would have been enough."

"You mean you don't intend to go back for the funeral?"

Philip looked up. "Now? All the way to France?"

Jonas responded by cocking his head and raising his eyebrows.

"Don't be absurd," Philip said. An ache was starting in his temple.

"How long has it been, Philip? A decade? You were pretty close to her, weren't you?"

"I suppose so. Yes. Despite everything."

"Are you all right?"

"A little numb, maybe. Taken off my guard." He paused. "It's Yvonne I feel for. She sounded . . . shaken."

"You should go, you know."

Philip began a vague protest about his schedule, his responsibilities, his patients. Jonas cut him off.

"Don't use work as an excuse. You know people would understand. Even patient-type people."

That much was right. What would it be, two or three days? Jonas could handle any emergencies. Work was not the problem. "It's ridiculously rushed," he said. "I'd have to leave tomorrow in order to make it."

"Great. Then you won't have time to fret about the flight."

He ran his fingers through his beard. "What I mean is, I don't see what it would accomplish."

"I guess you'll find out."

He shook his head. "Look, I didn't come in here for advice. I just wanted you to know." He took the last step toward the door and laid his hand on the knob.

"Is she still teaching?" Jonas wanted to know.

He stiffened. "Probably."

"Probably?"

The ache in his temple pulsed. "I mean, yes. I think so. In Rouen. At the university."

"Remarried?"

This was the last straw. He turned and looked Jonas in the eye. "How should I know? She hasn't gone out of her way to keep in touch. I don't exactly get their Christmas newsletter."

Jonas held his gaze.

Philip looked away. "Yes. They have a child."

The silence ripened.

"A daughter?" Jonas said. He raised his hands to defend against Philip's reaction. "We were both thinking it," he said. "One of us had to say it."

Not so, Philip thought as he stared down at the carpet. Jonas knew as well as he what a useful role repression could play in people's lives.

"You should go," Jonas said. "Take some time."

Philip closed his eyes and shook his head. No, time was the last thing in the world he was inclined to take.

Two

It was nearly dark when Philip trudged up the steps of the subway station, briefcase in hand. Halfway down the block he stopped at a Chinese restaurant, soon reappearing with a white sack. Two blocks further along he let himself into the brick apartment building.

In the mirrored wall of the entryway he saw a bearded man with tired eyes, over the crest of middle age, lugging a briefcase and a carry-out bag, his necktie askew. This image of himself was reflected again from the wall behind, back and forth between the two mirrors, producing an infinite number of Philip Adlers receding into the distance. Who was this man really? In the psychology of childhood development, the mirror stage was well documented: when the infant recognizes his own reflection, the identification plays a crucial role in the formation of the ego. But what about adults, especially those who are past their prime? When Philip glanced into a mirror these days, it was hardly identification that awaited him. Each time, the man looking back was a little less familiar.

Yvonne, too, would have aged. But she'd have managed it more gracefully than he—just as she did everything else.

He would send a card, some flowers. That much was possible. But she shouldn't expect anything more from him.

In the apartment upstairs he flicked on the light and entered a broad living room banked with windows, one side lined with shelves, the other adorned with framed photographs. Like his office, the apartment was filled with objects, but unlike his office, this more personal museum appeared to have been ransacked. Newspapers and discarded clothing obscured the sleek lines of the furniture. Used glasses and coffee mugs stood on the desk and end table. Dirty plates were stacked in twos and threes, silverware heaped on top. On the floor by the sofa lay shoes and slippers, abandoned where he had cast them off.

During the workweek, disorder established beachheads in Philip's life, creeping forward and outflanking him. Every weekend he beat it back to a safe distance.

"Edith?" he called as he parked his briefcase by the desk. "Edith? Where are you?"

Out of the dark bedroom trotted a slim Calico cat, a mask of black surrounding one eye, the other ringed with tan. She stepped primly forward, her nose twitching.

He held up the sack. "Chicken chow mein. Our favorite."

She rubbed against his ankles. Philip knew this was a simulacrum of affection, one designed to hasten the presentation of his offering, but he didn't mind. To the contrary, he relished Edith's uncompromising catliness, her unapologetic feline narcissism. By the measure of the Hare Checklist for anti-social disorders, all cats would be psychopaths. And yet, such endearing ones!

He scooped a serving of food into her bowl, and stroked the back of her neck as she began to eat. Dishing up his own serving, he carried his plate out to the sofa, settled in, and clicked the remote. On the screen an attractive woman stood before a group of assistants, writing on a white board as she brandished a Ziploc bag with her free hand. A detective series. Some mystery. He tried another channel, only to find a nearly identical show. The characters were interchangeable, the dialogue inane.

As he cracked apart the wooden chopsticks, a word leapt into his mind like a spark: *baguettes*. It was the French term—not just for long loaves of bread but also for these tiny utensils. A detail Yvonne had taught him many years ago.

How strange it had been to hear her voice again today. The tight vowels, the purring R. She had started to address him calmly in English, but after he spoke, something broke inside of her, and then only French had poured out, interrupted by heaving breaths. Even Yvonne's sob was familiar. How many times had he heard that in the months leading up to the divorce?

He stiffened. Probably she knew what effect her voice would have on him. Perhaps she'd slipped into French right on cue. He wasn't going to fall for it. She had no right to disturb him. No right to ask for anything anymore.

On TV a woman (was it the first one?) rode in a car with a burly black colleague, tracking a pick-up truck that had begun to accelerate. Tires squealed, and as the vehicle raced around a curve, two wheels lifting from the pavement, Melanie Patterson came to mind. A controlled skid. Side-slipping like that was dangerous. People died that way.

He clicked off the set and started his rounds through the apartment, collecting dishes and newspapers. The current issue of the *American Journal of Psychiatry* lay on an end table, the cover bearing a brown halo from a coffee cup.

The desk was strewn with the week's mail, including bills for magazines that had accumulated unread in a stack on the floor. He cleared off the chair and woke the computer. On the chess website there was an alert. Faruk89 had made a new move: Nf4. On the screen, where their dwindling armies occupied the checkered terrain, Philip reviewed the black knight's new position, squinting hard. What was Faruk89 up to now? It seemed like such a harmless position. A little too harmless. According to his profile, Faruk89 lived in Istanbul, and although they'd only recently been matched via the website, Philip already recognized him as a formidable opponent. Worst of all, he suspected that 89 was Faruk's birth year, the proverbial Young Turk reminding Philip he was losing his edge. So far he'd managed to keep the youngster at bay by springing surprises, making unpredictable moves that were highly risky but disconcerting. He'd have to give Nf4 some thought.

In the bedroom he plucked up dirty clothes under the watchful eyes of his parents, who presided in a photo on the wall, a shot of the three of them when Philip was only fifteen—Max stout in his black suit, his arm on his son's shoulder, his mother in that absurd hat, clutching his hand in both of hers, crowding against him with an eager smile. Cautious people, they'd been. *Don't be showy*, his father had always said. *Keep a low profile.* They'd lived through the forties, after all, had seen what could happen to their kind, and they'd taken self-effacement to the extreme, nearly allowing their branch of the Adler line to die out unnoticed.

In another frame the three of them stood under an oak tree after his college graduation, his parents already looking old. It was the last shot he had of the family together. Within eighteen months they would both be dead. Heart disease for one and cancer for the other, at least according to the certificates. Philip knew the real cause of death: terminal fretfulness.

He straightened the photographs on the wall and collected coffee mugs from the bedside table. The apartment was coming together. He'd do the laundry tomorrow, but in the kitchen he packed the dishwasher with a week's worth of plates and cutlery. The dishes looked especially plain this evening.

Nothing like the breakfast bowls they used to keep in the kitchen in Paris—creamy, gentle pieces, well proportioned, with a curve of just the right depth for two hands to cup around. For years he and Yvonne, and then Sophie too, had greeted the morning with those bowls, in the French way, filled to the brim with coffee or hot chocolate.

The dishtowel draped over his shoulder, he leaned against the counter like a man steadying himself at the railing of a ship.

It was after the death of his mother that Philip had left for Paris, taking on a residency at the American Hospital. It had felt like the opportunity for a new life, especially when, two months later, he met a French girl at a party. The start hadn't been promising. "Are you British?" she'd asked as he butchered her language. "No, American." "I see," she'd replied with a smirk, "I guess nobody's perfect." Yvonne didn't like Americans, felt they were shallow and had no sense of history. He'd labored hard to overcome that bias, finally earning her begrudging respect by sheer doggedness. And only later her affection.

All for what? So that they could march hand in hand toward the catastrophe that awaited them? *Nobody's perfect.* Perhaps he should have listened to that assessment on Day One.

From the coffee table he picked up two books and returned them to the wall of shelving, shoving them into the available crannies. Someday he would deal with this, too: the old set of encyclopedias, the obsolete textbooks, the well-thumbed novels. Nothing but ballast, all of it, ready to be tossed.

Take some time, Jonas had said. But time was Philip's enemy, and he did all he could to fill his schedule as tightly as these shelves.

Take some time.

He sighed. Anne-Madeleine had been a fine woman, full of spirit. And she'd accepted him, a foreigner, into her family—had eased his membership into the Aubert clan, with Roger, Évelyne, Flora, and their assorted spouses. And now she was gone.

Yes, Jonas was right: he should take some time. But only a little. Granting Anne-Madeleine his attention would be like pulling at a loose thread: the whole fabric could start to run. But he owed her this.

Kneeling down, he retrieved a leather-bound photo album from the bottom shelf and settled onto the couch. He rolled his tongue through his mouth, feeling the tug of an old thirst, but dispatched the thought as soon as he recognized it. No. Now he was to focus on the pages in front of him.

The very first images were shots of Paris: a broad avenue with mansard-roofed apartment buildings; a café bustling with customers and aproned male servers; statuary in a small park; a wrought-iron gate. Then came a much younger Philip Adler standing with a group outside a restaurant, his eyes on an attractive woman, dark-haired, with high cheekbones.

He remembered the excitement of that evening—the night he had first curved his hand around her waist. He recalled Yvonne's laugh, their shared sense that they were opening a door on something wholly new in their lives.

Then came the family home in Yvetot. Yvonne's brother, Roger. The party after her dissertation defense. A handful of wedding pictures fluttered by, then a jumble of shots of apartments and friends.

The album was an incomplete narrative, a blighted sample, like the scraps of family life a tornado strews over cornfields, miles from the disaster. Most of the photos were torn at the edges, bearing pushpin holes in their corners, or residue from Scotch tape—refugees from the earlier homes of bulletin boards, refrigerator doors, scrap books.

He skipped ahead and found the picture he wanted, showing Anne-Madeleine and her already elderly husband, Guillaume, on the front steps of the home in Yvetot, their children and in-laws gathered around.

Now Philip hesitated. He'd reached a limit, and if he went further the slope could become too steep. He risked losing his footing, and then the only way out would be through the very bottom. But like a drunkard already on his third drink, he had no power to stop. There was no sense pretending. He turned the page.

It was the picture of an infant: a slip of a swaddled body, lying on Yvonne's chest. Philip's eyes rested there for a long moment before he lurched ahead, turning the leaves of the album faster and faster, as though hurrying to be done with it. The infant grew into a toddler, the toddler became a preschooler. A few pages later Philip came across his younger self trotting alongside a ten-year-old girl pedaling madly on a bicycle. They were on a dirt path, the one he remembered from Yvetot. In this picture he reached out to the seat while the girl batted him away, wanting to do it all herself. Yes, he thought, that captured her spirit.

Through the next pages the girl matured. In one shot she stood in a tennis

skirt, racket in one hand, the other palm angled against her hip, an impertinent smirk on her face. In another she held up her right arm encased in plaster,
brandishing the cast like a trophy, her eyes wide and mocking.

The last one was a photographic trick. It showed the same girl in a double
profile, face to face, the two noses only an inch apart. As he tipped the page to
the right, he no longer saw the silhouettes, but rather the space between them,
a black, vessel-shaped outline. Faces or vase—that old illusion. He remembered how they'd set that picture up using a wardrobe mirror and work lights.
Yvonne had accused them of insanity, but he and his daughter had giggled
their way through, delighted with the result.

Then came the blank, black pages at the end, one after another.

Was it really his daughter he remembered, or just these reproductions of
her? In some way he supposed it didn't matter, for the mechanics of emotion
were the same. He knew how it worked. Stimuli reached his amygdala and
sent impulses to his hypothalamus, which in turn triggered the sympathetic
nervous system. His chest would contract and his pulse quicken, the result of
simple cause and effect.

Tucked inside the back cover were newspaper clippings, now yellowed and
brittle, and he unfolded them carefully on the coffee table, the snippets of
headlines forming a collage of words: *Sophie Adler . . . portée disparue . . . la
police enquête . . . Édouard Morin . . . inculpé . . . non-lieu.* Many clippings bore
the date: 1993. A few included grainy photos of his daughter.

He shook his head. He didn't need to read the articles. Fifteen years ago a
man named Édouard Morin had cut through his life like a scythe. What would
returning to France now accomplish?

In the fourteen years, ten months, and seven days since his daughter's
death, Philip had managed to recreate something resembling a life. It had
been a halting and fragile process, a bit like building a ship in a bottle when
you have neither the right tools nor the proper materials. But gradually he'd
assembled the masts and rigging of an existence, had glued the parts in place.
He'd even learned to deal once again with adolescent girls in his practice. Girls
like Melanie Patterson.

He knew perfectly well how trauma maimed people's minds, no less completely than weapons or heavy machinery mangled their bodies, leaving them
scarred and damaged. But sometimes it's better to hobble forward. After all,

you can't undo the past. A large part of Philip's job consisted of helping people come to terms with that lesson.

He looked at his watch. It was late. However, it was also Friday night, so he didn't need to worry about sleep. He might not feel good about it the next day, but morning was a long ways off. He could sit with the pictures just a little longer, and then he would lay it all to rest once again.

Three

The woman seated to his left had slumped against the window, snoring softly. The man to his right, a corpulent, unshaven specimen, chuckled out loud at a film on a tiny screen, shifting his elbow to conquer what remained of the armrest. Philip's knees were splayed to make room for the fully reclined seat in front of him. His long frame didn't fit well in these contraptions.

He hated flying. Feared it. It was an irrational panic, made no less dire by his knowledge of its irrationality. When patients asked for help with their own aviophobia, as it was called in the *DSM,* he tried to fob them off on a colleague. If they insisted on working with him, he didn't hesitate to pull out his pad and write them a script for Xanax. The more, the better.

So he was not heartened by the information presented on his personal screen. The last thing he needed was this constant reminder they were hurtling through the stratosphere at 553 miles per hour.

It had been a struggle to get out on time. Jonas had agreed to take care of matters at the office, and Linda was rescheduling appointments. Philip had called some of his more vulnerable patients himself to let them know he'd be away, that Jonas would be on call. He'd even e-mailed Faruk89 to let him know their game would be suspended. He didn't want to leave anyone in the lurch.

The Xanax left him parched, and it hadn't even taken effect yet. People around him had drugged themselves with wine and beer, even indulging in after-dinner cognacs. He'd felt a pull in that direction himself. After all, who would be the wiser if he had a drink here? Moreover, who could blame him? He looked about in hopes of spotting a flight attendant.

A woman in a blue uniform swayed down the darkened aisle collecting empty cups. When she reached Philip's row, he leaned toward her across the belly of his neighbor. "Any chance I could get a scotch?" he asked in a hushed tone. The words felt strange on his tongue.

"I'm sorry?" she replied in accented English. The thrumming of the engine had absorbed most of his request.

Her voice soothed something in him, and he reined himself in, amending his order as he translated it. "*Je voudrais un verre d'eau, s'il vous plaît.*"

She smiled. "*Vous parlez français.*"

"*Je le parlais,*" he replied, settling back in his seat. "*Dans le temps.*"

Je le parlais. That was about right. Not *I spoke*, but *I used to speak*. Conjugated in the imperfect, the tense of habitual activities and unfinished actions in the past—a past that still felt utterly remote, even while the distance separating him from it closed at over 500 miles per hour.

The flight attendant fetched him a cup and he took a long gulp. As she moved ahead and leaned toward another passenger, he admired her blue-uniformed flank, the curve of her calf. He closed his eyes. The Xanax was finally kicking in, forming a pleasing fog.

He drifted into a zone close to unconsciousness, deeper than reverie but not as remote as dream. It felt awkward in his mouth now, this language that he'd struggled to master, whose foreignness had been like an obstacle course leaving him bruised and scraped—but cautiously victorious. French had become for him a kind of *open sesame*, a charm revealing a magical cavern of otherness. When he'd gone to France—what was it now, nearly twenty-seven years ago?—he'd been looking to escape so many things: his family, his Jewishness, a failed relationship. He'd been modern enough and naïve enough—in short, *American* enough—to think that he could really get away, that he might actually refashion himself. Worst of all, he'd tricked himself into thinking it had worked. In Paris he'd branched out. He'd gone to museums and concerts. Everything was exotic. Simple trips to the grocery store or the bakery reserved small surprises. During his time at the American Hospital he'd met Yvonne, a girl from a good Catholic family who was writing her dissertation on Italian literature and making extra money from Spanish and English translations. She possessed magical powers: a simple gesture from her expanded the cramped social circles of Paris enough for him to slip in at her side. Yvonne had coached him in his French—which still came out like the pidgin of an immigrant laborer, but grew to become more than adequate, comfortable even.

For a while, anyway, he'd found his place.

The impact of the tires on the runway jolted him awake. He'd only slept in snatches, enough to leave him groggy and thickheaded. Or maybe it was the

Xanax. In the short exchanges at immigration and customs his French felt stiff. He was like the Tin Man, his jaw in need of a squirt of oil. Once beyond the security area, he stopped for a double espresso, hoping for a boost from the caffeine. But still he felt out of kilter, like a film where the sound lagged behind the image.

By three thirty he had picked up his keys at the Hertz desk and located the gray Renault Laguna in the parking lot, settling himself heavily behind the wheel. It was now nine thirty a.m. Boston time. He rubbed his palms against his eyes, then turned the key in the ignition.

The outskirts of Paris were a tight weave of traffic and it took an hour before the white tip of Sacré Coeur rose on the horizon. That was his sign to veer off to the west, looping around the city on the north. Progress was slow, and his grogginess didn't help. Twice he had to slam on the brakes to avoid rear-ending the car ahead. After nearly two hours, the traffic still clotted, fatigue overwhelmed him. Edging toward an exit, he pulled into a highway hotel and got himself a tiny room, outfitted like a well-appointed prison cell. He collapsed on the bed fully dressed.

He awoke feeling alert and ravenous, ready for the day. However, a glance at the clock produced a new wave of exhaustion: it was barely three in the morning. But then he'd lost the rhythm of sleep, was incapable of turning off his mind. He tried the relaxation techniques he taught his patients—to no avail. Finally he gave up and made coffee with the cup-sized machine on the desk, sipping while he looked over the handful of photos he'd brought along from the album.

By six a.m. he lay on the bed staring at the dimpled ceiling. He knew sleep was done with him, and it wouldn't be long before he'd be back on the road. Then he'd have no choice but to tough it out, lurching through the next twelve or fourteen hours, come what may. In some sense it was a relief to know he'd soon be underway, that the machinery of this ordeal was starting up. He'd push through, one way or another, and then it would be over.

He gave his eyes one last rest before it was time to go down for breakfast.

When he awoke again it was bright outside and the alarm clock showed 12:07. He cursed out loud as he rolled out of bed. In the mirror he scowled at the exhausted man with gray-streaked hair matted down by the pillow, the tidy outline of his beard blurred by two days of grizzled stubble. He showered and dressed, grooming speedily, shaving around his beard with a practiced hand. He knotted his necktie fast, leaving the ends lopsided, then shoved on his shoes. As he flicked the laces around in a flurry of tying, a snap sounded and his right hand jerked back, a strand of shoelace clutched in his fingers. Just what he needed. He flung the lace to the ground.

Then he caught himself. Irritation, disorientation, that faint feeling of sadness—the whole bouquet of chronobiological symptoms. Jet lag. He forced himself to breathe deeply.

Glancing again at the clock, he calculated the distance he had to travel and shook his head. There was no way he could make it in time for the funeral now, no way at all, and he had to let them know. He called from the phone in his room, and when he got Yvonne's voicemail, he left his message in English.

"It's me," he said. "I overslept. I'm sorry, but it doesn't look like I'll get there in time. I don't have a cell phone here, but I'll contact you as soon as I get in." He paused. "Bye-bye."

She'd say he'd done it on purpose, that oversleeping was a way of avoiding what he didn't want to face. Worst thing was, he wasn't sure she'd be wrong.

Back on the road it wasn't long before the first chalky cliffs appeared at a bend in the Seine, the gateway to Normandy. An hour and a half later, after Rouen, he left the *autoroute*, preferring the back roads, many of the intersections marked with stone crosses. The pavement grew narrow. He swept along the edge of a broad forest, then looped north, traversing villages and hamlets, some no more than a cluster of shuttered houses. Every few kilometers a new community appeared, the church steeple rising above the trees, followed by rooftops. He cruised through, unhindered by stoplights or roundabouts. The road curved easily, wending through parcels of pasture and woods, passing over threads of creeks. Lanky Norman cows grazed in the pastures.

After the turnoff for Le Mont de l'If, he entered the flat basin of Upper Normandy in the center of the coastal bulge.

Then, just before Yvetot, he spotted activity in a farm field to his left. A tractor idled amidst rows of turned earth, puffs of exhaust sputtering from its stack. On the cart path bisecting this plot of land two other vehicles waited, one a small car marked *Gendarmerie nationale*, a blue light blinking from a beacon on the roof, and the other a white utility van with its back open, a shovel leaned against its side. Further away, along the edge of the woods, a cluster of men stood together—farmers by the look of their caps and boots. He slowed the car to a crawl and watched as a stocky man in blue coveralls, an insignia embroidered on the front, stepped from behind the tractor, cradling a burden in his arms, hugging it close against his chest. Philip's first, incongruous thought was that the man carried, of all things, an *infant*. But the load in his arms was dark and hard, and the way he lumbered forward suggested a great weight. A stone, perhaps? The man in coveralls continued his unsteady trudge toward the white van.

Then, in his rear-view mirror, headlights flashed. A car had come up, and he was forced to accelerate, abandoning the odd scene. It wouldn't be the first time something in France had left him baffled.

As he crested the last hill, the square campanile of Saint-Pierre church rose in the distance, soon followed by the low, jagged skyline of the town as it appeared on the horizon, a familiar profile.

But the outskirts of Yvetot felt different. Formerly bordered by modest farms, the town had now attracted big box discount stores and a giant supermarket. Forlorn shopping carts sunned themselves in parking lots where Charolais cows used to graze. Service stations had replaced barns.

Perhaps everything had changed? But as Philip steered the Renault down the slope, winding toward the heart of town, bands of old slate roof and stone wall came into view. With each passing block he sensed another step of a reluctant awakening, like a tingling in a benumbed limb. After this ancient perimeter he encountered the more modern structures in the center, rebuilt after the German occupation. There stood the garish city hall, with its war monument of a soldier in a battle scene. Off to the left was Saint-Pierre, the oddly newfangled church, a giant cylinder of brick and glass, like a monstrous keg planted in the city center. Around the main square, small shops stood shoulder to shoulder.

Except for the flowerpots on the street corners and the presence of a few new storefronts, Philip would have sworn that nothing much had changed in the center. It was as if time had halted fifteen years ago, and now, finally, motion was resuming. A kicked ball suddenly unfroze and a young boy broke from his long pose to chase it. An old woman pulled back on her terrier's leash, yanking him from his long-held stance at a lamppost. The church bell chimed for the first time in over a decade.

It seemed ridiculous to consider this a homecoming. Philip had never spent long periods in the town where Yvonne had grown up, but a few times a year they would make the pilgrimage from Paris, bringing Sophie to visit her grandmother. He hadn't known the locals by name, but he would chat with the butcher and the grocer. There, just to his left, was the newspaper shop he used to frequent. To the other side was their favorite bakery. Over there stood the hardware store. Yes, he'd been something more than a tourist in Yvetot, and now its streets and buildings, even the curve of its road, surprised him with their familiarity.

He parked in front of the weary structure of the Hôtel la Cauchoise, one of the few buildings in the center that the Germans had neglected to destroy during the war. On the sidewalk he stretched his legs, checking his watch to confirm the magnitude of his lateness. Nearly four o'clock. He'd missed the funeral by over an hour, and he had to wonder: had it been worth coming at all? How would Yvonne react? He was half-tempted to climb back in the car and flee while there was still time.

The lobby of the hotel was dark with old-world wood smelling of furniture oil and mold. Overstuffed armchairs yawned in the shadows like Venus fly traps waiting for their prey. On the oak reception counter next to the service bell, two dead cockroaches lay back to back. Philip tapped the bell twice. Steps sounded down the hall, and an old barrel of a man arrived. He had a frog-like face, his chin lost in a wide neck, his eyes magnified behind wireframe glasses. He peered at Philip with suspicion, as though uncertain why a visitor with a suitcase might approach a hotel reception desk. Norman hospitality.

"*Oui?*" he inquired.

Philip uttered his name and the man examined him at length, unrushed, before finally waddling behind the desk and cracking open the reservation book, turning the heavy cover over the bodies of the roaches. "*Bien,*" he said, tracing his finger down the list of names. "*Adler, Adler . . . Voilà.*" He squinted at Philip again. "*Une seule personne?*"

"*Oui. Pour une nuit.*" One night should do it.

Once again the old eyes studied him. "*Vous êtes . . . Américain, n'est-ce pas?*"

When Philip confirmed this suspicion, the man nodded, then tried out his thickly accented English. "From New York? Chicago?"

"Boston," he replied, happy not to have to deal with French until he got more sleep.

"Of course. In *Mass . . . Massa-shou . . .*" He couldn't get his mouth around the sounds.

"Massachusetts," Philip pronounced.

"Yes. I'm afraid, my English is not so good."

"Nonsense. You speak quite well."

This compliment lifted some of the chill. The man introduced himself as Monsieur Bécot, and from behind his desk he produced a ragged assortment of brochures, slapping them down on the counter one after the other, reciting in a flat tone the litany of tourist sites in and around the town.

"I don't think I'll be needing these," Philip interrupted.

Bécot stared. "I see. Perhaps you have been to Yvetot before, Monsieur Adler?"

He hesitated. "I have passed through."

Bécot considered this answer. "*Bien.* Well, at least you should learn what to avoid. The Saint-Pierre church, for example." He shook his head in disgust. "*Quelle horreur.*"

Philip nodded. "I couldn't agree more."

Monsieur Bécot approved of this reaction, turned and withdrew a key from the pigeonholes behind him. "*Une très bonne chambre*," he announced. "*Au troisième étage.* And a message." He presented an envelope with Philip's name on it. The handwriting was Yvonne's.

He headed for the stairs, then paused and turned back. "One more thing, Monsieur Bécot."

His eyes thinned. "*Oui?*"

"I came across something rather odd as I entered town." He described the scene he'd witnessed in the field. The blinking lights, the man in blue coveralls.

By the time he finished, Bécot was nodding. "Yes, yes. I heard that old Masseau found one. Hit it with the tractor! Not a stone, Monsieur Adler, no. It is a, how do you say, a oh-bus."

"A what?"

"A oh-bus," Bécot insisted.

Philip rummaged through the shreds of his French. What did the man mean? An opus? A bus? Then it clicked. Bécot was using the French word, pronouncing it in English. "You mean an *obus*. A shell."

"That's right, a shell. *Artillerie*, you know. From the war."

"Here? So far from the coast?"

"*Everywhere*." Bécot's expression brightened. "The war left its souvenirs, Monsieur. At the Abouville church, you still find holes from bullets in the stone. On the road to Fécamp there is a bunker, almost all under the ground now. Every year, they find many tons of *obus*—shells—from the war."

Philip shook his head. That couldn't be right. "No, the man I saw, he wasn't wearing any protection."

"Hah. That is Tristan." Bécot smiled with approval. "He is a *démineur*, and always he says, not to bother. If the shell goes, then he goes too. So it is better to be *confortable*."

Philip tried to square Bécot's explanation with what he'd seen. Certainly he'd heard of old armaments washing up on the beaches, but how had he missed the everyday nature of farmers plowing up high explosives? The old complexity of France returned to him now, a world shaded with deep folds.

Bécot was still talking, and a word snagged Philip's attention. "I'm sorry. What did you say?"

"Bodies, Monsieur."

"What?"

"Skelets."

"Skeletons?"

"That's right." The old man hesitated, studying his guest. "Or parts of them," Bécot continued. "Now and then, they come up to the surface. If we can tell—German or American or French—off they go to the military cemetery. But sometimes they do not know, and then Rouen sticks in its nose. Rouen," he added with distaste, "wishes to be in charge of everything."

But Philip was no longer listening, troubled by the image.

The two men stood in silence. Bécot bobbed his head as though he'd just made a decision. "I can perhaps offer you an aperitif, Monsieur Adler?"

"No, thank you."

"*C'est gratuit.* No cost. A little *Calvados*, perhaps? Liqueur made of apples?"

"I'm afraid I don't drink."

The old man gave him a surprised, faintly pained look.

"Thank you all the same, Monsieur Bécot." Philip turned and started up the steps.

Before he was halfway up the flight, Bécot spoke to his back. "It must be very hard, I think, to come back to Yvetot after all these years. Monsieur Adler."

He turned to find Bécot eyeing him. Philip had missed something. Back in the States he prided himself on his powers of observation, noticing people's tics, reading them like the tells of poker players. But here it wasn't just the language that was different. So were the looks and gestures.

"I remember the story well," Bécot continued. "When I saw your reservation, I suspected. But Adler is not an unusual name. I was not certain it was you, even when you arrived. You are different. Older. But I do not forget faces or names, even from the newspaper. Even when a person hides behind a beard. It is you. I can tell."

Philip nodded slowly. "Yes," he said. "I'm afraid it's still me."

"You have come for Anne-Madeleine Aubert? For the . . . *enterrement?*"

"The funeral. That's right."

"You are too late."

"I know."

A new silence hovered between them.

"You should not have returned, Monsieur Adler."

Philip bristled. "And why is that?"

Bécot raised his palms in defense, but offered no reply.

So this was to be his welcome. Philip turned and mounted the stairs, ducking at low passages in the hallway.

The room was squashed under the mansard roof of the hotel, and it had the sloped ceiling to prove it. The bed occupied most of the space, a beige cotton coverlet hugging the corners of the mattress tightly enough to conceal the sagging basin of the middle. When he slid his carryon into the great wardrobe by the armchair, the door gaped back open, again and again, like the chin of a mouth-breathing boy. Near the bathroom, the odor of mildew grew stronger. Flanking the minibar stood a lame desk, one leg shorter than the others, pushed with its chair into a shallow alcove below a yellow-curtained window overlooking the main square. So this was Monsieur Bécot's penthouse suite.

He opened the envelope the old man had given him. Just a few lines in

Yvonne's hand. The ceremony had gone as well as possible, she reported, *despite his absence*. He could call her that evening if he felt up to it, but in any case would he please meet her the next day at the office of Maître Caumartin? She gave the address.

Maître, Philip realized, was a title given to a lawyer or notary. Whatever could she want of him there?

Dusk had settled by the time the Renault pulled up outside the Saint-Louis cemetery on the south end of town. Near the entrance leaned a centenarian oak tree, its stocky trunk dividing into branches that strained against their own weight, some sporting great wooden knobs where arboreal amputations had been performed long ago. Philip climbed out of the car and smoothed down his necktie. He buttoned his sport coat. From the back seat of the car he retrieved his camera and took up an armful of flowers, the cellophane from the florist crinkling in his hands. He made his way past the oak toward the iron gate.

The cemetery was vast, filled with rows of stone slabs, separated by thin bands of gravel. It was a far cry from the sprawling, green-lawned cemeteries of New England.

Amidst the individual graves and family vaults were occasional tipped crosses and flourishes of sculpture. Many tombs had been colonized by lichens or bore a blanket of moss. A life-sized maiden bearing a flag in one hand and an olive branch in the other stood as a lissome memorial for the war dead, her eyes cast downward in sorrow, her crown adorned with a five-pointed star, a sensual horror. What did she represent? The nation? Gratitude? The Angel of Death? All Philip knew for sure was that she'd gone to rust, with flakes of metal lifting off the rise of her breasts and the pleats of her robe.

Names reeled by with each step, the stones providing a directory of the families of Yvetot—Cottard, Bourdin, Massue, Rioult, Joret, Desplanches, Hesse. In this single stretch were dates spanning more than a hundred years. Old and new were interspersed, abandoned graves having been reclaimed to make room for new occupants, resulting in glistening new stones tucked between ruins. There were so many dead to accommodate.

A path led toward the back. After the maintenance shed Philip took a right. Halfway down the gravel alley, on the left, lay a brownish slab adorned with fresh wreathes and bouquets. The name Aubert ran along the arched top of the headstone, and engraved below was the inventory of remains, beginning in 1891. Below the name of Yvonne's father, who had died nearly two decades ago, came the last completed entry: *Anne-Madeleine Aubert, 24 janvier 1926–7 juin 2008*. Four other names appeared beneath Anne-Madeleine's, those of the now adult children, Yvonne included. Only the birth dates had been chiseled in.

He was sorry to have missed the ceremony, had hoped to pay his last respects with the others. No one had suffered from the events of fifteen years ago more than Anne-Madeleine. To be honest, he was surprised she'd lasted this long, racked with guilt as she was. He suspected she'd greeted death with something akin to relief.

"*Dieu te garde*," he said aloud. "You'll be missed." He contributed a bouquet of flowers to the growing collection, lightening his load by half. A second bundle remained.

He turned to the right, walking past two more stones until he reached the one he didn't want to see. This was a more modest grave, one of polished, reddish granite. At the bottom right corner he noticed a thin crust, the first foothold of lichen. A yellow rose lay on the top, still fresh. He added his own bouquet to the middle of the slab. Then he knelt, forcing his eyes upward to the inscription: *Sophie Marie Adler, 4 février 1979– juillet 1993*.

He'd had to argue with that stuffy old priest for them to include her middle name. That wasn't how it was done in France, Father Huet had said. But damn it, on this stone Sophie's entire life had been reduced to a dash between two dates. The very least they could do was to let her have her name.

All the old imaginings surged forth. Sophie writhing on the ground, struggling under powerful arms. Darkness. Cries. Dirt. Sweat. The tear of fabric. A man's back. Grunts. He pictured her straining to look over the man's shoulder, desperate to focus on anything other than where she was, something far away, something she could cling to.

All this because of one man. One boy. Édouard Morin had been only seventeen years old at the time. Since the murder he'd traveled from one institution to another, first in Paris, then near Versailles, then in Marne-la-Vallée. It had taken a long time for Philip to kick the habit of tracking Morin's whereabouts, a task that required fierce self-control and zero tolerance for relapse. He wondered if Morin had ever experienced a prick of remorse about raping and murdering a fourteen-year-old girl. He suspected not. The concept of guilt would have had no meaning for him. Not that remorse would change anything.

In the distance the iron gate creaked, the sound of another mourner headed for another grave. Philip struggled from his knees and brushed the grit from his trousers. With his camera he lined up a shot of the stone with his daughter's name.

It was a hollow gesture, this picture of an empty tomb. Sophie's body had never been recovered, and fifteen years ago this stone had been erected to screen that fact. Graves were always a presence pointing to an absence, but here that function was doubly true, the connection even more tenuous. He'd refused to take the picture before, wasn't even sure he wanted it now. But there wouldn't be another chance.

He turned, retracing his own footsteps in the other direction, heading back to the maintenance shed, back to the peeling statue, back to the military graves, back to the tipped stone crosses, back to the entrance, back to the giant oak, back to the car, back to the hotel, back to the message from Yvonne. Back to everything.

Four

As he slept that night, foreign words that had long slumbered now rustled in his mind, waking and taking wing. Along with language came images of Yvetot, dissolving into scenes from Paris: buildings, streets, places, people—all remnants from the past. In the theater of his mind an outdoor market buzzed with negotiations and the hawking cries of vendors. A bus roared down a broad boulevard. Then he found himself in a medieval knot of roads, the sidewalks narrow and empty, the scene oddly familiar. At the turn of an alleyway, he glimpsed a teenage girl, tall, dressed in jeans and T-shirt. Did he know her? She vanished around a building, and he struggled to follow, his legs numb and heavy. By the time he turned the corner, she was disappearing behind a line of trees. He forced himself on, pushing as if into a stiff wind.

The scene changed. He saw her pausing by a hedge where she flicked her darkening hair over her shoulder, glancing left and right before starting forward again, her small frame moving quickly, her thin arms swinging loosely in their joints. They were in a park now, or a garden. He had gained on her, was approaching from behind, was nearly within reach, and finally he stretched out his hand and touched her lightly on the back, making her wheel around.

It was black-haired Melanie, a scowl on her gaunt face.

He woke with a start, his legs entangled in the sheets. Where was he? Where was Edith? What was that moldy smell? From the middle of the spongy bed he surveyed the room—the writing desk, the wardrobe, the high window, the minibar—and his mind clicked: Yvetot. He flopped back on the pillow and stared at the ceiling, his mouth cottony, his head aching.

And what was he to make of that dream—the brackish waters of which had already begun to recede, leaving everything covered with a film of anxiety? Something about a park, a girl? He shook his head. Sleep amnesia they call it.

He showered and shaved, nicking himself as he curved the blade around the bottom of his beard. He coaxed his repaired shoelace into a bow. Then, as he pulled on his sport coat, the sleeve snagged on the wardrobe handle and a button broke off, rolling under the chest of drawers and leaving behind a tuft of threads on his cuff. So began the day.

In the end he hadn't had the courage to call Yvonne last night, not after his visit to the cemetery. So this morning he would meet her at the law office. That seemed appropriate. After all, his last encounter with her had taken place in front of a lawyer thirteen years ago, where their divorce had been gutted of passion, reduced to a matter of red tape.

She had always been one for order. According to her mother, when she was little, Yvonne had kept her dolls in military rows and organized all her books by size. Her school notebooks had been works of art, filled with fine, rounded cursive, her ink color-coded to signal key vocabulary words and quotes. In the family lore, Yvonne was the one who, at age ten, trained the Aubert family dog. At twelve she announced her plan to become a professor, and when her mother humored her and asked if she had anything specific in mind, Yvonne had proclaimed matter-of-factly that she would be a specialist of Italian literature. Her father had roared, but sixteen years later that prophecy came true. As it turned out, she learned a number of languages, even studying abroad in England and Germany, but Italian remained her favorite. Her doctoral thesis had dealt with renaissance poetry, leading to her first position at the Paris III campus.

As he drank coffee in the cramped breakfast room at La Cauchoise, Philip felt a rising tide of apprehension, and it occurred to him that it might not be too late to vanish into thin air, to return to Boston without seeing anyone. Wouldn't that be the best for all concerned?

He knew the idea was preposterous, entirely irrational.

Though he used to know the center of Yvetot reasonably well, the law office was several blocks away, on a street he'd never heard of. Monsieur Bécot provided directions, which Philip retained well enough to make it through the second turn, but then his internal map blurred. None of the roads in this town were straight, and they had a nasty habit of changing names every fifty or hundred yards.

He stopped twice for directions, and every time he parted his lips his accent betrayed him, unmasking him not just as a stranger, but worse, a foreigner. He'd come to the language too late, had never mastered the vowel sounds, the slide of the R, the disappearing H and S. Long ago, back when he'd traveled with Yvonne or Sophie, the escort of natives had eased his passage. Now, his accent drew him sidelong stares, as if he were a disfigured man.

The rue Launay proved to be farther away than he thought, and he arrived late at the brick building where the notary's shield hung over the paneled door. Before entering, he straightened his jacket and tie, but still felt rumpled. For Yvonne he'd been an attractive project, a handyman's special. When he arrived in Paris for his residency, both orphaned and freed by his parents' deaths, Yvonne had served as the principal architect of his reinvention. She bestowed upon him innumerable linguistic corrections while coaching him in manners and dress. She introduced him first to her friends, then to her siblings, and finally to her parents. She fashioned the two of them into a couple, and then by alchemical transmutation transformed that couple into a family. Only occasionally had he felt a twinge of anxiety, the way a magician's dove must sometimes wonder how long the spell will hold before it reverts to an ordinary handkerchief.

Such had been Yvonne's reputation for accomplishing whatever she set her mind to that it had come as a shock when the ultrasound suggested she was carrying a girl, despite her professed preference for a boy. Philip had half expected her to produce, by sheer willpower, a little member between the legs of the embryo. It turned out he wasn't far from wrong. Thanks to her mother, Sophie had grown into an independent, confident, and assertive girl, one who felt she could do anything. Which had been wonderful. But also part of the problem.

He rang the bell at the door and waited for the electric click of the lock. Inside the notary's office, the receptionist looked him up and down, her eyes stopping at the tuft of loose threads on his jacket cuff. He clapped his other hand over his wrist.

"Monsieur Adler," he said. "I am here to meet with Maître Caumartin. And Yvonne Adler." He corrected himself instantly. "Aubert. Yvonne Aubert."

"You mean Madame Legrand?"

Of course. He hadn't much practice with her new name. Although it wasn't new. She'd been remarried long enough for them to have a twelve-year-old daughter.

The woman led him down a corridor, and Philip felt his chest tighten. Voices leaked out from the door of a meeting room, one of them a woman's firm tone rising above the others, which he recognized at once. "Does everyone have a copy?" she was saying in French. And as he turned through the doorway, there they all were, the old cast of characters seated around a long, oval table. Dried up Évelyne was whispering to her skinny, balding husband, Sylvain. Next to pretty Flora sat the well-groomed Pierre. To the left Roger leaned back in his chair, his feet up on the table, his fingers pressed together, a half-amused, half-bored expression on his face. They looked the same, adjusted for age, having become somehow even more themselves.

A short, well-dressed man Philip didn't know sat to the right.

But it was Yvonne who drew his gaze. She stood with her back to him, her tall form buttoned in a brown Chanel suit, a bundle of papers in her hand. "I said," she repeated while brandishing the document, a hint of exasperation creeping into her voice, "Does everyone have a copy?" No one answered. Their eyes had all moved to the door, and now Yvonne turned. Her expression softened.

She was older now. Perhaps a bit weary. Yet still a handsome woman, square-jawed and erect. A smile came to Philip's lips.

Roger was scrambling to his feet, grinning. "*C'est le retour de l'enfant prodigue,*" he roared. Broad-shouldered and sporting a moustache, he was dressed less formally but more richly than the others.

"Roger," Philip said, stepping toward him, extending his hand.

"Bah," Roger replied, continuing in French. "My dear Philip—Anglo-Saxon to the core. Don't be ridiculous." He ignored the outstretched hand and gripped his former brother-in-law by the shoulders. Before he could protest, Roger had planted a kiss on each of his cheeks. "Nice beard, *Monsieur l'hirsute.*"

The others around the table were less effusive. Yvonne's sisters gave pinched nods of greeting, and their husbands acknowledged his presence with tight-lipped smiles. Sylvain was the first to break rank and reach a hand over the table. Soon Philip was making the rounds, shaking hands, kissing cheeks. Yvonne's younger sisters didn't seem overjoyed at this gesture of affection, but after all, they were, or had once been, family.

He took the long way around the table, postponing for a few instants the encounter with Yvonne. But then he ran out of hands to shake, and the room fell quiet.

"*Bonjour Philippe,*" she said.

Yvonne's voice transformed his name into a familiar cluster of taut French I's and pert consonants. He replied with a nod, clasping his hands, then wondering where to put them. The entire group was watching the spectacle of their encounter, but Philip didn't know the script. Over the years he'd learned many of the nuances of French intimacy—whose hand to shake, whom to kiss, when to use the formal *vous* or the casual *tu*—but no one had covered this particular situation in his training. What was the appropriate salutation when greeting your ex-wife for the first time in thirteen years? He was about to extend his hand when Yvonne gave him a clue, lifting her chin and inching forward. He approached to kiss her on both cheeks, skin against skin. Her fragrance was the same. There were fine wrinkles at the corners of her eyes.

"How are you?" she asked in French.

"I'm . . ." he began, finding himself confronted with too many contradictory and yet correct answers to this simple question. He blinked and looked over the table toward the others. "Well, for one thing, I'm *late*," he said with a laugh. He struggled to formulate a sentence, but the French wasn't flowing. "I'm sorry about missing the ceremony. But I suppose you're used to my tardiness. Old dogs and new tricks, you know."

"Old monkeys, you mean," Roger called from his end of the table. "That's the expression in French. We'll just have to brush up your idioms."

"Welcome back to Yvetot," said Yvonne.

"It's good to be here," he said. Platitudes. He had a storehouse of those at the ready. He looked around the room. "You haven't changed a bit."

"And still such an excellent liar," Roger proclaimed.

There was one person Philip hadn't met yet—the short, rather dapper man on the other side of Yvonne. The new husband.

"You must be *Hair-vay*," Philip said.

"*Er-vé,*" the fellow corrected with a broad smile, wagging his finger in the air. "Remember, my dear sir, the H is not pronounced in French." He bowed his head to accept Philip's unoffered thanks for the correction. "Dr. Hervé Legrand, at your service. Endocrinology. Infertility, mostly. Must say, I'm delighted to finally meet you. Awfully kind of you to make the trip." Hervé clamped Philip's hand in his own and shook. "I so look forward to speaking with you. Why don't you sit over here by me?"

And before he could protest, Hervé had guided him away from Yvonne's side, like a child being seated by the teacher's desk. A first husband's lot is ludicrous, just a hair's breadth from that of the cuckold.

Roger beamed. "So good to have you back."

"Is it?" Philip said.

"Of course! It was always so *useful* to have you in the family." His eyes sparkled. "It kept their minds off me."

Classic Roger. Part clown, part black sheep.

On the other side of Hervé, Yvonne leaned forward. "You had a good flight?" she wanted to know.

"Good enough."

"And you're staying . . . ?"

"At La Cauchoise."

"That old *trou à rats?*" Roger interjected as he checked the thermal pot for coffee. "Run by our local fossil, Bécot?" He poured himself a cup.

Philip turned back to Yvonne. "How was the funeral?"

It was Hervé who answered. "A pity you slept through it. Jet lag, I suppose? The ceremony was quite tasteful."

Roger nearly spat out his coffee. "Tasteful?" he retorted. "That old crock of a priest, Cabot, he got mixed up in the service. Part of it he did twice. Everything was out of order. We didn't know if we were coming or going. I tell you, if mother hadn't already been dead, this would have finished her off."

"Roger," Évelyne said, as if shushing a child. "That's not appropriate."

He ignored her. "The worst of it is that we'll probably find she left everything to the church. Wouldn't that just take the cake."

"Roger!" cried Évelyne.

He turned to his sister. "You know, you don't have to keep squawking my name like that. I'm as sorry as anyone that she died, but you have to admit, it was a pretty hilarious funeral."

Évelyne clamped her beak shut, not willing to admit anything of the sort.

Flora's face squeezed out a pained expression. "*Please* let's try to get along," she crooned.

The room roiled with tension, but when Philip exchanged a look with

Yvonne, she let a flicker of humor show in her eyes. It was like old times. For Philip, an only child, initiation into the Aubert clan had been an introduction into wonderment.

There was a lull in the conversation. "So," Philip said, "what exactly are we doing here?"

Various Auberts exchanged glances.

"Well," Yvonne began. "It had to be today, I'm afraid. Flora and Pierre have to leave tomorrow."

"*What* had to be today?"

Évelyne squinched her nose. "Didn't you tell him?"

Yvonne shrugged. "I wanted to explain in person. But then he missed the ceremony. And didn't call last night. And, anyway, it's not the kind of thing you do over the phone."

Évelyne rolled her eyes.

"You know, Philip," Roger began, "it's terribly nice of you to show up, considering we've only invited you so you can give away your money."

"My money?"

"Don't put it that way," Yvonne snapped at her brother. She turned to Philip. "Let me explain. There's a complication in Mother's will . . ."

"That's right," Roger continued. "What she means is that you've walked into a disinheritance."

"A what?"

"Not at all," said Yvonne to Roger. "It's just a formality."

"It's a scene straight from Balzac, that's what it is," Roger sang out.

Hervé stifled a grunt.

"Why do you *insist* on speaking like that?" Évelyne snapped at her brother.

"*Please*," whined Flora to no one in particular.

The husbands were savvy enough to sit back and wait for Yvonne to intervene.

Philip smiled. The Auberts were like an improv group that had worked together too long, falling back on routine types and scenarios regardless of the subject handed to them, delivering new lines with the same worn-out intonations and gestures. And Philip knew the roles. Yvonne, the oldest, who always found herself in charge; Évelyne, who resented Yvonne's leadership while not showing any aptitude for it herself; Flora, who fancied herself the mediator, but didn't have the patience for it; and Roger, the clever brat of the family, but also the showman, the clown, the one who distracted them from their squabbling. Even the spouses played their bit parts.

But some of the characters had gone missing. Not the least of which was Anne-Madeleine herself. And, in the more distant past, Guillaume, the white-mustachioed patriarch who used to preside over events like this. But the absence of the parents hadn't reassigned any roles.

There was another gap: as Philip surveyed the table his eyes stopped on the unoccupied chair next to Roger. "So where's Élisabeth?" he said, asking after Roger's wife.

Évelyne's jaw clenched, Flora looked down at the table, Yvonne brought her hand to her temple, and Hervé turned away. Even Roger looked pained, his jocularity waning. "Ah, Philip," he said, "I see you haven't lost your knack for finding the most embarrassing thing to say."

Which was true. Philip was as guilty as everyone else of playing old roles. As the therapist, his part had always been to produce the obvious questions that no one else would ask.

Before any more conversation could misfire, the door opened and the notary marched into the room. Maître Caumartin was a snappily dressed young man, junior to all those in attendance. In his hands he clutched a thick dossier with elastic bands closing the corners.

"Good morning," he called out to the group, gracing them with a smile that looked freshly applied. "I understand we're all present?"

When no one contradicted him he assumed his seat at the head of the table. Maître Caumartin arranged his forms and pens and stamps like theatrical props. He engaged in small talk with Yvonne and Hervé, warming up his audience. Finally he turned to the group at large, his eyes twinkling. Professing concern for *their* busy schedules and *their* presumable desire to move through the meeting quickly, he offered to get the process underway, and since no one objected during the instant he left for that eventuality, he flipped open the dossier and perused the first page of notes. "Ah, yes," he muttered in a stage whisper to himself. Then, looking at the assembled participants over the tops of his glasses, he asked, "Is Monsieur Adler here?"

"Present," Philip said, raising a finger.

"You are American, if I'm not mistaken?"

"That's right."

"Yes, I can hear it," he smiled. "Do you believe your French is sufficient for following these proceedings?"

"I think so," he replied. "My grammar's not perfect, but I understand pretty well."

Maître Caumartin leaned forward. "*Beecawz,*" he said in heavily accented English. "*Eef you wan, eye-uh can trance-late foe you.*" He grinned broadly at this accomplishment.

Roger sniggered.

"I think I'll be all right," Philip said.

The notary's shoulders sagged. "Very well." He fluttered his fingers over the papers like a pianist preparing to play. "Shall we begin?"

What Maître Caumartin had before him, Philip realized, was Anne-Madeleine Aubert's will, a long document that the law apparently required him to read out loud from start to finish. Philip's presence at the event made no sense to him. After all, he and Yvonne had been divorced for an eternity.

While the notary droned through the reading, pausing at the end of each section to see if there were questions, Philip stole glances at Yvonne. Age, he thought, that great illusionist. It plays so many tricks on us. Some people vanish entirely into the folds and creases of their advancing years, while others resist the tectonics of time. Yvonne was of the second sort.

She caught him spying on her and hunched her shoulders in a shrug of apology. Sorry for what, Philip wondered. For not explaining the nature of today's visit? For making him come back at all? For something else?

As Maître Caumartin wound through the convoluted syntax and the legal terminology, certain topics recurred, and a vague idea began to form in Philip's mind, fueled by what Roger had said.

"I'm sorry," he said, interrupting halfway through. "Do I understand correctly that I have some sort of claim here?"

Maître Caumartin was taken aback to find himself cut off, especially by the person least connected to the family. He turned to Yvonne. "Did you not explain?" he inquired.

"I'm afraid we didn't have time, Maître."

The notary nodded and stroked his chin, then undertook to answer Philip's question, putting it in layman's terms. Because his marriage to Yvonne had been under the settlement of joint assets, the *régime de la communauté de biens*, he still held some right to a portion of the inheritance. He cited two passages of the civil legal code as proof.

Even after the explanation Philip couldn't fathom it. If a divorced husband ended up owning some fraction of his ex-wife's mother's estate, he suspected he had ancient traditions or the Napoleonic Code to thank for it—laws that privileged the place of men, making it hard even today for a woman to squeeze a man out of her life. Or perhaps it was simply an error. Who knew for sure? He had always found the French legal system mind-boggling.

"But I have nothing to do with this," he objected.

"Of course he doesn't," Évelyne chimed in.

"Music to our ears," added Roger.

But it turned out not to be so easy to give away a legacy. After all, sometimes there were debts to be paid, and those, too, became the responsibility of the heirs. As the notary explained, for one to disavow an inheritance it was necessary for all the parties to agree, for everyone to sign, and for all the signatures to be certified.

When Philip prepared to ask another question, Maître Caumartin planted his elbows on the table and pressed his fingertips together, forming a tent over the papers. "Might we take questions later?" he said in a tone that made a lie of his smile.

Forty-five minutes later, the recital came to an end. There was property to be distributed among the heirs, not least of which was the large house at the edge of town. And what was to be done with Anne-Madeleine's car, which had been quarantined in the garage for the past two years? Could any of the old paintings be used to pay off taxes? Who had the authority to make which decisions? The crisscrossing voices rose in a clamor.

But Philip had only one question: Where do I sign? With a flourish, the prescient notary produced another document. This one would allow him to transfer his portion of the assets and liabilities, the *actif* and the *passif*, back to the family.

The din from the other discussions went quiet, and Philip felt all eyes upon him. He patted his pocket in search of a pen, and Yvonne touched his arm, offering him a black ballpoint. He nodded his thanks and turned to the signature page, pretending to skim the last clauses, tapping the pen by each bullet point, delaying the final gesture. This legal claim was his last, unexpected connection to this particular past.

And yet, his signature was what Yvonne wanted, which was all that mattered. He wrote out his name, then scratched his initials at the bottom of each sheet, feeling Hervé's scrutiny, perhaps even his breath, over his shoulder. When he was done, he closed his fist around the pen.

"Thank you," Yvonne said from behind.

There were other signatures, some photocopies to be made, but soon it was over. The notary shook hands with all those in attendance, issued a few parting comments designed to be charming, and saluted them collectively as he left the Aubert family to digest the transaction they had just concluded.

"See how fast he took off?" Roger said loudly as the door closed. "I imagine he has other cats to whip."

Other cats to whip. Philip remembered this one, the French version of *other fish to fry.* The language was full of such surprising turns of speech, and they were gradually coming back to him. The total immersion of the meeting had helped.

Chairs scooted, papers rustled, purses snapped.

"Well, that's that," Évelyne proclaimed, dusting off her hands.

"A pity, though," Roger said. "Money is what keeps families together."

Évelyne glared. "Do you try to be so crass? Or does it just come naturally?"

"What now?" Roger protested. "I'm just telling the truth. It's not my fault if the truth is crass."

Hervé joined in. "Not everyone thinks the way you do, Roger. Thank God."

"You really think there's more to family than cash?"

"Indeed I do," Hervé replied.

Roger fingered his chin while he pondered the statement. "Hmm. Then I suppose that means Philip should stay for dinner tonight. Since stripping him of the money doesn't really change anything."

Hervé's eyes grew large.

"Don't you think, Yvonne?" Roger added, all innocence.

Philip suppressed a smile.

Yvonne had been pulling together her papers, searching for her pen, patting the pockets of the Chanel jacket. Now she gave the current matter her full attention, turning to Philip. "Roger's right. Why don't you stay for the meal?

Since we didn't have a chance to see you yesterday?"

Not two hours earlier his goal had been to escape as quickly as possible, to flee back home. Now the web of familiarity caught at him. He begged off, protesting that his flight left the next afternoon.

"Nonsense," Roger pressed. "Everyone's still here from the funeral. We're having one final bash. It'll be like old times. Stay tonight and leave in the morning. You'll be at the airport in three hours."

"I already have a reservation near Roissy."

"Cancel it," Roger said. "French hotels are used to being stood up."

"Do come," chimed in Flora. "You can meet the children."

Philip turned to Yvonne for help.

"You should stay," she said.

He tried to read her eyes.

"See?" Roger added. "Everyone hopes you'll come. You do too, don't you, Hervé?"

Hervé scowled. "Yes," he said flatly. "Of course we hope you can stay for dinner."

Philip had to admire Roger's pluck. That's what had brought them together so many years ago: Roger's steadfast resistance to protocol, to being *comme il veut* instead of *comme il faut*. Yvonne used to have a touch of that, too.

"All right," he conceded. "I'll stop by for a little bit."

Back in his hotel room he sat at the wobbly desk, rolling Yvonne's ballpoint pen between his fingers. It was a simple, black-barreled job with a button at the top and the logo of the University of Rouen on its side. They probably made them by the thousands and sold them for two or three euros at the university bookstore. She wouldn't miss it.

The morning had been strange, filled with surprising memories, as if he'd pulled the stopper from an old perfume bottle, only to find a pungent ghost of fragrance within. He still felt the brush of her cheek.

Only Hervé had been truly annoying.

When Philip went down to let Monsieur Bécot know he'd be staying another night, the old man's expression darkened.

"You'd rather I left, wouldn't you?" Philip said.

"That is not for me to decide, Monsieur Adler." His nose approached the register as he amended the reservation. "But I know Yvetot. I have lived here all my life. I know the names, the people. At least the ones that are left. So many families are gone now. Yvetot is a dying town."

"I don't see what that has to do with me."

Bécot paused and looked up. "There have been so many problems here, you know. The Germans destroyed Yvetot. Then came the occupation. Then the collaboration. One pain after another."

"That was nearly sixty-five years ago."

Bécot flicked his hand. "What I am saying, Monsieur Adler, is that people in Yvetot are not interested in going back to the past. Just ask Monsieur Guérin at the archives in the town hall: no one goes there. People, they do not wish to be reminded of these problems. Especially by someone who does not—if you will excuse the expression—who does not belong here."

Philip's temper rose. So he was an unwelcome guest. Yes, Sophie's rape and murder had attracted the press, casting Yvetot in a bad light. The journalists had salted their articles with subtle insinuations, hinting that something was wrong in a town where such a crime could take place, where no one foresaw what a boy like Édouard Morin might do. Philip's return now picked open the old scabs of shame.

But after all, he told himself, it *was* Yvetot's fault. They should have helped Édouard Morin before it was too late. Instead, they'd refused to face the facts, had waited too long, and his family had borne the cost. And now they dared assert that he didn't belong?

"And you, Monsieur Bécot?" he pressed. "Is that how you feel?"

"Me?" Bécot's face was hard to read. "I run a hotel, Monsieur. It is my job to welcome people who come to our town. So I do not take sides."

"I suppose I should thank you for your honesty."

Bécot turned his attention to the register. "I wish you a very fine stay, Monsieur Adler. You will be at the Aubert home this evening, is that right? I look forward to seeing you at check-out in the morning."

In his room Philip attempted a nap before the gathering but only managed to study the flaking paint of the ceiling. The window was open, and the fabric shade of the light swayed with the breeze.

His mind refused to shut down. Everything in Yvetot reminded him of Sophie, and Sophie made him think of Morin. What, he wondered, would that boy look like now? What had become of his father, Olivier, that pitiful, apprehensive little man?

He closed his eyes, desperate for a nap, but sleep wouldn't come. Memories nuzzled at his mind's gate like kenneled dogs.

Five

The dinner proved to be a heavily populated event with a buffet laid out in the dining room of the Aubert home. The house was a stone structure, a hundred and fifty years old, three stories tall, large enough for a separate service stairway in the back, and rich with history. It had been spared by German artillery thanks to its location on the outskirts of town. During the Nazi occupation, officers had been billeted there, and according to family legend a certain lieutenant colonel had enjoyed taking target practice in the dining room. Now guests roamed about the spacious rooms of the main floor carrying plates and glasses, moving from group to group. Philip stepped gingerly through this familiar space. A few furnishings had changed since his last trip to Yvetot, but the portrait of Yvonne's father still glared down from above the mantel, and even now Philip couldn't tell if the old ghost approved of him.

He met Flora's and Évelyne's children, each name promptly displaced in his memory by the next. Overall, he marveled at how few of the creatures in this house he actually knew, or rather, recognized. There were multiple generations of Auberts, ranging from an unsupervised pack of five-and-six-year-old marauders to a herd of ancient, sexless ruminants who sipped at *digestifs* and exchanged mutters in hushed tones. The entire extended family was present, with one important omission: Roger himself. Mr. Incorrigible hadn't turned up yet.

He exchanged greetings with guests and strained to hear responses over the hubbub, nodding and smiling with special vigor whenever he had no idea what the other person had said. He was an expert at vague replies—one of the skills he sometimes practiced in sessions with patients.

Still, it wasn't long before the novelty of the American had worn off, and soon he ended up alone in an armchair in a corner, listening to the clinks of glass and silverware, wondering how long it would be before he could legitimately depart. The box of chocolates he'd brought had been plundered by the children. He was pretty sure Yvonne had never even seen them.

Hervé came through the room, and by the time he'd recognized the tall stranger sitting in the shadows, it was too late for either of them to pretend he hadn't. "You don't have a glass," he said with a pinched smile. "Can I fetch you something to drink? A Chardonnay? Something stronger?"

"No, thank you."

"Are you sure? There's an excellent Burgundy here." He was rattling through the bottles on the table, tipping them back to decipher their labels. "I don't know how familiar you are with fine wines . . ."

"I don't need anything, really."

"Nonsense. You really must try this Meursault." He was already pouring a glass.

Back home people might have taken the hint, but here Philip was going to have to be direct. "I don't drink," he announced, and Hervé gave him a surprised look. "They say there's a god who watches over drunkards," Philip continued, "but he didn't do such a good job with me. I have to look after myself."

"Ha-ha! I see," Hervé replied, overcoming the awkwardness of the confession. "Nicely put, I must say. Yvonne told me your French was pretty good, but still, I'm impressed. For an American."

"When you live somewhere for fifteen years," Philip replied, "you don't have much choice but to pick up the language."

"A bit of an accent, of course."

There it was—the jab.

Hervé was already off on another topic. "So tell me, is psychiatry in your family? What are you—a nephew or grandson of the great Alfred Adler?"

"No relation."

"I see." He leaned against the table, crossing his ankles. "But that is a Jewish name, isn't it?"

Such a question would never have been asked so baldly in the States. Philip responded in the affirmative and braced himself for more questions about his family's background, but in fact Hervé was already moving on. He was more interested in conjuring up questions than in hearing the answers.

"And what do you consider yourself?" Hervé said. "A Freudian? A Jungian? A Lacanian?"

"A pragmatist."

Already Philip was zeroing in on his diagnosis of Yvonne's husband. Definite narcissistic tendencies. Not pathological, of course, but measurable.

"I see, I see," Hervé was saying.

Philip tested his hypothesis by turning the conversation around and quizzing Hervé about his own work. Yes, he realized, this was the way for the conversation to flow. Hervé prattled on with no help, a conversational machine in perpetual motion. He had helped to found an infertility clinic in Rouen, and he had the entire history of that endeavor at the ready. "Seventeen years ago," he began, "we were on the cutting edge. In France infertility was taboo. People wouldn't talk about it with their doctors. Instead, they'd engage in all manner of hocus-pocus." He laughed. "Maybe you know of the sculpture of Victor Noir, in Paris?"

Philip allowed how he did not.

"A handsome fellow, killed in a duel. The funeral sculpture shows him lying on the ground, equipped with, shall we say, a special *bulge* in a particular area. Legend has that if women touch it with their lips, they'll be pregnant within the year."

"I have a hard time imagining women kissing a sculpture in the cemetery."

Hervé gave a sly smile. "Who said anything about kissing?"

On he went with facts and figures about infertility. Did Philip know that forty-seven percent of cases concerned the man? That it could be tied to stress and insomnia? In France the birth rate had been dropping—though not as much as in Italy, where in a hundred years all you'd find were cats!

"And yet," Philip said, "you and Yvonne only have one child, isn't that true?"

"I see what you're driving at. The cobbler should start by fixing his own shoes, is that it? But you see, Philip, reproduction is also a matter of choice . . ." On he went.

Philip's attention drifted back at the mention of Yvonne. "At first she wanted to live in Yvetot," Hervé was saying. "But, as you might imagine, it's rather hard to move here once you've lived in Rouen."

"Why is that?"

Hervé gave a condescending look. Only small children or Americans could not know the answer to such a question. "Let's just say that Yvetot only exists thanks to its location between more important places."

"Is that so?"

"Of course. The town was drying up after the textile industry collapsed . . ." He prattled on about the steady deterioration through the decades. Yvetot no longer produced anything of value, and now, like so many other small towns, focused on tourism. "So," he concluded with brio, "like certain mature mollusks that cease eating and survive only by digesting their own bodies, Yvetot has undertaken the moribund process of devouring its past." His polished delivery of this line suggested how often he had used it.

Philip had a pretty good idea now of the kind of man he was dealing with. Hervé was a know-it-all. He'd be able to crank out answers about any topic handed to him, whether it be pork-belly futures in Chicago or the history of Belgian missionaries in the Congo.

"You should meet Margaux," Hervé was saying. He craned about at the clusters of people. "She's around here somewhere. Delightful girl. Terribly good at school. Took first this year in science, you know."

No, Philip hadn't known.

"Of course girls are better at science than boys. The boys don't concentrate enough at that age. But they catch up later. You see, what happens is . . ." Hervé revved up another lengthy explanation.

"You know," Philip interrupted, "I'm fully aware of how awkward this situation is."

Hervé stopped and coughed. "I'm not quite sure what you mean."

"You don't need to pretend. You've been perfectly decent about it, *Hair-vay*," Philip continued. "But don't worry. You don't need to entertain me. You don't have to distract me or keep me from Yvonne. In fact, you don't need to worry about me at all. I'll be gone tomorrow, and that will be good for everyone."

Hervé suppressed a scowl and adjusted his sport coat. "I see."

"I just thought it would be best for us to be direct."

"Certainly. I appreciate your frankness. Well, I hope your visit has been worthwhile, Philip. Perhaps it will have helped you to turn the page."

The expression galled him. "Perhaps."

Hervé stuck out his hand. "I suppose we may never see each other again." He didn't seem distressed at the prospect.

"No. Probably not."

As Hervé moved on, Philip plunged himself into a club chair placed between two rooms, deep in the shadows. On one side the old-timers had sunk into overstuffed furniture. On the other, children were building a fortress out of sofa cushions. Philip eavesdropped on the various threads of conversation, but his language skills slipped as fatigue and jet lag overtook him. He felt like a phantom, barely visible to those in attendance, planted halfway between the geriatric wing and the daycare.

The younger sister, Flora, passed through, chatting with him briefly before leaving to check on little Georges, who had reportedly gorged himself on the chocolates someone had brought, and who now writhed with a tummy ache. Évelyne drifted by a couple of times, bony shoulder blades jutting from the open back of her black dress, nodding politely to Philip. When she finally stopped by his chair, he knew better than to take it as an act of charity. She smelled faintly of mothballs.

"Enjoying yourself?" she asked with a patronizing smile.

"Not particularly." He saw no reason to be coy.

"Have you said all your goodbyes?"

"Are you that anxious to get rid of me?"

"I'm just thinking how uncomfortable it must be to linger somewhere you don't belong." There it was again: the sentiment Monsieur Bécot had expressed.

"Tell you what, Évelyne," he said as he rose from his seat. "Let me freshen your glass. What are you drinking?" *Toe of frog?* he wanted to ask. *Eye of newt?* But he didn't know how to say these in French. He settled for: "Some kind of witch's brew?"

It wasn't a mature response, and it wouldn't help, but he couldn't always play the professional. Sometimes the doctor was in, and sometimes he was out. He left Évelyne grimacing, and in the middle of the next room, he crossed paths with her gutless husband, Sylvain, who shrugged a smile in his direction, as if to suggest that he didn't have the necessary authorization to visit.

Wine and liquor flowed in abundance. He breezed by the table set up as a bar, a rainbow of liquids and labels: Nuits-Saint-Georges, Sancerre, Pernod, Armagnac, Calvados, Poire Williams. There were times he still thirsted for a drink, but this wasn't one of them. What with the fatigue and the crush of memories, alcohol would finish him off. Besides, what the hell had become of Roger? It was just like his former brother-in-law to insist that Philip stay for dinner and then not show up.

He ensconced himself in another chair, even more remote, and attempted to vanish. He looked at his watch and wondered what time it was in Boston, but his brain failed to complete the calculation.

In the end it was Yvonne who came by. He watched her cross the living room, stopping twice to exchange words with guests. During these brief halts she shot a smile in his direction to make sure he understood she was en route. The brown suit from the morning was gone, replaced by a sleeveless blouse and a black skirt that stopped at the tops of her calves. Her dark hair was probably dyed these days, and he thought there was a bit more makeup than before. Still, if gravity had taken its toll on Yvonne, you couldn't tell by looking at her breasts or hips, or the underside of her arms. At least from a distance she looked remarkably preserved, while he himself had grown old.

She settled onto the arm of his chair, her thigh near his elbow. "Are you very drunk yet?" she asked him in French.

He inhaled her fragrance. It was hard to imagine that Yvonne and Évelyne were related. "No," he replied. "Not yet."

"I am," she confided. "Drunk, that is. What a horrible week."

"I can imagine." He paused. "I'm terribly sorry about your mother, you know. I always liked her."

"And she doted on you."

He hunted for something to add, but his mind was as empty as an old cupboard. Finally he turned up a crumb. "When is Roger going to get here? I'm still on Boston time, and I'm not going to last much longer."

She cracked a smile. "As you may recall, my baby brother can be a little unpredictable."

"What was all that about this morning? What's up with him and Élisabeth?"

Her expression clouded. "Bit of a quagmire, really. I don't fully understand what's going on. Roger puts on all these airs, but I don't think he's very happy. You should ask him about it."

"That would require his presence."

"Philip," she said suddenly, "you're coming apart at the seams."

He flinched. Was it so obvious?

"There, on your sleeve. All those loose threads."

He looked down at his cuff. "It's nothing," he said. "I lost a button."

"You should trim them."

He waved her away. "Really, don't—"

"You're always so ragged."

He was about to explain that he didn't typically travel through airport security with scissors, that he hadn't had time to worry about buttons and shoelaces, and that a few extra threads were the last of his concerns, when suddenly Yvonne leaned down, her blouse gaping at the neck. He caught his breath as she drew the sleeve up to her parted lips. There was a flash of teeth as she bit and pulled, tugging at the fiber.

"There you go," she said, surrendering his arm to him. "That tidies it up a bit."

Philip drew back his hand, coughed and looked away.

Two children raced into the room, stopping against the liquor table and making the bottles rattle before they charged out the other door.

"It's hard to see you again," Yvonne said.

He nodded. "I feel like I've stepped backwards in time."

"Yes," she mused. "But perhaps it's good. To let us close the door. Once and for all."

"Funny," he said, his lips pursing. "That's more or less what Hervé told me."

"Don't be too hard on him. He's not in an easy spot, either."

Maybe. Philip wasn't ready to give Hervé the benefit of the doubt. He guided the conversation into other territory, and soon Yvonne was telling him about her position at the University. Then she recounted the story of Hervé's creation of the infertility clinic, and in her words it sounded less entrepreneurial and more noble. Still, every detail strained his patience. He rubbed his temples. The well of his French was running dry.

"Yes," he said. "Everything seems to have worked out pretty well for you."

Yvonne agreed.

"And you have a daughter," he added bluntly. "Don't forget about her."

She paused. "That's right. Have you met Margaux yet?" She looked about the room. "I'm not sure where she's run off to."

How, he wondered, could she speak of daughters so nonchalantly? "Yes," he said. "I'd say you've made quite a wonderful little life for yourselves."

Yvonne's posture stiffened. "Do you hold that against me?"

"Not at all. It's just that we're different that way, you and I. I can't shut things away, close them off. You were always so much better at that."

Now Yvonne was standing. "It was fifteen years ago, Philip."

"Fourteen. And ten months."

He'd expected—perhaps hoped—to get a rise out of her, but instead it was a pained expression that formed on Yvonne's face. In fact, perhaps it was even pity? His neck flushed with heat. "At least I haven't forgotten," he said.

"And you think I have?"

He crossed his arms.

Her face contracted. Then she paused and forced herself to relax. She almost never lost her cool, after all, which Philip had counted among her most infuriating traits.

"You and I, we did what we could," she said to him. Her voice was collected.

He gave a small snort of indignation. Did she actually believe that? "No we didn't," he objected, too tired to play the game of politeness. "We gave up. We quit." He put his hand to his eyes. A headache was starting to bloom. It was bad enough being in this house, in this town. Did he also have to put up with Yvonne's self-serving revision of history?

"I don't know how you take it all in stride," he continued, unable to stop the ugliness in his own voice. "Or rather, maybe I do. Maybe that's the advantage of teaching literature: you learn how to lose yourself in fictions. You make believe."

"Philip."

"Don't *Philip* me." He was standing up now.

Heads were turning.

"Stop it," she said firmly. "You're embarrassing yourself."

He raised his voice another notch. "You crack open the books and let the metaphors buoy you up. I guess some people just read Dante, while the rest of us have to live it."

Yvonne started to respond but caught herself, resting her eyes for a moment before speaking again. "Thank you for coming this evening. And for making the trip. It meant a great deal to me."

"I'm not done," he snapped.

"It was nice to see you, again, Philip. Have a good flight back."

"Don't you dare walk away," he barked.

But she did dare.

"That's right," he called to her back in English as she crossed the room.

A voice in his head hissed at him to shut up. "Run along! Whenever it gets uncomfortable, just turn away."

She disappeared around the corner into the living room. Guests gawked at Philip, and he felt himself shrink from their eyes. Why had it been so important to antagonize her, to feel the old passion, that ancient anger? He'd blown on the dark coals and made them glow again.

Through the doorway he spotted Hervé heading in his direction, on a mission. Philip escaped down the back hall.

In the kitchen he surprised a group chatting around the coffee maker, leading him to zag to the right, toward the service staircase. He clomped up to the second floor, but even there voices echoed from rooms, so he climbed yet another flight up to the cramped third floor. Aside from storage areas, there was nothing but a single tiny bedroom up here, the old servant's quarters, a room he knew all too well. If nothing else, it would be a decent place to hide out for a bit. He made for the door at the end of the landing, twisting the knob and pushing it open.

There was a thump, followed by a yowl, a gasp, and the sound of tumbling furniture. An orange cat caught by the swinging door bounded over a night table and up onto the single bed. At the little writing desk an adolescent girl with dark hair had leapt to her feet so suddenly that her chair had tipped over, her mouth forming an O of astonishment. Philip gaped at the shape of her forehead, the curve of her nose, the roundness in the eyes. His focus sharpened. She looked to be eleven or twelve, startled, but not frightened.

"Excuse me," he stammered in French, staggering back. "I'm sorry. I didn't know anyone was here."

"This is my room," she replied with a hint of indignation.

He stared. "Your room?"

"When we visit *Mamie*," she replied.

Mamie? Grandma? Did she mean Anne-Madeleine? So this was Margaux, Yvonne's daughter. He paused and glanced about the walls. The room had changed. There were new posters, new furniture, new colors. "I'm sorry," he said. "I . . . I took a wrong turn." He backed out. "I shouldn't have barged in on you."

Now her face wrinkled in a look of concern. "Were you looking for something, *Monsieur?*" She studied him and her eyes widened with a kind of recognition.

Philip took another step back, and as he saw Margaux moving toward him, he turned and bolted, dashing down the hall to the stairway, taking the steps two by two, desperate to escape. It was crazy, really, this whole visit. What on earth had he been thinking? He charged through the kitchen, leaving astonished guests in his wake.

Outside the front door he collided in the dark with a couple coming up the walk, the man stinking of whiskey. Philip pushed past.

"Where do you think you're going?" called a voice in French.

He wheeled around. The man was Roger. A woman stood at his side. Not Élisabeth. Younger. Much younger.

"You can't leave now," Roger slurred, grinning. "I just got here. The party's about to begin."

Philip wasn't prepared to face any more drunken Auberts. He turned and strode to the jungle of cars, some parked at the base of the drive, others nosed onto the lawn. Under the trees where it was nearly black, he searched for his Renault. In the distance Roger exchanged whispers with his date. Footsteps crunched on the gravel, then a hand lit upon Philip's shoulder. He shook it off.

"What's going on?" Roger said.

"I'm going home."

"You must have met Évelyne's brats, is that it? Flora has a litter of them, too. It's enough to put anyone off. But you can't go now."

"Don't tell me what I can't do."

"Listen, Philip, you're just wound up. You need a drink."

"And don't tell me what I need."

Roger staggered after him through the tangle of cars. "Oh come on," he said, his tongue thickened with alcohol. "You're not being . . . reasonable . . ." He paused. "Look, I know, it's not easy coming back."

"Mind your own business, Roger." He'd located the car and was digging in his pockets for the keys.

"What happened? Was it Hervé? It's always painful to meet the man who's fucking your wife. Trust me, I know all about that."

"Leave me alone, will you? You don't know the half of it."

Roger scrunched his face in concentration, then brightened. "I get it. I know what has you all riled up. You met Margaux, didn't you?"

Philip jammed his key into the lock.

"That's it," Roger continued. "You met Margaux. And she reminded you of Sophie. Isn't that right? You felt like you were looking at your own daughter. Well, who can blame you? That's what I see, too."

Philip growled with frustration. Why the hell couldn't he get his key in the lock?

"Come on," Roger said, laying his hand on Philip's shoulder.

"Don't touch me, Roger."

"Don't be ridiculous!" He hooked his arm around Philip's shoulder, trying to draw him away from the car. "Come on back. We have things to talk about . . . important things."

Philip spun on his heels, facing that cocky grin. Then he shoved as hard as he could, sending Roger back with a cry as he fell to the ground.

"Roger?" called out a woman's voice in French. It was the girl he had arrived with, up by the front door. "Roger? Is everything all right?"

Roger plucked gravel from his palms. "Fine, my dear," he called into the darkness. "I'll be with you in a moment." He struggled to his feet. "We need to talk."

"What we need," Philip said, "is for you to leave me alone."

"You have things to get off your chest. And I'm such a good soul that I'm willing to make a sacrifice to help you. You know what I'll give up?" He continued in a confidential whisper, nodding in the direction of the front door. "Joëlle. I've been working on her for three weeks, and tonight was to be the night. But for old times' sake, I'll go out with you, instead."

"Go back to your party, Roger. Go back to your carousing. Don't let me stop you." Finally the key glided into the lock and he climbed into the car. He fired up the engine and shifted into reverse.

"We need to talk," Roger called out.

He began backing the car through the maze of vehicles.

"Philip," Roger shouted as the Renault pulled away. Then, when it was almost too late, he bellowed out a name: "Olivier Morin!"

Philip skidded to a stop. Roger had not said Édouard Morin, a name he thought of in one way or another every day of his life. No, not Édouard, the boy, but Olivier, the father, the one who'd fought to protect his son from the press. And from Philip himself.

Roger smiled as he swaggered toward the stopped car. "That got your attention, didn't it? Olivier Morin."

"What about him, Roger?"

"He's dead, Philip. A year-and-a-half ago."

"What's that to me?"

"Don't be stupid. You know he was the one keeping Édouard from talking. The one shielding him. But you could get to Morin now," he said. "I'm almost sure of it." Roger was delighted with himself.

Philip tightened his fingers on the steering wheel. It was the last thing he needed to hear. "I'm not interested in Édouard Morin," he said finally. "It's over. It's too long ago."

"Oh come on. Who do you think you're kidding?"

Philip revved the engine and backed the car onto the street as Roger lumbered forward in the shadows.

"What's going on?" Roger cried out. "Am I the only one who cares about that girl any more?"

Philip shifted gears and the tires screeched as the vehicle lurched forward into the night.

Back at the hotel Philip slipped in and grabbed the room key from its pigeon-hole behind the reception desk, heading upstairs before Monsieur Bécot could come out. He closed himself in his room with the lights off and sank down on the edge of the bed, his head in his hands. A glint of reflected moonlight caught his eye. The handle of the minibar. He turned away.

What a colossal miscalculation. He should never have returned. It was too much to bear. Sophie, Roger, Yvonne, Hervé, Margaux. In a word: Yvetot.

The next morning he rose late, his mind thick, a throbbing behind his eyes. As his thoughts cleared, the memory of the previous evening came back, and right along with it a deep feeling of shame. Had he really said those things to Yvonne? Had he actually knocked Roger to the ground? He rubbed his head. He was done making a fool of himself.

Skipping breakfast, he checked out of the hotel and threw his bag in the car, driving all the way to Charles-de-Gaulle without stopping. After turning in the keys at the Hertz drop-off, he began the reverse process of his travels, receiving his boarding pass and checking in, confirming his identity at passport control, and stripping himself of metal objects at security. Two hours before departure he had already sunk into a plastic chair in the waiting lounge, still off-schedule from the first half of his trip, hungry, unshaven, sullen.

More than anything, he wanted to sleep, to turn off his brain. He tried to find a position that might allow him to slip into unconsciousness, twisting in his seat, hunkering down, jamming his fists into his jacket pockets—where his right hand encountered a tubular object. He pulled it out and found himself staring at Yvonne's ballpoint pen. He rolled this black wand between his fingers, examining the university logo, slowly closing his fingers around it.

That girl in the room. *Were you looking for something, Monsieur?* Of course he was looking—had been for over a decade. But what about Margaux? What would it be like for a twelve-year-old girl to always know that her half-sister lay buried somewhere in the countryside nearby?

He'd been fretting about Hervé and Yvonne, sparring with Roger. All that was pointless. He might not put it so bluntly with his patients, but Philip knew how it worked. By the time a person is twenty, the die is cast, the capacity for change nearly exhausted. Adults don't count. It's the children who matter. The only ones who really do.

He shoved the pen back in his pocket, stood, and walked to the wall of glass looking out upon the runways. In the distance, planes took off and landed against a background of cobalt blue. A little later his own flight began boarding. The crowd thinned. Stragglers trotted down the gangway. There was a final boarding call. He heard his name paged. Eventually the doors closed. At 1:45 p.m., Air France flight 332 pulled away from the gate and taxied out to the tarmac, where it waited in a queue.

Philip watched from a distance as the plane began its violent acceleration down the runway, the nose lifting into the air.

At a payphone in the terminal, he punched in a number.

"It's me," he said when it picked up.

"Philip?" came Roger's stunned voice from the other end of the line. "Shouldn't you be over the English Channel right about now? Are they allowing phone calls from thirty thousand feet?"

"I couldn't do it," he said.

"Do what?"

"I'm sorry about last night."

"Don't mention it."

"And you were right about Margaux. She does remind me of Sophie."

"Me too."

"I'm coming back."

Roger was all attention. "Really?"

"Just for a day or two."

"Yes, of course. Just a couple of days."

"I don't know what good it will do."

"Nor do I. But we'll find out."

"So," Philip concluded, "it looks like you get to have it your way after all."

"*My way*," Roger breathed. "It so happens that's just the way I like it."

Six

Those first days he'd had the excuse of jet lag and the shock of rediscovery, but the time for maudlin overreaction was past. If he was going to stay in Yvetot, he might as well do things properly, and that would mean going back to the beginning and laying it all out as clearly as he could.

No one knew better than Philip how the mind darns over holes, stitching together the torn fabric of memory. Remembrances are always fictions. But that doesn't make recollection a bad place to start. Quite the contrary.

He spread out his cache of photographs on the writing desk in the room at La Cauchoise, where Monsieur Bécot had begrudgingly checked him back in. These were the shots he'd borrowed from the album at home: Sophie perched on her bicycle in one, gripping her tennis racket in another, then carrying her skis or holding up her arm in the cast. There was the trick photo with the two Sophies face-to-face. Viewing these images was a painful pleasure, one he ordinarily wouldn't have allowed himself. But if he wanted to make headway, he'd need to spend some time in this underworld, nudging old ghosts.

It had started on a Saturday at the end of her eighth-grade year. They were already late, Anne-Madeleine having expected them in Yvetot the night before, where Sophie was to spend the week. While Yvonne slaved over a conference paper on one of Petrarch's sonnets, Philip lobbied for them to light out for the countryside. Yvonne wasn't ready, wasn't even sure she could go, and this led to a tiff. She told him to go without her, while he insisted she could work from her mother's home. Right then and there, in the heat of the argument, they nearly canceled the whole expedition. But the end of June in the city was hot and humid, the countryside beckoned, and Philip had prodded and wheedled. Sophie teamed up with her father in tacit conspiracy, moping ostentatiously. This fresh-faced, spring-loaded girl, newly emancipated from school, needed room to run.

Later on he would torture himself with variants of that day. What if they had argued an hour longer? If they had delayed for another day? If a cool breeze had kicked up across the capital, making the countryside less seductive? But the facts were the facts. They had agreed on a revised plan. Yvonne would set aside her conference paper for one day. They would drive out and stay in Yvetot overnight, then return home, leaving their daughter behind.

During the drive, Sophie rode in the back, her feet up on the seat, her nose in a book. He remembered which one: the second volume of *The Lord of the Rings,* in French translation. Sam was her favorite character.

Under a thin gauze of clouds they pulled into the drive of Yvonne's childhood home, and Anne-Madeleine, aging but still spry, appeared on the stone steps. Kisses and greetings all around. Anne-Madeleine took Sophie's backpack, faking a groan at its weight, and the two of them headed off for the hideaway bedroom on the third floor. Philip and Yvonne snuck a bite in the kitchen, then walked under the lindens to stretch their road-weary legs. Yvonne took his hand, glad to be there despite her earlier resistance. That evening Roger showed up with Élisabeth on his arm, boisterous as ever, and at dinner while the wine flowed he'd gotten them all roaring with laughter, especially his favorite niece, Sophie, who reveled in her uncle's madcap stories, and who knew how to return the volleys of his wit, which Roger received with a caricature of indignation.

Throughout the evening Yvonne and Philip let themselves forget about hospitals and patients and literature. Who cared about conference papers? How could they have squabbled like that? During a gale of laughter Yvonne had pressed his foot with hers under the table, and a look in her eyes had made him eager for the hour when the guests would leave.

The next morning they rose late, breakfasting on jam and bread in the kitchen, washing it down with bowls of dark coffee. Yvonne was preoccupied once again with her work, holing up in the living room with her notes. Philip lent Anne-Madeleine a hand with hedge-trimming in the garden. Sophie had run off to the neighbors, searching for the twins she often saw during the summer, making her plans for this week in the countryside. They had a light lunch—a *salade niçoise,* he recalled—and then early in the afternoon he and Yvonne returned their bags to the car. He kissed his daughter on the cheek. She graced a poor joke of his with a laugh. And then they were off. In the mirror of the car he saw her wave as they rolled over the crackling gravel of the drive.

That was the image that stuck in his mind—Sophie's reflection in the rearview mirror, her hand in the air.

Not that night but the following one, after a long day at the hospital, while

Philip was deep in sleep, the phone rang at one o'clock in the morning, jolting them awake. He experienced the sudden pinching that accompanies wrong-time phone calls, a clutching in the heart. Anne-Madeleine's voice came over the line, strained and urgent. Even before he made out her words he understood the intonation.

That was the moment his life started to tip, beginning its long tumble into a void whose very existence he had never suspected.

Then came the night drive back to Yvetot, racing on the country roads, with Yvonne shrunken in the other seat. The roar of the engine. The faint squeal of tires on the curves. Their arrival. Anne-Madeleine, huddled on the sofa, anguished, crying.

Sophie had last been seen in the late afternoon when she wandered off toward the park, a soccer ball under her arm. Anne-Madeleine hadn't missed her until dinner, at which point she'd scouted out the streets, asked the neighbors, going further and further afield. By ten o'clock she'd called the police—who now wanted to talk to Philip.

Had he been with Yvonne all day? Was there anyone who could vouch for his whereabouts? Rage had flared inside Philip as he realized the nature of their questions. At the same time, his professional self understood. Statistically, yes, it would be a relative, a male relative. They had to ask. He gave them the information they needed.

Next came the updates about the search. Officers described the neighborhood sweep. Rouen had been alerted.

Philip listened to it all in a daze. Less than twenty-four hours earlier he had kissed his daughter on the cheek; now, at three a.m. he heard the police debate the merits of dredging the river. He felt sure there'd been a mistake, a miscommunication. Sophie would walk through the back door at any moment. She'd be found lounging in an attic room, lost in a book and deaf to the clomp of boots and the rumble of male voices below. His mind played tricks, generating one totally implausible—but arguably possible—explanation after another. The father trumped the psychiatrist, denying the fact of his own denial.

Around four a.m. Flora and Pierre showed up. Élisabeth had already arrived. Yvonne did most of the talking with the police. It was easier for her, he told himself, because of the language. He recalled Roger's arrival as the first fingers of dawn showed in the east.

And while they waited, time was becalmed. The sail of the minutes couldn't find the wind, the hours foundered on the rocks.

Then, late the next morning, one more police car rolled up, the gravel crunching, the sound of it somber. There was the look on the face of the captain, the first mention of Édouard Morin, the awkward, bug-eyed adolescent from a few blocks away, a boy Philip had actually met, had spoken with—*and had already begun to diagnose.* No, he was not autistic, as people used to whisper. The aloofness, the quirks of speech, the obsessive behaviors—the symptoms all pointed to something on the schizophrenia spectrum. Schizoid. That had been Philip's conclusion. Months earlier he'd announced this to Anne-Madeleine, to Yvonne. The boy needed care, treatment.

They'd shrugged it off. It wasn't for them to say. They didn't want to meddle in another family. It wasn't the French way.

For want of meddling, his daughter had died.

Of all things it was the father, Olivier Morin, just a little older than Philip himself, who turned his son in. Having grown suspicious after hearing about the girl's disappearance, the father had pressed the boy for answers. Édouard couldn't account for crucial hours, and bit by bit spatters of information came out.

Philip knew that a schizophrenic's world can be as tightly sealed as an oyster's shell. Édouard's confession consisted of short, staccato answers, sketching the events incompletely, like dots on a page that hinted at an image.

What mattered the most was what Morin wouldn't say, what even his father couldn't tear out of him: where it had happened. Or more precisely: *where she was.*

Don't worry, the police had said. They would find the body. And they tried. Days passed while they searched the house, the yard, the park, the sheds, the dumpsters. A diver was lowered into an old well. Dogs were brought in. Strings of volunteers stalked through woodlands and fields. There was no shortage of possible clues. After all, the woods were full of trails and footprints, litter and shreds of fabric. But one by one they led to nothing. Days turned into weeks. There were limits to how far one could search, and to how long people could care. Meanwhile the legal proceedings were underway, full of evaluations and reports, also headed nowhere.

Philip had trudged through those weeks, then months, as if in a trance, tortured by the suspicion that he could have done something, nagged by the intuition that he'd brought it all upon himself, that this was his punishment. For running away from the States. For turning his back on his past. For daring to start something new.

And then came the night, months later, when Yvonne finally uttered the words that had been gathering like a storm, ones she could no longer contain, and that represented the beginning of their end. *You can't change what happened*, she said. *You need to pull yourself together.*

Certainly she'd meant these words to be an outstretched hand, a lifeline. After all, she'd been through hell herself. But the fact that Yvonne could utter these words after only eight months, made her seem like a stranger.

As evidence, recollections are awkward and unreliable. Memory is the twin of imagination. However, as with lies, the sags and bulges of remembrance often show the general contours of the truth. As a psychiatrist it was Philip's job to peer under covers and masks, and to tap at the walls and floors of his patients' stories in order to locate the secret cavities and false bottoms.

To equip himself for his work he stopped at the supermarket just off the square. The abundance of purple-veined lettuce, meaty mushrooms, and misshapen quince fruits contrasted with the sparseness of the school supplies, now out of season. Unable to locate a single spiraled tablet, Philip settled for a girl's diary, a slender volume of pleasant heft, with a cheap leather cover dyed cornflower blue and sporting the imprint of a dragonfly. The binding was simple, but it opened easily and the ruled pages would lie flat. The diary's daintiness clashed with the task he needed it for, but it would have to do.

From the hotel he called Jonas that afternoon to let him know he'd be staying in France for a few more days. "Just to wrap things up," he said.

"You don't have to explain yourself to me," Jonas replied. "To Linda, maybe, since she has to talk to the patients. Me, I think you should take all the time you need."

Philip promised to return by the weekend. He couldn't afford to fall further behind. "The only one I'm really worried about is Melanie Patterson," he told Jonas. "We were making progress."

"Right," Jonas drawled. "I remember the broken glass. I guess things were going pretty well."

Philip asked him to have Linda schedule a phone session with Melanie. That way he could at least keep tabs on the girl.

There was a lull.

"How was it, seeing Yvonne?" Jonas began.

Philip winced. "I behaved rather badly. Let's leave it at that."

"You've piqued my curiosity."

He looked out the window at the chestnut trees on the square, their leaves rustling faintly in the breeze. "It's been uncanny, this return."

"Remember what Freud said: *Love is homesickness.*"

"Don't forget the phone session with Melanie," he said. "Ideally in the next couple of days."

"Time to redirect, is that it? You've always been the Artful Dodger. Yes, I'll have Linda set things up."

At the end of the day Philip drove north toward Fécamp to meet with Roger, motoring through the pastures and woodlands in a red Smart Car that was so cramped his hair brushed against the roof. He passed through grayish stone hamlets with enigmatic names like Ypreville and Le Buc, each one more deserted than the last. Then the villages began to grow again. A gas station appeared, along with cross streets. Soon there was enough traffic to warrant roundabouts and traffic lights. The road rose over the crest of a hill, revealing the vista of an actual downtown curled around a port. The ocean was gray-green and choppy, and the air carried a hint of salt.

After locating a parking spot near the Aubert real estate agency, Philip began extracting himself from the car, backing out the door and unfolding his lanky body as if in a breach birth. He knocked the crown of his head against the frame.

"Nice wheels," said a voice behind him. It was Roger, leaning against the doorway of the agency, one hand in a pocket, a smirk on his face. "Style and power rolled into one. Though I would have gone with black, myself."

"I didn't have a reservation," Philip said, rubbing his scalp. "So what do you expect? The woman at the rental counter saw how tall I was, and she hunted for her most uncomfortable vehicle."

"It's like they say. Everything's smaller in France—from cars to food servings to the size of women's breasts. I guess that's what makes us quaint." As Philip approached, Roger wrapped his arms around him and squeezed hard. "A bear hug," he proclaimed. "One of the few useful things I learned in the States."

"I've hardly been away twenty-four hours."

"What can I say? You're my brother-in-law."

"*Ex*-brother-in-law."

"Don't drag me into that. You and Yvonne may have divorced, but *we* didn't." He clapped his hands together. "So much to talk about. Shall we go for dinner? It's a touch early, but I know a place."

"I don't mean to pull you away from the office."

Roger pushed out his lips and shrugged away the question of clients. Business was slow. He bemoaned the plight of the real estate market and the tightfistedness of the Fécampois. While Roger began to lock up the agency, a full-bodied woman with close-cropped hair appeared around the corner, striding in their direction. Philip was just beginning to recognize her gait and button nose when Roger jangled his keys and turned.

"Élisabeth," he cried. "My dear, look what I've found. It's Philip."

But Élisabeth looked to be in no mood for chatting, and as Roger stepped forward to greet her, she raised her hand and administered a powerful slap. He staggered back, cupping his hand around his cheek.

"Ça," she announced, "*C'est pour Joëlle.*"

Roger gestured but found himself at a loss for words. It was as good as a confession.

She halted in front of Philip, flicking her hair back. "Hello, Philip. I heard you were in town. I'm sorry you had to witness that." She leaned forward and kissed him on the cheek.

"Nice to see you, Élisabeth. Your right hook is in good form."

She gave a wry smile. "You'll excuse me for not staying to chat right now. I'm afraid I'm rather upset."

"I understand. Or, at least, I'm beginning to."

With a final dark look at Roger, she turned and marched away, her heels tapping sharply on the sidewalk.

Philip turned to his brother-in-law and folded his arms over his chest as he waited for an explanation.

Roger pressed his fingertips to his cheek and flinched. "She bruised more than my arrogance."

"Care to tell me what's going on?"

"It's complicated," he said. "Let's just say that I probably had it coming."

The restaurant was full of dark wood, mirrors, and ladder-back chairs. Roger had settled in on the other side of the linen-draped table. A huddle of glasses waited at each setting, along with more silverware than Philip knew what to do with.

He leaned across the table. "So what's going on with you two? Are you divorced or not?"

"Oh, you know. Pretty much."

"You can't be *pretty much* divorced. It's one or the other. And I take it Joëlle isn't the first one Élisabeth has caught you with." Roger was deep into the wine list, scrutinizing it like a gambler with a racing form. Finally he waved the waiter over and placed his bet.

"That's another thing," Philip started. "You were plastered last night."

"What can I tell you? I like to have a good time. That shouldn't come as news to anyone."

"When a man can hardly stand up straight, it's beyond enjoyment."

"Might I remind you that if I had difficulty remaining vertical, it was because my brother-in-law knocked me to the ground?"

Philip leaned back. "What's going on with you?"

Roger gave him a hard look. "It's really none of your business."

The wine arrived and Roger went through the ritual of tasting. This sacrament complete, the sommelier began to pour. Too late Philip realized the first glass was his own, and he gestured for the server to stop.

"You can't refuse that," Roger said. "It's a Volnay."

"Thank you, but no."

Roger eyed him darkly until the sommelier retreated, then leaned forward. "Is this a new bad habit of yours, not drinking?"

Under his beard, Philip felt his cheeks redden. "For nearly five years now."

"You used to enjoy a good glass."

"A bit too much. I finally took control. You might consider that yourself."

Roger rolled his eyes. "Good grief. What did you do? Go to meetings? *Hello, my name is Philip, and I'm an alcoholic?*"

He gritted his teeth. "Yes. Something like that."

Roger sighed. "Hmm. That explains a few things. Well, let the unhappiness of the one cheer the other." He emptied Philip's glass into his own before sipping off a mouthful of the ruby liquid. He savored it with exaggerated pleasure.

At moments like this Philip understood why the Aubert siblings found Roger so exasperating. Histrionic personalities could be charming—as long as you didn't mind the self-centeredness, the theatricality, the immaturity. Still, Philip partly envied him. Roger was willing to question assumptions and buck the trends. Even now, nearing fifty, he could still wriggle into the costume of the maverick.

"So," Roger began. "Does Yvonne know you're back in town? Or rather, that you failed to leave?"

"Not yet."

"You can't keep it a secret, you know. Not around here."

"I'm afraid she's going to ask me what I'm doing, and I haven't figured out the answer to that question." He gave Roger a knowing look. "One thing I've learned is to be prepared before speaking to Yvonne. Your sister isn't always the easiest woman to deal with."

"Doesn't come as news to me. Still, try not to be too hard on her." He planted his elbows on the table. "I'm not saying that because I'm her brother, you know. Far from it. But you don't know all she went through. I don't mean just Sophie. The divorce, too. If I had a cent for every time I had to hold Yvonne while she wept . . ."

The vision of Yvonne sobbing on Roger's shoulder flashed through Philip's mind, but it felt false, artificial—a Photoshopped image, one that clashed with the sleek and controlled woman he had seen at the party just the other night. "She seems to have gotten over it," he stated. "She's built herself a new life. One that doesn't resemble the old one."

Roger snorted. "You mean her marriage to Hervé? Yes, I'd say he's pretty different."

"It's natural enough. She'd had her fill of foreigners, so this time she married a man from home."

"Home?" Roger's smile broadened. He glanced right and left as if checking for eavesdroppers, then leaned in. "I wouldn't repeat that too loudly. Hervé may be a Norman, but he hails from Rouen, and in small towns like Yvetot and Fécamp, Rouen is considered the enemy."

Philip stroked his beard. "So she wanted a place to live that was different from both Paris and Yvetot. Something that was home, and yet not home. Rouen must have seemed like a successful compromise."

"Perhaps. In a way."

"But then there were things she couldn't control. Like Margaux. My guess is she was hoping for a boy. Anything to avoid reminders."

"Can you blame her?"

Blame was not the name for the emotion Philip felt. "I don't hold it against Yvonne that she wanted a new life. I just resent her for being so damn good at it."

While they ate, Roger turned to the topic he'd brought up the other night: Olivier Morin. Just over three years ago the man had retired from his position as a press operator at a local printer. Not long after that, word got around that he had cancer.

"The pancreas," Roger said. "As you can imagine, it didn't take very long. But to be honest, I didn't feel too sorry. He was an odd little fellow, and there's no doubt that he'd had a hard time of it because of his son. I don't think he actually minded dying. But afterward, I got to wondering about what his death would mean. He'd worked so hard to protect Édouard, barring all access to him. And suddenly that obstacle was gone."

"So you made some inquiries."

Roger nodded. "Not right away. But then I realized you'd be coming back for Mother's funeral."

"And what did you learn?"

Roger paused to fill his wineglass, taking another long sip, holding the fluid in his cheeks before swallowing. "As you probably know," he began, "Édouard passed through a number of clinics. Turns out he's back in the region, in the psychiatric hospital outside of Rouen. It took a while to get hold of the right doctor. But I finally got there. He's under the care of a fellow named Suardet."

Philip prompted him. "And you've spoken with him?"

"He was a bit reluctant at first, but, well, you know me." Roger grinned. "I know how to stroke people the right way. In the end he agreed to look into it. He wasn't sure offhand what the legal situation was—that is, whether there were any restrictions about who could see Édouard. And, of course, a meeting could only occur if Morin himself consented to it. Today, since you were coming back, I left another message for our good doctor—along with your number at the hotel. I don't suppose he called yet?"

Philip shook his head.

"That boy, he must be thirty years old by now," Roger said.

"Thirty-two," Philip muttered, lost in thought.

"That sounds about right."

"Not about. Exactly."

Roger took another gulp of wine. "Anyway, now that the father is dead, the door to the son is open. Theoretically, at least. So what do you think? Will he agree to meet?"

In his mind's eye Philip saw Morin's face as it was at seventeen, bug-eyed under his shocks of dark hair, nervous, his gaze skipping from side to side, his lips clamped in a grimace. The last thing Édouard Morin wanted back then was to meet anyone at all, and Philip saw no reason for this to have changed.

"No," he said. "I don't think so. There's no possible benefit for him."

Roger frowned. "But there's also no risk," he said. "I mean, he's not going to get into any more trouble. Wouldn't you think he'd want to clear the air after all these years? That he'd sympathize with your situation?"

"I don't think compassion is an arrow he has in his quiver."

Roger looked deflated. He contemplated his empty plate.

It was Philip who spoke first. "You know, back when the case was dismissed, what struck me most was the legal term."

"What do you mean?"

"They called it a *non-lieu*. I understood the case was being dropped, but I wasn't familiar with that word. French was such an annoyance then. You can't imagine what it's like not being able to follow the legal proceedings for your own daughter's murder. *Non-lieu*. To me it just meant *no place*. As if they were saying that the murder itself had never occurred. Or that the case didn't belong in the court. But most of all it described Sophie: it was she who had no place, wasn't anywhere. Without her body, the whole process had been performed around a void, a vacuum. Nothing but a name."

Roger nodded, draining the end of his wine. "That's French law for you. We excel at taking the obvious and making it obscure. It's a national pastime."

The waiter came by with coffees, along with a snifter of Calvados. Roger swirled the golden liquid in the ball of his glass, lifted it to his nose and inhaled.

"Tell me," Philip said. "Are you the one who left the flower on Sophie's grave?"

The snifter paused beneath Roger's nose. "Listen, I was already there for Mother's funeral, so it was just a few steps away. Don't start thinking I make daily pilgrimages." He took a gulp of the digestif as if to wash the taste of sincerity from his mouth. He sighed. "You know I was supposed to have dinner with them that night, don't you?" He closed his eyes. "If I hadn't canceled, she'd never have gone off on her own. She'd still be alive today."

"You don't know that," Philip murmured.

"And do you know why I canceled?" Now he turned his eyes to the ceiling. "Because of Élisabeth. An opportunity came up for an evening of romance, and because I always do whatever my prick tells me, I canceled on my niece." He stared into his cup. "While Édouard Morin bludgeoned her with a stone, I was busy fondling Élisabeth's tits."

"No one expects you to be a monk, Roger."

"Hah. No danger of that, I suspect."

A sense of understanding settled on Philip: the rose on the grave, Roger's keenness to help, perhaps even his difficulties with Élisabeth—a relationship damaged by the very tragedy whose occurrence it facilitated.

"What it comes down to is this," Roger continued. "I'm sure I am far better suited to unclehood than to fatherhood, but if I did have a child—what I mean is that if I had had one—well, let's just say that I'd have wanted her to be like Sophie."

He raised his hand and called for the check.

It was night before Philip started the return drive to Yvetot. Occasional headlights flickered and grew, blinding him before vanishing. At intersections in dark-windowed hamlets he slowed to a crawl, craning to recognize his route.

While he drove, it was the image of Yvonne sobbing in Roger's arms that stuck with him. At least she, too, had suffered after the divorce. For all these years he had wrapped himself in a cloak of grief lined with regret. But that mantle was cut wide enough to accommodate others in its folds.

The road dipped into a dark swale, woods rising up along the shoulders, ghostly trunks glowing in the headlights of the Smart Car before receding into black as he passed. Maybe here, he thought. Perhaps Édouard Morin had dumped Sophie's body in these very woods, just a hundred yards to the right or the left. Why not? As well here as in a thousand other groves or gullies.

All the old imaginings. Every rise of earth turned into a potential grave.

Might there be a chance of finding something? If so, he'd have Roger to thank. Roger, who had kept him here, who was offering his support, but who himself needed help. There was a darkness in his brother-in-law he didn't recognize from before. His impertinence had gone bitter. Irony had aged into sarcasm.

The steering wheel slid under his fingers as the road straightened, the beam of headlights returning to the painted lines. He passed through the village of Ypreville, following the main street as it veered through a labyrinth of buildings. At the town hall the road split in three directions, slips of signs bearing unpronounceable Norman names—Yébleron, Daubeuf, Sorquainville. He inched the car forward, scanning the stone walls for hints of his route. Finally the light swept across a battered metal arrow, nearly broken off its post, the point mashed: Yvetot.

In the dark lobby of the hotel Monsieur Bécot drew his room key from the pigeonhole behind the reception desk, along with a small sheet of paper.

"While you were out," Bécot reported, practicing his English, "you had a telephonic call." He handed Philip the page. Then, with distaste, he added, "From Rouen."

Philip unfolded the sheet, his pulse quickening. It was from Suardet, the doctor Roger had contacted. A meeting with Édouard Morin was possible. Philip read the note twice, unsure if he should let himself believe it. There was no benefit for Morin in such an encounter, and yet here was his acceptance, transmitted by Suardet and recorded in Bécot's unsteady hand. After nearly fifteen years, Philip would find himself face to face with the assassin of his happiness. Suardet even proposed a time, impossibly close: ten o'clock the day after next.

Bécot leaned forward over the oak counter. "It is all right that I ask a question, Monsieur Adler?"

"Certainly."

"This Monsieur Morin," he said. "It is not Édouard Morin?"

"I'm afraid it is."

Bécot's large head sagged. "Monsieur Adler," he said. "This is not my business, I know. Maybe I should not say anything. I understand what you do here. Everyone in Yvetot can understand. But we have a proverb in France. *Ne réveillez pas le chat qui dort.* Do not wake the sleeping cat. The past is past."

"Sometimes the cat wakes up on its own, Monsieur Bécot. Isn't that what you told me about fields in Normandy, about all the remains from the war? That which is buried comes to the surface."

Bécot shook his head.

"Personally," Philip added, "the proverb I prefer is, *pour faire une omelette, il faut casser des oeufs.* To make an omelet, you have to be ready to break a few eggs."

"A very fine analogy, Monsieur Adler," Bécot said with a strained smile. "Very clever. But remember who said it: Robespierre, during the Revolution. Do you wish to end up like him?" He drew his index finger across his neck.

Seven

Stripped to his undershirt, Philip sat on the sagging bed in the room at La Cauchoise, the old phone pressed to his ear. Through the open window a rustle of roosting doves came from the gutters on the roof. It was closing in on midnight. He'd been talking to Melanie for over half an hour, and things weren't going well.

"I *don't* want to talk about it," she was saying.

"Well, Melanie. No one's forcing you."

"*You're* forcing me."

He sighed. Overhead a moth threw itself against the fabric shade of the ceiling light, again and again. He knew how it felt. "So, how am I forcing you?" he said at last.

She snorted. "Right. As if you don't know. You, like, tell my dad I'm not getting better. You tell him I'm not trying. And then he makes me do more sessions."

"Melanie, I don't tell your father what we talk about. You know that."

"*Right.*"

Philip could picture her rolling her eyes, flicking back her hair. He wondered if she was in her full Melanie Patterson regalia, covered in black right down to the dots of polish on her fingernails. Maybe for a phone call she didn't feel the need to don the whole Goth uniform of anguish.

It was time to nudge things in a new direction.

"What are you so angry about?" he asked her. "Are you mad at me for leaving?"

He heard a puff of indignation. "I don't care *what* you do. You don't have to ask me for permission. Nobody else does."

He frowned. What was she referring to? Melanie's father traveled a good deal for his new company, but Philip suspected she was talking about more than a feeling of abandonment. What else happened without her permission? He considered Neil Patterson—the controlling nature, the ego. The kind of attitude that led to inadmissible behaviors.

He ran his fingers through the nap of his beard. Yes, this seemed possible, entirely too possible. And what of Melanie's mother? A cow-eyed, anxious woman, she'd been the one to push for treatment. Probably she'd had some inkling of the nature of this trouble. But no, Cindy Patterson couldn't be counted on for much more.

He tried to bend the conversation in this direction.

"Do you trust me, Melanie?" he said into the phone.

"Trust you to take my dad's money? Sure."

"Now why would you say that?"

"Because I've seen what he pays you, you know. He told me. I guess he, like, wanted me to see how much I was costing."

Philip winced. Patterson shouldn't have done that. It wasn't wise—not unless you were trying to make a sixteen-year-old girl feel guilty, and then use that guilt to keep her under your control. In which case it was a very clever idea indeed. He wondered how long it would be before Melanie could speak about him.

Tick, tick went the moth above him, still seeking a breach in the light shade.

"Well, let's talk about that," he offered, trying to rescue what he could. "How did it make you feel to see what your father was paying me?"

"I don't really give a *fuck*," she said, wringing the word for all its juice.

"But it sounds like you do," he said.

"That's *bullshit*."

"Then why did you bring it up?"

There was a pause, and he could almost feel the phone shiver in his hand.

"I *hate* this," she seethed.

"You hate what, exactly?"

"I hate *everything*."

"What do you mean by everything, Melanie? Could you be more specific?"

"No," she cried. "I can't *be more specific*. Why can't you just leave me alone!"

He tried to keep his voice level. "Because I want to hear what you hate."

"I don't fucking *care* what you want to hear. You want to know what I hate? I hate these goddamned sessions. I hate having to waste my time sitting here. I hate *you*, if you really want to know. That's what I hate."

He needed Melanie's face, wanted to see what her body had to say.

"Can I go now," she said through her teeth. It didn't sound like a question.

"We still have twenty minutes."

"What, so you can earn what, like, another thousand bucks? What's the matter? Are you running short of money on your little French vacation?"

He felt a pinch. "I'm not on vacation, Melanie. You know I wouldn't have left if I didn't need to."

"Oh, *right*. Of course. It must be super-important."

She'd found a lever, and Philip felt the balance in the conversation tipping. "You know I can't talk about this with you."

"Oh, sure. I get it. It's all, like, *do you trust me, Melanie?* But it doesn't go in the other direction, does it? When I ask a question, it's all hush-hush. Everything you do is top secret."

Philip pressed his thumb and forefinger against the bridge of his nose. A pain was blossoming behind his eyes. She had a point of course, but he couldn't start telling patients about his private life.

Up above, the moth had slowed in its attack on the light shade, circling more erratically. Maybe it had learned its lesson, was ready to cut its losses. Maybe it was just exhausted.

"Look," he began. "I wish I didn't have to be away right now, but I do. That doesn't make our sessions less important to me."

"Yeah, right," she said blandly. "Whatever."

Her tone irked him. "No, not *whatever*," he said. "Why do you think I've arranged to keep our sessions going like this?"

"I'm so grateful." Her voice was listless. "Thanks a billion."

"Stop pretending it doesn't matter to you."

"But it *doesn't*," she said.

His shoulders tightened. "Melanie."

"Don't you get it?" she continued. "*I couldn't care less.*"

"*Melanie.*"

"So you should just enjoy your vacation. How's your tan?"

"Stop it."

"I hear they have all these topless beaches over there. I bet you like that, don't you?"

"Damn it, Melanie." He threw his head back and clenched his teeth. Did the girl understand nothing? Why did she behave like this? After everything he'd been through, all he'd done for her, the life he'd given up, the trouble he'd taken, *this* was how she thanked him?

Then a long breath escaped from him. He understood. His shoulders sagged. How could he have been so blind? She had transferred her feelings about her father onto him, and now, pressed into the paternal role, he had taken up his own part in the script. He couldn't deal with this. Not now. It was too heavy. He didn't have the strength.

"Are you still there?" she was saying, her voice balanced on a wire, trying to show how little she cared while checking to make sure her audience was still in attendance. "Doctor Adler?"

It was all he could do to squeeze out a few words. "I have to go."

"But you said we had twenty minutes." The taunt had vanished from her voice. She knew she'd struck a nerve. She just didn't know which one.

He kept his voice steady. "Something's come up. We'll do another call soon."

"But I . . ."

"I have to go. Goodbye."

He hung up. Sitting on the edge of the bed, he lowered his head into his hands and massaged his brow with his fingertips. Now there was this to untangle as well.

A white mass fluttered on the floor to his left, stopped, then fluttered again. The moth rose halfway to the lamp before falling back to the ground. It couldn't let go, and not letting go was killing it.

Eight

Sleep restored a hint of hopefulness. He would schedule a new call with Melanie. And he had another task now, a larger one, one he had the skills for. From long experience with the monologues of patients, he had learned how to recognize patterns in the shadows of symptoms. He wouldn't have much time with Édouard Morin, but if there was anything to listen to, he stood a chance of hearing it. He had one day to prepare for the encounter.

Huddled under the too-low showerhead in the hotel bathroom, the water sputtering onto his chest, he was in the midst of contemplating his plans when a bump sounded in the bedroom. A moment later it came twice more, suggesting that it wasn't a bump after all, but rather a thump—or a knock. Dripping, wrapped in a towel, he emerged, fumbling on the nightstand for his glasses, which fell to the floor just as the knocking resumed. He turned the knob and cracked the door open to reveal the blurry figure of a woman in a yellow blouse and summer-weight skirt. Even without his glasses on she looked uncomfortably familiar.

"So much for goodbyes," Yvonne said, her voice sharp.

He straightened. "Actually, I don't remember any goodbyes. The last I saw, you were storming away from me into a crowd of people at your mother's house."

"That's right. Shortly before you assaulted my brother in the driveway."

Philip paused. "Give me a minute, will you?" He closed the door, pulled on a pair of trousers and plucked a shirt from the open suitcase. Hunting for the glasses that had tumbled from the nightstand, he felt a crunch underfoot, nearly snapping the hinge of the frame. When he put them on, they rested crookedly on his nose. He let Yvonne in as he finished buttoning up his shirt, somehow finding himself with one more hole than he needed.

He gestured around the room. "Welcome to Monsieur Bécot's finest suite."

The bed was unmade, and dirty laundry lay strewn about like flotsam on a beach, but not all the disorder was Philip's: the sagging window curtain came courtesy of La Cauchoise, as did the tipped desk, and the ancient armoire that yawned on its defective latch.

"True," he continued, clapping his hands together. "The glory is somewhat faded, but—"

Yvonne interrupted him. "When you left the house the other night, I didn't expect to see you again. For a long time."

He couldn't hold her gaze. "I was going to call you today. I swear I was."

Her blank look invited him to try again.

"How did you find out?" he said. "Was it Roger?"

Her eyebrows rose. She'd file away this fraternal infidelity for future reference. "It's a small town," she answered.

All right. Now he at least had some idea of the speed of Yvetot's rumor mill.

Yvonne walked to the window, trailing her fingers across the writing desk, just inches from the black pen. "Would you kindly tell me what you plan to do?"

"*Plan* is too ambitious a word."

"By which you mean that you don't know?" She turned. "That doesn't sound like you, Philip."

There was no easy way to buffer the information. "I'm going to see Édouard Morin." Yvonne's eyes flared and her lips parted. He hurried to continue. "A single meeting," he assured her. "No one has been able to speak to him, and now that his father has died—"

"Don't you *dare*."

Philip closed his eyes. "Look," he began.

She clenched her hands into fists. "Just what do you think this will accomplish?"

"What can it hurt?"

"Answer my question."

"You answer mine," he shot back.

Yvonne put her hands on her hips. "All right. What can it hurt? How about *me and my family?* I don't want to put them through this. I don't want to deal with it. I don't want my daughter to have to—"

"Tell me, which daughter are we talking about?" he said. "Just to be clear."

He regretted these words right away.

When she spoke again, her voice was measured but tense. "Listen to me, Philip," she said. "What you and I lived through was a ghastly thing. Something no parent should have to face. But it was fifteen years ago. Going back to it will solve nothing. Will *change* nothing. Why on earth do you want to dredge it all up again?"

Philip found this question incredible. He and Yvonne were like two separate universes obeying entirely different physical laws. In hers actions were balanced by reactions, matter was conserved, and time marched forward in a single, irreversible direction. His own was filled with dark matter and supernovas, riddled with wormholes that tied space and time together in a Gordian knot. That these two universes had once been joined seemed unthinkable to him now.

His first impulse was to argue. But what headway could he make? Even he had to admit that Yvonne's view of the world was more practical. Part of him even wished he could be like her. However, it wasn't a thing you could choose.

Muffled voices sounded in the hallway—the chambermaids checking for rooms to clean. He waited for their voices to recede.

"Answer one question for me," he said to Yvonne, keeping his voice low. "Every time you look at Margaux, isn't it Sophie you see?"

"For God's sake, Philip," Yvonne replied in a hushed cry, "don't talk like that. Can you imagine? It's difficult enough for Margaux to have this story lurking in her background. The last thing she needs is for it to all come to the surface."

"Maybe that's exactly what she needs. To have this ghost exorcised, once and for all."

"Don't you dare presume. This is my daughter you're talking about."

He sank onto the bed and stared into the ragged carpeting between his feet.

"How did you do it, Yvonne?" he said. "How did you move forward? I need to know. Because even after fifteen years, I've not been able to close that door."

Yvonne turned to the window. For a long moment she stared out over the square. "I could do it because I'm not you," she replied. "It's what funerals are for, Philip. They provide closure. They help you to forget a little bit, enough so that you can move on."

"The funeral was a sham. There was nothing to bury. It was like a dress rehearsal."

She turned. "Then all funerals are shams. What you bury is never what you lost. You know that as well as I do."

He ran his hand over his beard. "I know how pointless this is. The body is just a shell. A mortal suit of clothes." He pulled at his misbuttoned shirt. "Though I must say, mine pinches at the shoulders these days and needs to be let out a bit at the waist."

She allowed herself a hint of smile.

"So you're right," he continued. "It shouldn't matter. What's the difference between Sophie's bones and some old rocks and twigs? Nothing much. I fully appreciate that it makes no rational sense. And yet I can't *not* do this." He looked up at her now. "Do you see that?"

The anger in her eyes had waned. "You shouldn't have come back, Philip."

"Give me two days. Let me go through the motions. Then I'll leave. Three days at the most. We both want the same thing, don't we? To put an end to all this?" He paused. "I'll be discreet."

A laugh escaped from Yvonne. "You have many qualities, Philip, but I don't count discretion among them."

He cracked a wry grin. "That's fair. I don't have a good track record on that score. But I'll make a special effort."

They stood in silence until it was time for her to go. Halfway out, she stopped and turned. They were face to face, inches apart.

"If you're going to remain in Yvetot," she said, her voice low but imperious, "I want you to be *invisible*. Do you understand? I want to see nothing, hear nothing. Do what you have to do, then leave. Don't interfere with us. Can you manage that?"

He swallowed and nodded.

Satisfied that their transaction was complete, she gave a last look about the room.

"Do clean this place up, Philip," she said. "It's a mess."

He watched her stride down the hallway toward the stairs, her calves flexing with each step. He felt short of breath.

Philip straightened out the buttons on his shirt, but the results were hardly satisfactory. Each day left him more ruffled than the last, and he'd reached the outer limit of presentability. The lumpy knot in his shoelace didn't help, nor did the missing button on his jacket sleeve, the scab from yesterday's shaving accident, or the new Band-Aid repair job on his glasses. Having originally packed for three days, his clothes were on their second wind and in need of laundering. He pried a recommendation from Monsieur Bécot and found a launderer just off the main square, where a chubby, surly woman agreed to take his bundle.

More than clothing, though, he needed a plan, and for that he required coffee and a table. Down the street, a bar-café called the *Tord-boyaux* occupied a wedge-shaped building at the corner of the road. Through the glass door he made out a cluster of men at the bar, served by a bovine woman. A short fellow with a tweed driving cap was chatting with animation, gesturing broadly to the group in illustration of a tale. He drew a quip from a gangly man in a police uniform, and laughter rippled through the roughly attired group—at least until Philip entered. Then all eyes rotated toward him and a hush settled over the group.

The *Tord-boyaux* smelled of beer and body odor. Plywood shelves behind the bar bowed from the weight of bottles. A green and red Pernod clock hung on the wall, the minute hand missing. Aside from a list of beverages pinned to the left of the bar, the only decoration on the walls was a laminated poster of mountains—inexplicably the Rockies rather than the Alps or Pyrenees—imperfectly masking the lumpy plaster where a window had been walled up some years earlier.

"*C'est ouvert?*" Philip asked, though it was a foolish question. The proof stood before him in the form of flesh and blood, in the glasses and cups resting on the zinc counter, or even in the wisps of cigarette smoke floating in flagrant defiance of the no smoking sign.

The *patronne* answered with a reluctant nod, and Philip made his way past the group of mostly unshaven men, taking a small table in the corner.

At the bar, conversation was slow to resume, the fellow with the driving cap speaking in hushed tones. There were sidelong glances in his direction, followed by mutterings.

Monsieur Bécot may have been right that no one wanted him in this town, but Philip wasn't to be dissuaded. Soon fueled by espresso, he pulled out the blue diary he'd purchased at the supermarket and opened it to two blank pages. On the left side he wrote the heading "Boston," and on the right "Yvetot." The first list was short. He needed to keep in touch with Jonas about the office. He had to prevail upon his neighbor to continue feeding Edith. And he wanted Linda to schedule another phone session for him with Melanie Patterson.

The second list was more substantial. Before the meeting with Édouard Morin, he wanted to pick up a digital voice recorder, for it was often useful to listen to conversations more than once. Also, managing communications would be tricky without a cell phone. Last of all, he was running low on cash.

Then there was the item that connected the two pages: the flight back. Today was Wednesday, but it was hard to predict when he'd be ready to leave. It all depended on Morin—on what the man might have to say. This was the one category he had no control over. Philip wrote Édouard Morin on his list, following the name with three question marks.

When he paid for his coffee at the bar, the customers lapsed again into funereal silence, pretending to ignore his presence. The *patronne* slapped his change on the counter, and before the door had fully closed behind him, the murmurings began, one alcohol-raked voice after another. The volume increased.

He started his tasks. At the phone store an acne-covered sales boy sold him a cheap Nokia, activating it for local service. Next he stopped at the ATM by the bank, replenishing his supply of cash.

The voice recorder proved to be a more difficult object to locate in such a small town. He made the rounds of the few shops carrying minor electronics—the tobacconist, the newsagent, the optician—each proprietor unable to produce such a device, or even to suggest where to find one. Their answers to his questions were rapid, clipped.

He got the message. He wasn't welcome in Yvetot. He would find friction at every turn. The laundry woman had grimaced at his shirts, and at the *Tord-boyaux* they begrudged him even his coffee. Only the boy in the phone shop seemed to have missed the memo.

He had nearly given up his search when he passed the hardware store just off the main square, where a husky young shopkeeper clung high on a ladder, repainting a sign where the old name HESSE was leeching through and haunting the newer name like a ghost. He recalled this store in its earlier incarnation, years ago, as a den of nails and farm implements, run by a gruff and ancient man.

In the display window among assorted gadgets, there lay an old recorder, the size of a pack of cigarettes, still wrapped in cellophane.

"What can I do for you, Monsieur?" the man called down to the top of Philip's head.

When Philip began to ask about recorders, the salesman stiffened at the American accent. He claimed not to have anything of the sort.

"But you do," Philip protested, pointing. "Right there. In the window."

"Oh, you wouldn't want that. It's so old! It's been there for years. Who knows if it even works?"

"I'll take my chances."

"Well," the man started, "I . . . I'm afraid I need to finish this sign right now. Perhaps after lunch . . ."

Philip rolled his eyes. More stonewalling. If he backed down before such pettiness, he'd never get anywhere. There was no one else on the street, so he grabbed a rung of the ladder and gave it a vigorous shake, rattling the bucket of paint.

"What are you doing, Monsieur!" the man howled, his brush tumbling.

"I said I would like to make a purchase."

"But I told you—"

Philip cut him off with another shake of the ladder, ignoring the cries until he heard the sound of boots descending the rungs.

Ten minutes later he left the hardware store, the recorder clutched in his fist like a trophy.

That afternoon he called Roger in Fécamp to let him know about the meeting, declining his brother-in-law's offer to accompany him. No, he repeated: this visit he would do alone.

In his hotel room, he laid open the blue diary and took notes, attempting to anticipate the turns the conversation with Morin might take. The most likely scenario was that he would refuse to speak about Sophie directly. If Philip could guide the conversation along the perimeter of the issue, he might spot truths stirring inside, just as one glimpses wildlife deep in a forest while strolling along its edge.

But such delicate control usually required a profound understanding of the other person, and Philip didn't know this man. Mostly he remembered the boy's eyes, large and bulging under the shock of black hair, as if they could scarcely bear what they had beheld, shifting their focus in a skittish gaze that touched upon objects fleetingly. In the past, Morin would rarely meet the eyes of others—especially when the person in question was the father of his victim, and particularly when this father sat across from him in the same chamber, such as the day when a black-robed judge named Tremblay uttered the word *non-lieu* that formalized the dismissal.

Nevertheless, even through the mask of detachment, Morin's stark intelligence had been evident. Philip would now be venturing onto Morin's territory, as in a game where the opponent holds all the advantages, including the most powerful option of them all: the simple refusal to engage. In chess, Philip would familiarize himself with his opponent over the course of several games. Here he'd have only one chance.

Toward the end of the day he wandered through the streets, taking it slowly in the heat of early summer, mulling over possibilities. Yvetot was a weary town. A few storefronts were empty, and several buildings cried for repair. Stucco crumbled from walls, revealing more primitive construction underneath. Even the roads were cracked and full of potholes.

Outside Saint-Pierre Church a rotund priest wearing a white chasuble scurried about, chasing away a pack of children who had clambered up the wall near the entrance. While the priest scolded one boy, another crept up from behind and yanked on his robe, making him whirl about like a black top.

He hiked all the way out to the Aubert home, dark and shuttered now that the clan had dispersed. Probably Yvonne would soon put it on the market, and that would be the end of it. He walked on, past the park, and eventually rounded back toward the town center. The great canopy of an oak rose before him: Saint-Louis cemetery.

The dislocations of jet lag had altogether departed, French flowed more fluidly from his lips, and the labyrinth of streets less frequently surprised him. He had his bearings. He was ready.

Nine

The psychiatric facility lay several kilometers to the south of Rouen, toward the top of a broad hill. As he walked up from the parking lot, Philip surmised that it dated from the turn of the century and had probably first served as a sanitarium for respiratory ailments. A two-story wing unfurled from each side of the central administrative block, with a score of high windows interrupting great stretches of wheat-colored stucco. A frieze flecked with *art nouveau* motifs ran in a band beneath the ledge of zinc roofing, conferring upon the structure a kind of pleasantness, the decorative feel of a large but modest hotel—one with bars on most of the windows.

He'd arrived early, and Suardet's assistant parked him in the empty waiting room while final preparations were made.

The oddness of the situation rattled him. He'd seen plenty of Édouard Morin fifteen years earlier, usually at a distance. At one point, in a hallway outside the judge's chambers, he had sat almost within reach of the rapist, filled with the urge to lunge for him, to wrap his fingers around the prominent Adam's apple of that delicate neck, killing Morin before the guard could pry him away. Philip had had his medical training, and he knew exactly where to collapse the larynx. A few minutes later the opportunity to kill Édouard Morin had slipped away. A bailiff led them into the chambers of the investigating judge, and the elderly gentleman explained his decision. Despite Morin's confession, he would not stand trial and he would not face incarceration. He would instead become a ward of the state with *extended medical care*, until such care was deemed unnecessary. That's when he pronounced the dismissal, the *non-lieu*.

Professionally Philip had understood, expected, and even agreed with this outcome. The specifics of Morin's diagnosis were not part of the public record, but he'd seen enough of the young man to have a good idea of the circumstances. Institutionalization was the obvious solution, and had Philip been called in as an expert witness on such a case, where someone else's daughter had been murdered, this was precisely the opinion he would have rendered.

But it was not someone else's daughter. And instead of serving as an expert, Philip played the role of the father. He'd found it hard to tear his gaze away from Morin during the proceedings, studying the boy's eyes, his thin fingers, his slender neck.

France no longer practiced capital punishment, but until a dozen years before Sophie's murder the official instrument of death had remained the guillotine. Philip had caressed this image in his mind. Part of him—the larger part—wanted to slay Édouard Morin. *Slay*. He had uttered that single syllable again and again, savoring the slide between the S and the L, the sound itself enacting the slicing and severing he dreamed of.

Now, in the waiting room, he checked his watch. Suardet was running late. His gaze settled on the window overlooking the hills.

And then there had been the father, Olivier Morin, the small and awkward man, trying to protect his son from the maelstrom of public attention. A press operator at a printer, Morin was more at home with machines than with the vortex of events into which he'd been catapulted. The poor fellow had been overwhelmed, allowing himself and his son to be shepherded by the lawyer through a process he didn't fully understand.

On more than one occasion the two men had come into contact. He'd seen Édouard's father shield his eyes from the flash of cameras outside the courthouse and shrink into himself during the hearing. The son may have been dazed and nervous, but the father was entirely broken.

He remembered with particular crispness the afternoon when Olivier Morin entered the deserted cafeteria at the courthouse. He and Yvonne were huddled over vending machine coffees between sessions. After glancing in their direction, Morin had retreated to the far corner of the vast room, sinking into a chair.

Yvonne had clutched Philip's arm when he stood, trying to hold him back. There was no reason for them to address the man whose son had murdered their daughter. But Philip had pulled himself free and walked across the room. The other man had looked up and gaped, amazement in his eyes, tinged with trepidation. Perhaps he was waiting for Philip to strike him. Or worse. But Philip wanted only to speak. He took a seat. They were both in a terrible situation, he said, both destroyed by the fate of their children. He wanted Morin to know he didn't hold him accountable for his son's actions.

Olivier Morin hadn't responded, had merely continued staring at the table-top. The two men remained together in silence for several minutes, and when

Philip finally rose to leave, he extended his hand. The other father looked at it, thunderstruck by this generosity, before reaching out to shake.

Now Olivier Morin was dead, and Philip imagined how his existence must have thinned during the years following the case, layer after layer eroded by incessant waves of anxiety until there was nothing left.

The receptionist appeared at the door of the waiting room. The doctor was ready.

Suardet was a stout man with a brush of a moustache, sitting in his shirt-sleeves behind a heavy desk. Philip presented his card, and the doctor studied it, glancing back as he sized up this transatlantic colleague. Philip knew that older doctors sometimes resented the younger ones, and Roger had intimated that this would be especially true in Rouen. But Philip wasn't here to pass judgment. The circumstances were familiar to him: a facility with too many patients and too few doctors, where mostly they made do with medicating symptoms rather than solving problems. It felt like home.

They exchanged a few pleasantries about the profession. The medical community in Rouen was not large, so it didn't surprise Philip to learn that Suardet knew Hervé Legrand. This meant that information about the visit would leak back to Yvonne's household. Confidentiality was a relative term.

"It's a good thing you speak French," Suardet said as he rocked back into his chair. "So much of the literature is in English these days. I find it terribly annoying."

Philip felt no need to defend his national tongue, and the doctor gave an approving smile as he pressed his hands together. "Before we undertake this meeting, I thought you and I should have a chat. I don't mind telling you, Doctor Adler, that I advised Monsieur Morin against this encounter."

"And why is that?"

"I appreciate the situation you find yourself in, but my first responsibility must be to my patient."

"Of course."

"And I see no therapeutic benefit to this meeting. I don't know what Édouard Morin was like fourteen or fifteen years ago. He wasn't my patient then. But today he is a difficult person to interact with. It's hard to know exactly how he feels about things."

"Perhaps he feels nothing."

Suardet conceded that one could get that impression, but he didn't believe it to be accurate. In fact, he compared Morin to a man who had been skinned alive, with nothing left to buffer his nerves. "The slightest contact touches him intensely," he explained. "So he attempts to touch nothing. This avoidance may give the impression of insensitivity, but I take it to be a form of protection. A shell, if you will."

"Why are you telling me this?"

Suardet leaned in toward him, his blue eyes glowing below silver eyebrows. "Because I don't intend to allow you to torture my patient, Doctor Adler. That's why."

"I'm not looking for revenge."

"Then what?"

Philip clasped his hands. "Édouard Morin murdered my daughter," he began. When the doctor began to protest, he cut him off. "I'm not talking about the legal definition of guilt. This is not an accusation, merely a description of what Morin himself has said. He made no secret of it during the court proceedings. But there was one piece of information he refused to reveal: What he did with the body." The last word felt awkward in Philip's mouth. He was still not used to speaking of his daughter this way, as a corpse, a lump of meat. He hoped he would never grow used to it.

If Suardet was shocked, he didn't show it. "And why do you think Morin will help you now?"

Philip shrugged. "I don't see why he would. But then, why did he agree to meet at all?"

Suardet stroked his jowls as he pondered the question. "I can only suppose it has to do with his obsession with order. He likes to dot every i. Perhaps he sees this meeting as a way to wrap something up."

Philip recalled the obsessive-compulsive behaviors Morin had exhibited during the inquest. He couldn't speak unless the chairs were lined up properly. Unless each ball of paper had made it into the wastebasket. Unless the ripple in the rug was smoothed and the rug itself straightened. Unless the judge's robe sat evenly on his shoulders.

It wasn't uncommon for obsessive-compulsive behavior to accompany schizophrenia disorders. They were, in the parlance of psychiatry, comorbid pathologies. Philip was not privy to the specifics of Morin's official diagnosis, but the labels were not important. He remembered the symptoms: social dysfunction, the absence of real emotion, an unusual relationship to language, an excessive focus on detail.

As they entered the meeting room, Philip surveyed the space. Accessed by a door on either side of the white conference table, the narrow chamber served as an interface between two worlds, a point of overlap between the realm of patients and that of doctors. Around the Formica-topped table stood five plastic chairs with tubular legs and hard feet that scraped on the tiled floor. A round clock hung high on one wall. The plaster of the ceiling was cracked. Otherwise, the room was without ornament—a far cry from the cabinet of curiosities that was Philip's office in Boston. Here one found nothing to excite the imagination, and it occurred to Philip that this was precisely the goal.

When Suardet led the patient in through the other door, Philip's first impression was that the gangly seventeen-year-old had been replaced by someone else. Although he walked with the same high-stepping, birdlike gait, this person had filled out. He'd become a man. His hair, though still black, was receding and revealed a broad swath of forehead. Of slender build, Édouard had developed a stoop, and the slackness of his body left a bulge around his belly. The transformation shouldn't have surprised Philip. Since his return to France every encounter reminded him how much time had elapsed. Everyone had aged—Roger and Yvonne, Évelyne and Sylvain, Philip himself. Still, Morin's metamorphosis had been more dramatic. He had entered his first institution in late adolescence, emerging from the ward now in mature manhood.

Only Sophie never aged.

Morin took a seat across the table. His eyes, though more heavily lidded than before, were the same—overly wide, still intense. The Adam's apple, less prominent than in the slender neck of the teenager, still bobbed with the frequent gulps. Beneath the superficial changes resided the same individual. Of that Philip was now sure.

Morin raised his right hand to the exact point on his forehead where his hairline began, and with his fingertips he smoothed the thinning strands backwards, although as far as Philip could tell, nothing needed straightening. His gestures were precise, delicate.

Dr. Suardet moved toward the head of the table, in the position of the mediator.

Morin stared at Philip, unblinking, and Philip found himself imagining Sophie on the ground, batting upward with her hands. Dirt on her face, leaves and bits of bark in her hair. A scream. Was that how it happened? His imagination was all too fertile. It could provide endless variations.

Morin's lips were closed in a placid expression, and Philip wondered how to start. Beginnings can be so crucial, like openings in chess—or, as Yvonne used to say, the start of a sonnet: all the rest flows from the first verse. Usually Philip relied on his most powerful therapeutic tool: silence. He would wait for the patient to speak. But here he had come as the supplicant, and he thought it wise to begin with a conciliatory gesture.

"*Je vous remercie—*" Philip said, beginning to thank Morin for agreeing to the meeting.

"You can speak your own language, you know," the other man said, breaking into English.

Philip paused. "I beg your pardon?"

"*O en español. En su país creo que se habla mucho.*" Morin left a beat, then switched again. "*Oder hätten Sie lieber Deutsch?*"

Philip turned to Suardet for assistance. The doctor folded his thick arms over his chest. "Édouard has an interest in languages," he explained in French. "He has put his time to good use, you might say."

"Thanks to you, Mr. Adler," Morin said, continuing in English, "I have much time to occupy. I am pleased to have the opportunity to practice my English with a native speaker." His tone was stilted and bookish, although the grammar was rigorously correct. His odd accent hovered between American and British, inflected with traces of French.

"I will not be of much assistance in English," Suardet said in French. "But it's up to you. I will attempt to follow."

Philip weighed the options. Forcing Morin to express himself in a language that was not his own could give Philip a tactical advantage, flushing the other man out in a territory where the nooks and crannies were less familiar.

"I have no objection," he responded. "Your English appears to be excellent. In fact, if you don't mind, I would be glad to record a sample of it." He reached into his pocket and withdrew the digital voice recorder. He looked at

Suardet, who made no protest, and he placed the device in the middle of the table.

Morin smiled. "I know why you are doing that. You don't need to pretend, Mr. Adler. I am not an idiot." Once again he raised his hand to his hair, gently brushing backwards with his fingertips. Then he reached for the recorder, moving it to the dead center of the table, and lining it up. "Do you mind? If we're going to have that out, we may as well keep it straight. It's best to keep things tidy, don't you agree?"

"Sometimes," Philip replied, "we have to live with a certain amount of untidiness."

"*Qué lástima!*" Morin said with a smile. "You speak like my dear Dr. Suardet. Tell me, Mr. Adler, did you have a good trip? Were your travels incident-free?" There was a preciousness to Morin's voice. "Incident-free," he repeated, raising his finger. "Like smoke-free, error-free, chemical-free, duty-free, tax-free, alcohol-free, sugar-free. There are so many freedoms in English, aren't there?"

There was something almost Germanic about Morin's accent, the way every S hummed like a Z.

"My travels were fine."

"I'm glad to hear it." Morin studied him. "On the subject of your journey, there is one thing I have been wondering about."

Philip allowed the silence to hang in the air. He gestured with an open hand, inviting Morin to continue, and Morin smiled.

"Don't worry, Mr. Adler. It's not that important. I just wondered, did you take the 18:50 train from Paris last night, arriving in Rouen at 20:02? Or the train this morning, the 7:53, arriving at 9:01?"

"Neither."

"Now there you surprise me. Certainly you did not choose the 19:50? That would have brought you to Rouen at a most inconvenient hour. And the others are so much slower. Unless you arrived yesterday afternoon. Perhaps to engage in some tourism? Rouen has much to offer in that department."

"I drove. From Yvetot."

Morin shook his head in disappointment. "Train travel is a superior form of locomotion. And it is so much better for the environment. You have seen, I am sure, how concerned we are for the environment in the world today?"

"I've noticed that," Philip replied, still trying to get a bead on the oddities of Morin's voice. It wasn't just German that tinged his accent. The buzzing Z was everywhere: *sorry* turned into *zorry*; *seen* became *zeen*; and *concerned*, *conzerned*. He wondered if it was actually not an accent at all, but rather a speech impediment. He didn't recall any such thing from fifteen years ago.

Morin stared, but Philip could tell that his gaze had shifted lower, to Philip's neck or shirt pocket. He had a vaguely pained expression, but then looked up again. "You took the *route nationale*, through Barentin, of course."

"No. The back roads."

"I see. Passing by Le Mont de l'If."

"That's right."

"Your Mountain."

"I beg your pardon?"

"An *if* is a tree, Mr. Adler. A yew, in English—yew, you, you and me. Le Mont de l'If: Yew Mountain, You Moutain, Your Mountain. Unless you'd prefer The Mountain of If. The Mountain of Possibilities. That is an evocative name, don't you think?"

"I wouldn't know."

He sighed. "Unfortunately, there is no mountain at Le Mont de l'If. It's nothing but a long hill."

Morin's speech was halting and singsong. The intonations were all wrong. "I am very fond of cartography," he continued. "Doctor Suardet may have told you that I have something of a passion for maps."

Suardet perked up as he heard his name. He was struggling to keep pace with the English.

Philip folded his hands on the table. "No," he replied. "I was unaware of that."

"Well, it's true. France has 36,682 independent municipalities, more than in your entire country, Mr. Adler, despite the fact that France is one seventeenth as large as the United States. I can identify all 3233 municipalities in Normandy, and many from the surrounding regions. I am working on the rest."

Zurrounding, Philip heard. *Working on the rezt.* "Very impressive," he said.

Morin glanced down at Philip's throat again. "Would you mind very much, Mr. Adler?"

"Mind what?"

"I hate to be a pest. But would it inconvenience you to button your left shirt collar? Only one side is buttoned, you see. That is uneven, which I find quite distracting."

Philip paused. Without haste, he reached up and fumbled for the collar.

"Thank you very much. I do think it's best for things to be neat. While we are on the topic, there is something the matter with your glasses."

"That's right. I broke them. I had to tape the frame together."

"How unfortunate." He huffed out a breath. "I suppose there is no fixing that now." He frowned. "You know, I've often thought that if things had gone differently, I would have liked to work with the cartographic service."

"However," Philip said, "things did not go differently."

"Indeed." Morin paused. "You know, you really should have come by rail. It has been a very long time since I last rode on a train. However, there is a line that passes not far from here. Within eyeshot of the clinic." He cocked his head. "Can one say that in English, Mr. Adler—eyeshot?"

"I don't believe so. No. You can say earshot, but not eyeshot."

"Because eyeshot is in the dictionary, you know."

"Then I must be mistaken."

"But I have not seen it used in my readings. The Internet would be useful for this kind of search, but unfortunately they do not seem to trust us with the Internet here." He turned to Suardet. "*N'est-ce pas, cher docteur?*"

"Tell me, Édouard—may I call you that?" Philip said.

"I would prefer not. I don't think we are on a first-name basis."

"Monsieur Morin, then. Tell me, do you know why I am here?"

"Not to help me with my English?"

"No."

"And probably not to discuss train timetables," Morin replied.

"No."

"I suppose it is also not to debate the advantages and disadvantages of various forms of transportation?"

"Not that either."

Morin pressed his hands together and furrowed his brow in thought, then looked up. "Perhaps it is to reminisce about Thursday, July 2, 1993, that sunny—though somewhat humid—day when I had sexual intercourse with your daughter, whose skull I then beat with a rock until she was dead in order that she should not tell on me?"

The room lapsed into silence, disturbed only by the sound of the clock. Philip clenched his fist under the table and ran his tongue over his dry lips. "That's right," he replied. "That's the topic I wish to discuss."

"Doctor Suardet mentioned something about that. Unfortunately, I don't think I can teach you anything new. Unless you have forgotten some of the details from fourteen years and ten months ago."

"No, I have not forgotten."

"I suspected as much. Neither have I. What good memories we both have. So what can I do for you?"

Philip leaned forward, keeping his eyes on Morin, who smoothed down his hair once again.

"Something is out of place," Philip said.

Morin's eyes widened slightly, then narrowed, as if he were pondering an interesting move. "I beg your pardon?"

Philip didn't reply.

"Out of place?" the younger man repeated. Then he looked to the side and spat out a series of phrases, "Out of kilter. *Sghembo. Nicht an der richtigen Stelle. In loco falso. Égaré. Descolocado.*"

"Yes. That's right."

Morin's Adam's apple dipped. "That is certainly an intriguing assertion, Mr. Adler. One could think about it a good deal. Morning, noon, and night. I love that expression. Don't you? *Morning, noon, and night.* It has a wonderful rhythm to it." He paused. "But in the end, I think you are wrong. Nothing is out of place."

Philip certainly hadn't expected Morin to open up easily, but the breeziness with which he deflected questions and dominated the conversation irked him. It was time to flex a bit of muscle. He exchanged a glance with Suardet, and the doctor nodded his assent for Philip to continue.

"Tell me, Monsieur Morin, why did you agree to meet with me?"

Édouard settled back in his chair. "To see. To hear what you would say."

"So, as a form of entertainment."

"I suppose you could call it that."

"And is it working? Do you find this amusing?"

"Quite," he replied with a smile. "Otherwise at this hour I would be required to participate in arts and crafts, you see. There is nothing more pathetic than a room full of idiots with round-tipped scissors, I assure you."

Philip pressed his fingertips together. "My job consists of listening to people," he said. "And if twenty-five years of practice has taught me anything at all, it's that people speak for one reason, and one reason alone."

"All right," Morin said. "I'll play along. What is that reason, Mr. Adler?"

"It's because they have something to say."

The two men stared at each other. Suddenly Morin laughed.

"And what would I have to say?"

"Perhaps something that was left out fifteen years ago."

"I don't think so."

"For instance, something that might be askew?"

"No," Morin insisted, an edge to his voice. "I told you. Nothing is out of place."

"Are you finding our conversation less entertaining now?"

He looked aside. "Rather, yes."

"Then why stay?"

"I shouldn't. It is a waste of my time. And time is such a precious thing, it should never be spent carelessly."

Philip left a pause. "I can tell you what's wrong," he said. "And I can help you fix it."

Morin relaxed, leaning back in his chair again. "Do you play poker, Mr. Adler? Because I have read several books on this subject. Many people believe it is a game of probability. But that is incorrect. I wish it were, in fact, because I am very good with numbers. And yet the experts agree that poker is a matter of making one probability appear to be another. It's what they call bluffing."

"This is not a bluff."

"Then why don't you tell me what is out of place, Mr. Adler?"

Philip let another silence hang. "My daughter," he said.

Morin's face clouded. "I very truly beg your pardon?"

"My daughter's body. It's not where it belongs." He watched Morin gaze back at him. "Doesn't that nag at you? You who likes things so tidy. Hasn't that bothered you all these years?" He paused. "I'm not asking for much,

Monsieur Morin. Just a little help finding her remains. So Sophie can get to the right place."

Morin's brow furrowed briefly, and then he laughed again. "Yes, that certainly is bluffing. Quite exactly."

The laugh galled Philip. He would have liked nothing better than to take a swing at Morin, but he kept the mask of his calm in place. "It costs you nothing," he said. "There's no risk to you. Just let me put my daughter in her grave. This is not a legal matter. I have no power to help you or harm you. I am asking you this only as a father."

Morin's eyes darkened and he looked away.

"As a father looking for his child."

The other man cupped his hand over his jaw, as though cradling a toothache. He turned to Suardet. "Can you believe this, Doctor? *Pouvez-vous le croire?*" He turned back to Philip. "Trust me, my dear sir. There is nothing out of place here. Everything is where it belongs."

Philip was running out of tools. He couldn't think how to keep Morin engaged, and he needed to avoid pleading. He kept his voice level. "No one can do anything more to you. The courts have already ruled. All I want is to lay her to rest."

Morin pursed his lips and leaned forward. "I understand. I really do. You feel you need to make things even. You like order, too. But it's the problem of remainders, Mr. Adler."

Philip stiffened. "What do you mean?"

He opened his hands to explain. "You know: remainders. You divide a number, seven by three, but it doesn't fit. There's something left over. That's why I find numbers like pi so interesting. Or the square root of two. They call them irrational numbers, although in some ways they are the most rational of all, for they can only exist in the mind, or perhaps in heaven. In the real world we don't like remainders that trail off forever. You know what we do when that happens?"

"What?"

Morin pulled back. "Come now, Mr. Adler. You know what I'm talking about. When we divide a number and the remainder is too long, we cut the numbers off. It's called *rounding*. That's how we make theory fit with reality. That was a very hard lesson for me, but I think I've learned it. Sometimes one really does have to round. Do you see what I mean?"

"I see that you're avoiding the topic."

"But not at all," Morin puffed. "This is precisely the topic. You're the one who brought up the question of order." He threw up his hands, turning to Suardet. "What a pity. I had hoped for better. I think I may as well return to my hole." He stood up.

Philip took a shot in the dark. "Tell me, Édouard, what was it like for you to lose your father?"

Morin's look hardened. "*Cállate*," he snapped in Spanish. "*C'est un sacrilège. Du weisst nicht wovon du sprichst.*" He massaged his jaw again as he rotated through languages.

"Settle down, now," Suardet grumbled, looking at his watch.

"I only mentioned your father," Philip continued, "so you could understand my own concern. How would it make you feel if you didn't know where your father was buried?"

Morin glared. "You have no right to speak of my father, Mr. Adler."

"I knew your father. Not well, but I spoke with him. He was a good man."

"Stop it," he snapped. "It's a desecration in your mouth."

Philip had found a nerve. He knew he'd only have a moment before Suardet intervened. "Help me," he said to Morin. "And perhaps I can help you."

"I don't need anyone's help," Morin glowered. "It won't be long now anyway. And then I'll be with him."

"What do you mean?"

"Oh, don't pretend you don't know," he spat. "Everyone knows."

Now it was Suardet's turn to raise his hands in frustration. "Good grief! Not this again," he sputtered in French, turning to Philip. "He's convinced he has cancer. In the tongue. But it's ridiculous. Entirely psychosomatic."

The announcement took Philip by surprise, but suddenly the humming accent made sense, along with the way Morin clutched at his jaw. If there was a tumor, the nerves might have been damaged by treatment. Even the shape of the tongue might have been altered, affecting his ability to produce certain sounds.

"It started over a year ago," Suardet continued. Then he addressed Édouard. "There's nothing the matter with your tongue, and you know it. We've done all the tests."

"Don't hide it from me," Morin shot back. "I know I'm rotting away. I can feel it. Why do you insist on treating me like a child?"

Suardet snapped his pen down on the table and sighed. "We are done, here, gentlemen. I have a full slate of patients to see today."

"Just a few more minutes," Philip said.

"I'm sorry, Mr. Adler," Suardet replied, already rising, moving to Morin's side. "I have work to attend to."

As Morin headed for the door with Suardet at his side, Philip scraped his chair back and rose to his feet. "Édouard," he said. The other man stopped. "Please."

Morin turned and examined him, breaking into a smile. "Have a good stay in Yvetot, Mr. Adler," he said. "This region is full of history. Perhaps you will avail yourself of your holiday to learn more about it."

"I am hardly on holiday."

"I myself am particularly interested in the Second World War. Like the rest of the north, Yvetot was under German control, you know."

"I don't care a whit about German history. I care about my daughter."

Morin stared at him, then winced and drew his hand back up to his cheek. He stepped back to the table, planting his hands on the top and leaning toward Philip, peering into his eyes before standing upright again. "You think I am your enemy, Mr. Adler. But I am eager to help you. Believe me, everyone should know about history. When the Germans approached Yvetot on Monday, June 10, 1940, the inhabitants were very clever. They changed some of the road signs in the countryside, moving them or turning them around. People did this to send the Germans in the wrong direction, to slow them down. A wonderful idea, don't you think?"

Philip took a deep breath. He had tired of the game.

Suardet tugged at Morin's elbow, but he refused to turn. "And then the Germans set up blockades around Yvetot," he continued, "on the roads to Sorquainville, Malamare, and Adonville. They were blocking access to the coast, stopping the French retreat. But some people knew better than to approach the blockades. They just went around them on the smaller roads. They knew the land. They found other ways. Isn't that fascinating?"

Philip didn't answer.

"I have appointments to get to," Suardet called out, and again he tried to guide Édouard toward the door.

"You are wrong not to care about this, Mr. Adler," Morin said. "History is an excellent teacher."

Dipping his head in farewell, Morin finally yielded to Suardet, turning and exiting from the room, bouncing along with his happy gait.

The doctor closed the door and turned back to Philip, shaking his head. "You've had your meeting, Monsieur Adler. Don't say I didn't warn you in advance."

He ate lunch alone in a bustling café in Rouen, staring blankly at his food. In the blue diary he jotted down thoughts with Yvonne's pilfered pen. The meeting had been the most bewildering conversation of his entire practice. As he tried to distill what he'd learned, he faltered. His notes were a jumble, a log of odd phrases and strange behaviors.

Was any of it significant? Morin had spoken to him in a language that was not his own, and errors or quirks may merely have signaled lapses in his English. Unless he could calibrate himself to Morin's brand of English, Philip wouldn't be able to tell which apparent mistakes might have hit secret targets—mis-accomplishments produced by the unconscious.

Before heading back to Yvetot, he wandered through the old quarter of Rouen, mulling over the encounter, filtering the torrent of images. He passed by medieval half-timbered houses, then under the arch with the gilt Renaissance clock, and through the square where Joan of Arc had been burned alive. He'd not been in this city for over a decade.

In any case, Morin had been not been the cowed, timid soul he had expected. At times he exuded exaggerated confidence. There were flickers of rage. But no shame that Philip could detect. *Intrigued* was the word. Yes, Morin had been intrigued to meet the father of his victim.

And Suardet had been right. He was not an apathetic schizoid, as Philip had assumed all those years ago. He was instead schizotypal—so sensitive that he had built up a bulwark of language to protect him. There was even a hint of magical thinking, and Philip wondered if he had delusions. That could account for the pain in the tongue, which produced the speech impediment, or the accent—the buzzing of the S. Suardet had said they'd run all the tests, that there was no physical problem.

The cobblestone alley opened to the plaza where Rouen's great cathedral rose overhead, broad and tall, its weathered stone darkened by the centuries, teeming with a bedlam of ornaments. High across the front stood a gallery of crowned statues—kings of France or of the Bible, he didn't know which. He entered.

Philip had brushed up against Catholicism by way of Yvonne, handling it like one more foreign language he would never make his own. The lexicon of this tongue took the form of sculpture and rose windows, visible words that twined into awkward phrases he could barely decipher. The murmur of stone and glass recited the acts of God the creator, then the story of Adam, the father of all mankind. Floods mixed with massacres and rebirths. In one window Abraham brandished a knife over Isaac's head; in another, a tree of descendants sprouted from the fertile loins of Jesse. Then a younger story joined and repeated the first—that of the child destined to be lost.

Before the north portal Philip paused to study the bas-relief of the Last Judgment. The lowest panel told of the resurrection of the dead, where revived cadavers clambered from sepulchers. Above was pictured the weighing of souls. At God's right hand the blessed stood in orderly beatitude, awaiting entrance to heaven. To the left, grinning demons prodded the hordes headed for damnation. Some of the condemned shielded their faces with their hands while others offered bags of gold to bribe their torturers. One woman gaped, her stone face frozen in the realization that all hope was lost. Souls stewed in a cauldron held in the maw of a gigantic beast. A young man roasted on a spit. Demons tormented men on the wheel or devoured them whole. A weird, squat devil, nothing more than a sneering stomach on legs, surveyed the work of his fellows, ready to engulf whatever might offer itself to him.

And at the very bottom of this hell, one desperate soul had evaded his captors, seeking to claw his way up the other side and sneak back into the realm of simple purgatory. A damned man unwilling to settle for his lot. The sculptor had portrayed him falling back into the fires just as he reached the brink of salvation.

Shoehorned back into the Smart Car, he curled through the streets on the way out of town, driving by a handsome nineteenth-century building converted into a medical clinic. He slowed. It was Hervé's group, the reproductive specialists. So this was where Yvonne's husband coaxed new life out of barren souls.

Yvonne's existence in Rouen had seemed somehow abstract to him before, but the clinic with the Legrand name made it real.

Stopping at a gas station he consulted a phone book and picked up a map of the city. Then he set out again. The roads twisted as the terrain rose away from the Seine, and soon he arrived at the university campus at Mont-Saint-Aignan, an assortment of charmless brick-and-glass structures. One of these buildings would house the language departments. For all he knew, Yvonne was in a classroom right now, leading a group of skinny, intense students through the mysteries of Petrarch.

He finished by tracking down the house where she and Hervé lived, a two-story brick structure of standard Norman construction, with a small yard enclosed behind a stone wall and a metal grill. Gazing through the bars of the gate from his car window, Philip made out rose trellises splayed along the south side of the house. A plump cat lay in the sun, licking its front paw.

While sitting in the car outside Yvonne's house, Philip opened his blue diary to a new page. Clicking the pen absentmindedly, he thought for a long while, finally writing one word: *Yvonne*. Nothing else came to mind.

The jacket cuff below his closed hand still lacked a button, and he recalled the sharp image of his ex-wife bending over and biting off the threads.

Two blocks down, a city bus passed through the intersection, and a moment later an adolescent girl with dark hair turned the corner, headed in Philip's direction. She was dressed in skintight jeans, a school backpack slung over her shoulder as she walked jauntily, white cords dangling from buds in her ears. For an instant it was Melanie Patterson that came to mind, but of course it was Margaux, whom he'd not seen since the party, now coming home after school. Something about her—he thought it was her gait, perhaps the length of her stride or the way she carried her arms—reminded him of Yvonne.

He'd promised to be discreet, and yet there he was, practically staking out Yvonne's home, with her daughter less than a block away. It was reckless, pointless. Or worse: maybe it was deliberate. Yes, that made more sense. How stupid of him! It was perfectly transparent: he'd dallied here precisely because he knew he might catch a glimpse of Margaux, a ghost of Sophie, herself haunted by the very girl she resembled.

How could Yvonne bear to let her walk alone like this? How could she allow Margaux to wander out of her sight? And how could Roger—who still left flowers on Sophie's grave—stand to watch another niece strolling about without a worry in the world?

He started up the car and pulled away, whizzing past Margaux a moment later, forcing himself to keep his eyes on the road. He was reasonably sure she hadn't noticed him.

Ten

Once he left Rouen in the distance, the road sank into wooded stretches of countryside, and dwindling sunlight flashed in the gaps between branches. It was compact landscape, every meter accounted for, and yet the terrain varied considerably, changing from manicured meadows with tall, lazy cattle, to handsome stands of oaks clustered between fields, interrupted by rugged strips of forest cut through by streams and creeks. Half an hour later, just before the hills opened to the plain, he passed the turn-off for Le Mont de l'If. What had Morin called it? The Mountain of If, the Mountain of Possibilities. Yvetot felt like the opposite.

As he pulled up in front of the hotel on the Place des Belges, Roger stood outside the brasserie giving a two-fingered salute to a man just taking his leave. By the time Philip parked and came over, the visitor had disappeared. Monsieur Bécot was right: people in Yvetot wanted nothing to do with him.

"So you still have friends in this town?"

"Oh, yes," Roger replied. "Old connections, you know. Ancient. That was a school chum from about a hundred years ago." He clapped his hands together. "So, how did it go? Tell me everything." He steered Philip into the brasserie, toward a table with two beer glasses, leftovers from his last meeting.

"I think I'll switch to whiskey," Roger told the waiter. "Something tells me I'm going to need it." He turned to Philip. "And you? Ah, I forgot. Monsieur doesn't drink."

Roger downed his glass in two gulps and ordered another. "I'm ready. Speak. What was it like seeing Morin again, after all these years?"

"Unnerving."

"I can imagine."

Philip gave him the overview, describing Morin's behaviors, his fixation on order, the play with languages, his apparent illness. Then he pulled the digital recorder out of his jacket pocket.

"If you want specifics, I have them right here."

"Aha," replied Roger with satisfaction. "I should have known that the American eye for technology would prove useful."

For the next twenty minutes the two men sat hunched over the device. Philip found it instructive to listen again, wincing as he heard his own botched moves. Morin had been cleverer than he'd expected.

"One thing is certain," Roger said when they finished. "Morin's English is extraordinary. Better than mine, and I spent two years in New York. I must say, I find that rather annoying. He learned it just from books, did he?"

"Language is apparently one of his obsessions."

"Along with railroads and geography. Not to mention history—all this nonsense about the Germans and their roadblocks."

Philip gave him a look. "You mean it's not true?"

Roger shrugged. "It could be. After all, the Germans were crawling through this area." He gestured away from the table, designating all of Normandy. "But why such strange little details? Where did he say the roadblocks were? Sorquainville, Malamare, and some other godforsaken village? Sorquainville is on a side road in the direction of Fécamp." He jabbed a thumb over his shoulder, to the north. "I'm not even sure where the others are located. But I'm pretty confident none of them made it into the history books. I suppose he wanted to show off, demonstrating his command of the map of France. Total gibberish if you ask me."

Philip ran his fingers through his beard. "I don't know. People always have some reason for what they say."

"Now you're speaking like Élisabeth."

"Well, it's true. People don't speak nonsense."

Roger folded his arms across his chest. "She has this theory that I don't actually know what I want, especially right after I tell her explicitly. She says I don't know my own mind, that I'm always of divided opinions." He raised his eyebrows. "And she has offered to formalize this division surgically. I believe the technical term for the operation is castration."

"I'm not kidding, Roger."

"I'm not sure she was, either. Still, I don't go in for all this talk about hidden selves. It smacks a bit too much of ghost stories, or religion. In fact, it turns us all into potential patients for you lot!"

Philip tipped back in his chair and clasped his hands over his stomach. "Tell me, how often do you do the drive between Yvetot and Fécamp?"

Roger's eyes narrowed. "Why do you ask?"

"How often?"

"I don't know. Four or five times a week."

"I see," he nodded. "You know the road pretty well by now, don't you?"

"Of course. I've driven it for years. I could do it with my eyes closed."

"Do you get tired of it?"

"No," he said, shaking his head. "Not really. If you're trying to point out stresses in my life, it's not going to work. The truth is, I find the drive relaxing. I think about all sorts of things. Work I have to do. Vacation plans. Or, well, to be perfectly honest, women."

"And before you know it, you've arrived in Yvetot. Is that right?"

"Precisely," he smiled smugly.

Philip leaned forward, planting his elbows on the table. "So tell me: While your mind is busy wandering through trysts and real estate transactions, who's driving?"

"What?" Roger's smile weakened.

"You heard me. You said you don't pay any attention to the road. Your imagination wanders, and before you know it, you've arrived at your destination. What became of the thousand decisions you made along the way—where to turn, when to slow down, how long to wait at the intersection? That's not even counting all the tweaks of the steering wheel, each one crucial to keeping you on the road."

Roger scowled.

"Once you stop to think about it," Philip continued, "you have to accept the obvious conclusion: while you are occupied with your daydreams, some-one else is at the wheel."

The same thing happened, he asserted, in all speech and actions. Most of our behaviors are performed without conscious thought, the result of multiple drivers, each with his own style. The trick was to identify these different logics. From there, Philip began to lay out the repetitions he'd detected in Morin's speech. Certain themes had bubbled up to the surface, along with linguistic oddities that were every bit as strange as the physical tics. Even the occurrence of foreign phrases seemed orderly, appearing at moments of stress. Repetition was no guarantee of a meaningful pattern, but it was a start.

"That's all well and good," Roger said. "But I don't see where it leads."

"I've been thinking about that. We need to gather as much information as possible. It's hard to predict what will be useful, but an obvious step would be to review the police and court records."

"If you can get them." Roger reflected for a moment. "I suppose another idea would be to talk to Father Cabot."

"The priest?"

"That's right. The same one who bungled my mother's funeral. He's a bit of a dunce, I'm afraid, but in these small towns there's little that escapes the ears of the clergy. The highway to heaven is the Church, after all. And the confessional is its tollbooth."

Philip shook his head. "A priest won't breach confidentiality. Besides, I gather that the locals aren't eager to help me out."

"So I hear," Roger said. Philip looked up in surprise. "Yes, that's right—word gets around. Local ties never die out, you know, and I have my sources." He poked with his finger to punctuate his point. "You're right that people aren't keen to have this old business dredged up. And who can blame them?" He paused. "But Father Cabot is a different fish. First of all, he's not from Yvetot. And he can get a bit too chatty."

"All right. I'll give him a try."

"Will you be needing me?"

"Not right away. I don't want to take you away from your work."

"Well," Roger said, "given the state of the market right now, that's not much of a problem." He gave a sheepish grin. "But I do have one client who's heartbreakingly attractive. And recently divorced. I don't think she can actually afford anything, but I'm going to drive her around for a few showings. Maybe we'll finish around dinner time. And then—"

Philip reached across the table, covering Roger's hand with his own. "You should call Élisabeth, Roger. That's what you should do."

Roger's smile vanished and he drew his hand away. "I know. I know." He looked annoyed. "Life is full of things I *ought* to do. I just don't manage to get around to them often enough."

It was late when the two men parted, and Philip walked back to the hotel by way of side streets. Yvetot was different in the chocolaty shadows of night. Quiet and suggestive. Streets curled off into darkness, alleyways opened where least expected. The town had the wrinkles and folds of a brain.

Roger's philandering troubled Philip. It bespoke a fear of closeness but also the need for attachment. Élisabeth's fate was to be cast away, reeled in, and cast away again, in endless repetition. Didn't this ambivalence also explain Roger's move to Fécamp? It buffered him from Yvetot, while allowing him to maintain connections on his own terms. So much for the insouciance of the past. Now Roger's charm had turned cautious. In many ways, he was no longer the same person as before.

Of course, who was? Not Philip. Even Édouard Morin had changed—still a bundle of peculiar behaviors, but somehow stronger, cannier. His time in custody had given him the chance to develop a protective carapace.

No one had been immune to the passage of time. When Philip considered his own arrival in France nearly thirty years ago, after his parents had died, he recalled the sensation of imminence, of promise. He'd begun learning, expanding, taking risks, meeting people. Soon he'd founded a family of his own. But that past lingered in his memory like a dear old pet shoddily stuffed, with patches of fur dropping off and the mount coming loose. After Sophie's death Philip had grown circumspect. In the end, his childhood caught up with him, and he heard his father's voice in his head. *Don't be showy. Keep a low profile.* What did you expect, his father would have said. Philip had dared to raise his head, and this is where it got him.

When he entered La Cauchoise to collect his room key, Monsieur Bécot nodded toward the dim lobby.

"You have a visitor, Monsieur Adler," the old man said.

Hervé Legrand reclined in an armchair, his legs stretched out, crossed at the ankles, his hands clasped. The fingers of a doctor, Philip noted. Perhaps he'd brought a scalpel along.

Hervé uttered a *bonsoir* as he came to his feet, standing a full head shorter than Philip. He extended his hand, a taut smile on his lips. He looked tired, a virile growth of stubble darkening his cheeks.

"*Hair-vay,*" Philip said. He saw the other man flinch at the pronunciation, but he didn't bother correcting it. "You just happened to be passing through, I take it?"

Hervé issued a small chuckle, barely a catch in his throat. "No, no. I made a special trip to see you. I've been waiting for some time."

"I was out with Roger."

Hervé frowned. "How nice."

"What can I do for you?"

There were no other clients in the lobby of the old hotel, but Monsieur Bécot remained alert and attentive at the reception desk.

"It's such a pleasant evening," Hervé said. "Why don't we step outside?"

The Place des Belges was nearly vacant, rimmed by a few parked cars. The lighted windows of restaurants shone from beyond the trees, but most of the shops were now shuttered. Hervé lit a cigarette, drawing in a deep breath and releasing the smoke in a thin stream. "Look, Philip. We're grown men. I want to be direct with you."

"That sounds good."

"I know you've had your meeting with Édouard Morin."

"I must say, I'm impressed with how well everyone keeps tabs on me." Philip chose his words carefully. This wouldn't be a good time for his French to falter.

Hervé took another long drag. "It was a long time ago, Philip. I know this is not what you want to hear, but the best thing would be to forget about it. Let go of what you cannot fix."

"I've tried that. It hasn't worked. Not for me." He watched Hervé size him up, could see him calculating his next move.

"I'm sure you'll appreciate that I can't have you dragging my family through your problems. Margaux, most of all, shouldn't have to deal with these stories."

It was a clever choice. She was the last one Philip wanted to hurt. Because he didn't like having to agree with Hervé, he introduced a wedge. "Tell me, did Yvonne send you?"

Hervé straightened. "No. I saw no need to trouble her with this. Yvonne is upset enough as it is."

"So you've taken it upon yourself to protect her. From me."

"I wouldn't have put it that way. But the fact is that someone had to step in."

"How chivalrous."

Hervé paused. Then he turned and faced the square, taking another long draw on his cigarette.

The show of composure irked Philip. He disliked Hervé. Or rather, he begrudged him for succeeding where Philip had failed. And yet, he couldn't fully disagree with this man who had replaced him. He understood the protective impulse Hervé felt for his wife and daughter—for his life—and in his shoes Philip would have done the same thing. At least Hervé was taking action, which was more than Philip had done, back then, when disaster threatened his world. No, he couldn't fault Hervé. No more than he could yield to him.

"I've put a process in motion," he said. "And I'm going to see it through."

Hervé nodded, still facing the square.

"I'll do what I can to keep things under control," Philip continued. "I don't want to hurt anyone. But if I can get to the bottom of it all, surely that would be a good thing for everyone."

"Personally," Hervé said, "I fail to see what it would achieve."

Philip's neck went hot. Was it so very hard to understand?

"Even if you find what you want, Philip, what good will it do? We're both medical men. You know as well as I that it's—"

Philip raised his hand to stop him. He knew exactly where Hervé was headed, and he didn't want to hear it. "I'm also not going to retreat," he told him. "Not now. Not yet."

Hervé stared into the darkness. "Very well." Now he turned to Philip and looked him in the eye. "But I'm not willing to stand idly by. Keep that in mind. If you disrupt our life, Philip, if you endanger the happiness of my wife or daughter, I'll come at you. With everything I have." He spoke matter-of-factly. "There's nothing I won't do to protect my family."

"Is that a threat?"

Hervé considered the question. "Yes. I suppose so. I think you should take it that way."

"I see," Philip nodded. "At least we understand one another."

Hervé studied the end of his expiring cigarette and dropped the butt to the ground, grinding at it with his heel before marching off into the dark.

In his room Philip set himself up at the writing desk, wedging an old magazine under the short leg to level it. He was exhausted, overwhelmed with images, words, memories. But he had to set it all aside for his call with Melanie—for another conversation he wasn't ready to have. He laid out pen and paper. A glass of water was at hand. At ten o'clock sharp he dialed the number and waited for the connection to go through. At first he thought she'd picked up, but then realized it was only the recording. It came almost as a relief.

"This is Melanie," came the impertinent voice. "I've either missed your call or dissed it. If you want, you can leave me a message. But no promises about calling back."

After the tone sounded he explained that he was sorry he'd interrupted their last call, and he urged her to get in touch with Linda so she could set up another time. Before signing off, he hesitated. "Take care of yourself, Melanie," he added.

He had a hunch that Melanie had been there, refusing to pick up. Was she trying to punish him? He was wrong to have singled her out from among all his other patients. She was no more at risk than they, and he had nothing special to offer her.

He saw now that his motivations had been far from noble. Melanie and Margaux and Sophie were overlaid in his imagination, blending into a single girl. You didn't need a degree in psychiatry to figure that out—or to see that it wasn't healthy, not healthy at all.

Eleven

His plan to return to Boston by the weekend now seemed fanciful. Perhaps it had never been realistic. Perhaps that was how he'd tricked himself into staying.

The events of the previous day were still sharp in his memory. The meeting with Édouard Morin loomed largest, but there were other topics calling for consideration as well: Roger, Margaux, Hervé, Melanie. And Yvonne. The longer he stayed in Yvetot, the more restless she would become, and the greater the danger of a confrontation. Excuses might extend his credit, but what he needed were results. In that case, any argument Yvonne presented would evaporate. She might even feel a touch of gratitude.

The conversation with Morin was the beginning of a foundation, but he would need stones and mortar. The court records would help, along with the old press clippings. And Roger had suggested that he speak with Father Cabot.

As he left the hotel, he let Monsieur Bécot know he'd be staying on, and the old man shook his head, replying in stilted English. "Every day which passes, you ask to spend another night. I thought you did not like Yvetot, Monsieur Adler."

"It's growing on me."

The other man squinted at the expression.

Philip hesitated. "Tell me, Monsieur Bécot, where would I find old newspapers? Does the city save them anywhere? At the library, perhaps?"

"I have the past week or so in my office, if you would like."

"Older. Years older."

Bécot's expression darkened.

"Yes, I'm afraid so," Philip said. "I'm still trying to wake the sleeping cat."

"Monsieur Adler," Bécot began, shaking his head over the register. "I wish you the best in many things, but not in this. I'm afraid I cannot help you."

"Look, Monsieur Bécot. I'm not going to leave until I've studied everything. The sooner I get what I need, the sooner Yvetot will be rid of me."

"Monsieur Adler, I don't think you understand." He cast an uneasy glance through the empty lobby. "People in Yvetot are growing impatient."

"What people?"

Bécot didn't want to say, claimed he couldn't be sure about anything in particular.

Philip put it to him point blank. "You, for example, Monsieur Bécot? Are you telling me I should leave?"

No, no, it had nothing to do with him. But people in town, they didn't want the old stories resuscitated. The situation was—he cast about for the right term—uncomfortable.

"Uncomfortable?" The flimsiness of the word irritated Philip. He leaned over the desk. "Tell me, Monsieur Bécot. You were here during the war. You lost friends and family members. Some of them were never recovered—like the ones you described before, the bodies that come to the surface in farmer's fields."

Bécot nodded and swallowed, and Philip continued. "If someone told you now, nearly seventy years later, that it was possible—conceivable—that one of the people you had lost could be found, at least a trace of them, what would you do? What would your answer be? That nothing should be disturbed, because it's not *comfortable?*"

Bécot blanched. When he finally spoke, his voice cracked. "For newspapers, you could try the library, with Madame Boquet. They don't open until ten, and I don't know how far back their copies go. The *Fanal d'Yvetot* is no longer printed, though I believe Monsieur Harancourt still keeps many of the old issues in his home. For most old papers, though, your best option is Monsieur Guérin."

The name clicked in Philip's memory. Bécot had mentioned him before. "The fellow at the local archives."

"That's right."

Philip's voice eased. "Thank you, Monsieur Bécot. You're a veritable fount of knowledge."

The old man grimaced. "You . . . you helped me to remember."

City Hall was an imposing Second Empire structure, the words *Hôtel de Ville* engraved in three-foot-tall letters beneath a plain-faced clock at the top of the façade. On the plaza outside, there towered the bronze sculpture of a soldier, the metal weathered green and black, a monument to the First World War. Inside, the information desk at the entry was unmanned, so Philip wandered down the hallways, following the signs for the *archives cantonales*, trudging down to the cellar and ending up in a broad, windowless chamber filled with well-ordered shelves bearing identical cardboard boxes with handwritten access numbers. He called out twice to no avail and finally passed to the other side of the counter, looking deep into the darkened hallway, at the turn of which light glowed. Following the passage, first right, then left, he entered a second chamber, much less orderly than the first. Here the plywood shelves overflowed with books, sacks, lamps, tarps, clocks, empty picture frames, bundles of letters, and various figurines. Sundry other objects peeked over the lips of old fruit cartons. A deep shelf held fragments of ancient statuary, including one nearly complete sculpture of a winged child, its forefinger lifted to the pert smile on its lips as though it were shushing him.

"Don't say a word," a voice breathed from across the jumbled terrain of the room. It was a thin man sitting hunched over a workbench, his hands angled under a magnifying glass clamped to a stand. He maneuvered a pair of needle-nosed pliers over a brass cylinder. After pressing, he gave the tool a twist, and there came the zing of spring steel unspooling and seizing against metal.

"*Voilà!*" he proclaimed as he set down the pliers and examined his handiwork. Only now did he turn his lively eyes to Philip, blinking at him as he lowered his spectacles from his cloud of white hair. A disassembled clockwork lay spread out before him.

"Some of these mainsprings," the fellow said, "they can be quite dangerous, you know. The larger ones, that is. People have lost digits at it." He held up his right hand, showing an index finger only half as long as the others. Then the finger slowly grew before Philip's eyes as he unfolded it from its bent position. The man laughed. "So far, so good." He hopped off his stool. "Still, I don't suppose you've come down here for a lesson in clock repair, Monsieur. Did you get lost in the corridors?"

"Not at all. I followed the signs. Monsieur Guérin, I presume?" He extended his hand.

"Hah! *Monsieur Guérin, I presume.* Very good. Like Stanley meeting Livingstone in Ujiji. Yes, I suppose it is a bit of jungle down here. You must be Bécot's American. Monsieur Adler, is it? I've heard all about you."

"I'm not surprised. Evidently all of Yvetot is on the lookout."

Guérin chuckled. "Yes, I'm afraid the *Yvetotais* can be like that. A bit inquisitive. Never cared for it myself. A bunch of busy-bodies, that's what they are."

Philip nodded at the disemboweled clock. "I'm sorry to interrupt your work."

"Nonsense." He gestured at the deserted surroundings. "As you can see, the archives are not exactly a hub of activity." Guérin flashed a smile. "Which leaves me with plenty of time for my hobbies. Of course, Rouen pays for it all, so we don't really mind. Any time we can spend money from Rouen, people in Yvetot are content."

"Very practical," Philip conceded.

"So, you are here for the purpose of research, are you?"

Philip nodded, and Guérin led off toward the main office, leading him back through the wilderness of boxes, clocks, and terra cotta statues.

At the front desk Philip explained what he was after, starting with information about Olivier Morin's death.

"No problem at all," Guérin replied. "All the death certificates are here, along with obituaries from the newspaper."

"There's more."

"Let me guess. His son, Édouard? Just so you know, Monsieur Adler, I understand your interest in this case."

At least Philip wouldn't need to pretend.

Guérin strode over to one of the shelves and skimmed the labels. "I have a special carton with clippings about crime in Yvetot," he called out. "However, I'm not sure that everything about the Morin case is included there, for it wasn't *just* criminal, was it? There were those other issues, the psychiatric ones, which made it hard to know where to classify everything. But I should be able to turn up some items of interest."

"I don't suppose you have access to the court records?"

Guérin turned and raised his hands in distress. "Alas, no. For that you must go to Rouen. But these other documents I can provide."

He set out on an expedition through his wilderness, whistling while he worked, bringing his quarry back to the counter piece by piece. Before long there came the hum and flash of the photocopier. In under half an hour he had produced a tidy folder of documents.

"Here is everything I have to offer," he explained as he handed it over. "All in all, there was more than I remembered. For the court documents and police reports, though, I'm afraid you'll need to pay a visit to the Bureau of Records at the courthouse." He raised a bony finger. "I should warn you that the personnel can be rather prickly."

"Because it's Rouen?"

Guérin's eyes glinted. "You're a quick learner, Monsieur Adler."

"I'm just hoping the papers will still be available."

"You needn't worry about that."

"Really?"

"Trust me. You can't obliterate the past. This is one area where the French have considerable expertise."

"You think? So far, everyone in Yvetot seems committed to the cause of amnesia."

Guérin considered the point. "Yes, I see what you mean. There can be a bit of that, too. Still, remembering and forgetting . . ." He weighed the words with his hands. "They're not so different, perhaps." Philip arched an eyebrow, and Guérin continued. "There is a famous example from long ago. During the Revolution. Perhaps you know about it?" When Philip confessed his ignorance, Guérin clapped his hands together, shifting into the second gear of his storytelling. "You see, when the king and queen were executed in Paris, their bodies were thrown into graves filled with quicklime to speed the decomposition. The people wanted to erase everything. Just as they tore down the Bastille, so they wished to wipe out the royalty, and not just their bodies, but even their memory. Louis XVI was never to have existed."

"But there would always be the grave, the tomb."

Guérin drove a finger into the air. "That's just it! There was a tomb, and yet *not* a tomb. The royal couple was both hidden and not hidden. Both forgotten and remembered." At Philip's expression of confusion, Guérin pressed on. "They buried the king in the same place as hundreds of other victims, in a common grave. The queen came some time later, in the same way. There were no markers, no names. They disappeared without a trace. Just two trees lost in a forest."

A wrinkle formed on Philip's brow. "You said the past couldn't be obliterated. But your story shows the opposite."

"Not at all. You see, many years went by. We had the Empire of Napoleon. Then, much later, the return of the royal family. The new king was desperate to recover the remains of his brother, and it happened that one man knew where the bodies were located. He had guarded this secret for years, waiting for the opportune moment. They dug where he told them to, and they found the royal remains. Despite the quicklime, the bones were intact. Can you imagine? Twenty-two years later?"

Yes, he could imagine. "But how . . . how could they recognize them? If it was a mass grave, how did they know which bones were which?"

Guérin's eyes glowed as he wagged a finger. "An excellent question. It was the rubber in the garters, Monsieur Adler. The royal garters of Marie-Antoinette!"

Back at the hotel Philip shut himself in his room and stretched out on the bed. Guérin's story had left him unsettled. Applying the lesson of royal corpses required traveling through the memory of Sophie's death and, what was perhaps worse, imagining once again the irrevocable corruption of her flesh.

Like everyone, Philip had a pool of memories he couldn't bear to hold in mind: the time as a child when he'd run barefoot and driven a rusty pin all the way through his middle toe, the day he'd found the family cat dead in the middle of the street—followed by any number of painful, embarrassing or deeply humiliating moments in his life. Sophie's death was lord and master of all these smaller pains, but it followed the same logic. Memories like these bobbed up at unexpected moments, leaving him wincing until he could banish them back to the depths.

Forcing himself to work, he went through the folder Guérin had provided. It was filled with clippings from the papers—both *Fanal d'Yvetot* and the regional *Paris-Normandie*. There were even brief reports in the national press. The articles came in chronological order, starting with the report of Sophie's disappearance, then breaking the news of the police investigation, the detention of Édouard Morin, the preparations for the trial, the declaration of the *non-lieu*, and finally a trickle of squibs over the years whenever Édouard Morin was transferred from one institution to another. The series concluded with Olivier Morin's obituary.

Many of the early clippings included photos, grainy halftone shots that still managed to portray the terror in Édouard Morin's eyes. It was an early, unformed version of the man Philip had visited at the psychiatric hospital in Rouen—though with the same fragile neck, the same wide eyes. He'd been so young! Philip imagined the boy's growing awareness that his life was toppling into a hell of his own device.

There were two different pictures of the father: a close-up shot taken on the day of the arrest, and another showing him from a greater distance as he entered the courthouse in Rouen, his right hand raised in an unsuccessful attempt to block his face from the camera. Philip stared into the pained eyes of the father, wondering how it must have felt to surrender his own son to the authorities. He thought again of the day they had sat together in the courthouse cafeteria. If only Olivier Morin had spoken to him! They shared something, after all: they had each lost a child.

And then there were the pictures of Sophie, the same image copied again and again, first when she'd gone missing and there was still hope, then afterward when reports about the inquiry appeared. Over time the articles dwindled in size, finally fading to nothing.

Although Monsieur Guérin had framed the photocopier on specific articles, bits and snippets of surrounding material appeared in the margins, ranging from news items to weather reports to coupons to classifieds. The same sheets that drummed the news of Sophie's death offered slices of Yvetot's life, and Philip found himself awash in memories he hadn't expected: the construction of the new school, the autumn of abundant rains, and at the end of the year, the departure of the parish priest, the one who had presided over Sophie's funeral, for a new position in Rouen.

What surprised him most about these records was their thinness. The different newspapers had cannibalized each other's prose, more eager to fill column inches than to shed any new light. Nevertheless, the articles provided a structure of names and dates, and he transcribed these facts into the blue diary. He had to start somewhere, and if he could compile all the information in this one set of pages, perhaps the details would form their own web of connections.

Then came a powdery photo from the *Fanal d'Yvetot*, a shot of the funeral, that ginned-up ceremony that started at the church and ended at the Saint-Louis cemetery, where they'd stood about the vacant grave listening to Father Huet's stiffly formal service. There Philip was in the middle, at Yvonne's side, his hand clutching hers, the invisible germ of their separation already sprouting. What thoughts occupied his bowed head? It was a somber group assembled in that field of crosses, starched-looking men and downcast women. Behind them to the right stood the grainy figure of a man, his legs slack as if ready to buckle, one hand pressed against his brow, the other arm draped over the shoulders of a woman who braced him. It was Roger with Élisabeth. At the time Philip had been too stricken to consider the grief of others, but this photograph showed a man he barely recognized: a brother-in-law who, fifteen years later, would still lay a yellow rose on a girl's tomb. Who, like Philip, still felt responsible.

Guérin's file was a start. The next step was to contact Rouen for access to the legal documents. On the phone, a sharp-voiced woman in the Bureau of Records grew impatient as he stumbled over the technical vocabulary in French. "*Comment? Quoi?*" she kept asking as she tried to penetrate his American accent.

All he wanted to know was if it might be possible to procure a copy of a dossier dating from 1993. *Possible?* she asked back. Of course it was *possible*. As long as he had a court order and had filled out the appropriate forms—without which it was quite *im*possible. When he pressed for details, she responded pointedly. "Monsieur, it's not my job to provide legal assistance to the general public. If you need help understanding French law, I suggest you contact a French lawyer." After that simple pronouncement, the line went dead.

Roger had suggested he try Father Cabot, so at noon he reinserted himself into the Smart Car and revved it up. But as soon as he pulled away from the curb the vehicle started to buck as if the pavement had sprouted bumps and ridges overnight. A flapping noise came from the front, and when he stopped to investigate he found that both front tires sagged like misshapen snails of rubber. In his entire life Philip had never experienced a single flat tire, and now, at the same time, he had two!

Then he understood. As Monsieur Bécot had warned, Philip's welcome in Yvetot had worn thin. He glanced about in search of culprits. One fellow strolled by whistling an aria. Women pulled groceries in carts, all of them oblivious. So he leaned on the horn, letting it bleat without interruption as heads turned. He kept at it, determined to blare the horn forever if that's what it took, and a few minutes later the white and blue police car rolled up at his side. The window went down, and Philip recognized the balding officer who frequented the *Tord-boyaux*.

"Anything wrong, Monsieur Adler?" he said, not even pretending he didn't know who Philip was.

"Someone has slashed my tires. I'd like to file a report."

The officer gave him an astonished look. "Are you sure?" He climbed out and examined the damage. "The thing is, Monsieur Adler, I don't see any cuts. It must be a leak, don't you think?"

"Two tires at once? You're telling me this is an accident?"

The officer scratched the thin hair at the back of his head. "Yes sir. That's my professional opinion. What else could it be? These cobblestones, they're hard on a vehicle, you know." He pointed up the street. "You'll find a service station just a few blocks that way. They'll be most helpful, I suspect."

He ended up paying for a truck to come with a pump, and then—should he have been surprised?—the tires held the air just fine. The coveralled mechanic gave a shrug. Maybe the seal between the rubber and the rim had been compromised, only to reform in the summer heat. Who knows? He'd seen stranger things than this in his day.

In short, there was no way to prove that the car had been vandalized, and Philip struggled to contain his irritation. He was still smoldering by the time he made it to Saint-Pierre Church.

The main door led directly into the giant rotunda of the nave. Tall windows spangled with colorful glass displayed abstract mosaics of light: martyrs paired with the symbols of their sacrifice. Behind the altar hung a towering cross from which a splayed and frail Jesus looked down with forgiveness. At the entrances to the side chapels, racks of electric votives flickered mechanically.

Philip loathed this building. He fixed on the pew where he'd sat the day of Sophie's funeral, and he recognized the area where the footsteps of pallbearers and the casters of caskets had worn the carpet thin. He remembered just where that old priest had stood, gesturing theatrically throughout the homily. He was glad to be dealing with a different man now.

He found Cabot in the sacristy, seated at a table, a napkin tucked into the collar of his cassock, his fork poised over a half-devoured meat pie, a bottle of red wine at the side. He was a corpulent man with a puffy face and a large nose veined with purple. The crown of his head was bare, almost like a monk's shaved tonsure, though the hair was thinning up front, too.

"Excuse me, Father," Philip said, the title strange on his tongue. He'd never grown used to this oddity of Catholicism—the conferral of fatherhood upon men sworn to celibacy. "I'm sorry to interrupt you, but would you have time for a question or two?"

Cabot eyed his dish and his rounded shoulders sank. "Do you mind if I continue with my lunch at the same time, Monsieur? Ordinarily I wouldn't ask, you understand, but it's such a busy day."

"Of course."

"Well then, please, pull up a chair." He took a steaming bite as he eyed his visitor. "You're the American, aren't you?" he said as he chewed, jabbing his fork toward Philip.

"That's right."

"I thought so! I'm pretty good at figuring out accents. It's Monsieur Abbler, isn't it?"

"Adler."

"What kind of name is that, anyway? German?"

"Of a sort, yes."

"And you're a psychologist, aren't you?"

"Psychiatrist."

Cabot fluttered his hand, dismissing the distinction. He smiled. "We are colleagues, my dear Monsieur Adler." When Philip cocked his head, Cabot explained. "Don't you see? Instead of the psychiatrist's couch, I use a confessional. Though I must point out one little advantage on my side." He pinched his thumb and forefinger together to show how small, though very real, the advantage was. "The psychiatrist does not give absolution." He chortled. "And yet, we're both savers of souls, aren't we?" The priest seemed satisfied with this parallel.

"Father, I don't mean to keep you for long."

Cabot glanced at his watch while he chewed. "I do have a meeting at two o'clock. With the roofers, you know. So annoying. It's leaking again. All along the south side. And they just repaired it last year. Supposedly all new copper." Philip attempted to speak, but Cabot continued. "How does copper leak, you might well ask?" He used chunks of baguette to sop up the sauce from his pie. "Can water simply pass through a sheet of metal? Do they think I'll take it as one of God's miracles? Even this bread does a better job." He stuffed the spongy mass into his cheeks, still managing to talk. "Roofers are scoundrels, the lot of them."

He washed down the bite with wine and stifled a burp. "Still, I suppose that's not what you're here to see me about, is it, Monsieur? Perhaps you'd like a mass for your daughter? As long as you're in town?"

"I take it you know my story."

"Well, it all happened long before I was brought in. I was in Lisieux before, you know. A wonderful little city—a pilgrimage site, thanks to Saint Teresa. But yes, I've heard about your daughter, may she rest in peace," he said, crossing himself.

"Now I'm looking for her body."

Cabot's eyes grew large. "What do you mean? She's right there in Saint-Louis cemetery. I've seen the grave myself."

"It's empty, Father. Her body was never recovered."

The priest's eyes widened further. "I had no idea. How very unfortunate."

"Begging your pardon, Father, but it's worse than unfortunate."

"Of course. A terrible thing," Cabot mused. He wagged his head to the left and right. "Still, I suppose all true believers owe their salvation to an empty tomb."

Philip decided not to pursue the reference. If he wasn't careful, they'd be lost in digressions. He turned the discussion in the direction of Olivier and Édouard Morin.

These names reined in Cabot's attention. "As for the boy, I never even knew him. Knew *of* him, of course. But those events, they took place so long ago."

"You were acquainted with the father?"

"A bit. Olivier Morin, he wasn't what I'd call a devout Catholic. Not that he was alone in that respect. Oh, Monsieur Abbler, you would hardly believe the state of my flock in Yvetot. It's not my fault, mind you. Indeed, I'd like to think that in some small way I've held the line here—perhaps even improved it since the day of Father Huet. But all over France we are losing parishioners to other pursuits. Sports mostly. Do you know what happens to church attendance every year during the weeks of the Tour de France? It's appalling!"

"Olivier Morin," Philip said, prodding the priest back on track.

"Right. Well, for a long time he didn't come to Saint-Pierre at all. I knew who he was, and he did start attending mass during that last year, while he still could. He had the cancer, you know. You'd be amazed how many people return to the church then," he commented with annoyance. "I know what they say—better late than never, but still, it's rather galling."

Philip began an awkward interrogation, trying to learn what he could about Olivier Morin. What was the man like? Who were his friends? What were his habits? But most of his questions stumped the priest. Cabot could speak at great length about Yvetot families and rumors—even if he muddled some of the details—but about Morin he knew little. The man had never lingered after services, never taken confession. He participated in no parish activities, and Cabot wasn't aware of any close connections. The Morin family was at the end of its line—another piece of evidence supporting Monsieur Bécot's theory that Yvetot was fading toward extinction.

"But are you saying," Philip pressed, "that Olivier Morin had no friends at all? What about at his funeral? Who attended it?"

Cabot wrinkled his brow. "You'll have to forgive me, Monsieur Abbler. There are so many ceremonies. Weddings, funerals, baptisms, confirmations, first communions . . ." Then his eyes brightened. "But now that I think about it, I do recall Monsieur Morin's funeral—because it was so odd."

"Odd?"

"Excessively. There was no one there at all, you see. Not a soul."

Philip nodded. Because of his son, Olivier Morin represented a tear in the social fabric, and the community had done what it did best, what it did to all outsiders, to everyone who made trouble: it had ostracized him.

That evening he called Roger. The visit to the archives figured in his report, but he glossed over the photograph that had captured Roger's grief at the cemetery. He would spare him that particular pain.

When he described his flattened tires, his brother-in-law listened with interest.

"It sounds like you're becoming unpopular, my friend."

"Unless you count Monsieur Guérin. He didn't seem to mind me."

"You would think," Roger continued, "that they might be struck by the irony of it. Deflating your tires certainly sends a signal, but it doesn't exactly help get you out of town." His voice turned somber. "Still, it shows that people are growing impatient."

"I won't stay any longer than I have to. But everywhere I turn there's a new obstacle." He related the exchange with the woman at the Bureau of Records, and Roger gave a bitter chuckle.

"I love that!" he said. "*No legal assistance for the general public.* If that isn't the job of the public courthouse, then I don't know what is."

"In any case, I don't know what to do, Roger. We have no court order. And given how slowly things move in this country, I shudder to think how long it would take to get one."

"Don't worry about that," Roger replied. "We'll get your precious documents. And we won't need a court order."

"How do you expect that to happen?"

Roger sighed, and Philip could picture him shaking his head. "You know, you lived in France for many years, but in some respects it was all in vain. You remain very much an American. It's perfectly charming, I assure you, but quite ineffective. In France, when you desire something that is not allowed, you should never request it over the phone."

"Is that so?"

"Indeed. And above all, you must not request it with a foreign accent— especially not an American one."

Philip tensed up. "I don't have a great deal of choice about that," he retorted. "It's not my fault I sound like an American. I don't know why the French are so sensitive about that. The accent doesn't change what I say."

"That's where you're mistaken. Accents are our way of determining the origins and the social class of the speaker. Is he French or foreign? Is he from Paris or Normandy? From Rouen or Yvetot? Does he work as a doctor or a farmer? You see, accents tell us whether you are inside or outside the group, which in turn determines what we think a person has to say—and what right he has to say it. In many situations, accent is more important than the words themselves."

"Terrific. Where does that leave me?"

"It leaves you needing someone who can speak with the proper voice. In short, it leaves you with *me*. We will travel to Rouen together, and we shall return with the documents we require."

"Are you sure you have time?"

"Who has time for any of this? And yet time is what it requires."

It was such a plain observation that one could almost overlook its generosity. "One last request," Philip said. "Would you mind not mentioning any of this to Yvonne?"

"Why on earth would you think I'd tell her anything?"

"I don't know. Because she might ask? Because she's your sister?"

"But she is also an ex-wife, and that places her in a separate category altogether. Ex-wives are a species requiring very particular handling."

Twelve

After dinner Philip returned to his hotel room and reviewed his notes. The results from the day now occupied several pages in the blue diary, and these columns of ink created at least the illusion of accomplishment. Flipping through, he happened upon Yvonne's address, copied from the phonebook just the other day.

When she'd come to visit him, she'd stood in this very room. They'd been together, separated by inches, by the sheerness of fabric.

Philip had vowed to keep a low profile, but now he felt a craving, a need to meet with her again. Might he chart a course through all the tension and resentment? And if he did, what awaited him on the other side? The images that paraded through his mind were positively torrid.

Before going to bed, he tried another call to Melanie Patterson, and to his surprise, she picked up.

"Oh. It's *you*," she said by way of a greeting. "Again."

Her tone was high-pitched and impertinent, but the hints of Boston in her voice soothed him. It felt like home. Moreover, he could speak to her in English, while during most of his day he had to scramble through a linguistic obstacle course. And despite everything, he liked this girl.

"Melanie," he began, smiling into the phone, "how are you doing?"

"Yeah, well, you know," she replied.

"You've been hard to reach. Didn't Linda try to set up an appointment?"

"Only like a zillion times."

Vintage Melanie. "Can we talk?" he wanted to know. "Do you have time?" He carried the pen and notebook over to the bed, swung his feet up and sat leaning against the headboard.

She emitted her trademark snort. "Do *I* have time? The question is, do *you* have time?"

He deserved that dig. "Yes, I'm sorry I had to cut our last call short."

"You don't have to, like, *apologize* to me," she said, her voice oozing with apathy. "I'm sure there are lots more important things to do off in Paris."

"I'm not in Paris. And no, nothing is more important."

"Yeah. Right."

There it was again, the lack of trust. But could he really blame her? Something had happened to Melanie in the one place where trust should never be broken—the home. And now, after weeks of microscopic progress in their sessions in Boston, just as they'd started to build a relationship, he'd left her in the lurch. Just as everyone else had. And now, here he was, literally phoning it in.

"Hel-*lo?*" she called out. "Are you still there?"

The absurdity of the imbalance between them had never struck him so clearly. He needed to give Melanie something. Trust was a bridge built from both sides of a chasm, meeting in the middle.

"Because if you aren't," she continued, "I've got stuff I gotta—"

"Melanie," he interrupted. "I haven't been entirely honest with you."

There was a silence on the other end. He could imagine her sitting up straight, weighing his words.

"What do you mean?" she said, stretching the syllables with suspicion.

"You're right. I am here in France because of something important. More important than I can describe. I'm sorry I had to interrupt our sessions for this, but that's what happens sometimes. Reality gets in the way."

There was a pause. He could tell his frankness had taken her off-balance.

"What is it, this important thing?"

"I'm afraid I can't tell you much about it."

"Oh, I get it," she said, her tone bouncing back. "It's super-important, but not for delicate ears. Is that it? Well, that's all very interesting, Doctor Adler, but—"

He made a snap decision. "It has to do with a thing that happened long ago. And now a chance I have to . . . to do something about it."

Once again the line went quiet, and Philip tried to read the silence. Blind to her gestures and her expressions, he relied all the more heavily on sounds and their absence. He heard a shuffling on her side.

"To . . . fix it?" she said.

"Not quite. But to make it better. To make it . . ." He searched. "Bearable."

There was a pause. "I see."

That was as far as Philip was willing to go. These revelations were already pushing the limits of professional conduct. He backed into less threatening territory. He told Melanie a bit about Normandy, describing the countryside, the cows, the sea, the food—even giving her a rundown of the motley regulars in the *Tord-boyaux*, at one point eliciting a squeak that sounded suspiciously like a rusty laugh. He kept track of the topics, scribbling a list of key words down on a page of the diary.

And from there he asked about her own family's vacations, and eventually Melanie uttered a cluster of tentative sentences. The sneer in her voice ebbed. There were still areas of resistance. When the conversation brushed up against her father, Melanie slowed down and veered away—only to return from some other angle. Philip was familiar with the dynamic: the will to communicate was knotted together with the need to censor, like two powerful animals yoked back to back, pulling in opposite directions.

As they neared the end of the hour, he knew he'd have just one chance to address the real topic. Speaking about her father directly would be pointless, but perhaps they could approach the problem by way of a symptom, by discussing the ways she hurt herself. He dreaded transitions such as this—those moments in sessions when he had to risk all the capital he'd built up.

"Before we finish," he began, "do you mind if I bring up another topic?"

In an instant, the tension was back. "What do you mean?"

"I don't want to play games with you, Melanie. We have work to do, you know. I thought we might talk about something else. Your eating, for example."

She said nothing, and Philip jotted a note on his page.

"Or rather," he continued, "your *not* eating."

"I've already told you," she bristled. "I'm *not* talking about that."

He sighed. "I don't mean to make things difficult. I really don't. But we can't avoid it forever."

The line went quiet, but at least she didn't hang up.

"I'm not judging," he continued. "I'm just trying to understand. Why don't you start by describing to me what your meal schedule is like? Are there specific foods you try to avoid?"

"It's is none of your business. Don't you *get* it? It doesn't mean *anything*. You sound just like my dad."

"Is it hard not to eat?"

"I'm just not *hungry*, okay? Why can't people, like, *accept* that?"

"Are you still vomiting?"

She didn't answer, which Philip took as a yes. He continued. "Do you have any idea why you worry so much about how you look?"

"I couldn't care *less* how I look."

"Is that why you dye your hair black? Why you buy all black clothes? Because it seems like you're very concerned to show how much you don't care."

Even from thirty-five hundred miles away Philip could feel the electricity. He wrote down "importance of appearances" and underlined it twice.

"Tell me," he continued, "do you have your black fingernail polish on today?"

"*Stop* it," she snarled. "You don't know what you're talking about."

"Why does this make you so angry?"

"I don't eat because I don't *want* to eat. What's your *problem* with that?"

"But why don't you want to eat? Everyone wants to eat."

She snorted again. "Obviously *not*."

"Well, then, if you don't want to eat, what do you want?"

"I'm *not* talking about this anymore."

"What do you want, Melanie?"

"I want to be *left alone*."

"Melanie?"

"Go to hell! Go to fucking hell!"

Every word from the girl's mouth pulsed with pain, but Philip knew he had to push. He was close to the abscess, and he pressed the blade. "Tell me what you want, Melanie."

"What do I *want?*" she cried into the phone. "I want you to fuck off. I want you to stop calling me. I want . . . all these people . . . to stop wanting things from me!"

He heard her gasp on the other end. Was it for surprise at what she had said? Or simply a breath between stifled sobs? He was about to ask, when suddenly the line clicked. She was gone.

His first impulse was to call her back, but he doubted she would answer, and it could make him look too keen, putting her in control. The smart play would be to give her a day or two to cool down and collect her thoughts. Then they could speak again.

Her complaint of *all these people* meant just one person, he was sure. They were approaching the wound. Melanie herself would have recognized this by now. It was a delicate and dangerous stage, and Philip would need to give their next conversation a great deal of thought.

Thirteen

The next morning he folded himself back in the Smart Car and headed for the countryside, hoping the fresh air and the curves would stir his thoughts. Asphalt widened and narrowed, linking villages that sat like beads on a rosary. Sunshine glinted on the slate roofs and burned off the fog in the fields. Pastures alternated with lush groves. The land about him was happy with life.

Returning by way of the Fécamp road, he once again traversed Ypreville, pausing at the complex intersection by the town hall—the road toward Yvetot weaving around the corner, while arrows to Toqueville and Sorquainville angled right and left. The last name stirred his memory, and he realized that Sorquainville was one of the towns mentioned by Morin when he spoke of the German roadblocks.

He took the turn, heading eastward on a ribbon of asphalt that rose into fields as flat as water. A broad pasture extended on his right, a herd of white cattle lounging in the sun. To the left lay a field of sorghum. He passed a stone cross at an ancient intersection, and as the road wore even thinner, he found a smattering of stunted houses clustered around the remains of a church. Here he brought the car to a full stop and climbed out.

Sorquainville was nothing but a juncture of family farms, a hamlet owing its existence to an intersection, the roads leading almost nowhere. In the direction from which he'd come, Philip saw the distant rooftops of Ypreville. In the other he made out a line of trees. A cow lowed in the distance. Chickens clucked. Somewhere a dog barked.

As he stood on the gravel before the pitched steps of the locked church, he had to wonder. A German roadblock on the road to Sorquainville? The destination wasn't worthy of blockading. It was barely a dot on the map, a nearly nonexistent plot of turf located on the brink of habitable space. He found it impossible to imagine Sorquainville having any military importance at all.

Back at the hotel, Monsieur Bécot was on the phone at the reception desk, visibly worked up, speaking too fast for Philip to understand. When he hung up the phone, he turned to his American guest, his enthusiasm for once overwhelming his prudence.

"It has happened again, Monsieur Adler," he cried out in English.

"What do you mean?"

"Another *oh-bus*." When Philip still didn't understand, Bécot gestured with both hands, as if presenting an invisible ball. "You remember? An *obus*. A shell left over from the war. You didn't believe me when I told you how many pieces still come out of the dirt. And yet, here is another one. I say they are like souvenirs. This time it was in Duclin's field, just a few kilometers away. The old boy went over it with his tractor. He is in the hospital now!"

Philip squinted. "You mean it actually went off?"

"Oh yes," Bécot replied. "That is Normandy for you. They say we have another forty years of . . . what do you say? *Surprises*. They wait for us, and one by one we find them."

Bécot was prattling on and Philip nodded vaguely, his thoughts already adrift. Yes, that's the way it would happen, he told himself. Fifty years from now, in some farmer's field or in the excavation for a foundation, Sophie's remains would turn up. No one would understand. There'd be some shrugging of shoulders as the bones were exhumed, and then they'd be carted off to a common grave.

He turned back to the desk. "Monsieur Bécot, I need to pick your brain."

"This story," Bécot said, still smiling to himself. "It will be in the newspaper. You wait and see."

Philip leaned in. "I've just returned from a drive, Monsieur Bécot."

"That's very good, Monsieur, but I am telling you that—"

"On the way back, I took a little detour. I stopped at Sorquainville."

"Sorquainville?" Bécot drew back, a perplexed look on his face. "Why would you go to Sorquainville. Nothing is there." He reassessed. "Not unless you wish to buy a chicken from Monsieur Jouvet."

"I have a question for you about that town. Back in the war, when the Germans arrived, I understand they put up roadblocks."

Bécot blinked at Philip. "Well, yes," he said. "That was at the beginning. When the phantoms arrived."

"The what?"

"Général Rommel, with his *Panzers*. The people called them *la division fantôme*—ghosts—because they moved so fast, no one knew where they were. The Germans, they did what you describe. They closed roads to keep French soldiers from getting to the coast."

"Do you happen to know where those roadblocks were located? For instance, would there have been one on the road to Sorquainville?"

Bécot gave a sour look. "But *what* road to Sorquainville? Monsieur Adler, there is no road to Sorquainville from Yvetot. You must go through . . ." He checked his internal coordinates. "Through Ypreville," he said. "Or from the other side."

"I see."

"Besides," he continued, raising his hands over his head and shaking them. "Why block the road to Sorquainville? No one goes there."

Philip nodded. "That's what I thought." He paused. "What about Malamare and Adonville?"

Bécot was dumbfounded by this display of obscure names. He looked torn between curiosity and anxiety. "Monsieur Adler," he said, "I am going to show you how wrong you are. Perhaps that will put a stop to this." He led Philip back into the office and drew an ancient Michelin map from a drawer, the colors bleached with age and the creases barely holding. He unfolded it on the desk as carefully as if it were the Shroud of Turin.

Tracing his finger across the paper, he pointed the towns out one by one. There was no doubt about it: Malamare and Adonville were as forlorn as Sorquainville. They appeared in the smallest print Michelin deigned to use, with only a crook of road leading through them. One was in the direction of Le Havre, though several kilometers off the main road. The other was along the way to Dieppe.

"I assure you," Bécot said, "the Germans put no blocks in those places. They wanted only big roads—ones that are perhaps not far from these villages, but certainly not these."

Philip studied the map. The three towns Morin had mentioned were like the points of a triangle, each one in a different direction from Yvetot.

"I'm sorry to disappoint you, Monsieur Adler," Bécot continued. "But I tell you for your own good. These towns. They barely exist. They mean nothing. They are no place."

No place. It was nothing more than a coincidence of language, but Philip was incapable of ignoring the echo: *non-lieu.*

Notes had accumulated in the blue diary with the dragonfly cover. However, with each pass through the recordings of the meeting, and through Monsieur Guérin's files, Philip came out with a thinner harvest. There was a presence in Morin's speech, a language beneath the language, like something hidden that wanted to be found. But it was too partial: a sieve of words. Philip's own recollections were insufficient to fill the gaps. Much had seeped away over the past fifteen years, and his memory was like the ancient map Bécot had shown him—a speckling of dots where all the connecting lines had faded.

For a while he sought to avoid the obvious conclusion, but there was no use denying it. He needed more—and not just the records from the courthouse. He would have to see Édouard Morin again. Given Hervé's connections in the medical community, it wouldn't be possible to keep a second visit quiet, which meant that he'd have to tell Yvonne. A delicate task. He imagined the local bomb disposal expert disarming old shells in the field. That was the kind of touch he'd need.

On the morning of the courthouse expedition, Roger pulled up in front of the hotel in his blue BMW. The window glided down.

"Do you mind if I drive?" he called to Philip. "We could take your car, but I fear you'd have to strap me to the roof."

On the way to Rouen Philip told Roger about his stop in Sorquainville, as well as his discussion with Bécot. It supported Roger's belief that the list of towns was the product of an unhealthy mind, a kind of deliberate obfuscation. This left Roger all the more perplexed when Philip announced he would request a second meeting with Morin.

"Why would he say anything new?"

Philip hedged. "I don't have clear expectations."

"I get it: a fishing expedition. You drop your line in the water and hope something strikes."

"More of a trawler. I'll scoop up everything and then sort through the catch."

Roger banked hard around a curve. "You're a strange one, aren't you, Philip Adler? I admire your diligence. I was all in favor of pumping Morin for information, but I had rather hoped he'd be a bit more helpful."

"Perhaps," Philip said into his window, "we're just not listening right." Yes, it all came down to listening—to what psychiatrists sometimes called the *third ear*, a special organ attuned to subtle patterns. Mental illness was a private code that grew like ivy, twining along the limbs of language. Philip's job was to hear the flutter of those leaves, to trace the vines, to discover the roots and sustenance.

He frowned. If the task was listening, he was ill equipped for Morin's foreign tongues—the bursts of German, Spanish, Italian, and Latin. Even Philip's French was a mess—his accent a disaster, his grammar a wreck. Morin had agreed to speak in English during the first meeting, but there was no guarantee he would do so for a second. Language offered a wilderness where Morin could seek shelter.

In order to recognize patterns and see connections—to listen—Philip had to be able to understand. Which meant he needed help from someone who had the skills he lacked. His heart quickened as he realized who it had to be. She was the obvious choice. But he wasn't sure how to make the request from a safe distance.

The *Palais de Justice* of Rouen was a flamboyant medley of towers and arches, pinnacles and arcades, gargoyles and ornaments—a stone monster built with one clawed foot firmly planted in the late Middle Ages, a second just over the threshold of the early Renaissance, and a third in the realm of architectural miscellany, where curlicues, restorations, and annexes grew like galls in the wounds suffered by the edifice over the course of five centuries. The jumble of the outside reflected the labyrinth of corridors coiling through its innards like an irritable bowel, bulging here and there into stone diverticula.

They wound their way through the hall, up Stairway A to the third floor, and down a long corridor. A tall, two-paneled door bore the engraved sign: "*Bureau des Archives*" and showed the hours of operation: "*9h00–19h00*."

Roger paused before they entered, holding Philip back. "One small detail," he said.

"What?"

"Let me do the talking." He fluttered a hand to counter Philip's objection. "Remember: accents."

Philip grumbled but agreed, and with this matter resolved, Roger pushed through the door into the office. A long counter stretched across the room, separating clerks from the public they were to serve—although both categories were currently hypothetical, as not a soul was visible. From the cubicles in the back, a woman's voice droned. She appeared to be recounting her weekend.

Roger closed the door, shuffled his feet, coughed, and engaged in all the small sounds of human presence until finally the voice slowed, hesitated, and stalled. A drawn-looking woman appeared from behind the divider, her hair pulled back as tightly as piano strings, graying roots showing in the part. She straightened her skirt as she approached, then shimmied onto a stool behind the counter, crossed her arms, and focused on the papers in front of her. Although she sat only three feet away, she had not yet acknowledged their existence.

"Excuse us for bothering you, Madame," Roger smiled, finally drawing her attention. "We were hoping you might be available to assist us. You see, we hope to acquire a copy of the records pertaining to a legal case."

The woman studied him, then turned her thin eyes toward Philip, examining this strangely tall specimen as if he were a weed asking to be pulled.

"Might that be possible?" Roger nudged.

She pursed her lips. "Judgments are a matter of public record," she said. "You'll find them in the *Registre des jugements*."

"Of course," Roger replied. "But you see, we are looking for more than just the judgment. We need transcripts, motions, police reports—all the trimmings."

When she spoke, her lips barely moved. "For that you'll need to start at the Bureau of Legal Affairs, Monsieur. Stairway D, second floor."

Roger jabbed a finger in the air. "And yet, we have just been to the Bureau of Legal Affairs in Stairway D," he lied. "It is they themselves who sent us here." He broadened his smile.

The functionary's eyes had narrowed to slits. "What exactly are you looking for?"

"Merely the file from the case of Monsieur Édouard Morin, from the fall of 1993."

"And you have an authorization for this? A formal request?"

"I confess we have nothing formal at the moment. I had hoped it might be possible to dispense with such additional steps, and that—"

"No," she said, cutting him off. "That will not be possible."

"Goodness," he exclaimed. "It's so rare these days to find a civil servant who knows the rules as well as you do. Certainly not those jokers over in Stairway D. I wonder if you might be aware of any process by which the matter might be expedited. Perhaps there is a fee?" He was reaching for his wallet. "I'm afraid I only have cash . . ."

Her pause inspired hope that she might consider Roger's offer of a bribe, but she refused him with a certain relish. "No, Monsieur," she said with a smile. "I'm afraid not."

The screech of a scooted chair sounded from another cubicle, and a younger woman appeared briefly, giving a timid glance in their direction as she dropped a bundle of paperwork into an out-basket, then disappeared.

Philip knew the category for people like this Cerberus of public records: malignant narcissist. Roger would never get past her so easily.

He stepped forward, ignoring Roger's glare. "We fully understand, Madame," he said. From these first accented syllables, he knew she'd recognized his voice from the phone call. "We certainly wish to follow the appropriate procedures," he continued. "And I believe we can get ahold of the legal document rather quickly." Roger began to speak up, but Philip silenced him with a look. "Our lawyer is here in Rouen," he continued. "We have only a little time, but perhaps we could return in a couple of hours." He glanced at his watch. "About one o'clock? Would that be convenient?"

The woman leaned forward, her smile razor thin. "I'm afraid that would be most *in*convenient. I will be at lunch at that time."

"How unfortunate," Philip exclaimed. He turned to Roger. "I suppose it will have to be another day, don't you think?" He turned back to the counter. "Thank you so very much for your assistance."

He dragged a stunned Roger into the hallway.

"What did you do that for?" Roger hissed. "I nearly had her!"

"Don't flatter yourself. She wasn't going to crack."

"You don't know that," he grumbled.

"We'll be returning at one o'clock."

"What good will that do? You heard yourself. She won't even be here then."

Philip pointed to the hours posted outside the door. "And yet, the office itself will be open. The she-devil will be at lunch, and someone else will be at the counter—probably that poor young woman who has to listen to her all day long, and who will be delighted for us to treat her as a human being for fifteen minutes."

Roger's jaw opened, then closed. "That's not half bad," he said, though it clearly pained him to admit it. "I'm afraid I may have—what did your president use to say?—*misunderestimated* you."

"In the meantime, we have a project to attend to."

Fifteen minutes later, seated at a table in a café, Philip drew a blank sheet of paper from his briefcase. Starting about a third of the way down the sheet, he proceeded to write out a semi-official request for the documents.

Roger squinted as he tried to read the text upside down from his side of the table. "But you're writing it in English."

"All that matters is the appearance of authority. In my limited experience, little is more important to French bureaucracy."

Roger nodded at this assessment, impressed.

Philip continued. "Administrations are hierarchical systems, and therefore narrow. Your run-of-the-mill civil servant can't possibly know what signs of authority are appropriate to each culture. Our job is to create something that corresponds to her imagination. A letter from a doctor—especially a psychiatrist—will carry some weight."

"That's quite good," Roger concurred. "Say, I'd suggest that you make the English rather complicated."

"Of course. Then we'll find a place to type it up."

"Nonsense. In France an official letter must be handwritten. Typing is too impersonal. And I suggest you use that nearly indecipherable hand of yours."

"Unintelligibility equals authority?"

"Don't you find?"

So Philip wrote out an elaborately phrased and hieroglyphically scrawled request for the records pertaining to Édouard Morin. "What do you think?" he said, showing off his handiwork.

Roger's brow furrowed deeply as he tried and failed to read it. "Excellent. But are you sure you want to circulate counterfeit documents?"

"But it's not a counterfeit—not quite. It's a letter written by me, signed by me and for my benefit. They don't need to know that I am both the doctor and the concerned party. Of course our friends up in Stairway A won't know that, and we won't go out of our way to point it out. All we need is to persuade the woman at the desk."

Roger rubbed his jaw. "Probably. But the bureaucracy is a complicated machine. You never know who might take a closer look at it. Say, be sure to make your signature large and florid. That always makes a good impression."

At a photocopy shop down the street Philip took scissors to one of his business cards, cutting it into fragments which he scotch-taped onto a sheet of paper, approximating the layout of letterhead. After a test, he slipped the handwritten letter into the paper tray, printing the mock letterhead over the request. Even Roger had to admit that it looked professional.

"But something's missing," Roger mused. "Would you happen to have any American currency?" Philip produced a fifty from his wallet. "Nothing smaller?" Roger asked him. "Such a waste."

He took scissors to the bill, cutting out the seal of the Department of Treasury, gluing the tiny emblem onto the letter beneath Philip's signature. "Such fine paper they use for American bills," he said with admiration. "It feels so official." He held the sheet up to the light, frowning like an artist considering finishing touches. Then he borrowed the rubber address stamp from the proprietor of the shop, and punched it over the seal and signature, twisting it slightly to smudge the lettering.

"Nothing is official in France without a stamp," he said.

The words "*TechnoCopie—Rue des Bons Enfants—Rouen*" would be legible to anyone looking closely. Which meant: no one.

A little before two o'clock they trotted down the steps of the *Palais de Justice* with an enormous packet of photocopies supplied by a less fierce, more compliant woman at the Bureau of Records. As they departed, the sour harpy of the morning crossed their path in the other direction, returning from lunch. Her icy stare followed them as they rushed ahead, and they didn't turn back.

To celebrate this documentary triumph, Roger dragged Philip off to a bar where he downed one Belgian beer after another, Philip accompanying him with tonic water. The more Roger drank, the more he spoke about Élisabeth, insisting that he was not going to let her interfere with his bachelor lifestyle—a lifestyle that served him well, thank you very much, and that needed no fixing, especially not at the hands of a woman who had booted him out of her own life several times, which showed how poorly qualified she was to give advice. How could anyone expect him to live with a woman like that? He could take care of himself, couldn't he? Each question came like another card at the top of a teetering structure.

"Is it really me you're trying to convince?" Philip asked.

And the house of cards collapsed. Roger stared into his glass.

"What is it you really want?" Philip asked.

"I only wish I knew." He took a deep breath. "All my problems come down to women. Think of it: if I hadn't run off to shag Élisabeth that night, your daughter would still be alive."

There it was. That old chestnut. "Of course," Philip replied. "Just like me: if I'd not returned to Paris. Or hadn't brought her out to Anne-Madeleine's in the first place. Or had taught her to stay at home with dolls and tea parties. We can play the what-if game all day, but don't think you can win at it. It's a contest everyone loses."

Roger hung his head. "You know what? I saw Élisabeth the other evening, and for a little while I remembered—vaguely, mind you—why it is we got married. But the next morning, not so much. That's how it goes, back and forth. Again and again. It's dragged on like this for years now. All in all, I find it terribly distressing."

Philip fingered the edge of the file from the courthouse, as thick as a dictionary. "Well, at least there aren't any children involved."

"Of course there aren't."

His combative tone gave Philip pause. "Do you wish there were?"

He harrumphed. "You know what? I'm done talking about this."

"Ignoring problems won't make them go away."

"Could have fooled me," Roger shot back. "It seems to have worked pretty well for you over the past fifteen years."

Philip absorbed the blow. He'd touched a nerve, and now he let a long silence hang between them as Roger's shoulders rounded.

His head bowed, Roger rasped out a question. "Hypothetical. Say a man walks into your office one day. Tells you he hates his life. Wants to begin anew. What advice do you give him?"

Philip paused, trying to catch his brother-in-law's eye. "Well," he began, "I'd tell him to start with something small. Something he knows he can handle. Once he has mastered that, he should add one more thing. And then one more. That would be it. Start small, and make one change at a time."

Roger stared blankly at the table, nodding.

Philip left him to sober up in the city center while he hiked the steep hill into the neighborhood where Yvonne and Hervé lived. By the time he reached the two-story brick house, he'd broken into a sweat, and he stood to cool off, not wanting to appear as desperate as he felt. After all, he had no backup plan if Yvonne refused him. Only she had the language skills, and only she understood the context. No one else came close.

When the doorbell went unanswered, his shoulders lightened. A reprieve. He checked his watch. It wasn't even four o'clock yet, and chances were good she was still at the university. She used to prefer her classes early, but perhaps her habits had changed? Any one of a thousand things might have delayed her. Still, if he waited long enough, she was bound to turn up. He walked around to the metal gate for the backyard, which he found unlocked. Lime green grass, primly mowed, carpeted the yard, while on the trellises along the south the roses had started to bloom. The gardens displayed the abundance of early summer, thriving on warmth and humidity.

He took a seat at the patio table, settling in to begin the courthouse file while he waited. The girth of the packet both daunted and promised: surely, in the ocean of those hundreds of pages, something useful would bob to the surface.

He set out the diary and pulled out Yvonne's ballpoint pen, ready to record his thoughts. There were administrative filings of all sorts, but the heart of the matter lay in the police statements, the helter-skelter collection of evidence and testimony, closer in time to the events themselves, making these pages especially precious. Compared to the carefully edited legalese of the later documents, these were the subconscious of the case, churning in their uncensored disarray.

Everything began with the original missing person report filed in Yvetot after Anne-Madeleine's call, late on that July night—at an hour when, as they would later discover, Sophie already lay dead. Somewhere. These first sheets captured the messiness of the original panic: when she'd last been seen, when Anne-Madeleine first grew worried, where she had looked. The police notes listed what Sophie had been wearing—and the simple mention of his daughter's lavender T-shirt triggered a surge of memories, images of closets and dressers, laundry and messy bedrooms. Philip smelled now the peach-scented shampoo she'd used all that year.

There was the handwritten chronology, with items crossed out and corrected, reconstructing Sophie's last known hours. Then came the list of people she knew in town. The whereabouts of all the family members—Roger and Élisabeth in Yvetot, Flora and Pierre in Rouen, Évelyne and Sylvain already living in the south. And then the lists of friends and neighbors, the broadening circle of all those who knew Sophie, who might have had their eye on her. *Who?* That had been the question of the first hours, and every name had rung with guilt.

The printed words began to dance before Philip's eyes, and he turned from the pages to anchor himself in the present. But Yvonne's middle-class backyard offered no haven, filled as it was with the telltale traces of family life. A rusted bucket sat in the flower bed, a pair of dirty gloves draped over the side; under the hedge lay a partly deflated soccer ball; the lawn mower stood ready to serve, its electric cord trailing off like a long tail; three empty glasses waited patiently on a tray by the back door. These mute signs of domesticity pitched about him like buoys on a rough sea, and plunged him into a froth of memories: the Aubert home in Yvetot, with the police milling about in the entryway; Anne-Madeleine crying; Yvonne sitting with him in the stillness of the living room; the arrival of Élisabeth, Roger joining them later; the phone ringing and not ringing; the thoughts of Sophie before, during, and after. And, last of all, that old sensation of slipping back into the dark waters of his own imagination, now strangely troubled. Something was amiss—out of place or out of sequence—and he couldn't put his finger on it.

"Can I help you?" came a voice in French. He spun around in his chair to see a girl with long, dark hair standing at the gate. It was Margaux. Yvonne would be furious. How stupid of him not to realize that she might appear first!

"Terribly sorry," he stammered, rising to his feet. "I shouldn't have come into your yard like this. I hope I didn't startle you."

"Yes, a bit," she said tentatively.

"My apologies. Let me introduce myself. I—"

"I know who you are. We met at that dinner. At *Mamie's* house."

"That's right."

"You're the American. *Maman's* first husband."

He nodded, unable to turn his eyes from her. "My name is Philip. Philip Adler."

Margaux walked into the yard, dropping her school backpack on the ground. She pulled out a chair from the other side of the table and slid onto it. "So, you're my . . ." She scrunched her brow. "My stepfather? No, that's not right, is it?"

"No."

"Father-in-law?" She frowned. "That's not it, either."

Perhaps in some language there was a word for the father of your dead half-sister, but Philip couldn't find it in French. "I'm . . . nothing . . . that is, I don't think there's a term for it."

Margaux looked unsatisfied with this hole in language. Then she sighed and accepted it. Looking around, she scanned the garden. "Have you seen Rodolphe?"

"Who?"

"Our cat," she explained. "He's usually in the garden. But he stayed out all night, and I was worried about him."

"No. No sign of him, I'm afraid."

She turned back to him. "You're here for Mother, aren't you?"

"That's right. Do you expect her home soon?"

She shrugged. "Perhaps? It's hard to know for sure. Sometimes she gets home quite late. She has all these meetings."

Philip's mind raced. This was a mistake. He shouldn't be talking to Margaux. He shouldn't have come at all. He rose to his feet. "I'll stop by another time." He started scooping his papers into their folder. "I don't mean to be in the way. If you could just mention to your mother that—"

"Tell me," Margaux interrupted. "Do I look very much like her?"

He froze. "I'm sorry?"

She cocked her head. "Like Sophie. Do you think I look like her?"

Philip tried to swallow and failed.

"Because I think so," she continued. "I've seen pictures of her, you know. *Maman* doesn't say anything, of course, but every year, I think I look more like my sister."

Margaux had fetched tumblers of water from the kitchen, into which she'd dolloped raspberry syrup from a can, carefully transporting the overfull glasses to the patio on a tray. Philip had spread out the pictures from his wallet, the shot of Sophie on the tennis court, the one from the mountains, another showing her straddling her bicycle.

"How'd she break it?" Margaux asked, pointing to the shot where Sophie raised a plaster-covered arm in triumph.

"Skiing. Took third place in a race, then couldn't stop at the very end. Rather disastrous."

"And *this* one?" She picked out the trick photograph of the two Sophies facing each other.

"It's what you call a Rubin's vase."

She crinkled her nose. "A *what?*"

"You've seen these before." He used his finger to draw on the surface. Look at the outline of the faces, and then at the black background. What do you see?"

"Oh, now I get it. Two faces or a vase. You're right, I *have* seen this trick, just not as a photograph. It's like the picture with the old witch. If you look at it just right, it's a beautiful young woman."

"That's right. Designs like this, they're tests of perception." Margaux squinted. "In psychology," he explained. "They show how people perceive the world. In the case of a Rubin's vase, you can only see one thing by *not* seeing the other."

"What do you mean?"

"Look at it again. You can focus on either the vase or the faces, but you can't see both at once."

She stared at the image, canting her head.

Philip continued. "She loved optical illusions. So we made that one together."

"You mean, on the computer?"

"No. The old-fashioned way, with film." Everything Philip said seemed to puzzle Margaux, and he realized how much time had elapsed since he last had a child to talk to. In the meantime, the world had changed. Margaux belonged to the first wholly digital generation.

"With *film?*" she said, marveling as if he'd spoken of writing on papyrus.

"You see, we set up a mirror," he explained. "And lit it just right. It's Sophie and her reflection." How he had relished explaining old-fashioned things like this! It had been one of his principle jobs at home, regaling Sophie with stories of what things had been like in the prehistoric past of his youth. There was nothing he liked better.

"But that's so complicated," Margaux said. "With film, you couldn't see your pictures right away, isn't that so? I don't think I'd care for that."

"Oh, there are advantages."

She looked up. "Like what?"

"All sorts of things."

Margaux folded her arms, waiting for a better answer.

And eventually he found one. "You take more care with things if you know you don't get a second chance."

She considered the comment, finally deeming it satisfactory.

A cream-colored cat emerged from the rhododendrons and rubbed up against Margaux's bare ankles.

"There you are!" she exclaimed, scooping the cat into her arms.

"Rodolphe, I presume?"

"Yes," she said as she rubbed the cat's belly. "This is Rodolphe. Big, fat Rodolphe."

Then, over Margaux's shoulder, Yvonne's face appeared in the kitchen window. Astonishment rapidly surrendered to outrage, and she glared at Philip with a look that held an entire inquisition, one that boiled down to a single question: *how dare you?*

Margaux was still talking. ". . . off in his jungle," she said, completing an observation.

He turned back to her. "I'm sorry. Whose jungle?"

"Rodolphe's," she said, her tone scolding him for his inattention. "He likes to go on safaris during the day. He's a great hunter, although you wouldn't think it to look at him, the fatso! But quite often he brings back his catch."

"Nothing too big, I hope," Philip muttered. "No gazelles?" Yvonne was twitching her head to the side, gesturing for him to leave. Pretty soon she would storm the backyard if he didn't get away.

Margaux was laughing. "No, not yet."

"I need to get going," he said, rising to his feet.

"But . . . but you wanted to see Mother."

"It will have to be another time. Roger and I are headed back to Yvetot this evening."

"Uncle Roger?"

"That's right. He came into town with me."

"Will you be coming back?" Margaux asked.

"I don't know. Not right away."

"I'll tell *Maman* that you came by."

"Please do. Give her my regards."

"I will," she said with importance, as though entrusted with a mission.

Margaux rose from her seat as he opened the gate, and she stepped toward him, lifting her chin. It took him a moment to understand. It was the gesture of parting, the child presenting her cheek for the *bise*, that little hint of a kiss. He felt a pinch in his chest as he bent down to brush his face against hers. Her lips emitted a smack. Then they repeated the gesture on the other side.

"Your beard is prickly," she giggled, rubbing her cheek.

He didn't get very far. By the time he came around the front of the house, Yvonne was outside, ready to pounce.

"Before you say anything," he began, but those were the last words he uttered for several minutes. She lambasted him, her volume growing as she dragged him down the street, out of earshot of the house. They stopped at the end of the road, at the roll of the hill, all of Rouen in the distance below them, the central spire of the cathedral as straight as an arrow.

She was livid. He'd gone against *all* the terms of their agreement: staying too long, surfacing too much, and now approaching the one person she had sought the hardest to protect. What did he think he was doing?

"I was looking for *you*," he finally managed to insert. He gestured back to the house. "I certainly hadn't expected Margaux to show up like that. Look, Yvonne, I tried to extricate myself, but it wasn't easy."

"Rubbish," she shot back. "You say goodbye and you tip your head. It's not so hard!"

"You don't understand. She was asking questions. About Sophie."

Yvonne's shoulders tightened and her nostrils flared. "How *dare* you bring that up? After all I told you."

He raised his palms. "It wasn't me. She's the one who asked. She wanted to talk."

"How can you even suggest such a thing," she cried.

"Yvonne, there's a ghost in your house that you won't even acknowledge. Margaux has questions, and it doesn't help for you to pretend there's nothing to say. You can't forbid her curiosity."

She gasped a breath and looked away. Her body was still rigid, but Philip sensed her fury subsiding. He realized he had to seize the opportunity of this ebbing.

"I need your help."

And he started to explain. While he spoke she stared out over the rooftops of Rouen, bathed in late afternoon light. He told her about his first visit with Édouard Morin, how it had felt to sit across from the man who had killed their daughter, and what he had said. He recounted the obscure references, the wild digressions, the dodges into other languages. He repeated as closely as he could Morin's cavalier description of their daughter's rape.

Finally he came to the point: he planned to visit him again.

"Absolutely not," she hissed. "You said you would see him once and then leave. You're growing obsessed, Philip. Just like before."

"There's more," he pressed. "I need you to go with me." He gestured to counter her objection. "Hear me out. Morin, he dips into all these languages. I need you. I need your expertise."

She shook her head violently. "It won't accomplish anything. Philip, it's done. It's over. It's not reversible."

"Another thing," he said. "It's Morin's accent. I can't figure it out. It sounds almost German. And yet *not* German. I don't know what to make of it."

"What does it *matter?*" she cried.

"I'm just trying to understand, Yvonne."

"But understand what? Why?" She stood with her hands clenched, her body knotted. Philip tried to think of something that might soften her pose. Long ago he would have taken her hand, might even have enfolded her in an embrace. But those solutions were forbidden to him now. Instead he let silence do its work. Stillness could produce calm.

"You're wasting your time," she said finally.

"Maybe," he acknowledged.

"All this nonsense about accents." She exhaled. "Why do you care?"

"I don't know. Teach me."

She paused, shook her head again. "It's ridiculously complicated. There are too many variables. Who can say? Some people can never change their accent, others don't want to. Sometimes you end up with a blend. Look at me. I started with Italian, and in Italy they say my accent is French. Then I learned Spanish, and in Spain they say I sound Italian."

He didn't dare move. "This is why I need you," he said. "You'll hear things that I won't."

She gazed at the ground between her feet.

"Please," he said. "If it produces nothing, I will leave. I swear I will."

She shook her head vaguely. "You have no idea what you're making me do, Philip. If you did, you wouldn't ask."

It was the opportunity for him to back down, to withdraw the request. But instead, moving with caution, the way one reaches for a metal pot that may be hotter than it looks, he lifted his fingers to the edge of her arm and touched. When the contact didn't burn, he allowed his whole hand to come to rest there. Yvonne's posture began to soften.

Fourteen

It came as no surprise that Suardet objected to Philip's request. The first meeting had left Morin agitated, and the doctor had no desire to deal with the consequences of a second encounter. However, bolstered now by Yvonne's support, Philip was in no mood for negotiation. Suardet's preferences were immaterial. Édouard had a right to hear about the offer, and while the doctor could advise him as he wished, it would ultimately be Édouard's decision. Philip made that point clear over the phone, and Suardet left the conversation grumbling but compliant.

There was other business to attend to, some of it tied to Boston. Linda had arranged a phone session with Melanie, and he added it to his schedule. He was ready for this call. Moreover, he needed it. In France everything had a way of slipping beyond his control, but this thread kept him connected to Boston, to his work, to the one thing he knew he could do well. In their next session he would inch Melanie toward speaking of her father. It would lead to outbursts, confrontations. He could predict the tenor of their exchange—could practically hear the howl of her insults. But it would be in a language that he knew, with patterns he could predict. He could do it.

The best way to help Melanie after that would be for him to return to Boston, and the fastest way to Boston was to finish his business in France. So he turned his attention back to Sophie, laying out the collection of resources on his bed at the hotel: court records, police reports, photos, transcriptions, newspaper articles. It would take days to study all the new material from the courthouse, but even as he skimmed them now he sensed a deepening texture. The recollections that had faded to the thinness of an artist's sketch began to take on detail and color, hue and shadow. He recalled the distant church striking three a.m. while Yvonne sobbed in Élisabeth's arms. There was the stoic exhaustion in the eyes of the brigadier who provided the hourly reports. Then, as first dawn tinted the horizon, there was Roger bounding up the front steps, taking first his sister in his arms, then Philip.

Everything was coming back. Too hard, too fast. He needed to organize his thoughts. Turning to a fresh page in the diary, he wrote SOPHIE MARIE

ADLER across the top. Printing in capital letters made her name somehow more formal and distant, and this helped him retain his focus. Then, as he examined the documents and listened again to the voice recorder, he added words to the page—terms from the court reports, names of people and places, dates, repeated themes, the real or imagined pain in Édouard's tongue—until Sophie's name was surrounded by a galaxy of signs. Some words he linked by lines, forming half-constellations. Yet the facts felt disparate and diffuse. If some logic tied all these elements together, or linked them to the happenings of fifteen years ago, Philip hadn't yet understood it. He needed a kind of Rosetta Stone, a dictionary for the hieroglyphs of Morin's expression. He suspected that the key lay in the nexus of obsessions with places and words and sounds. The question was, would Philip even recognize this key if he saw it?

He rocked back in his chair, studying the ceiling. The dead ends of Sorquainville, Malamare and Adonville perplexed him. Monsieur Bécot's description of the nothingness of these towns didn't square with Morin's account. Certainly Édouard was accurate in some respect: the Germans had indeed traversed Yvetot, fanning out in the direction of the coast and erecting roadblocks to slow the French retreat. But these checkpoints had not existed in the locations he'd asserted. He'd taken the historical record and skewed it, edging the truth to the side, referring to hamlets just barely off the routes the Germans had actually occupied.

He scrubbed at his eyes with the heels of his palms, then called down to the front desk and asked for a sandwich to be sent up. While eating, he listened again to the recording from the meeting with Morin, tracking the logic from topic to topic: from foreign languages to travel, trains, geography, toponymy, vocabulary—and then to Sophie, the assertion of order, the allusions to poker, the religious imagery, the switching of languages.

It felt like a succession of detours, delaying the arrival at a point Édouard both did and did not want to reach.

By mid-afternoon he'd added only a handful of tentative observations to his notes, some of which he had later crossed out.

It was time for a walk.

He started out across the main square, where mothers pushed strollers and an old man walked a dog. Smells crowded the air, the scent of fresh bread billowing from the bakery, floral odors wafting from the gardens, the bitter stench of bitumen rising from a street repair. Chestnut trees along the boulevard were in full bloom, and greenery sprouted from cracks in stone walls, decorating even the signs of Yvetot's deterioration. Philip strode past shop windows, angled down along the train station, and then headed east, going as far as the old Aubert home. The shutters on the living room were now open. He knocked at the front door, but no one came. The door was locked.

As he stepped down toward the drive, the image of his brother-in-law came back to mind. The night after Anne-Madeleine's funeral, it was right here that Philip had rushed past Roger and Joëlle. Fifteen years earlier, Roger had embraced him on these same steps at the moment of another death. Both scenes had taken place at this location, practically on the Aubert threshold, a point of arrivals and departures, both meetings coming at twilit hours—at the fall of deepest night and the break of day.

Was that right? Something about this recollection felt incomplete.

As he mused, Philip looped back toward the town center, passing by the hardware store where the shopkeeper had finished repainting his sign and the ladder had come down. For now only the name MANTET was visible, but Philip suspected it was just a matter of time, and the older name would bleed through again.

As he walked by the Saint-Pierre church, he glimpsed Father Cabot heading for the doorway, a baguette under his arm. The priest waved to him. Several children played soccer on the crescent of lawn in front, and a zealous kick sent the ball bouncing in his direction. Philip trapped it and knocked it back as the boys called out their thanks.

The people of Yvetot were getting used to him. He no longer felt so out of place.

Then he headed south, and on either side of the narrow street archways opened into courtyards, some revealing dilapidated structures, others leading to what looked like small manor homes.

He couldn't have plotted this route on a map, but Yvetot held a strange familiarity for him now. It was a town Philip knew poorly but that felt akin to a home—one replete with secret passageways and unexplored chambers.

A canopy of leaves loomed, the broad foliage of an old oak tree. By the time he reached the gate he realized where his legs had taken him: the entrance to Saint-Louis cemetery. He had not set out with this destination in mind, but it shouldn't have been a surprise. It was further proof of what he'd explained to Roger: we are not always in charge—sometimes someone else is at the wheel. No, his arrival at this destination was hardly the result of chance.

His mind paused over this term. Chance. *La chance.* The word was a point of overlap between the two languages, but they were false friends. In English chance referred to utter randomness, all things haphazard, while in French its twin designated good fortune, luck—that swell of confidence that whispered to you, suggesting that no matter how you throw the dice, they will turn up sixes. No, he didn't expect ever to enjoy that feeling again.

Pushing through the gate, he stepped onto the gravel path and walked along the elongated tombs. They reminded him of playing cards, laid out in the fashion of the memory game he used to play with Sophie, dealing out the deck face down in rows, and taking turns in the hunt for pairs. Here too one might lift up a slab and find something akin to a face card, different branches of the same family scattered as if some divine hand had shuffled the oversized deck.

There was no clear logic to the organization of the graves. The dates spanned over two hundred years, old tombs alternating with newer ones. He knew how it worked. Abandoned graves were gradually reclaimed by the city, and then the plot was recycled. The old had to make room for the new, even here.

He was nearly to the maintenance shed when he paused, and it took a moment for him to understand why he had stopped at a particular gray sepulcher. The stone had no flourishes of sculpture. The tomb wasn't ornate, or even well maintained. Neither grander nor more extravagant than the others, it sported a list of several descendants. What had caught Philip's eye was simply the date associated with the most recent addition: *Julien Hesse, décédé le 27 mai 1993.* The same year as Sophie, just a little over a month earlier. She had been but one of many. People in Yvetot were queuing up for a spot in this garden for the dead. The family of Julien Hesse had barely had time to retreat from the cemetery before the Adlers and Auberts made their way in. Even death had scheduling problems.

He marched farther along the gravel, coming to a stop before the reddish slab he'd contemplated only a week earlier. The flowers he had left, along with Roger's yellow rose, were dry and wrinkled. There again was the name, all in capitals, just as he had written it in the diary:

SOPHIE MARIE ADLER

He admired the texture of the letters, deeply engraved in the stone, marking Sophie's name by voids. It all felt hollow to him now. An empty name above an empty tomb.

It was at that moment that the idea surged up. It appeared first like a dark, unrecognizable presence, and Philip sensed a connection with the jumble of information he'd accumulated over the course of the day. The letters of Sophie's name, first estranged, had begun to feel newly familiar. They reminded him of the meeting with Morin, of words that had been spoken. The silhouette of an idea flitted like a sylph through the shadows.

It had to do with the roadblocks Morin had described, the ones whose existence Monsieur Bécot had adamantly denied. In Sorquainville, Malamare, and Adonville. That was the order Morin had listed them in, Philip was sure. If they were fabrications, why would Morin have chosen these particular names—ones that harbored an echo Philip could almost hear, ones beginning with the letters S, M, and A?

For those, he realized as the nausea rose within him, were the initials of the name before him now: Sophie Marie Adler. Indeed, more than initials: even the second letters matched.

It could have been coincidence. Philip couldn't deny it. Chance—hazard or luck?—might have formed this parallel, just as two sticks falling from a tree might happen to form an X where they land. But if he was to believe Bécot and the maps, Morin had nudged history. Because the facts hadn't suited the story he wanted to tell, he had shaved off certain details. It amounted to a kind of *rounding*, which was precisely what Morin had described. Reality sometimes required adjustments, and it became acceptable to trim the edges, eliminating remainders. By tweaking geography and history, Morin had managed to send a message.

S M A. Philip had marked these initials on the labels of endless pieces of clothing for summer camp. Anne-Madeleine had embroidered them on a pillow for her room. Yvonne had formed them with brass letters for their daughter's bedroom door. Sophie herself had inked them in the corner of innumerable art projects.

A shiver ran through him as he realized that Morin had intended for him to make this connection. Philip had underestimated the situation. It was more complex than he had imagined. More subtle. Behind the singsong voice and the birdlike gait, there was a canniness to Morin that Philip had not appreciated. He would have to be more careful. Much more careful.

On the way back to the hotel, ideas swirled through his head like starlings. He needed a new paradigm, a different way of thinking. Only then might he have a chance of understanding.

Stopping in at the *Tord-boyaux*, he slipped past the group of regulars clustered at the bar, paying no heed to their silence as he made for the table at the back of the room. He didn't listen to the conversation resume, didn't hear the door opening and closing. His mind was elsewhere. He pulled out the diary and scribbled rapidly on a new page, underlining passages and stroking exclamation marks in the margins, trying to keep pace with his thoughts.

The *patronne* plodded over for his order.

"A beer," he muttered without even looking up. It was only after she turned away that he realized what words he had spoken. Once again his mind had tried to ambush him with old habits and reflexes. Now was not the time to lose control. He called her back and revised his order to coffee.

He wrote feverishly, his fingers trembling as they clutched at the black pen. For the first time since arriving in Yvetot, he'd made a connection.

Half an hour later he strode back to the hotel, finding a new message awaiting him at the front desk: Doctor Suardet had called, and Édouard Morin had agreed to a second meeting. The news could not have been better, nor could it have come at a more favorable time. He called Yvonne from the lobby to let her know the schedule for the encounter.

Charging up the stairs to the third floor, he took them two by two. Things were finally looking up! He was onto something. It was time to call Roger. His mind was overflowing, and he needed to share his ideas.

However, when he opened the door to his room, a strange odor greeted him, and the light failed to go on when he flicked the switch. Something had gone wrong with the fixture that hung from the ceiling, which now had changed, drooped lower and gently swayed, the simple fabric having blossomed into a bouquet of yellow, red, and black tufts, all sprouting from a wad of plumage held together by two gray rods at the top, like some outrageous, oversized woman's hat. As his eyes adjusted to the dim, Philip saw that the rods had claws, and the two gangly flaps were wings, feathers splayed at the tips. The room stank of barn and flesh, and from the stub at the bottom of this misshapen mass something dark oozed and dripped, pooling on the floor. Dark spatters dotted the rug and the cream-colored bedspread, as well as a section of the wall and even the papers on the desk.

A gnarled shape the size of a child's fist rested on the floor, a jagged crest of red along one portion, with a wedge of hard brown that opened like parted lips. Embedded in the middle was a glossy pellet that looked remarkably like an eye.

Fifteen

After untangling the wire binding the rooster's corpse to the light fixture, Philip wrapped the bloody carcass in a bath towel and stormed down the stairs. At the front desk Monsieur Bécot was just finishing his spiel about sightseeing to a young couple when Philip thudded the reddening bundle onto the hotel register and peeled back the flaps. The visitors blanched, and Bécot put on a passable imitation of astonishment, stammering that no, he'd seen nothing, nothing at all! And yet he'd been on duty all afternoon. No one could have gotten a key to the room.

It hardly mattered if Bécot was telling the truth. Philip knew what he was dealing with: another message from the people of Yvetot.

Over Bécot's objections, the police were called, and twenty minutes later the same all-purpose officer as before showed up, his cap in his hand as he scratched his scalp and surveyed Philip's room, hotel personnel crowded at the doorway.

"You're not going to tell me that *this* is a coincidence," Philip challenged.

"No sir," the man replied. "It sure doesn't look like an accident to me."

"So what are you going to do about it?"

The fellow pondered the question, glancing back at the throng of onlookers in the hallway. "Well, Monsieur Adler, I guess I'll have to cite you for damages."

Philip flushed red. "What?"

"There's no sign of forced entry, sir. Monsieur Bécot himself says no one came by." He shrugged. "What else is one to think?"

"You're saying I slaughtered a rooster in my own hotel room and strapped it to my light fixture?"

Philip glared at Monsieur Bécot in the doorway, waiting for him to intervene, to tell this officer that his conclusions were absurd. But Bécot returned the look impassively. He'd made it clear from the beginning that he wouldn't take sides in the matter of Adler versus the town of Yvetot—certainly not publicly. Philip wouldn't be able to expect much assistance from him.

"Perhaps you'd like to check out of the hotel, Monsieur Adler?" the policeman suggested. "This room doesn't look very pleasant."

"Not a chance," he answered through his teeth.

As the chambermaids stripped the blood-spattered sheets from the bed, Philip stood outside the hotel, scowling as passers-by crisscrossed the Place des Belges. No one looked, but he knew all eyes would be on him as soon as he turned his back.

Where had this scrutiny been fifteen years ago? No, when it concerned a member of their own community—even someone like Édouard Morin—they knew how to turn a blind eye.

Needing to get away from Yvetot, he drove up to Fécamp, where he met Roger at a terrace café at the edge of the port. The air was thick with the smell of fish, gulls screeching high overhead.

Somehow Roger had already heard about the rooster. "I don't like the direction this has taken," he mused.

"It's the louts from the *Tord-boyaux*. I know it is."

"Perhaps. But even if you're right, they're just carrying out actions that others would endorse. You've not made any friends around here, Philip. I've warned you about that. Even with my connections, there's only so much I can do."

"Don't worry about me." He gulped down the last of his coffee. "I'm not your responsibility."

"Aren't you? I'm the one who talked you into staying. But perhaps it's time to reassess. You're putting yourself at risk. And for what? There's not much to show for it." When Philip refused to concede the point, Roger clarified. "And by *not much*, I mean *absolutely nothing*."

Which is when Philip explained to Roger about the cemetery, about the link between Sophie's initials and the villages Morin had mentioned.

Roger's eyes narrowed. "But that's absurd. Surely you can see that."

"I'll verify it with Morin soon, but it's a connection, Roger. A first one. There will be more."

"*Might* be more," Roger corrected. "But what else *might* be around that corner? Next time it won't just be tires or poultry."

"I'm not stopping now. There's too much at stake."

"But how will you—"

Philip leaned in. "I wasn't there for her then. I'm not going to leave her now."

Roger's shoulders sagged and he settled back in his chair.

While they sat in silence, a whiskered snout appeared from under a pile of fishing net on the quay. The rest of a brown rat emerged, and it scuttled along the stone edge, as busy as a docker, pausing at each of the mooring bollards.

Roger was the first to speak. "I've always admired your determination. Your focus."

"In my business we call it a compulsion."

"Well, I suppose I have my share of those—though mine are not quite as noble." He sighed. "Perhaps if I were a little less *compulsive*, I wouldn't have been off with Élisabeth that night. I'd have been where I could have done my niece some good."

"It's not your fault."

"No, of course not. No more than it is yours. But not being at fault doesn't make you feel any less guilty, does it?" He left space for an objection. "No, I didn't think so." After checking his watch he pulled himself to his feet. "I have a client, I'm afraid. Well, perhaps *afraid* isn't the term. She's quite lovely." He shelled a bill from his wallet onto the table. "It's tomorrow that you and Yvonne see Morin? Why don't we meet for dinner in Yvetot, and you can tell me all about it." Then he leaned in over Philip. "And do tread softly, won't you? I got you into this thing, and I'd sure as hell like to see you make it out." He gave him a wink, then headed down the sidewalk.

Philip drove south out of Fécamp, a bitter taste rising in his mouth as the first signs pointed toward Yvetot. Did he really need to return to that purgatory? Thank God for Roger. At least there was one Norman who wasn't afraid to buck the trend, who was willing to acknowledge—even exaggerate—his own responsibility. Roger had always been there for him. Had always been ready to help.

Once again he recalled his brother-in-law climbing the steps of the Aubert home in the rosy light of pre-dawn, pushing past the police to reach the stricken parents. That was the image. Wasn't it?

Then a gap appeared along the edge of this memory. Something didn't fit. There was a wrongness to it. Suddenly Philip felt short of breath.

Yes, Roger had been there for him. For both of them. But not in the middle of the night. He had not arrived at the same time as Élisabeth. No, Roger had appeared later, as dawn was breaking. That, at least, was Philip's recollection.

But if Roger and Élisabeth had been together all night, as Roger insisted, why would they have arrived separately? And above all, why would Roger have described it otherwise?

He chided himself for formulating such questions. It was insane! Because of Roger, he had stayed in France. Thanks to Roger he'd made progress. Roger was the only one who had offered him a shred of help.

Nevertheless, doubt had worked the edge of its lever into his thoughts, and once he had asked himself these questions, he was incapable of un-asking them.

He didn't call Yvonne. Talking to her about Roger was unthinkable.

More surprising, though, was the fact that she didn't call him. He'd assumed word would spread about the feathered warning in his hotel room, but apparently information flowed at different speeds depending on the direction. While his own actions belonged to the public domain—broadcast live throughout Normandy—measures undertaken by the Yvetotais were cloaked in the silence.

Perhaps it was just as well. He didn't need complications now. So, after the chambermaids finished their work—at Philip's expense—he made a show of staying on the premises, taking his meals in his room and working late. He hoped at least to have fueled some chatter in the *Tord-boyaux*.

Sixteen

The next day he drove to Rouen under a hazy sun. The university campus, perched on a hill over the town center, churned with students in short-sleeves, jeans, and pencil skirts—walking with the easy gait of gods enjoying their well-formed bodies. Pulling around the central fountain in the Smart Car, Philip spotted Yvonne alone at a curb, dressed in a white blouse and mid-length skirt, gazing vacantly toward a stand of trees. A leather messenger bag hung over her shoulder, a stack of typewritten pages bulging under the flap. She was on her way to meet with her daughter's murderer, but she also had papers to grade.

He had half a mind to cruise on by. Did he really need to pluck Yvonne out of this successful present and parachute her into the past? Then she turned and raised her fingers in a gesture of greeting, and a pleasing shiver ran through him as she climbed in. He recognized the way her body settled in the seat, and he caught a whiff of perfume, a sweet but nutty fragrance. Everything was different—the car, the campus, the era, the destination—and yet absolutely the same: here he was, stopping for his wife at the end of the day, on their way to encounter, however indirectly, their daughter.

He handed over the files of newspaper clippings and court records, which Yvonne rested on her lap, fingering only the edge of the top folder.

Threading the vehicle through the trickle of pedestrians, he navigated away from campus, heading the car down the road that would loop past the city center, then south toward the psychiatric hospital.

She gazed out her window, not speaking.

"How was class?" he asked. When she didn't respond, he added, "I don't even know what you're teaching."

"Don't try to make small talk, Philip," she said. "You're taking me to see the man who raped and murdered our daughter. I'm not in the mood to chat."

He wound them through the congested city center, and soon they were entering the countryside.

Yvonne broke the silence. "In fact, I didn't teach."

He nodded. When she'd told him to pick her up on campus, he'd marveled at her ability to carry on. This sign of humanness was reassuring.

"I thought I could," she continued, talking into her window, "but I was wrong. I sat in my office. Students knocked on my door, and I didn't answer."

He nodded.

"Do you know what I was thinking about?" she said. "Paper dolls. Do you remember? How she loved to make those when she was little? And then she'd unfold all the figures. A string of little people."

Yes, he remembered.

"So I sat in my office. With scissors." She turned away. "Cutting god-damned paper dolls."

He reached out to rest a hand on her knee.

As they traveled into the hills Yvonne turned to the folders, lifting open the first cover and staring down. She leafed through and Philip watched out of the corner of his eye, the pages sweeping against her blouse, settling over the curve of her thigh. When she came to the press clippings from Monsieur Guérin, she paused over a grainy photograph of Édouard Morin.

"He's changed now," Philip said. "Not entirely, of course. But be prepared."

The court records held no interest for her. Nor did the police reports. In the end she came to the envelope where Philip kept his photos, and these she lingered over. The bicycle. The ski hill. Sophie's arm in a cast. The Rubin's vase.

Tufted pastures flanked the road. Ancient Calvary crosses of stone rose from the weeds at the older intersections. They were close to the hospital now, and the car dipped in a swale, hugged a turn, then rose up again.

He explained how the conversation with Morin would go. It was important to follow the plan. Philip would lead, and Yvonne was to remain in the back-ground. She would listen and, when needed, translate. She might hear things that Philip did not, but they would review those points later, after Morin had left the room.

They came to a stop in the parking lot at the base of the slope leading to the hospital. From the car Yvonne looked up at the great tan fortress of stucco, the white shutters gleaming in the sun.

"I can take you back right now," Philip murmured at her side. "We can let the whole thing drop."

"I said I'd do it. And I'm here." She turned and met his eyes for the first time since climbing into the car. "Let's get it over with."

At the surprise addition of Yvonne, Dr. Suardet grumbled and flapped his arms, complaining that it was irregular, not what they'd agreed to. In the end, though, he had to relent, presenting his decision as a tremendous gift. Philip understood the real motivation: Suardet and Hervé were distant colleagues, which made it awkward to refuse anything to Madame Legrand.

They found themselves in the same conference room as before, decorated only with that most essential tool of psychiatry: the clock on the wall. Édouard Morin waited for them, seated on the other side of the table, stiffly erect in the same plastic chair, dressed in a collared shirt and gray trousers, his blank face scrubbed of emotion. The extraordinary sameness of the situation didn't surprise Philip. It reminded him of the repetitive nature of his sessions with patients—the same people in the same positions saying the same things at the same hour of the same day, week after week. In his practice he sometimes found himself lulled by this sense of routine. The individuals reclining on his couch might all have different names and stories, but they conformed to patterns of interaction that he could mostly predict.

Changes, however, could make patients uneasy, and Morin scrutinized Yvonne, at first uncomprehending. His eyes widened, and his Adam's apple dipped with a swallow. He started right away in English. "It's Madame Adler, if I'm not mistaken?" he said, each S humming.

Yvonne leveled a cold stare that even Morin couldn't hold.

"Madame Legrand," Suardet corrected.

"What's she doing here?" he demanded.

The doctor hesitated. "It's just a conversation, Édouard. Nothing more."

Morin stared down, studying his fingers splayed on the surface of the table. He didn't nod his assent, but neither did he voice an objection.

Suardet moved to the head of the table. "Let's get started," he said.

Philip pulled out a chair for Yvonne.

"Excuse me, Mr. Adler," Morin said, raising a finger. "But that should be *your* place. Madame Legrand will be very happy next to you, I'm sure."

"I see. You want me in the same seat as before, is that right?"

"Don't you believe that is best? I think you'll be much more comfortable in that chair. That is, if Madame Legrand doesn't mind?" He continued to speak in English, even though French was native to everyone in the room but Philip.

Yvonne moved stiffly, her expression fixed, taking her seat, slipping the messenger bag off her shoulder and resting it on the floor.

"She is so much older now," Morin whispered loudly to Philip.

Philip paused. "You're older too, Édouard." He pulled out the voice recorder.

Morin tilted his head, speaking to Yvonne as though addressing a formal guest. "Mr. Adler invited you along to help him with language questions, didn't he? I understand you're very good with languages."

Yvonne remained silent. She was more controlled than Philip had expected, her body rigid, each gesture deliberate.

Morin turned back to him. "Isn't that right, Mr. Adler?" he asked with insistence. "You've brought her for the languages?"

"Something like that."

At the end of the table, Suardet drummed his fingers.

Philip pressed the button on the digital recorder and placed the device in the middle of the table, rotating it slightly. "Do I have this lined up the way you like it?" he asked.

"Very nearly, Mr. Adler. Very nearly. I appreciate your attention to my odd little habits." Morin reached forward and adjusted the recorder microscopically. "That's better, I think. Of course, nothing is ever perfectly aligned, isn't that true? But still, we have to do what little we can, don't you agree?"

"Perhaps."

Morin was breathing more easily now. Everything was in its place. A small smile spread across his face. "I know you think it's excessive, my attention to orderliness. But we are all bedeviled by disorder in our lives, and it only makes sense to reduce it whenever and however we can. That's my opinion. And yet, I am fully aware that, even now, we are surrounded by disorder. We are divided between *pair* and *impair*—what in English you call *even* and *odd*. But true evenness does not exist in the world." He gestured about the room. "These chairs are not straight. This building is not level. From my window the horizon tips slightly to the south. Even our bodies are not perfectly symmetrical. Reality is, by its very nature, odd. Not perfectly divisible. Like a wheel that is warped, out of true. Do you see what I mean?"

Philip pursed his lips. "I'm not sure that I do. Perhaps you could explain it to me."

Morin brightened. "You like it when I talk, don't you, Mr. Adler? You think I may tell you more than I intend. I don't mind explaining my feelings about this, though. It's quite simple. All I mean is that evenness is an ideal, a utopia. Reality is always a little bit off. Things don't ever square up. In short, the world is not tidy, by which I mean that there are no equations without remainders." He stopped to think. "The question is, what is your tolerance for unevenness? How much leeway will each person allow? How much play in the system is acceptable before you have to intervene and straighten things out? Each person has different limits for that. I, for example, like things to be quite close, which most people find excessive. But I'm sure you have your limits, too, Mr. Adler. We reach a point when the disorder becomes unacceptable, and finally we have to act. Then one simply does one's best. You make things as even as possible. Perhaps that is what you are doing now." He lifted his chin. "Tell me, Mr. Adler, how do you feel about this issue?"

"We're not here to discuss my feelings."

The two men studied each other. Édouard glanced again at Yvonne, still rigid and silent in her chair. He turned back to Philip and leaned toward him over the table. "So tell me, Mr. Adler," he said confidentially, "are you fucking her?"

Even Suardet understood this question, and the words sent a ripple through Yvonne's statuesque pose.

"No," Philip replied icily. "I am not."

"I see," Morin continued, settling back. "I hope you don't mind my asking. It's just that if you were fucking her, I'd want to be aware of that. I think it's good to know where everyone stands. Don't you agree? I'm not fucking anyone, in case you want to know." He looked first at Philip, then at Suardet, and then managed to turn his eyes briefly upon Yvonne. "Frankly, I think she's a little old for me."

"We're not interested in who you are fucking, Édouard," Philip said.

"What a pity. Well, if we are not going to discuss fucking, Mr. Adler, to what do we owe this additional visit? I don't suppose it's a medical call, is it? You're not going to take a look at my tongue? It continues to bother me—a painful burning sensation—and Doctor Suardet won't do anything for it."

Suardet rolled his eyes.

Philip shook his head. "No, I've not come for that."

With two fingers Morin pressed on his cheek, probing it gingerly before turning his attention back to the table. "That's too bad. By any chance have you researched the word *eyeshot* for me? It's really quite annoying not to know how—or even if—that word is employed. There are so many terms in the dictionary, and it's hard to tell which ones are truly alive and which ones are dead. Dictionaries are like communities, you know, and they have their own little graveyards."

Philip paused. "I have no answer for you there."

"How disappointing. And so?"

"Yes?"

"Why have you requested to meet with me again?"

"Actually," Philip replied, "I thought it was you who might like to meet."

Morin reached up and smoothed down his hairline. He cracked a smile. "I'm sure I don't know what you're talking about."

And this was where the dance began. Philip had decided not to tell Morin what he understood about the connection between Sophie's initials and the towns he had named. Just how much of that communication had been intentional was unclear, so he sought to demonstrate interest without revealing understanding. Patients often struggled with their own ambivalence, wanting him to divine what they themselves could not say out loud. His tactic was to feign even greater ignorance than was the case, which sometimes flushed patients out of hiding, forcing them to greater explicitness.

"You seemed to enjoy telling me about the region," Philip said. "All those references to trains and travel, not to mention language and history."

Édouard nodded. "I did mention that our region has a rich past. Very rich. I hope you have availed yourself of the opportunity to immerse yourself in it?"

"Not really. But I did find myself wondering about your infatuation with language. Where do you suppose that comes from?"

"I do have a bit of a weakness for it. I suppose *weakness* really is the term. Because of my interest in language, I probably end up saying too much. After all, *vir sapit qui pauca loquitur.*"

Philip turned to Yvonne.

"It's Latin," she stated without looking away from Édouard. "Wise is the man who speaks little."

A shadow of annoyance swept over Morin's face, then vanished. "Very good. Excellent, even. It's too bad you don't know Latin, Mr. Adler. Everyone should learn it. It's the foundation for so much."

"Tell me," Philip said, "why have you studied so many languages?"

"One must do something to pass the time, dear doctor."

"Could it be because each language expresses things differently?"

"I suppose that's one of the charms, yes."

"Do you think you're looking for one that expresses everything just right, that allows you to say things you can't otherwise communicate?"

He chewed his lip. "That's very poetic, Mr. Adler. But I'm afraid I am not adept at poetry. No, indeed, I think my linguistic interest is far more innocent. There's nothing one can say in a foreign language that can't be said in one's father tongue."

"Mother tongue," Philip corrected.

He blinked. "Of course. I'm sorry about that. I misspoke."

"That's understandable. Various languages use images of motherhood and fatherhood differently. That can be hard to master." Morin neither confirmed nor denied this, so Philip continued. "In some languages, for instance, the homeland is called the motherland. Isn't that right?"

"I suppose that's true," Morin replied.

"In others, it's called the fatherland. As in Germany."

"Why do you find this topic so intriguing, Mr. Adler?"

"I'm not sure. Perhaps because you spoke in such detail about the Germans the last time I visited."

"I'm afraid I don't understand."

"I think you do. It came after we discussed your own past, when I extended my sympathies regarding your father."

Morin twitched. "*Das hat nichts mit meinem Vater zu tun,*" he said.

Philip waited for Yvonne's translation.

"This has nothing to do with my father."

Morin raised his hand to his lips, parting them enough to allow his fingertip to touch his tongue. He winced.

"I know this is a difficult topic," Philip said. "You were close to him, and now he's gone. It's normal to be upset. I recall we spoke of your father at our last meeting, too."

"I would rather we change topics, Mr. Adler."

"Yes, that's what we did the last time. You began to describe the countryside around Yvetot, and told how, when the Germans arrived, people changed the road signs, slowing the German advance. Then you mentioned how the Germans set up roadblocks, forcing people to take alternate routes."

Morin's eyes glowed, but his voice remained flat. "That is mere history, Mr. Adler. Anyone could tell you that."

Philip had drawn him out onto the board, and he was ready to try a move. "By the way," he began, "I did look into your story about the German blockades, the ones on the roads to—what were they called?—Sorquainville, Malamare . . . and some other wretched place?"

"Adonville, Mr. Adler," Morin said curtly. "Adonville. You should pay closer attention."

"But it turns out you were wrong."

Morin's eyes grew large. "Do tell."

"Those villages are on small detours from the roads to Fécamp, Le Havre, and Dieppe, all located on the coast. Roadblocks were erected to stop troops from retreating to those ports. But Sorquainville was not a concern. Neither was Malamare, nor . . . that other town. What was it again?"

"*Adonville,*" Morin repeated with irritation. "What is your point?"

"My point? I don't have a point. I just thought you should be aware that your facts aren't straight. You care about accuracy, so I thought this would interest you."

Morin puffed with exasperation and stood up, beginning to pace on his side of the table.

Suardet shifted in his seat, frowning as he studied the two men. Yvonne remained immobile, the line of her jaw sharp.

"Frankly," Philip said, "I'd expected better from you."

These words halted Morin in his tracks, and he glared. "*Basta,*" he snapped. "*Non hai il diritto!*"

It was Italian. "That's enough," Yvonne translated. "You have no right."

Morin cocked his head toward her. "Madame Legrand, *l'aiutante.*"

"No right to do what, Édouard?" Philip pressed.

"*No tengo nada que decir.*"

"I have nothing to say," Yvonne relayed.

"Tell me what you mean," Philip said.

"*Lass mich,*" he retorted, pronouncing it *lazz*. "*Du kannst mir nicht vorschreiben, was ich machen soll.*"

"Leave me alone," Yvonne said, her voice sharp. "You can't tell me what to do."

"But I *am* telling you what to do. Speak to me."

"No," he yelled, his nostrils flaring.

"Yes. *Now.*"

"*Du bist nicht mein Vater!*" Édouard cried, smacking his fist on the table.

"Settle down!" Suardet called out.

Yvonne hadn't translated Morin's last phrase, but Philip didn't need her to. He had heard these words in English so many times, from so many people, and in so many ways over the years, that he recognized it almost by intonation alone. And every single time a patient of his bellowed this at him, insisting that Philip was not their father, it meant that, in fact, he *was*. At least by substitution. It was the transference, the displacement of a relationship from a person who was absent to one who was not.

And now, just as suddenly, Morin's emotion vanished. Calm settled over him, he slipped back onto his chair, and he clasped his hands on the table.

"*Siga, estimado doctor, no tengo miedo de nada.*"

"Continue," Yvonne reported. "I am afraid of nothing."

"Nothing? Not even of speaking your mind?" said Philip.

Morin leaned forward and studied him. "*Molto,*" he uttered slowly. "*Molto interessante. Herr Professor, ich bin sehr beeindruckt.*"

"Very interesting," Yvonne intoned. "I'm impressed."

Philip struggled to keep pace with the shifting languages. Yvonne's translations, he could tell, were abridged. "What about it, Édouard," he said. "Do you have anything left to tell us?"

He tipped his head back, looking at Philip as though from a great height. "Why do you imagine I would do such a thing, Mr. Adler? Because of your psychological games?"

"Because there are things you would like to express."

Morin sneered. "You think you understand me because I'm like one of your patients. And yet, I am *not* one of your patients, Mr. Adler. I am very different from your patients. For one thing, not one of them has raped and murdered your daughter. Isn't that right?" He frowned. "Unless you have other daughters?"

Philip stiffened.

"What about Madame Legrand?" Morin said, speaking as if she were not present. "Perhaps she has other daughters?"

So Morin knew about Margaux.

Philip cast a sidewise glance at Yvonne. If anything, she was even more rigid than before, frozen in place, only her eyes afire.

Morin continued. "You think you can read me because you know the patterns. But sometimes we see patterns where we want to. Instead of discovering them, we *project* them. Don't you agree?"

"I'm not here to answer your questions," Philip said.

"Is that so?" Morin replied. "Because I think it is quite exactly for these questions that you have come. You're interested in the answers, too. I can tell." He studied Philip carefully. "We're not so different, you and I." He indicated Yvonne with a nod. "Her, not so much. But you . . ."

"You don't know a thing about me," Philip said. "Stop trying to turn the tables." His neck felt hot. "I want to know the next step, Édouard," he said, his voice inching up the register. "I want to know what you did with my daughter's body."

"You have made your desires quite apparent, Mr. Adler. In fact, you are yourself quite apparent. Do you see what I mean? Apparent—a parent? And nothing com*pares* to a *par*ent. Oh, I share the erring despair of parents. They aim to repair the irreparable."

Philip gritted his teeth. "Enough of your rhymes."

"Tell me, do you know the myth of Procrustes, Mr. Adler?"

"I'm not looking for a lesson."

"How about you, Madame Legrand? No? According to the stories of Ancient Greece, Procrustes was a thief. He strapped his victims onto a special bed he made. I picture it much like a rack. Nobody fit his bed exactly. Some people were too small, so he would turn the crank to stretch their limbs. Others were too big, and for these he would use a saw to trim their arms and legs." He stopped to ponder his phrasing. "Is *trim* the right word? It sounds so much like a haircut. Maybe *cut* or *hack* is a better term. Or how about *lop?*" When no one answered, he continued. "Anyway, I have always thought of the story of Procrustes as a lesson in practicality. In theory we want the world to fit a certain ideal. But in practice, when all you have are round pegs and square holes, sometimes we have to force things a bit. Don't you think that's true, Mr. Adler?"

Philip was about to reply when another voice hissed at his side in French.

"*Salaud.*"

It was Yvonne.

Philip reached out to her, but she batted him away. "I didn't come to listen to this," she said. "For a pathetic little man to talk about cutting and lopping, as if we didn't know what he meant by it."

"Yvonne," Philip started.

"Shut up, Philip," she told him, her face suddenly ugly.

"Madame Legrand," Suardet began.

"*Laissez-moi parler,*" she barked, and Suardet backed down.

Morin had leaned back, taking in the scene. When Yvonne turned to him again, he dropped his gaze to the table. "At last," he said. "Someone who's willing to speak plainly." His taunting tone returned. "I have to admire your frankness. So like your daughter, you know. The first one, I mean."

"Look at me when you speak," she ordered.

"Madame Legrand," he began, "I don't think—"

"Look at me," she repeated slowly, as though issuing a threat.

Morin raised his head and for a moment his gaze flitted over Yvonne before he turned away.

She continued. "You don't know the first thing about my daughter."

"Oh, but I see the family resemblance," he said to the floor. "Like mother, like daughter, you know."

A cruel smile curled Yvonne's lips. "And like father, like son, don't you think?"

Morin's eyes flickered. "What do you mean?"

"I knew him well. Your father. Quite well."

"Yvonne," Philip murmured again.

"Don't you want to hear about it, Édouard?" she pressed.

Morin scowled. "That's enough, Madame Legrand. *Es gibt Grenzen, die man nicht überschreitet.*" He wrenched his attention from her and turned to Philip and Suardet, switching to an exaggerated British accent, the vowels flattening and the R's vanishing while the buzzing S remained. "I'm *teddibly* zorry, chums, but I believe we're done. I'm not at *libuhty* to *discuzz thizz* any *fawther*. No *fawther* at all." He winced from a pain in his mouth, as if he'd bitten his tongue.

"What's the matter, Édouard?" Yvonne said. "After all, you had your way with my daughter. Isn't it natural that your father should have taken an interest in the mother?"

Philip moved to intervene, but Yvonne stopped him with a glare. Suardet fidgeted and grimaced, unsure how much leeway to allow the wife of Hervé Legrand.

Morin looked at her with contempt. "*Puttana.* He wouldn't have touched you."

"*Tu crois?*" she said, inching forward on her chair. "Do you need details? Where we met? How often we did it? How he slipped his hand up my skirt . . ."

Morin flinched with each detail. "*Mentirosa!*"

". . . between my thighs."

"*Come osi parlare così?*"

"*Carogna,*" she spat back.

"*Du hast keine Ahnung—*"

"*Und du keinen Schneid!*" she snapped, leaning in. "You see, you can't go scampering off into languages anymore. How does it feel, not being able to get away?"

Morin wheeled around to Doctor Suardet for help.

"Madame Legrand," Suardet began.

But Yvonne was done listening. "And what about this, Édouard?" she continued, sitting erect, drawing her shoulders back. "Don't you want to know how he took me?" She leaned forward and looked lengthily into Morin's eyes. "He wasn't very good," she said in a confidential tone, "if you care to know. But he wanted it so badly."

There was a pause, and then Morin uncoiled like a spring, lunging toward Yvonne and administering a backhanded slap that sent her to the ground, her chair clattering against the tiles. She reached up to shield herself from the next blow, but Philip was already between them, shoving Morin against the wall.

Suardet cried out as he scrambled to restrain Édouard, who yelled again.

"*Puttana!*"

Philip's body tingled with an energy he barely recognized, and now he bore down on Édouard, entangled with Suardet. Grabbing him by the shoulders, spinning him around, he thrust the man against a pilaster in the wall with a solid thunk of bone. Now, at last, was his chance. Now, at last, he'd let this dog of a man know how it felt. One blow was all it would take, the skull caught between a fist and a column of cement.

On Morin's stunned face understanding bloomed. There was no hint of fear. Instead, his lips parted and he lifted his chin, turning slightly to the left and closing his eyes. It was a look of acquiescence.

"Adler," cried Suardet in protest, but it was no longer needed. Philip had released Morin, roughly but without striking. He stumbled backwards.

Footsteps thundered in the hall. Attendants were on their way.

He helped Yvonne to her feet, one arm looped around her waist, the other under her arm. A line of blood trickled from her lip. Her blouse gaped open, the top button torn. Édouard struggled to free himself from Suardet, and she glowered at him in silent triumph, her eyes as dark as pits.

Back in the parking lot, Philip guided her, seating her in the car, and locking them in. He had no idea what to do next, where to go, and his fingers jittered as he tried to insert the key into the ignition. Yvonne seemed dazed, a strangely satisfied look on her face.

The scene from the ward was a blur. Morin had assaulted her, and then Philip himself had responded with violence. In nearly thirty years of professional practice, he had seen his share of brutal confrontations, but not once had he participated in one.

His job was to remain detached, to keep his perspective. Only from a distance would he be able to see the patterns. But every time he found himself with Édouard Morin, the iron bands around his heart loosened, making room for passion.

He looked up the hill at the hospital—a calm, implacable building. Was anyone injured? Wouldn't Suardet have to call the police?

And what was he to make of Morin's weird submission as Philip had raised his fist—like an animal accepting its own sacrifice?

He turned to Yvonne, the sphinx sitting in the seat next to him. He had planned the meeting with Morin down to the last detail, knowing how he would struggle to keep the lid on his own emotions. But in fact it was Yvonne—the one who had banished the past from her life—who had finally allowed her well-tailored present to split apart. This was his fault. He was the one who had forced her into the confrontation. If he hadn't pushed, perhaps she would have soldiered on to the end.

He wondered now about her cold demeanor on the drive out. Her calm. Her determination.

"What happened in there?" he asked.

"You weren't getting anywhere with him," she replied, staring straight ahead. "I saw an opening. And I took it."

"You were supposed to wait, to—"

"There was no sense in waiting," she countered. "He was thrown off-balance."

"Because of the language?"

She turned to him. "Because of me." She paused. "The mother of his victim. But it's not just that. It's more general." She looked at her hands as if they were sullied. "It's women he can't abide."

Philip leaned back in his seat and drew a deep breath, trying to assemble the pieces of a thought. It took two or three tries before he managed to construct the next question. "Was this your plan all along?" he said.

She leveled a hard look on him. "No. That was not my plan." She reached down and opened the flap to her messenger bag, dug through the papers, and withdrew a pair of long-handled shears, the blades glinting in the dusk. An image leapt to Philip's mind: paper dolls. She'd brought the scissors from her office.

"If you must know," she stated flatly, "*this* was my plan." She let the scissors drop back into her bag. "It turns out I didn't need them."

He stared. At one point in his life he'd thought he knew this woman. But now everything was slipping from his grasp. Morin's languages, Yvonne's actions, his own conduct, even Roger—it had all veered out of control. Everything was misfiring, hitting beside the mark.

"Don't tell Hervé," she said, her eyes fixed on the windshield. "Or Margaux."

Of course he wouldn't tell. But Hervé would find out on his own, wouldn't he? After which Margaux would hear, and then all of Rouen, all of Yvetot.

He'd seen the communications network in action. It would start in minutes and reach the most remote outposts of central Normandy in a matter of hours.

However, thirty minutes later, when he pulled up at the curb in Mont-Saint-Aignan, the Legrand house appeared undisturbed, sedate, like every other structure on the block. In the dusk, Hervé's green Mercedes slept out front, and through the front window he saw Margaux splayed on her belly in front of the TV, kicking her feet together in the air. So Suardet hadn't even called.

Before letting her go, Philip pulled out a tissue and dabbed away the blood that had dried at the corner of her lips, cupping his left hand against her cheek. She licked away the remaining trace of red and waited for his assessment.

"Better," he murmured.

After climbing out of the car, she walked to the house without turning back. The front door opened and closed. Moments later a light went on in an upstairs window. The TV continued to play. Nothing else changed.

Yvonne had assailed Édouard Morin, cutting him with words better than she could have with a blade. She provoked an attack, and Philip himself had hurled Morin against a wall. But no one had found these events worthy of reporting. Had Suardet elected to spare Yvonne? For Hervé's reputation? For his own?

There were no good explanations, or if there were, they eluded him now. Meanwhile, other images had staked a claim on his mind: he and Yvonne were now bound by a secret. He imagined her body, remembering how he'd grasped her in Suardet's conference room, drawing her away, one arm around her waist, the other around her back, pressing her to him, her blouse open. It had felt like an embrace.

He pulled the Smart Car onto the curling road that led toward the darkened center of Rouen, barely able to steady his hands on the wheel.

How little we know, he thought, even about those we love. A small number of individuals will translate murderous impulses into action, but can anyone predict who will cross that line? Not Philip. Not even after all his years in the profession. Countless times he'd been called upon to give expert testimony about the mentally ill, usually to answer some variation of a simple question:

is this person a danger to himself or others? Sometimes his response was easy to formulate. Sometimes not. And sometimes he got it wrong.

But Yvonne? There was a darkness inside her he'd not suspected. He'd misunderstood, miscalculated. Now he imagined her at her desk, finishing a string of paper dolls and studying the shears in her hands, opening and closing them as she admired the blades. Then she'd have tucked them into her bag.

The shadow of the cathedral loomed to his left, and Philip drove on, curving through the roundabout. Then another familiar building appeared: Hervé's clinic, lights still blazing. He slowed to contemplate this sign of Hervé's success, this monument to his ability to produce life where nature had failed, and he felt a swell of jealousy. What wouldn't Philip give to experience fatherhood again—even if just for a day, an hour?

The main door of the clinic opened, and out strode a well-dressed fellow, a touch of swagger to his step. Yes, Philip thought, like that man, right there.

He blinked and leaned into the windshield. It was Roger.

His first impulse was to stop and call out. But what was Roger doing here, of all places, visiting a man he professed to regard with contempt? Philip rounded into a side street and cut the engine, watching while his brother-in-law sauntered up the walk. As Roger arrived at his BMW, a frown formed on his lips, and he plucked a narrow card from under the windshield wiper. Then he rolled his eyes and tore the citation in half, letting the pieces flutter to the ground. He climbed into the car, revved the engine, and pulled away.

First Yvonne, and now Roger. Was nothing as it appeared?

He started out after the BMW, pushing the Smart Car to keep pace as they entered the countryside. Roger's distant taillights vanished over hills and around curves, appearing for brief moments. In Yvetot, as Philip arrived at the Place des Belges, Roger was just walking across to the brasserie. And when he entered the restaurant himself, just moments later, his brother-in-law was already seated, draining a glass of wine.

"Sorry," Philip said. "Have you been waiting long?"

Roger shrugged with what might have been exaggerated nonchalance. "Half an hour? But don't worry—I had good old Saint Émilion to keep me company." He patted the open bottle and refilled his glass.

Philip's shoulders tightened. Should he challenge this lie? What did it mean that the visit with Hervé was to be kept a secret? He watched Roger pour himself another glass, but his gestures seemed suddenly wooden, his expression too fixed. It was as though Philip had stepped to the right or the left, only to discover the edge of a mask.

He, too, could play a role. As they ate, Philip eased into his report about Morin, charting a careful path. While Roger listened and drank, Philip recounted the meeting, expressing in detail the digressions, the excursions into other languages, the obsession with even and odd, the references to places and people. But he also edited, skipping over the lewd questions, the gestures and twitches. Most of all, he trimmed the culmination—Yvonne's verbal attack, and Morin's physical response. That news didn't need to get back to Hervé right away.

As he concluded this cautious summary, Roger downed his last glass and gave his head a heavy shake. "Bullshit," he grunted.

"I'm sorry?"

"It's a load of rubbish. The languages, the accents, all the dodges." He stumbled over the last word, slurring it. "Sure, you can read something into it if you want. But at some point you have to take things at face value."

Was this meant to provoke him? "You're drunk, Roger. You drink too much."

"Of course I do." He made a flourish with his hand. "And you drink too little. It all evens out. But being drunk doesn't make me wrong. You're reading tea leaves, and you know it."

Philip chafed. "You don't need to tell me about projection. After Sophie's death, every back alley looked like a dumping ground. Every bulge in the earth became a makeshift grave. *Maybe there*, I'd say. *Or there. Or there.*"

"But you've just proved my point. You turn nothing into something."

"Is it projection to find headless poultry in your hotel room?" He didn't add: or to discover your brother-in-law consorting with the enemy?

Roger turned somber. Yes, the slaughtered rooster was a real problem, and he'd come up with a solution. It would be best to give Yvetot a little breathing room, to take a break from La Cauchoise, at least for a couple of nights. He proposed putting Philip up at Anne-Madeleine's. Since the funeral, the house was empty and quiet. No one would even know he was there.

No one, Philip thought, except for Hervé. He considered balking, but then decided to play it out. Whatever was afoot, he'd have the advantage of knowing more than Roger thought. Besides, once word got out about Yvonne's attack on Morin, it might not be so bad to have a buffer.

It was late when they left the brasserie and drove out to the old Aubert home on the outskirts of town, a hulking presence set back from the street at the end of its gravel drive.

Soon they were inside, clicking on the lights. Roger left the shutters closed. "No need to advertise our presence," he said, his voice echoing off the walls. He gestured about the shadowed living room. "Make yourself at home. As much as you can, anyway. You can pick up your bags at La Cauchoise tomorrow."

He clattered about the kitchen. A few canned goods stood in the pantry. Bedding would be in the linen cupboard upstairs.

"Anything else I can do for you?" he asked with a yawn, handing over a house key.

It felt like a leading question. No, no, he said: Roger had done quite enough. And Philip locked the door behind him.

The hollowness of the old house deepened after Roger's exit, and the dust covers on the furniture aggravated its emptiness. He already felt like a ghost in Yvetot, and the prospect of a night in the house of his dead mother-in-law, in the very bed he used to share with his ex-wife in the guestroom, didn't help. The structure was a century and a half old, and it emitted its share of creaks and groans.

Over the mantel hung the portrait of old Guillaume, still judging Philip with his unswerving severity. The Aubert patriarch felt like France in miniature, the pattern of kings and emperors trickling down into the very structure of families. To think that some people believed that a revolution had changed all that!

He toured the deserted rooms, reacquainting himself with the house he had once known so well. Years ago it had been the hub of the Aubert clan—an always lively place filled with high-spirited people. Now it had gone as still as a museum, and Philip tried not to disturb the relics. He limited himself to the kitchen, the bathroom, and the guestroom on the second floor. Thanks to this rule he resisted the urge to venture up to the very top, to the little bedroom Sophie used to occupy when visiting Anne-Madeleine, the room later taken over by Margaux.

The only signs of recent activity appeared in the living room, now cluttered with boxes. Yvonne had started the sorting process as they prepared the house for sale. Behind the doors of the buffet, he discovered a vast selection of liquor and liqueurs, all the raw materials for social gatherings. The sight of the whiskey triggered a pinch in the back of his throat. But he pressed the buffet doors closed again, sealing that vault.

Why had Roger wanted him here, of all places?

He checked his watch. On top of everything else he had the appointment with Melanie Patterson later this evening—the call they'd been building up to—and he would need to be ready. How could he hold a phone when his hands still tingled from the brawl with Morin, from the weight of Yvonne in his arms? Everything had turned unreal, impossible. Roger himself had become opaque.

If he was to give Melanie his full attention, he needed to purge his mind of the day's events. In the guest bedroom he played back the recording of the meeting with Morin, transcribing phrases into the blue diary, noting changes of tone. When he came to foreign languages, he marked down what little he could, trying to capture Morin's unusual pronunciation, adding the translations Yvonne had given him afterwards. *There are borders one shouldn't cross*, Morin had insisted, and Philip couldn't agree more. But everyone seemed to be crossing them.

At the same time, images of Yvonne unspooled in his mind: her ugly look at Morin, the gaping blouse, the blood streaming from her lip. He was still astonished by it all. Something had been unleashed inside of her. It worried him and thrilled him, which he knew to be foolishness. He had no claim on her. It was Hervé who had everything—even a daughter.

He ran his hands through his hair. Fathers and daughters, sons and fathers, husbands and wives. It all came down to this. *Du bist nicht mein Vater*, Morin had said. Along with Melanie: *You're not my fucking father*. Or even Margaux: *Does that make you my stepfather?* But no, Philip was childless and orphaned, no one's father, no one's son. Even Guillaume Aubert, dead and gone, hanging over the mantel, was more of a father than he.

A knot formed in his stomach. There was one possible connection, one relationship he didn't want to acknowledge. Filial rather than paternal. *We're not so different, you and I*, Morin had said. An absurd statement, but one that also rang true. The sentence had lingered in his memory, and his mind gnawed at the words patiently like an old dog with a bone.

He forced himself to concentrate on his notes. He saw now how Morin had bolted in new directions, ducking into different languages, leaving Philip dizzy with unexpected detours that led to side streets, and from there into country lanes and dirt roads, through the innumerable Sorquainvilles of a deranged mind.

When he replayed the passage with Morin's English accent—or a wild blend of British tinged with French and humming S's—he tried to transcribe it phonetically. *I'm terribly sorry, chums*, he heard, writing "teddibly" to show how each R was tapped. "*Zawry*, chums," he wrote. "I'm *nawt* at *libuhty* to *discuzz thizz* any *fawther*. No *fawther a-toll*."

And above all the others came the nagging question: Why, when Philip had prepared to strike him, had Morin not defended himself? He could have protested or cried out. And yet he had practically leaned in for the blow. Only one explanation seemed plausible. Behind all the posturing and arrogance, Édouard Morin wanted to be punished.

Seventeen

It was midnight when he called from the guest bedroom in the Aubert home, family photographs staring at him from the walls, a vase of dusty silk flowers parked in the center of a doily on the oak dresser. A window rattled from the wind. He had the cell phone in his hand, the diary of notes laid open on the bedspread before him. He closed his eyes as he reviewed his plan. When he opened them, he was ready.

The phone rang eight times before Melanie picked up.

"So," she said. "Another long-distance call. You should double my rate."

"Hello Melanie. How are you doing today?"

"Oh, I'm great. That's why I have to keep talking to a shrink. All my friends think I'm a nut job. So does my dad. So, yeah, I'm pretty much hunky-dory."

Philip paid less attention to the words than to the intonation, the subtle inflections in the timbre of her voice. The barbed wire was up. It would be hard to get close. "Don't worry," he said. "You're not a nut job."

"Sorry, but you're not exactly, like, *objective*. You get paid to say that."

"You're not a nut job," he repeated. "You just don't know what you want. You're confused."

"And I suppose you're going to straighten me all out. Good luck with that little project. Send me a card when you finish."

He figured she was still mad at him for the last time. While he considered his options, the wind kicked up again outside, and beams creaked in the attic.

"How are things at home?" he asked.

"What about you?" she said, her voice flat. "How's everything in French-land?"

He wondered how hard to push. "Well," he began, "if you really want to know, it's a rather barbaric place. At least the little corner of it that I've been occupying."

"Not much of a vacation, huh?"

The images of the past forty-eight hours filed through his mind. "You could say that."

"And that thing you were trying to fix?"

"Not going well, I'm afraid."

"How come?"

There she was again, prying away. "It's complicated, Melanie," he said.

"Meaning you're not going to tell me, right?"

He sighed. "I can't get into this. It's not—"

"If you can't even fix yourself, I don't know how you expect to fix me."

She was already starting to irritate him. "You don't know what you're talking about, Melanie."

"And you don't know how to listen."

"What's that supposed to mean?"

"People try to tell you things, but you don't even hear them."

His eyes narrowed. "What don't I hear?" he asked. "Give me an example."

"Give me an example," she repeated mockingly. "Right. Like you need proof."

Taunting was the last thing Philip was in the mood for. He'd gotten his fill of it from Édouard Morin. "This is going nowhere, Melanie. Maybe we should just try again some other time, when you're ready to—"

"It's all because of the girl, isn't it?" she blurted out.

The words caught his breath. He was sitting bolt upright, the phone clenched hard. "How do you know about that?" he demanded.

"Like it's not obvious."

"Who told you?" he snapped. "How do you know about Sophie?"

"Is that her name?"

"How do you know about this?" he said, his voice rising.

She snorted. "You don't have to be a genius. It's *always* a girl. What's the matter? Don't you even go to the movies?"

He drew the phone away from his ear and tried to ease his breathing. There it was, his example of how poorly he listened, how quick he was to project his own thoughts on other people's words. Everything was blurring together.

She spoke again. "So what is she, some long-lost girlfriend?"

His eyes fell on the images hanging on the bedroom wall, family photos, peopled with faces he didn't wish to see. Even from picture frames on the night table, eyes looked up. There was nowhere safe to turn.

Another gust of wind pressed against the house.

"What's going on?" she was saying. "Are you still there?"

"I'm here."

"Who's Sophie?"

He gritted his teeth. "We're not talking about this, Melanie."

"She must have really gotten under your skin, right?"

"Knock it off, Melanie. It's ancient history."

"How ancient?"

"*Very* ancient. Time to talk about you now."

"And this thing you're trying to fix, it has to do with the girl, right?"

He rolled his eyes. He saw what was going on. She didn't want to talk about her father, so she'd latched onto another story, one dealing with another person's pain.

"So now you're trying to get her back?" She paused for an answer, and when none came, she forged ahead. "I bet she doesn't want a thing to do with you, does she? And I bet you really miss her. Don't you?" She paused before prompting him again. "Don't you?"

He rubbed his temple. Such incessant digging. But she was just a young girl trying to understand affection. Underneath the sarcasm and jabs, Melanie Patterson wanted to believe that something not foul might exist between a man and a woman. She hungered for this possibility.

He wasn't going to let her into the private territory of his life, the part staked with no trespassing signs. But he could give her the general sense of the landscape.

"Yes, Melanie," he said, feeling his throat swell. "I miss her."

There was a silence, and Philip knew she was absorbing this confession of emotion. When she spoke, he heard an ache in her voice.

"So . . . what are you going to do?"

He cast about for the vaguest possible formulation. "I'm trying to talk to a man who knows something I need to learn."

"Something that will help you?"

"I think so. I hope so."

"And he won't tell you?"

Philip paused. "He wants to say something, but I think he . . . doesn't know how to express it."

The line went quiet, long enough that Philip feared the connection had been lost.

"Like me," she breathed.

"What?" he flinched. "No. Not like you, Melanie." Any comparison between Édouard Morin and Melanie Patterson was unthinkable, repulsive. "Not at all like you."

"And how's it going with this man?"

"Not well. Not well at all."

Another pause. "Also like me."

"Stop this, Melanie."

"Maybe it can't be fixed. Not everything is fixable, you know."

"What do you mean?" What was she talking about? Him? Or her?

"Nothing," she said quickly.

"What's not fixable?" he pressed. He sensed the conversation slipping from his grasp.

"Sometimes it can't be done."

"Tell me what you're talking about," he pressed.

"I gotta go," she said hastily.

"Hang on a minute."

"*Seriously.*" It sounded urgent. "I still have stuff to do before I'm done."

"Hold on!"

"Goodbye, Dr. Adler," she said, a quaver in her voice.

"But . . ."

There was a pause on the other end, followed by a click. She was gone.

Eighteen

The next morning he awoke from troubled dreams to find the Aubert home undisturbed: the doors still locked, the shutters closed. What else had he expected?

While the coffee machine burped and steamed in the old kitchen, he fired off a text message to Linda so she'd have it as soon as morning rolled over Boston. The call with Melanie had left him uneasy. She was in a difficult patch, and he didn't know what to give her. His third ear had gone deaf. Briefly he considered handing her case to Jonas, but no, this was his own responsibility. They had made headway—had at least worked out rules for speaking that no longer included the hurling of objects. Fobbing her off on someone else now would jeopardize it all.

He returned to his room at La Cauchoise to shower and change. The laundry had come back and he drew a white shirt from the bundle, now a dingy shade of gray, the fabric stressed, as though it had been pounded with rocks at a river's edge. The tips of the collar were worn, and every button along the front was cracked.

As he tied his shoes, the second lace snapped. Two for two.

Then, right on cue, a knock came at the door. What surprise had Yvetot cooked up for him today? More butchered animals, or would they have grown more ambitious? He opened the door, steeled for a confrontation, but it was only his breath that he lost. Yvonne stood before him, dressed in a sober skirt, her purse clutched in her hands. She had regained her composure, had become Madame Legrand once again. Her eyes roamed over the unmade bed, the half-open suitcase, the files and papers strewn over the writing desk, and she raised her eyebrows.

"You should have called in advance," he said. "I'd have polished the silver."

She gave a tight smile, which made her wince and raise her fingers to her lip.

"Still tender?" he asked.

"A little."

"Well, I could say *that'll teach you*, but I suspect it won't."

He stepped to the window. Down on the sidewalk in front of the hotel, a man raised his hand to his mouth and a puff of smoke emerged. Hervé.

"What does he know?"

"He asked me how the meeting went, and I told him the basics. What he needed to hear."

"Suardet never called?"

She shook her head. "It wouldn't make him look very good, would it—the way things slid out of control?"

That much was true. But what about Édouard? Suardet couldn't keep him from speaking out. Since Philip's arrival in Normandy, not a single step had escaped notice. How was it that this incident, the most violent, could go unreported?

In the distance the bells at Saint-Pierre began to ring the hour.

Yvonne looked down. "But people are talking, Philip. You know what it's like here. All the old wounds are opened up."

"Is this you speaking? Or Hervé?"

"Both." She looked at him now as though studying his face for signs of wear. "At the beginning, I thought you'd be here a few days and that would be the end of it. Life would return to normal. But you didn't leave. And look what it's led to. Even I don't understand what you're hoping to accomplish."

"You saw Édouard Morin."

Yvonne paused. "I have to think of Margaux. She hears all the talk. About Sophie. About you. About us. It's tearing her up."

Philip closed his eyes and felt the crumbling inside. He himself could take it. But Margaux? He imagined her listening to rumors at school, each word reminding her that the rotting remains of her sister—a girl who resembled her, who had been almost her age—lay somewhere in the vicinity. Did she have to live with these sickening details, every single day?

And yet, if it could actually be resolved, once and for all, wouldn't that benefit everyone?

"Say the word," he murmured. "If you want me to go, I'll pack my things. I'll be gone by tomorrow."

She drifted toward the window and stared out over the skyline. Finally she turned to him. "I need to know. Do you really think there's a chance? Don't lie to me, Philip."

There wasn't a shred of hard evidence to suggest he was any closer now than fifteen years ago. But over the past few days he'd sensed the presence of a possibility, a kind of unraveling.

"Yes," he said, meeting her gaze. "I can't put my finger on it, but I think there's a chance."

He watched her eyes search his face for a sign.

"Then find her," she said. "But do it quickly."

"What about Hervé? Margaux?"

"Find her," she said again. The meeting was over. She had picked up her purse.

At the door Yvonne offered her cheek, and he didn't refuse. After his lips left her skin, he slid his hands down the small of her back, and Yvonne allowed him to draw her closer, tucking her head under his chin. He inhaled the earthy scent of her hair. For a moment they were parents again. They'd made a decision together about their daughter. He closed his eyes and held her as long as he dared.

After she left, he watched through the window as she emerged below. Hervé turned, flicking his cigarette into the gutter. He took her by the arm.

The meeting with Édouard Morin had cracked something open inside of Yvonne, and this bought Philip a little time.

His glasses perched on his nose, he turned to the long process of reviewing documents and recordings, spreading his archive over the spare furnishings of the hotel room. In the diary he circled phrases that had the ring of importance, linking passages by arrows and numbers. He noted symptoms in Morin's speech, words and phrases that bobbed upon the surface of his language like ocean buoys. Particularly wondrous were the linguistic pirouettes—dazzling displays of wordplay: the apparent and despairing parents who sought to repair the irreparable. Then had come the flourishes in Spanish and Italian and German, not to mention the British accent.

Everything circled back to the one soft connection he had made: Sorquainville, Malamare and Adonville. Alphabetically these towns evoked his daughter's name. Geographically they mapped a vast triangle within Upper Normandy. Historically they were meaningful only as substitutions for more significant locations. These towns called to mind the years of the war, which in turn was tied to Morin's frequent use of German—and perhaps even to the reference to the fatherland.

What he couldn't pin down was the logic that bound these elements together. Too much was missing.

So far he'd been standing at the edge, but now he needed to creep into the forest of symbols. To understand more deeply, he would have to stop thinking *about* Édouard Morin, and begin to think *like* him. There was no simple recipe for producing this shift. All he could do was pore over the documents and hope, aiming for a kind of free-floating attention that could glide over the evidence before him, catching on the burrs of oddity or sliding on the smooth spirals of repetition.

At the same time, the problem of Roger tugged at his attention. No, normally it was no crime for a man to visit his sister's husband—but when it was a question of Hervé, that circle became harder to square. Roger had other connections, too—local ties so close that he had learned about the beheaded rooster before Philip even told him. And now that the mask had begun to slip, everything took on a different hue. Philip's mind raced: the yellow rose on the grave, the plaintive insistence that Philip stay in Yvetot, the troubles with Élisabeth, and the carousing. Everything led back somehow to that one night in July of 1993, the one which Roger claimed to have spent with Élisabeth— except that when the family gathered around the police in the small hours of the morning, the two of them had arrived separately and hours apart.

That was how he remembered it. Or imagined it. Where was the line between projection and reality? Paranoid delusion, he often told patients, is nothing more than an exaggerated assessment of probability. That definition sounded glib to him now, skirting the real issue: how do you know when you yourself have crossed the line?

He aired his rattled mind on another long walk, circling through town, jostling ideas with each stumbled step on the uneven cobblestones. Eventually he passed by the *Tord-boyaux*, and a flush of defiance filled him. Yvetot had no hold over him. He pushed through the door and trudged past the surly regulars at the bar, taking up his post at the back table. From there he surveyed the group, staring down their awkward glances. It was the old crew—the greasy-haired one with the tweed driving cap, the tall police officer, the men in farmer's clothing. Sophie's grave didn't qualify him for membership in this community. To them he was a trespasser. But he wouldn't scare easily. They had no understanding of how little he stood to lose.

He could have returned to the Aubert home for the night, but he was keen to stand his ground. Roger wasn't very happy about his decision to return to La Cauchoise—nor was Monsieur Bécot—but Yvonne's support had conferred upon him a new truculence.

The next morning, after fitful sleep, he shuffled down to the breakfast room and found Roger waiting for him, already ordering a fresh pot of coffee.

"No," he was saying to the serving girl's question. "No milk is necessary. A good cup of coffee should never be adulterated with other substances. Adultery should be reserved for more important matters. Don't you agree?"

The girl went beet red. "*Oui, Monsieur,*" she murmured before bustling away.

Philip sat down cautiously while Roger raised a pre-emptive palm. "Don't start with me, Philip. That was nothing more than banter, which is a national sport in France. And as the health professionals keep saying, sport is good for us."

"I didn't say a thing."

"Well, your puritanical thoughts are rubbing off on me," he muttered. "I've even been feeling guilty about my infidelities to Élisabeth. You know, I really wish I could return to Catholicism. It has a wonderful way of handling guilt. The priest waves his magic wand—well, it's really his fingers moving in the sign of a blessing—and *poof!* Guilt is gone." He helped himself to half of Philip's croissant. "So you made it through another night? No horse heads planted in your sheets? No exploding packages? I do worry about your staying here."

"I imagine Hervé would agree with you," Philip replied.

Roger looked surprised at the comparison, then smiled. "But there's a difference. Hervé is worried about you remaining in the western hemisphere, whereas my concerns are more local. Mind you, it's not Hervé's fault that he's combative and disagreeable. It's the trait of short people—not to mention people from Rouen. I tried to warn Yvonne about this years ago, but she wouldn't listen."

"She came to see me, you know."

Roger arched his eyebrows.

He decided to take a chance. To see if Roger was serving as a conduit to other sources, Philip would have to put it to the test. He studied his brother-in-law's expression as he recounted Yvonne's visit, telling how she'd urged him to continue, contradicting the message Hervé had charged her with.

Roger gave a low whistle of admiration. "My sister? I have a newfound respect for her."

Although he was practiced in the detection of lies, Philip recognized none of the symptoms in Roger's response: no crossing of arms, no fidgeting, no loss of eye contact, no change of voice. Whatever was going on with Roger would need to be excavated more carefully. What came to mind was the chessboard, the old game with Faruk89. Play the expected moves, he told himself, and wait for an opportunity.

In the meantime, he needed Roger. Édouard Morin had shown he was waiting, that he had things to say. But without Roger's help, it would be difficult, perhaps impossible.

"There's a problem," he said while Roger loaded jam on the horn of his croissant. "I have to speak to Morin one more time, but Suardet isn't going to allow it."

"Why is that?"

"Things turned . . . rather ugly last time. I'm not proud of it, but Suardet isn't going to want a repeat performance."

Roger went pensive, then waved away this difficulty with a flap of his hand. "Don't be ridiculous. I'll just have to be persuasive."

"You think you should call him?"

"Call? Nonsense. People can refuse you anything over the phone. We'll drive out there and spring it on him. That way it's much harder for him to turn us away. We'll talk our way in."

"You don't mind? It seems like a long shot."

Roger leaned over the table. "You forget. Talking is my specialty."

Philip was reluctant to leave his car in Yvetot, where out-of-town vehicles tended to attract odd accidents, so the two men—one tall, the other broad—

packed themselves into the red Smart Car and headed out on the back roads. South of town they threaded their way through a herd of black-faced sheep, and later through a peloton of middle-aged cyclists, swaying as they pumped their way up the steady incline.

Less than an hour later they arrived at the wheat-colored hospital, where Roger's silver-tongued strategy might have worked if there'd been an ear to listen to him. But Suardet was not even on the premises, and to Roger's further disappointment, the receptionist was a young man, immune to his charms. The fellow paged through the calendar, offering to schedule them for an appointment. How would Tuesday of next week suit them?

Out in the hallway Roger mulled over alternatives, considering how best to track Suardet down. Meanwhile, Philip was trying door handles in the corridor.

"What the devil are you doing?" Roger said.

"It can't hurt to look around."

A few doors were unlocked. They surprised two physicians in the midst of sessions with patients, a third on the phone, and a fourth dozing in his chair. Finally they located a break room containing a vending machine, a row of lockers, and a broad table littered with plastic cups.

Philip began opening locker doors, eyeing the contents like an actor in a costume shop.

"Say, you know I'm not a stickler for rules," Roger began. "Far from it. But those are private belongings."

"Suardet isn't available," he replied. "And I'm running out of time." He pulled a white lab coat out of a locker and measured it against his chest.

"Philip? Don't you think this is a tiny bit insane?"

"Then we're in the right place, aren't we?"

"And perhaps slightly illegal."

Philip turned to him, straightening up. There was no time to argue. This was the test. Where did Roger stand? "Are you in or out?" he said, crossing his arms as he waited for his brother-in-law to make up his mind. The answer, whatever it was, would be useful.

Roger wrestled briefly with his conscience. "All right!" he said, throwing his hands in the air. "I guess this is what they call American ingenuity." He helped Philip into the lab coat.

In another locker they located a clipboard. At the end of a hallway, they found the entrance to the secure part of the facility, where Philip caught the door behind another physician.

Roger stayed behind as the lookout.

He found Édouard in a remote corner of the library, a vast hangar of a room with industrial carpeting and racks of shelving. It smelled vaguely medicinal. Among the few patients scattered throughout the reading area, Morin sat alone with a large volume split open on the table before him. Though dressed in the same simple uniform as always, he appeared more ragged than before, the white shirt rumpled, his hair less perfectly groomed. And when he looked up, startled by the arrival of an unannounced guest, Philip could tell he'd not slept well, his usually prominent eyes dulled, his features drawn.

"Mr. Adler. I did not expect to see you again so soon." His tone was flat, each S buzzing. He peered past Philip in the direction of the door, swallowing twice. "Madame Legrand is not with you, is she?"

Philip shook his head. He took a seat across the table. It was the same configuration as the meeting room, but closer, more intimate. A worker wheeled a book cart past them, and the two men waited for him to disappear.

"You've come without Doctor Suardet in tow," Morin said. "Don't you think he'll mind being left out?"

"I thought it might be best to meet one-on-one," Philip replied. "Perhaps you can speak more freely." He tried to keep his tone even. Suardet might show up at any moment, but if Morin sensed he was rushing, it could derail the discussion. "I know you have things to tell me, Édouard, and this is your chance." He pulled out the voice recorder, placing it between them and pressing the button.

As if in slow motion, Morin raised his right arm, reached forward, and nudged a corner of the device. Then he brought his fingertips to the point of his hairline and smoothed back his hair.

"That's better," he said. "Don't you think?"

Philip didn't reply.

Morin gestured at the volume in front of him. "I have just been reading about the Mesolithic era, Mr. Adler. Do you know about that? It is the period between the Paleolithic and the Neolithic. This is a wonderful encyclopedia, although not entirely without error. I am currently up to the letter M."

"I don't care about that."

"I try to be regular with my studies. Otherwise one never gets one's work done, don't you find?"

"I'm not here to talk about your readings, Morin."

He shook his head. "I don't know how you can be so disinterested in things, Mr. Adler. Books have so much to teach us, if only we had the time to—"

"But of course we don't always have time."

Morin stared. "I don't suppose," he began, "that you've had a chance to look into the word *eyeshot* for me?"

The conversation was falling into the same weary themes.

Philip's cell phone buzzed in his pocket, and he flicked it open to read a one-word message from Roger: *Suardet*. The doctor had arrived.

"Tell, me," he said. "Why did you attack Yvonne the other day?"

Morin forced a smile. "Well, Madame Legrand was rather *exercised*, wasn't she? Though I suppose she had her reasons. It cannot be easy speaking to the murderer of your daughter, can it?"

As he watched the Adam's apple bob in Morin's fragile neck, Philip thought of the urge he'd suppressed fifteen years before, when he'd had the chance to take the younger version of this man by the throat.

Morin raised his chin and leaned forward, looking him in the eye. "I don't think anyone here would stop you," he said, as though reading Philip's thoughts. He glanced at the other patients in the library. "Especially not this lot. They're a rather sorry bunch."

He ignored the invitation. "I'm tired of this, Édouard. Why have you agreed to these meetings if you're not going to tell me anything?"

"But Mr. Adler, I've told you—"

"No. You've *spoken* a great deal. But you haven't told me a thing."

Morin frowned. "It's not easy, Mr. Adler. Often it is better to say things in a tongue that is not one's own—even though they say that languages are unfaithful, that translation betrays. You know: *traduttore, traditore.* And we all know what becomes of traitors of the fatherland."

"What's your point?" Philip said.

Now Morin leaned forward, taking on a conspiratorial tone. "You and I,

Mr. Adler, I think we understand each other. We share an appreciation for a certain kind of tidiness. You like things to be even, and you have a hard time accepting the situation when they are not. Am I right?"

Philip refused to play this game. "If you have something to say, now is the time to say it. I will not be coming back."

A pained expression flashed across Morin's face. "I'm doing my best, can't you see that?"

"Frankly, no."

Morin's eyes were tired. "You know, we share more than you might think. Almost a kind of brotherhood. For example, the interest in language? All the different ways people have of expressing themselves—it is endlessly fascinating, don't you agree?"

Suardet would be there any moment, and they were looping through the same old pattern, performing the same roles as before. Philip needed to change the dynamic, to alter the script. An idea came to him—risky, but possible.

He rose to his feet. "Well, I'm afraid this wasn't a very good idea, after all," he said. "I won't say it was a pleasure meeting you Édouard. It's unfortunate that we couldn't help each other. I won't be bothering you again—I head back to the States soon."

It was the trick of the interrupted session—taking time out of the hands of the patient, forcing him to choose. He turned and started for the door, walking in an unhurried gait. Five paces, six. Soon he was nearly halfway there.

"*Wait*," Morin called, his voice pained. "Wait. One more thing."

But Philip didn't stop—not until he heard the shuffling of the chair and Morin calling out once again.

"Mr. Adler!"

Now, along with everyone else in the library, Philip turned.

Morin was standing, his arms dangling at his sides. "Although I can tell you exactly nothing, or nothing exactly, I would like to say a few words." He paused to massage his jaw, then uttered a single phrase with torturous care. "The kernel of our grief."

Philip took a step closer. "What is that supposed to mean?" It was a nonsense phrase, not even a full sentence.

Instead of replying, Morin continued with his careful articulation, cradling his jaw with his hand. "I am . . . the boy of my father."

Philip's eyes narrowed. "What does that have to do with anything?"

"The apple . . . fell near . . . the tree. And a king gave . . . law by an oak." The words tripped out one at a time, each of them making Morin wince with pain.

"Monsieur Adler," yelled another voice. It was Suardet. The cannonball of a man had bolted through the glass doors of the library, and he was bearing down quickly. "*That's quite enough!*"

But Morin raised a finger and swallowed hard. "We each carry a burden." Through the pain in his mouth he forced out one more phrase. "And the Calvary . . . a likely mount."

Philip took Morin by the shoulders now, shaking him. "What are you talking about? Tell me, before it's too late."

But now Morin slumped back into his chair. "I have said everything I have to say, Mr. Adler. Which is perfectly nothing. That is all I am permitted to do. I am done."

Suardet was there, grabbing Philip's arm. "Monsieur Adler," he roared.

The doctor hauled Philip and Roger into his office, upbraiding them with such a torrent of reprimands that Philip could barely keep pace with the French. Roger, on the other hand, now pressed into the role of spokesperson, remained composed, responding with great congeniality to Suardet's outrage. He was right, Roger agreed. This went well beyond the pale! They had no business pulling such a stunt! And no, Roger could not think of a single good reason not to report this incident to the police—although, he observed, it might reflect poorly on the Legrand family, to which he was related. But whatever the doctor thought best, of course!

At first Roger's acquiescence enraged the older man, but eventually it left him without anything to push against. Like a bug turned over on its back, Suardet slowed down, and when he tired of thrashing, he stopped. The two men left his office convinced they would never be welcomed back, but almost certain that Suardet wasn't calling the authorities. Of course, Hervé would hear about it, and what action he might take was another story.

Nineteen

At the beginning of his stay Philip had sworn to be discreet, but it was hard to imagine how he might have done a worse job of making good on that promise. He and Roger were barely out of Rouen before their cell phones started ringing. Yvonne's home number showed on the screens, but Roger warned against answering. It would be Hervé on the other end, he was sure.

As the car eased into the countryside, Roger pressed for the report. "So. What did you learn?"

Philip hesitated. The answer could go in multiple directions. "It's hard to say," he replied. "More word games. I'll need to listen to the conversation again before I know if was worth it."

This visit had also taught him something he didn't mention now: Roger would back him up, at least in these circumstances. Wherever Roger's story led, it was separate from that of Édouard Morin. The more he learned, the more confused Philip became.

When they arrived in Yvetot, Roger urged him to camp out at the Aubert home, where no one would think to look, but Philip refused. All his papers were at the hotel. "Besides," he said, "what's the worst that can happen?"

"The worst? How about the best? At the very least, Hervé will have called the police in Rouen, and Rouen will call the police in Yvetot. It could be very unpleasant."

Philip pictured the same gangly officer arriving at his hotel room door—the one who'd brushed aside the vandalism of his car as well as the beheaded rooster dangling from his light. He wouldn't mind having it out with that fellow.

Miraculously, though, Yvetot was quiet upon their arrival. Father Cabot was sweeping the walk in front of Saint-Pierre, shoppers had queued up at their preferred butchers and bakers, strings of teenage girls strolled arm in arm.

No police waited for them at the hotel—just Monsieur Bécot watching a soccer game in the back office. And as Philip creaked open the door to his room, he found his affairs untouched, free of feathers, blood, and body parts. Roger left to fetch sandwiches, but still no one came to his door. He wasn't so naïve as to believe he'd gotten off scot-free. Some response would be in the works, and the longer it took, the more horrible it would be. He needed to move quickly now.

The faint recollection of an obligation nagged at the back of his mind—another task to attend to, one he was forgetting. But for now he worked at the wobbly desk in his room, playing the conversation back on the voice recorder, twice, then a third time, trying to note every detail that snagged on the barbs of his attention. In many respects, this last encounter with Morin had been the same as all the others: the bizarrely buzzing pronunciation, the pain in the mouth, the recurring questions. But Philip's understanding of these repetitions had evolved. At the first meetings, he had taken Morin's haughty tone as a sign of indifference or insensitivity. Then it came across as a kind of fearlessness. Even an invitation to violence. However, if Édouard suffered from crushing guilt, why would he need someone else to punish him? He was smart enough. The hospital might use blunt utensils, might not hand out shoelaces, but Morin could have found a way.

He tipped back on his chair and studied the clouds through his open window. A mottled one in the shape of a rabbit slid into view.

I'm doing my best, Morin had said. *I've been telling you all along.* Should such a statement be taken at face value, or was Morin playing more games? Toward the end, when Philip had threatened to leave, real urgency had tinged Morin's words. But even after the jumble of painfully expressed phrases, he'd denied having told him anything at all: *I have said everything I have to say— which is perfectly nothing.*

That perfect nothingness amounted to six phrases, which Philip transcribed one after the other on a page of the blue diary:

> The kernel of our grief.
> I am the boy of my father.
> The apple fell near the tree.
> A king gave law by an oak.
> We each carry a burden.
> The Calvary, a likely mount.

They read like aphorisms. And each one had made Édouard wince with its telling, as though from the pain in his tongue. What made these phrases so important? Certain themes resonated with other topics dear to Édouard: his father, of course, but also religion and grief. And under it all, wasn't there the same preoccupation with *evenness*, each phrase pairing two elements—kernels and grief, kings and oaks, apples and trees? The images struck out in different directions, but they were also connected, different articulations of similar ideas. It was the logic of this sameness that he would need to understand.

His cell phone rang. This time it was Yvonne, calling from the university. Hervé was furious, she said, had flown off the handle when he heard about the stunt at the hospital, had stormed about the house. He'd even accused her of being involved.

But that wasn't her main concern. "What did you find out?" she asked.

"I don't know yet. I'm working on it."

"And where are you? Hervé says the police haven't been able to find you."

Philip looked about the room as though something might have changed to cloak his presence. Everything was in its place: the ratty curtains, the gaping armoire, the grim mini-bar. He'd not gone invisible. "I wasn't even aware I was hiding," he replied. In fact, the hotel had been oddly quiet.

He promised to call her as soon as he knew anything more, and after a silence meant to sound tender, he signed off. He thought of Margaux. She was the one he was working to help now.

This reminded him of his other task: Linda was supposed to reach Melanie, and she should have contacted him with the details for their next session. He sent another text message to Boston.

At his desk he focused on the accumulation of notes in the pages of the blue diary. Somewhere in this book lay what he needed to know. How, though, was one to recognize it? A phrase like *I am the boy of my father* was of sound logic at the same time that it revealed nothing. After all, every son is the boy of his father. And yet, by stating the obvious in slightly unusual terms, Morin had conferred upon it an air of mystery.

Perhaps Morin's aphorisms were distractions from more important messages that were not even verbal—such as the grimace that occasionally rippled across his face as he spoke, reminiscent of the tortured look captured by the newspaper photographs in 1993. These expressions might be nothing more than the sign of his own distress, the slipping of the mask of his composure, or even the result of the pain in his mouth. But perhaps they were flashes of guilt, synchronized with particular words.

Roger showed up with sandwiches. "This town," he cried. "Finding lunch in the mid-afternoon is akin to an Olympic feat."

"I spoke with Yvonne," he said, halting Roger in his tracks. "Hervé called the police, but no one has come knocking. How do you explain that? I thought they'd be delighted to run me out of town."

Roger fluttered his hands. "The authorities work in mysterious ways. Perhaps we have not yet reached the critical moment." He settled into the musty armchair, his feet up on the bed.

Philip studied him. Never had he understood so clearly how much trust was a function of necessity. Yesterday at this hour he'd been questioning Roger's motives, his very character. Although not a single one of his questions about his brother-in-law had been answered, he now saw those doubts as luxuries to be indulged at another time.

He showed Roger what he knew, replaying the latest conversation on the recorder as he walked through his notes. They both were drawn to the six cryptic phrases at the end. Morin claimed to have said nothing, but he'd taken a great deal of care in saying it.

So they debated the function of these pronouncements, wondering whether they offered anything more than a simulacrum of meaning. It was possible for utterances to point in two directions at once, Philip insisted, and Morin's own diversions provided a fair illustration: Sorquainville, Malamare, and Adonville had led to Sophie at the same time they pointed away from her, like a form of misdirection.

Such doubleness was part and parcel of Morin's language. *I am eager to help you*, he had said, only to contradict himself in the next breath: *I have said everything I have to say, which is perfectly nothing.* How could both of these statements be true?

Roger sputtered with exasperation. "It reminds me of learning my catechism as a child. The less you understood, the more important it was supposed to be!"

The deliberate obscurity of the wording made the phrases heavy and dense. Moreover, they felt linked. What was a kernel if not a kind of seed—or a seed if not a kind of son? And then came the idea of the apple falling from the tree—sons tumbling from fathers—which led in turn to the phrase about a king giving law by an oak.

"Yes," Roger mused. "That's a royal image, and a saintly one at that."

Philip paused. "Saintly? How so?"

Didn't Philip know? Roger rubbed his hands together, delighting in American ignorance. The reference was common knowledge to every school-boy in the country: it was Saint Louis, one of the kings of France, doling out justice at the foot of an oak tree.

"And what was he sainted for?" Philip asked.

Roger shrugged. "What were any of them sainted for? Some terribly virtuous act, I'm sure—tagging along on crusades or burning heretics at the stake. Or, more likely, he produced a fortune for the pope. You know, the standard ways."

They examined the rest of the phrases in this light. *We each carry a burden* clearly evoked crosses to bear. The reference to the Calvary—"a likely mount"—suggested both innocence and sacrifice.

"It's all tipping in the direction of religion," Philip summarized. "Another of his obsessions."

Roger pulled back as if from something abhorrent. "I'm afraid that's not my area of expertise. Many years ago I served as an altar boy—pressed into service by my mother until I managed to get myself drummed out of the corps."

Philip put down his pen. "We need help."

Roger puckered his lips. "I hate to say this, but where does one usually turn for questions pertaining to salvation?"

Philip ran his hand through his beard. "You're not suggesting . . . ?"

"I'm afraid so. And I'd urge that we speak to him before lunch, as he's much less attentive after he's had a glass or two."

At Saint-Pierre they marched through the barrel-shaped building and crossed the altar to the sacristy. No one answered their knocks at the locked door. Roger's voice echoed as he called out for Father Cabot from behind the lectern. They checked the confessionals and side chapels. While Roger clomped down the stairs to peek into the meeting rooms in the basement, Philip waited above, standing in the middle of the nave.

This modern building was too fresh, contained too little knowledge of suffering to be of any use to him. No, Philip preferred the old churches—those that Yvonne had taught him to love. The ones with bodies buried under the slabs of the nave, names chiseled in the walls of the apse, and actual relics in the crypt. It wasn't so much religion he yearned for. It was history.

He studied the windows: Mary, Joan of Arc, Saint Peter, Saint Valery, Saint Wandrille, Saint Remi, Saint Audoin. It seemed that every saint in the book had made it here. Except for Saint Louis.

Roger came back up, shaking his head. "Off on some mission of mercy, no doubt. Or else home with his feet up. I doubt that man has ever been accused of working too hard. When France went to a shorter workweek, I don't think it dipped low enough to affect the priesthood."

"Guérin," Philip said suddenly. "In the archives. He might be able to help."

"An excellent thought. People say he knows everything."

If history was what Philip wanted, that would be their best bet.

On their way to city hall they passed the *Tord-boyaux*, and through the open door a voice rang out, calling for Roger. He hopped up the steps and reached in, shaking hands with the gangly police officer and the short, tweed-capped man. Something he said triggered laughter in the group.

"You actually know them?" Philip said when he returned.

"Not really," Roger replied with a satisfied smile. "A couple of them, yes. But as a Norman originally from Yvetot, I'm entitled to a lifelong membership in their club. We share a common history. Even the jokes are handed down from one generation to the next."

"And you shook hands with them? Even the mealy little fellow with the driving cap?"

"That *mealy little fellow* is the mayor of Yvetot. Try not to disparage our locally elected officials, Philip. It won't endear you to the Yvetotais."

In front of city hall, they passed before the monument to the First World War, the colossal soldier frozen in a huddled mass of dark green metal streaked with black. Downstairs they entered the tidy main office of the archive, threading their way between the shelves of boxes. At the reception counter, as Roger reached out to tap the service bell, muffled voices sounded in the direction of the storage room in the back. Philip led him down the narrow corridor.

"I'll take two," said a voice in French.

"Three for me."

"Dealer takes one. Now who's in?"

There was a clink of coins.

As they turned the corner of the overflowing shelves of bric-a-brac, the scene that met their eyes included Guérin, Bécot, and Cabot, all sitting around a game table, cards in their hands, coins and bills in the pot. It was Religion versus History versus Hospitality—and judging by the well-ordered stacks of coins amassed before Guérin, History was winning.

"*Bon sang*," cried Father Cabot, when he caught sight of the two men, leaping to his feet and stumbling on the hem of his cassock, cards tumbling from his hands.

"Hello, Father," Philip said as they approached.

"For the love of God!" went the priest. "Monsieur Abbler, don't startle us like that. I didn't hear anyone come in."

Bécot looked none too pleased either. "What are you doing here, Monsieur Adler?" he said, his voice strained. "And now you've dragged along Monsieur Aubert."

Only Guérin seemed genuinely glad to see them. "Gentlemen!" he sang out, his eyes gleaming under his cumulus of white hair. "How timely. Care to join us for a hand?"

"Just a harmless game . . . of cribbage, you know," Cabot said stepping forward to block the view of the winnings.

Guérin chuckled. "Cribbage? My dear Quentin, I think these fellows understand a wager when they see one."

"Well, yes, I suppose," the priest fumbled. "There is a religious aspect to betting, of course. Ever since Pascal . . ."

Guérin ushered the men forward for a flurry of handshakes and an exchange of greetings.

Roger peered about at the jumbled miscellany of the storeroom, examining the clocks and books and birdcages, and admiring with particular attention a plaster sculpture of a bare-breasted woman. "Quite a Cave of Wonders you have down here, Monsieur."

"You're the son of Anne-Madeleine, aren't you?" Guérin asked.

"Ah yes," said Cabot. "Tell me, Monsieur Aubert, how is your mother doing these days? Such a dear woman."

"How kind of you to ask, Father. She's doing as well as might be expected, under the circumstances."

"I'm so glad to hear it."

"You see, you buried her about two weeks ago," Roger added.

"Did I?" Cabot's ruddy complexion went violet. "Oh my, so I did. Do forgive me. There are so many, you know." His voice trailed off.

Philip and Roger accepted seats at the table and Philip explained their mission: they needed help tracking down some information.

Bécot grimaced. "Monsieur Adler," he said, shaking his head.

Cabot took this as his cue to exit. "Well, I doubt I can be of much assistance to you in such matters." He began to collect his remaining coins.

"Actually, Father," Roger interjected, "we need to enlist your help understanding a few articles of faith."

Cabot blanched as far as his complexion allowed. "Articles of faith?"

"We have questions about a Biblical reference."

"Well, of course. Certainly. As long as it's not too complicated. You see, it's a very busy day. In just a little while I have . . . I have . . ." He glanced at his watch. "I have . . ." He cast his eyes about the storeroom, and his voice trailed off.

Cabot helped where he could, but he explained that he was more of a shepherd than a scholar. At first he thought their question about Saint Louis had to do with the city in Missouri, which in turn he confused with the jazz and carnivals of New Orleans. Even when they got him focused on the right person, his knowledge of the specifics barely exceeded Roger's schoolboy image of the king giving out justice at the foot of an oak. He wasn't *entirely* sure what the grounds were for the king's sainthood, so he waffled, suggesting this and that, hinting that it was never easy to fathom the motivations of popes.

Roger enjoyed Cabot's floundering, and he tossed him questions the way one might lob anvils at a drowning man. "By the way, Father, I don't recall which pope that was," he said. "Or even what century. Could you clear that up for us?"

"Oh, well, I . . . I don't recall the exact year," Cabot said as he squirmed, looking at his companions in hopes that they might bail him out. Then his eyes lit up. "Henri," he said to Monsieur Guérin, "surely you have a book for this somewhere?"

And of course Guérin did. He pulled a volume from the dusty shelves and handed it to his friend. While Cabot thumbed through, Guérin leaned toward Philip. "Thirteenth century," he whispered. "I'd bet him ten euros."

"Boniface the eighth," came Cabot's victorious cry. "Now let's see," he muttered as he scanned the entry. "In 1297. That's when he was canonized. Oh my! The poor fellow died of bubonic plague. What a miserable finish for a king." He moved his lips and mumbled softly as he educated himself about the life and death of Saint Louis, eighth king of France in the Capetian line, occasionally emitting an "Ah!" or an "Oh my!"

Bécot disapproved of the whole business, eventually deciding to leave the others to their unhealthy pursuits. After all, he had the appearance of propriety—or at least neutrality—to maintain. He didn't want to be caught lending Philip a hand.

"Give it up, Monsieur Adler," he advised as he made for the door. "Don't disturb the past."

"Nonsense," Guérin countered. "That's what that past is there for. Come now, you old goat. Leave us in peace if you're not going to help."

Guérin escorted his friend to the exit, securing at least his promise of silence.

For the next hour and a half, the four remaining men labored in the archive, pulling down reference materials and puzzling through the bluffs and wagers of Morin's words, interrupted only by the growling of Father Cabot's stomach. By the middle of the afternoon, books and papers were strewn over the poker table. Guérin's neat cloud of hair had gone stormy from his tugging at it while he thought, and even Roger was looking less than dapper.

Morin had issued his cryptic statements in English, so Philip and Roger translated them for the others, often stumbling over the strange phrasing. It didn't help that Morin drew together so many disparate ideas. In addition to religious imagery there were the references to justice, trees, fruit and even probability. Sometimes a phrase appeared meaningful, but in too many ways. For instance, the *kernel of our grief* evoked mourning, a theme that meant something to both Philip Adler and Édouard Morin. Monsieur Guérin showed how these losses—the death of Philip's daughter and that of Édouard's father—coexisted in the town registry, where the names were separated by fourteen years and twenty-two pages. He handed over the book and Philip reviewed the scant records of these lives. There Sophie lay as an official record, reduced to two lines of type.

On the facing page Philip's finger fell upon another name he recognized—Julien Hesse, the man who had died just weeks before Sophie, and whose tomb he'd seen in the cemetery. It was the same name that had bled through on the hardware store sign. Yes, he was getting to know the families of Yvetot pretty well. Soon he'd be like Guérin, a repository of Yvetot family histories.

But these small discoveries led to nothing clear. Did the kernel of grief refer to Sophie? To Morin's father? Or to something entirely different? The phrase, like all the others, was so vague that it could indicate almost anything. Reading these words was like staring at Rorschach blots: the longer you looked, the more shapes you saw.

Philip noted a recurrence of contours in the references to saints and crosses and burdens and mounts. He quizzed Guérin and Cabot about the religiousness of the images. Might they not point to some specific sites in the region? Could Morin be hinting at a location?

"Religious imagery in Normandy?" Guérin exclaimed, and Roger and Cabot joined him in a hearty laugh.

"Look, Philip," Roger explained, "In this neck of the woods you can barely walk five paces without stumbling over something religious."

"Still," Guérin said. "You never know . . ." He pursed his lips and closed his eyes to think. "As far as I can recall, there are no churches near Yvetot with windows or statues of Saint Louis. What about you, Quentin? Anything come to mind?"

Cabot was again put on the spot. His eyes grew large. "Well . . . no. Not that I can think of, that is."

There was the old Saint Louis Chapel, in Rouen, Guérin mused. Also in Rouen they would find last judgment sculptures on the cathedral and Saint-Maclou church. But these were so far away.

"As far as crosses go," Cabot volunteered, "if you start tallying those up, where will it end? My goodness, this is Normandy. Think of all the churches, the cemeteries, the *calvaires*."

Philip interrupted. "What do you mean by the *calvaire*? Because Morin mentioned the Calvary, too."

"No, no, Monsieur Abbler," Cabot replied with condescension. "Not *le Calvaire*, the hill, but *les calvaires*, the sculptures. You know—the stone or wood crucifixes you find at intersections in the countryside."

"What was Morin's wording again?" Guérin asked, craning to see the paper.

Philip looked down at the page where he had listed the phrases: *The Calvary, a likely mount.* It was an awkward line to translate into French, and he hesitated over his choice of words. What did it mean for a hill to be *likely*? In what way is a rise in the earth related to probability or chance? He cast about for a way to render this phrase in French for Guérin and Cabot, fumbling over the options.

It was Roger who got there first, uttering the words: *une montagne de possibilités.*

The phrase echoed back to Philip in English with a strange familiarity. He had heard this phrase before, in Morin's own voice, at their very first meeting. He flipped through the pages of his diary, going back to the notes of his first meeting. There it was, written in the ink from Yvonne's pen. "Your Mountain," he muttered.

"What do you mean?" Roger said.

"That's how Morin described it. Yew Mountain."

"My mountain?"

"Or rather the *Mountain of Yews*. Like the tree."

"What tree?"

"The Hill of If, the Mountain of Possibilities."

Roger began to object to this string of absurdities, then stopped, his eyes widening. "My God. You mean . . ."

"Le Mont de l'If."

Philip steadied himself. It was the turnoff he passed nearly every day on the back road to Rouen. Not even a mountain, Morin had said, just a long hill. The connection was remote, spanning the very first meeting at the hospital and the very last. But wasn't that what Morin had insisted on? *I've been telling you all along.*

"That's it," said Roger. "That has to be it."

"Grab your jacket," Philip said. "We're going for a ride."

Twenty

Roger was struggling with the seat adjustment when Philip braked at an inter-section, resulting in a collision between his forehead and the glove box.

"Ugh. I should have insisted on driving," Roger said. "Then we wouldn't be stuck in this absurd little vehicle."

Philip didn't respond. Inside him stirred the sense of an ending, like the leaning rhythm of a coda or the final stanza of a poem. Morin's words had fallen together, pointing with sudden clarity. It was a lucky strike, a happy accident that yoked chance with opportunity, hinting at the possibility that was named Le Mont de l'If.

But how had he gotten this far? How had he made this leap? To his right, his brother-in-law wrestled with his seat belt, his elbow knocking the button that sent the window scrolling down. Philip found himself reassessing. Was it mere chance that Roger had nudged the search in the direction of Saint Louis and the Calvary? That he'd urged for them to look for Father Cabot? Or that he'd happened upon the translation of the *montagne de possibilités?* Yes, everything was fitting together except for one thing: Roger's role in this story. A shadow of caution swept across his hopefulness. But he had no other choice besides giving up, which was the same as no option at all.

Soon they were on the outskirts of town, then in the open countryside. Off to the right was the field where Philip had slowed on the day of his arrival, the place where the burly man in blue coveralls had walked out with an unex-ploded artillery shell cradled in his arms. They passed a strip of woods, and then the land began to rise. To the left a slim spur of asphalt curved up into the woods, a small arrow pointing to the destination: *Le Mont de l'If.*

The road here was unlined, barely wider than the car itself, rising along the crest of a slope bordered first by grassy fields, then by dark woods. The further they drove, the deeper the road sank into the terrain, the shoulders rising three, four, then five feet high, the road cutting like a gash through the land. Woods crowded the passage on both sides and trees tipped inward like rafters. Still the land rose, and finally the car climbed out, reemerging into a stretch of pastureland. A cluster of cream-colored cows congregated by the fence, one scratching her great neck against the barbed wire.

They passed by a low house with a slate roof. Then came a rattletrap out-building, followed by two more. At the summit of this gentle incline stood a lump of masonry still identifiable as a church, the structure bearing the scars of multiple makeshift repairs.

Philip pulled over onto a bald plot of beaten earth. They extracted them-selves from the car and looked around, taking in the surroundings. The church had been patched over the years, and then the patches had been patched, resulting in a façade of old stone pocked with stretches of red brick and even cement block. The south slope of the roof had been covered with squares of corrugated sheet metal, and on the remaining tiles tufts of moss competed with lichens for territory.

Across the street stood the ruins of a house, long ago abandoned. To the right leaned a block monument to those whom the hamlet had lost to the world wars. The names of six men, three from the same family, were inscribed upon it in worn letters.

A hundred yards up the road lay what could be called, by a stretch of the imagination, an intersection, though one of mostly theoretical value, catering to the hypothetical passage of unlikely travelers, and marked by a tall stone cross—a *calvaire*.

It was a forlorn dot of land. Le Mont de l'If made Sorquainville look like a city, Yvetot a metropolis. It hardly qualified as a place at all.

The word that came to Philip's mind was *non-lieu*.

He turned to Roger. Where would his brother-in-law lead if given half a chance? "What do you think?" he asked.

Roger blinked in the low sun. "I think that if I ever need to hide a body or two, Le Mont de l'If should be on my list."

Philip nodded. A ball had formed in his chest. It was the old feeling of proximity and imminence, stronger than ever. Along with it came a flutter of anticipation. Was this what he'd become—a man excited by the prospect of finding his daughter's decomposed remains? In his mind he ran through the series of snapshots—Sophie playing tennis, Sophie on skis, Sophie with her arm in a cast, Sophie mocking the camera. He pushed these images away.

"Where would you like to begin?" Roger wanted to know.

Philip surveyed the land under the setting sun. Le Mont de l'If wasn't high, but it was broad, and trees lined much of the road. Normandy had hundreds, if not thousands, of stone or wood *calvaires* marking intersections. Le Mont de l'If represented one chance among many. It reminded Philip of Guérin's old story about Louis XVI: You needed just one person who had kept the memory.

One person.

He turned and looked at Roger. "You choose."

Roger seemed surprised at this invitation but didn't argue. He stalked through the weeds, examining the terrain. The pastures and fields, he said, were out of the question: nothing could have gone unnoticed there. The only real chance was the long forested stretch they had driven through on their way to the top.

So they drove back to the start of the woods, and parked where Roger said. Here, too, it would be necessary to narrow the focus of their search, for the woods were long, and they extended a great distance to either side.

Roger recommended a first swath about fifty yards wide, starting just a stone's throw from the asphalt. Each took one side, Philip on the higher ground, Roger down below, and they began the slow crawl forward, walking in tight zigzags. Philip caught flashes of Roger's white shirt between the trunks of the trees lower down. The terrain here was uneven, and sometimes his brother-in-law would disappear for minutes at a time under the bump of a rise or in the V of a small ravine. Philip found himself a sturdy branch to serve as a walking stick, using it to steady his climb and to part ferns and underbrush as he examined the ground.

His mind began to lay traps for him. Every mound, every depression looked suspect. In the darkest thickets, where the ground was freckled with sunlight, twigs had a way of turning into bones. A rock became a skull. Any number of times he stopped and prodded the dirt with his branch, digging at the surface, only to find the soil hard, matted with roots. How long did it take for such organic cement to form? How long would the loose earth of a shallow grave retain any discernible difference from the rest?

And most of all: was he looking where Roger wanted him to?

The hillside was scraped and scarred with ridges, too rugged for anyone to clear for farmland. A few dry creek beds cut through the slope, and Philip scrambled down into each gully, poking at the sides. There were natural cracks and crevices in the walls, but no hastily dug sepulchers, as far as he could tell.

Behind a thicket far from the road Philip encountered a dry creek bed that led to a lumpy knoll rich with bulges of earth and tufts of vegetation. What might lie beneath this mound? Or that one? He probed with his stick.

When a branch cracked behind him, he wheeled about to find himself facing two men, unshaven, of uncertain age, standing just ten feet away. The first was as thin as a rail, the other huskier, with a long face. Both wore rubber boots and soiled trousers, topped with dirty blue sweaters—typical farmer's garb. The thin one carried a walking stick with a knob of metal at the end, and he smiled the way a dog bares its teeth. It was a windfall for them, a stroke of luck. All of Yvetot had grown impatient with the American, warning him and informing him, but he hadn't taken the hints. And now here he was in the woods, alone, far away from town. They gave each other a sly look. The husky one stepped forward.

"Halloo!" crooned Roger's voice from deep in the woods. Philip looked for him down the hill, obscured by brush. Roger called again, now closer. When Philip turned back, the men were gone.

When they met up, he didn't bother mentioning this strange encounter. He didn't want anything to interrupt them now. He had to play it out.

Roger suggested a second swath, fifty yards further in. "Maybe we should switch sides?" he suggested.

"Why is that?" Philip shot back, watching for his reaction. "Are you worried I missed something?"

Roger gawked. "Are you all right?"

"A second swath," Philip confirmed. "And we'll switch."

They started back in the other direction, deep in the woods. It was late now, and the sun was floating low on the horizon. Sometimes, as the ground dipped and rose, Philip found himself cast in deep shadows, the patches of darkness tricking him all the more. Outlines became more elastic, stretching to fit the elongated shapes of his imagination. The sensation of expectation gradually yielded to one of mere inevitability. All he needed to do was wait. Whatever he was looking for would find him if he gave it time.

Then he heard his name echo through the woods. Roger was high above, perhaps a hundred yards away, standing on the road and beckoning to him. Philip saw him cup his hands around his mouth, calling again. There was a tightness to his voice, but no urgency. Whatever Roger had to show him wasn't going anywhere.

His own lack of surprise stunned him. He'd felt it coming, the way one feels the winding of a spring.

Without haste, but never stopping, he mounted the hillside. His throat had gone dry.

When they met on the road, Roger just nodded to the right and led Philip up the hill into the trees. The underbrush caught at Philip's ankles, and he used his stick to push the clinging branches aside. He lagged behind.

Eventually they arrived at the edge of a small ravine. Philip looked to the right and left. Hadn't he already passed by here? Roger stepped and skidded his way down the embankment to the bottom, waiting as Philip followed.

Roger nodded toward the left, "I think you—"

"Shut up, Roger," he croaked as he pushed past.

A hole, overgrown with brush, showed in the flank of the ravine. Speckles of sunlight filtered through the brambles, and inside the cavity Philip made out the unmistakable contours of bones. A human skeleton. His vision blurred, then cleared. He'd done the anatomy classes all those years ago. It hadn't been pleasant, but he knew how to do it. You focus on the details, that was the trick. You don't look with the eyes of a father. You look with the eyes of a doctor.

Not three feet in, a broad gray skull loomed, half covered with dirt. The sockets of the eyes gaped, the rise of the nasal passage opening between them. The jaw stood slightly ajar, all the teeth present.

So this was where it happened. Where Morin had pinned her down. This hill, these trees, that stump—they were the last objects she saw. Perhaps it was with one of these stones, perhaps this one right here, that he had bludgeoned her.

A hand fell upon his shoulder, and he wheeled about. A maudlin look of sorrow furrowed Roger's face. Philip wrenched himself away.

"What's the matter?" Roger said.

His fists felt massive, like great weights swinging at the ends of his arms. "Are you happy?" Philip barked. "Now that I've found her? Now that you've guided me to her?"

"What?"

"Is there more, Roger? Anything else I should know?"

"Have you cracked? You're totally raving."

"Am I?" Philip stepped toward him. "I know about you and Hervé," he announced.

Confusion spread over Roger's face, followed by a wave of understanding. He blanched.

"I've put it together," Philip continued. "All of it. The roses. The guilt. Why you and Élisabeth arrived separately that night."

Now confusion returned. "What night?"

"Spare me!" he spat, turning now to focus on the cavity in the ravine. His daughter was the one who needed him now. He'd deal with Roger later. Brushing aside loose earth, he got a clearer view of the ladder of ribs, bowed upward. The sternum appeared to be intact. There was the clavicle. Many of the bones, no longer tethered by soft tissue, had come apart, but their position was clear enough. He saw the scapula, followed by the humerus, leading to the radius and ulna of the forearm. Through the front of the thorax, he made out the curved line of vertebrae embedded in the dirt.

And then his knees gave way and the great tightness in his chest loosened. His breath came heaving back. Something was wrong. Everything.

"What is it?" Roger said.

He struggled. "It's . . . not her." He turned and stared as his brother-in-law.

Roger shook his head. "You don't need to do this yourself, Philip," he murmured. The tone was patronizing. "We can call for help."

"I mean it. It's not Sophie."

"What?" Roger was dumfounded. "How can you say that? How could you know."

"The arm." His voice had regained its force. "Her right arm. Don't you see?"

"See what?"

"It's not broken."

It was the skiing accident, the three months Sophie's arm spent in a cast. Inside this cavity of dirt Philip had seen the bone, and it was smooth. It had never suffered a break.

Philip let Roger do the digging. He himself felt drained as never before. During the partial excavation of the bones, he forced himself into the role of a medical professional, confirming his conclusion. The skeleton was far too large to be Sophie's. It was male. And he was pretty sure the bones were too old. Then they found the metal buttons and, finally, a squarish tag made of tin, perforated so the bottom half could be snapped off, a text stamped into it: DESPLANCHES RAYMOND 1939.

A different child, lost to other parents of another era.

It was what Bécot had been telling Philip all along. Artifacts from the war—shells, mines, and bodies—kept coming to the surface, even now. Who knew what scene had played itself out on Le Mont de l'If some sixty-five years ago? After what skirmish had this French soldier dug himself into the loose ground of the gully, or what shell had buried him here? Did it happen at the time of the German advance, during the occupation, or in the midst of their retreat?

They touched as little as possible. Roger tied three sticks together to form a tripod marker at the edge of the embankment. They would leave the job of collecting these remains to another authority. Their job was simply to point the way.

Roger took the wheel for the return to Yvetot, and Philip leaned his head against the window, glad for the deepening twilight. While resting his eyes, he murmured an apology to Roger. What had he been thinking? Everywhere he turned he'd seen things that weren't there.

Roger shifted into higher gear. As they reached cruising speed and the engine thrummed, he began his own soft-spoken explanation. Philip had nothing to be sorry for. To the contrary, he was right. On the night of Sophie's death, Roger had not been with Élisabeth.

"Then where?"

He darted a glance at Philip. "Hervé's clinic. A medical workup. Let's just say there was a problem." He shifted in his seat. "You know. The seed wouldn't take."

"You mean . . . ?"

"Yes, that's right," he muttered. "I sowed, but there was no harvest. A pitiful count, if you want to know. Hervé was doing the whole workup—sleep disorders and all. He's very thorough. Still makes me come in for an annual checkup. Just had one the other day. I hate those visits, but I think Hervé enjoys giving me the results. Says I could just as well join the priesthood."

Philip draped his hand over his brow. What a fool he'd been. It all made sense. The shame of Roger's infertility, the loss of the chance at fatherhood, the discord with Élisabeth, the yearly visits—all leading to carousing and philandering, the way a dying oak casts out one last profusion of acorns. In the midst of it all, Sophie had become the stand-in for a daughter Roger never had.

"Yes, I should have told you," Roger continued. "It was stupid. Embarrassing, if you prefer. You can check with Élisabeth." He hesitated. "You can even check with Hervé if you need to."

Yes, he could check. But it was just ordinary enough to be true. Which meant that Philip had missed the mark in almost every imaginable way. Now he saw how his mind's ability to trick him was inexhaustible. He'd prided himself on his ability to differentiate signs from things, to detect subtle rhythms in speech, to recognize meaningful tics. But Yvetot had bested him. This town was nothing more than a giant Rorschach test, and each blot of ink morphed into fantastical creatures of his own making. So much for objectivity. Science is just passion dressed in a lab coat.

Worst of all was the return of doubt. For fifteen years he had known the fact of Sophie's death, and yet, without the presence of a body and despite everything reason told him, some spark of hope had lingered, fueling an ember that could smolder for days or weeks before flaring up into the blinding certainty that the universe had got it wrong. For an instant he would believe that the error had been fixed, the world trued up, and Sophie was about to prance around a corner, eternally the same. Then the flash would subside, plunging him into darkness once more, leaving only ardent cinders.

For a few moments in that fold of earth on Le Mont de l'If, he'd experienced a new sensation. Neither hope nor despair. Mere relief. And the instant he realized his error, the spark had reignited.

They reached the southern end of Yvetot, and soon they were outside the hotel.

Roger offered to stay, to get them something to eat, but he didn't argue when Philip declined. He said he'd swing by the police station on his way out of town to report what they'd found. And he'd call Philip in the morning.

Philip held himself together as he climbed the steps to the hotel, managing a silent nod to Monsieur Bécot as he picked up his key. Upstairs he didn't bother flicking on the light, but once the door was locked, he released a long, wheezing breath. Sitting on the edge of the bed, he dropped his head into his hands, staring into the darkness at his feet.

His throat ached with a thirst that water could not quench.

As though obeying a greater force, he leaned forward from the end of the bed and opened the door to the minibar. The pale light illuminated his face. Inside, a squadron of metal-capped bottles stood like midget troops, ready for action. He reached in. Hell, he'd earned it. No one could say otherwise. He twisted off the top and eyed the golden liquid.

His cell phone rang. There was no one in Yvetot he wanted to talk to, and his first impulse was to let it go. But he recognized the number. Good old Jonas! Just what he needed. A voice from home, a few words from someone who understood him. He put the untouched bottle down on the nightstand and answered the call.

"Jonas," he cried. "I can't tell you how glad I am to hear you."

"Yes, me too," Jonas replied, his voice flat. "I'm sorry to call you like this. Do you have a minute?"

The tone put Philip on his guard.

"I need to talk to you," Jonas continued. "It's about Melanie Patterson."

When he entered the *Tord-boyaux* it was nearly midnight. The crowd was larger than during the day, though some of the patrons at the bar were the same, including the tweed-capped man Roger had identified as the mayor. Clusters of mostly male drinkers occupied three other tables. The room smelled of stale beer and smoke.

Silence rippled across the room as he came through, group after group going quiet. Philip felt the eyes upon him, but he didn't care. Let them do their worst. He ignored them all and stalked to the back, planting himself on a chair in the corner. When the *patronne* lumbered over, he didn't even hesitate.

"*Je voudrais un whiskey*," he said. Then he called her back and modified the order. He'd take the whole bottle.

The *patronne* didn't flinch. Who knows? Perhaps in Yvetot customers regularly ordered three-quarters of a liter of alcohol and drank themselves into a coma. That appealed to him. A coma sounded just about right.

At least Melanie had not succeeded. In the hotel room Philip had needed to steady himself on the bed while Jonas described how it happened. He'd been so shaken that it took a moment for the words to catch up with him, for him to realize she hadn't actually killed herself. During that prolonged instant, before he'd understood the crucial fact of Melanie's survival, he'd closed his eyes and felt himself in a free fall. He couldn't face losing another one.

A broad cross-cut through the left wrist. Not vertical—although that may have been sheer ignorance on her part. And Melanie was a quick learner.

As he drank, glass after glass, he felt himself begin to fade. The scotch made him translucent, almost transparent in this crowd. Heads that had turned to follow his arrival gradually rotated back to their original position. A few whispered comments sounded, a chair screeched against the tile floor, a call went out for another *demi*. Soon the café was alive with chatter. In the back, beyond the perimeter of animation, Philip slowly worked his way through his potion of forgetfulness.

He eyed the amber liquid in his glass, holding the tartness of each gulp in his mouth before swallowing. Then he let it burn.

They'd been making such progress. Just the other night they'd had their most honest conversation ever. They had moved forward. In his memory Philip replayed fragments of the conversation, holding words up to the light of his mind to see what he had missed, seeking the subtle inflections that might have hinted at what was imminent. Every utterance now seemed to carry a darker lining. *I still have stuff to do before I'm done*, she'd said. Done with what? And what else? Sometimes, she'd said, he didn't listen right. Sometimes he missed what was important. Not everything is fixable.

It was all there, and he hadn't heard. Melanie had been craving his help, and he'd failed her.

This on top of everything else. Morin. Le Mont de l'If. Bones. Yvonne.

It had been a fool's errand, this return to Yvetot. That night in Boston two weeks ago when the phone rang, Yvonne's voice had stirred something that slumbered inside him. It was like the rousing of a giant in a fairy tale, where the lumbering creature sets on a rampage, crushing everything in its path, stopping only when its appetite has been sated. But this giant was insatiable. It hungered for something it couldn't have.

He should never have answered that call. He should never have opened his eyes. What had Bécot said when he first arrived at La Cauchoise? *Ne réveillez pas le chat qui dort.* Let a sleeping cat lie. There he'd been in his apartment in Boston, old Edith curled up and purring at his side. And he'd let the cat stir.

He left the café at closing time, turning toward the hotel. Then came a stretch he would remember less clearly. At some point he staggered across the square, passing by shops, the bakery. His left knee hurt. He may have taken a fall or two. Yvetot was unsteady, listing. The pavement shifted under his feet, and so he sat for a while on the bench in front of city hall, by the war monument. He'd seen this sculpture a hundred times. A thousand. Mounted on a massive stone pedestal it showed a soldier of vast proportions, a helmeted colossus striding forward, wrapped in a greatcoat, his eyes lifted to the sky. And now Philip saw for the very first time that in his arms, the soldier cradled a small, limp body. Of all the possible representations of France's bloodiest war, someone had selected a scene of rescue.

His vision blurred, then cleared. It wasn't a child at all. Embraced against the soldier's chest and slumping over his shoulder was a sheaf of grain—an agricultural motif for all the young lives reaped in these fields. The shadows had played part of the trick and his mind had done the rest. You see what you want to see.

Eventually he tipped himself into motion again, staggering down the street, past the old hardware store, coming back around the big-bellied church, faintly illuminated by floodlights. Then it had been a series of back streets as he stumbled south along a road, watching as an enormous shadow loomed up before him, a monstrous silhouette, taller than a building, arms outstretched to embrace him. It was the shape of the tree outside the cemetery, black against the black sky. He followed the stone wall to the entrance, but the gate wouldn't open. Rattling it did no good.

Then he pitched off in another direction. Maybe he'd light out for the countryside. That's what he should do: keep walking. Go and never return. To hell with this town. To hell with people studying his every move. To hell with Hervé and Roger and Yvonne and Margaux—to hell with it all.

But the streets were up to their old deceptions, knotting themselves even more than usual, looping back toward the middle each time he thought he was headed for the open road.

Then he felt the nip of familiarity. He knew this street, this hedge. His legs were acquainted with the unevenness of the sidewalk. Even the shapes of the cars lining the street were known, friendly. Under his feet he felt the gravel of the driveway, and he knew the lawn, those front steps, the shuttered windows. It was the Aubert home, empty and asleep.

There was no need to find his way back to the hotel tonight. He dug in his pocket and pulled out the key Roger had given him.

Flicking on a table lamp inside made the downstairs navigable. The dust cover Roger had pulled off the sofa still lay in a heap on the floor. The cardboard boxes sat by the bookshelves, their flaps outstretched like wings. But something had been moved. In the kitchen the breakfast dishes were gone. Had Roger washed them? He didn't recall. Then, as he passed by the narrow opening of the service stairway he saw a glow upstairs. How stupid of him: he must have left the light on in the guestroom the other night. Someone could have seen it.

But when he reached the second floor no lights were lit. The glow didn't come from there, but from farther up, dimly illuminating the stairs, leading the way to the compact third floor, the level that held nothing but the tiny room with the dormer. Sophie's bedroom.

He tried to blink back the effects of the scotch. A creak sounded as he mounted the steps, but the old house was so full of noises that he wasn't sure what had produced it. As he turned the corner of the landing he saw the simple fixture in the third floor hallway above him, brightly lit. He continued his ascent, soon reaching the top. With an outstretched finger he flicked the switch down and the light went out. He flicked it up, and the light went back on. This was no dream. Physics worked too reliably.

At the end of the hallway the door to Sophie's bedroom stood barely ajar, a tall slit of darkness showing from within. It transfixed him. His heart pounded. But at the same time he had absolutely no doubt: he was going to open that door. There was no way not to do so.

Stepping forward, he reached out and the panel yielded under his finger-tips, swinging silently inward as the light from behind swept across the little desk, the chair, the rug, and finally the bed.

His breath caught in his throat. A body lay under the covers.

No, two bodies.

His eyes adjusted to the dimness. Huddled together on the single bed were Yvonne and Margaux, asleep.

Twenty-One

The moment Philip awoke, he regretted it. Beside the throbbing in his head, his tongue felt swollen, and a pain drilled into the small of his back. His knee hurt. He wasn't sure where he was, or what time of day it might be. Jet lag all over again.

Still reclined, he looked around, wincing at the crick in his neck. Instead of the high little window of his hotel room, here there was a broad expanse of glass, a thin soup of sunlight leaking around the edges of shutters. To the left were bookshelves. Voices sounded from another room, a ribbon of light shining beneath the door.

Then he remembered: it was the old house. He was on the sofa in the living room, the heavy dust cover pulled over him as a blanket. The rest came back to him in reverse order: Yvonne and Margaux, the scotch, Melanie Patterson, Le Mont de l'If, Roger, Édouard Morin.

He struggled to his feet, still dressed, needing only to pull on his shoes to complete the bedraggled uniform. He followed the sounds into the kitchen, surprising Yvonne and Margaux as they whispered over breakfast.

"He's up," Margaux cried, and she hopped off her chair to present her cheeks for Philip's morning greeting. "We've been tiptoeing around," she said. "It was quite a surprise to find you here this morning. We weren't expecting that."

Then she was back at the table, spreading jam on her toast and chatting nonstop. What a coincidence that they would both show up on the same night! How strange that he hadn't brought a change of clothes with him! Hadn't he been surprised to find them there? Didn't he hope they would keep the old house?

Yvonne was more reserved. Dressed in jeans and a cardigan, her dark hair unbound, she avoided his eyes, busying herself by sponging up crumbs from the table, then setting to scrubbing the morning's dishes with rapt attention. When Margaux dashed upstairs to change for the day, neither of them rushed to break the silence.

"You've been drinking again," she said finally.

He winced. Five years he'd kept himself under control. Five whole years. But there was no use denying it. He'd tumbled from the tightrope of sobriety, taking a spectacular spill.

He related as concisely as possible his chain of disasters.

"My God," she breathed as he told her about Le Mont de l'If, the bones. She sank onto a chair at the table, staring vacantly.

"The rest of the night," he continued, "well, it only got worse." He didn't care to discuss Melanie. Yvonne already had all the explanation she needed.

"So you ended up here," she said. "You had a key to the house?"

"Roger. He brought me here the other night. To keep me out of harm's way."

She nodded. "Not a bad idea. Ever since the stunt you pulled at the hospital, Hervé has been beside himself."

Philip didn't plan to be a problem for Hervé much longer. He understood the warning sign of the whiskey, of his own drunkenness. He'd have to get out soon while he still could.

"What about you?" he said. "What are you and Margaux doing here?"

She ran her fingertips along the edge of the table. "I needed . . . a little space," she said. "We came for the weekend."

Philip allowed himself a flush of privilege. For the moment Yvonne had turned away from Hervé. She was right there, sitting only an arm's length away.

Alone with her in this familiar kitchen, drinking coffee from these cream-colored bowls, he hovered between ease and awkwardness. When had he last sat at a breakfast table with Yvonne while a girl's footsteps pattered upstairs? He felt like a doppelgänger of his former self.

She stood and straightened the chairs, then vanished upstairs.

The silence was broken by his cell phone. It was Roger.

"Good grief," Roger began. "Where on earth are you? You had me worried. I just stopped by the hotel. Bécot told me you went out late and never came back in. And yet your car is still parked outside."

"I'm at your mother's place."

"Ah," he drawled, relieved. "I was worried Hervé had laid his hands on you."

"I managed to get myself into plenty of trouble without his help."

"Shall I swing by and pick you up?"

Philip declined the offer, then paused. "I'm pulling the plug, Roger. I can't do this anymore."

There was a silence before Roger spoke. "Look. Yesterday was bad."

"You don't know the half of it." Philip told him about Melanie Patterson, about her attempt to take her own life, about his own failure to predict it. Then there was the whiskey, the plunge into that familiar abyss. "You don't understand," he continued, curtailing Roger's protest. "I have other responsibilities. Back in Boston. I'm out of time, and I have less than nothing to show for it. I'm done here. I'm spent. And I've only made things worse."

Roger tried to argue, but Philip held fast.

There would be loose ends to tie up: airline tickets to purchase, goodbyes to be said. And this morning the police needed to fill out their report about the discovery on Le Mont de l'If, for which they required Philip's statement.

"Do you want me to come by?" Roger offered.

"I can get a lift." There was a pause on the other end of the line, and Philip supplied the explanation. "Yvonne's here."

Roger let out a long "ah."

"It's not like that."

"Of course not. I didn't say anything."

When he arrived back at La Cauchoise, Roger was engaged in conversation with Monsieur Bécot. The story of the previous day had swept through town like a galloping tide, and the man was hungry for details.

"Monsieur Adler!" Bécot called out as Philip approached. "I have heard it all. Imagine, right at Le Mont de l'If, not far from Monsieur Houellebecq's farm. After more than sixty years. And to think—the body of Raymond Desplanches! I knew him—or rather, his younger brother. He was from Auzebosc, just a few kilometers away. And his cousin lived right here in Yvetot. We always wondered what became of him."

Philip nodded stiffly. The story held nothing but horror for him now, and he had no patience for Bécot's fascination. Leaving Roger to finish the story-telling, he climbed the stairs to his sanctuary: the too-soft bed, the mildewed little bathroom, the ill-fitted window, the sack of dingy laundry, the sordid minibar. He showered and changed, then marched back down the uneven stairs, having made himself as presentable as possible in another gray-tinged shirt. His shoelaces still bulged with knots.

Roger accompanied him to the police station at the Hôtel de Ville. The man waiting for them was the lanky, long-nosed officer Philip had knocked heads with before.

"Good God," Philip muttered. "Anyone but him."

"Don't be so judgmental," Roger said under his breath. He called out to the approaching officer. "Good morning, Francis."

The officer gave a deferential smile and a bob of the head, shaking Roger's outstretched hand. "G'morning, Monsieur Aubert."

"Francis Boucher," Roger said, presenting the man to Philip. "Recently promoted brigadier in the Yvetot police."

"I've already had the pleasure of his acquaintance," Philip said icily.

"Not to mention," Roger continued, "a schoolmate of mine, from a thousand years ago."

Boucher pulled off his cap and scratched behind his ear, smiling at Roger's happy recollection. He reached his hand out to Philip, grinning broadly. "Good morning, Monsieur Adler. Nice to see you again, Sir."

Philip declined to shake, but instead of taking offense, Boucher laughed. "Oh, that's right. I suppose I owe you an apology, Monsieur." He chuckled again, and Roger joined him as Philip's scowl melted into a frown of perplexity. "You see," Boucher continued, pointing his thumb over his shoulder, "Monsieur Aubert here, he told me to play my cards close to the vest. He wanted me to keep an eye on you, but only to intervene if it was necessary."

Philip felt off-balance. "What are you talking about?" He looked at Roger, who winked back. "You don't mean . . . ?"

"That's right, sir. The tires, well, that seemed harmless enough, so I didn't want to pursue it. The rooster, though, that was something else. Still, I hadn't seen anything firsthand, and it wouldn't have helped to make enemies. So I thought it would be best to start with quiet inquiries."

Roger stood with his hands stuffed in his pockets, a satisfied look on his face. "Didn't you wonder why the police never came to your door after you wormed your way into the hospital? When Rouen called down here, it was Francis who took the call."

"Oh, don't mention it," Boucher said modestly. "I would have done that anyway—it was Rouen after all. The best news, though, is Raymond Desplanches, or what remains of him. You've brought one of our boys back, Monsieur Adler! That's bound to help. Word's already gotten around."

"It doesn't matter," Philip said. "I'm leaving."

Roger's smile soured. "You're still stuck on that idea?"

Philip turned to Boucher. "You need a statement from me?"

"Yes, please. It shouldn't take very long. But Rouen is quite insistent about it."

Boucher booted up an old computer, cracked his knuckles, then hunted and pecked his way through the menus until he found the right place to start. One by one he filled in the fields, typing up the answers with his index fingers. In Normandy they were so used to bodies and armaments coming to the surface of the earth that they had a specially designed form for it.

"There won't be any trouble about this from on up the line, will there, Francis?" Roger asked at the end.

"Oh, no, sir. I know how to file this so they won't ask any questions."

"Good man."

Boucher looked up at Philip. "They think we're a bunch of bumpkins down here, Monsieur Adler. In Rouen, they fart higher than their ass—pardon the expression—but we know how to handle them."

Roger clapped Boucher on the shoulder as they took their leave.

At the brasserie, Roger ordered a half bottle of Burgundy to accompany lunch, but when Philip grimaced, he paused, swallowed hard, and canceled the order, asking for mineral water instead. "You know, no one can blame you for falling off the wagon," he said. "It was a hell of a day. I knocked back a few myself." A wrinkle formed across his brow. "Of course, I always knock back a few." He picked up his glass of water, and studied it as if it were an unfamiliar beverage. Then he took a long sip, evidently not displeased with the taste. "You know," he said finally, "it's curious how ordeals like this push us back into old routines, isn't it?"

"What do you mean?"

"Well, you went and hit the bottle last night. Me, I called up Élisabeth." He cautioned with his hand. "Now, don't start reading all sorts of nonsense into it. It was just a call. But after our little adventure on Le Mont de l'If, I experienced this rather desperate longing for . . . well, I guess it was for *home*. And the craziest thing came to mind." He stared at the table. "I don't think she was delighted to hear from me," he said, "but at least she didn't hang up."

Could it be that some good might have come of this disastrous trip? For Philip it had been nothing less than a tortured odyssey. But if Roger was returning to port, that was some consolation. What was the old saying? Let heaven exist for others, though my own place be in hell.

That afternoon he called Air France. It was the peak of high season, and it would take two days and a small fortune to get a seat. He didn't care. Ever since ancient Greece, people understood that the dead had to pay their own passage to the underworld—and just as with Air France, the price had never been negotiable.

His cell phone buzzed several times during the day, showing Hervé's number, but he didn't answer. Roger called, but he let that one go, too. He wasn't in the mood to talk. At least, not in Yvetot or Rouen. It was time to turn his attention to the future. He phoned Jonas and let him know the time of his return flight. He got the update on Melanie. She was stable. He should give her a call soon, Jonas said. It might do her some good.

Unable to bear sitting alone in another restaurant while the eyes of Yvetot feasted on him, he slipped out and picked up sandwiches to eat in his room. Seclusion had other advantages, too. There was no sense denying that the old thirst demanded to be quenched. It was the mathematics of alcoholism: the difference between zero and one was a leap of astronomical proportions, but one to two was only a mincing step. He purchased another fifth of scotch at the supermarket. Alcohol would lubricate the clockwork, accelerating the spin and whir of the minutes, easing his wait until departure. After a solitary dinner he twisted the metal cap off and poured himself his first shot, and by the time the knock sounded on his hotel room door, just after ten o'clock, he'd already made serious headway. Nevertheless, he opened up, only to find Hervé Legrand standing before him, his feet spread in a pugnacious stance.

"You've ignored my calls," Hervé stated. "I tried you several times today."

"Good evening, *Hair-vay*." The words slurred in his mouth.

"*Er-vé*," the shorter man snapped. "When are you going to get that right?"

Accents. Pronunciation. Soon he'd be on American soil and no one would ever complain again about the way he spoke.

Philip stepped to the side to allow Hervé into the room, watching him cast his eyes over the mass of documents littered throughout.

"Yes," Hervé said, as he spied the open bottle, "I heard you'd been hitting the sauce again. Old habits die hard, eh?"

"What do you want, Hervé?"

"You just couldn't let good enough alone, could you?"

"I guess it all depends on what you consider to be good enough, doesn't it?"

"Don't be smart. All of this nosing around. And then that ridiculous scheme at the clinic. It's a personal embarrassment to me. Not to mention the shenanigans at Le Mont de l'If." He shook his head in disbelief. "You're making a fool of yourself. Moreover," he said, jabbing with his finger, "you broke our deal."

Philip looked down at Hervé's finger on his chest. "We had no deal."

"You promised you wouldn't upset my family."

"Your family is upset enough already," Philip retorted. "You didn't need me for that."

"You don't know what the hell you're talking about."

"Don't I?" He smiled. "Tell me, Hervé, where did Yvonne spend last night? Wasn't at home, was she?"

This pleasing comment brought Hervé to a halt, producing a new and fiercer look. The other man stepped back, looking Philip over as though measuring him.

"I've been extremely patient with your interruptions in our life," Hervé said, articulating the words sharply. "But that's over. I want you out of here." He left a pause. "Don't cross me, Philip. I know about all the irregularities. There are people in Rouen who can make things very difficult for you. Get out of town. Now."

"Or else?"

His hands closed into fists. "Or else I'll do what I need in order to protect my family."

Philip's first inclination was to snap back, to plant his hands on Hervé's shoulders and push hard. But then a different impulse overtook the first. *To protect my family*, he had said. Yes, there was a family at stake here. A daughter.

And as Philip thought about Margaux, the whiskey-induced swagger evaporated. There'd been Sophie. And Melanie. He had tried to help them all, but it was no use denying the results. Philip's touch was poison. For the time being Margaux was still safe, and at least Hervé knew how to defend her.

His arms, yearning to take a swing just a moment ago, now dangled at his sides. There was no sense resisting. He had his reservation back to Boston. He'd already given up.

"Don't worry," he said, his voice heavy. "You're right. And I'm packing it in."

Twenty-Two

It was closing in on midnight when he finally took his old position at the writing desk, steeling himself before placing the call. No board of ethics would find him at fault, but he knew where the responsibility lay. He'd been too absorbed in his own life. Too distracted. Too much a person, and too little a doctor. He had failed her.

He drew his hands back over his temples, running his fingers through his hair. It was time to put on the mask of the professional. He picked up the phone and dialed.

At the sound of her voice he gritted his teeth but managed to answer.

"Hello Melanie."

"Doctor Adler? Is that you?" Her voice was small.

He took a deep breath. "Are you comfortable?"

"I s'pose. As much as you can be when your wrist is, you know, all mummied up."

He pressed his lip between his teeth. "So, have they stuck an IV in you?"

"Yeah. Took 'em a while to find a vein."

"I hate those things." He cast about for a topic. He could do this. "And you're all alone now?"

"Well, Mom and Dad, they went down to the cafeteria. Thank God. And I don't have to have a roommate. Double-thank-God."

It was the same old Melanie, but she'd turned softer. He wouldn't push her, not today. The trick was to keep it light. Light he could handle. But then, before he had time to speak, a great gasping sound wheezed over the phone. It was a suppressed sob.

"Oh, Doctor Adler," she said, choking back the tears. "I'm such an *idiot*."

Philip drew the phone away from his mouth. He closed his eyes and felt himself breathe.

"It's all right, Melanie," he said when he could. "You're going to be fine."

"I couldn't even do *this* right."

"Don't say that."

"It's so *embarrassing*."

He needed a lever to lift her up, to lift them both, and he opted for irony. "Embarrassing? What do you mean? Trying to do yourself in? Or bungling it?"

It worked. Melanie gulped, and when she replied her tone was trying to meet his. "Geez," she said. "I mean, take your pick, right? How hopeless is that?" She blew her nose.

"Listen, Melanie. We've all been there. Not everyone acts on it, but everyone considers it."

"Even you?"

"Even me."

"Huh. Well, go figure."

He let her finish pondering his humanness. "So tell me," he said. "Have they given you anything to relax you?"

There was a rustle of sheets. She spoke in a hushed voice. "Well, they tried to give me some pills. But I don't do drugs. Honest, I don't. You probably don't believe me, but it's true. So I barfed 'em up right after the nurse went out."

That's my girl, he thought. "I see."

"What about you?" she said. "Do you do drugs?"

There she went again, trying to pry into his life. But there he was, still tipsy from the scotch, six time zones away, and conducting professional sessions from a bedroom in a third-rate hotel.

"I drink," he confessed. "Sometimes." He let the news sink in.

"Does it help?" she said finally.

"Not really. For a while I think it does. But it doesn't. What about you? Does cutting help?"

"About the same."

"Uh-huh."

A silence hung between them.

"Well, I'll be back soon," he said. "We can start up our regular sessions if you'd like."

"Wow. How exciting."

"Though if you'd rather work with someone else, I understand."

"Gee, I don't know. We've done such a great job, haven't we? I mean, just look how well I've turned out."

"Melanie."

She stopped. "All right. I'll try. No promises, but I'll give it a go."

He listened to the steadiness of her voice and thought she meant it. There might be other crises in store for them later, but he was pretty sure they'd made it through this one.

"Mind if I ask you something?" he said. "Last time we spoke, you told me that I don't listen well. That I don't hear what people have to say. What exactly did you mean by that?"

"I shouldn't have said that. I'm sorry."

"It's all right. But what did you mean?"

She hesitated. "Oh, you know. It's just a thing."

"What kind of thing?"

"Well, it's like . . . Do you play music, Doctor Adler?"

"You mean an instrument? No, I never learned."

"Boy, are *you* ever lucky. I did like a million years of piano. What a drag. But my teacher, well, she was pretty nice. I mean, it wasn't her fault I was hopeless. I hit all the notes and stuff, but she was never happy. She kept telling me not to rush. *Slow down*, she'd always say. And then one day she told me this thing I'll never forget. Remember, she said, the rests are just as important as the notes. Isn't that nuts? I mean, I always thought of the rests as marks to skip over, things to ignore. And then she came up with this zinger. I'd never thought about them that way. Some people, well, I figure they have a lot of rests. I dunno. Maybe that sounds stupid."

"Not at all."

The conversation lulled.

"Like that," she said. "Just now. That was a rest."

As they approached the end of the conversation, she slowed and veered. He could tell she was working up to something.

"Doctor Adler?"

"Yes?"

"I guess it's pretty hard to—" she began, then stopped. She tried again, more bluntly. "You know what my problem is, don't you?"

Her problem, he told himself, was down in the hospital cafeteria with her mother. "Yes. Yes, I think I do."

"And you know why it's . . . hard to talk about, don't you?"

"Yes. I know about that, too."

She paused. "I kinda figured you did."

Twenty-Three

The next morning, when he announced his departure to Monsieur Bécot in the breakfast room, the old man's smile faded.

"I'll be sorry to see you go, Monsieur Adler."

"Two weeks ago you were sorry to see me arrive."

Bécot wagged his head. "I know, I know. But since then, well, I've gotten used to you." He brightened. "And then you brought us back Raymond Desplanches! That was a sleeping cat, and you were right to wake it."

"So at least I've done a little good."

"Yes, but . . . there was more to do."

"True," Philip nodded. "I had wanted everything finished, but instead I am finished with my wanting."

Bécot sighed as he topped off Philip's coffee.

After breakfast he closed himself in his room. From his window he watched Yvetot come to life. The weekly open-air market was set up on the Place des Belges, a long alley of covered stands with vendors hawking everything from fruits and vegetables to frying pans and shoes. A knife-grinder had set up his wheel under one of the chestnut trees. Nearby a caner was at his stand, repairing a chair.

Standing at the window, Philip picked up his phone and called Roger. It was time for the ritual leave-taking.

"I was afraid that would be you," Roger said when he answered. "Tell you what, let's have dinner tonight. A farewell."

"I need to pack."

"Pack? What do you have? Three shirts and a pair of shoes? And frankly, you'd be better off tossing it all and starting fresh. We really should talk about your wardrobe at some point."

From his window Philip watched a gaunt cat approach the back of the butcher's stand down at the market. It poked its nose under the flap of the tarp, then slipped inside.

"Roger, please. Let me slink away."

The fact was, he'd already made the psychological break. His body was stuck in France until the next day, but his mind had crossed the border. All that remained was the cleanup crew, charged with erasing the trace of his passage.

"Fine," Roger said with defeat. "Be that way." His tone turned somber. "I worry about you, my friend."

"The feeling's mutual."

Down in the market the cat bolted through a seam in the tarp and vanished under a car. A woman in a bloodied apron pushed open the flap and scanned the surroundings, scowling.

Philip spoke. "Can I give you a little unsolicited advice?"

Roger sighed. "I supposed I'm not allowed to say no, am I?"

"I don't know if you'll work things out with Élisabeth or not. But whatever happens, don't end up alone. Don't let that happen."

"Hah. That's a bit like the straw and the beam."

"What?"

"Or whatever the idiom is in English—the tea kettle calling the pot black, or some such thing."

"We're not comparable, Roger. I'm in a whole different league. But you? You can still alter the course of your life."

The cat was trying again, this time at the fishmonger's. It crept toward a heap of trash, nuzzled between the crates, and soon trotted away, its tail erect, a red and stringy mass dangling from its mouth.

Roger was talking. "I seem to recall someone telling me that *anyone* can chart a new direction," he said. "What was the idea? You start with something very small—one thing that you can change. And you move on from there."

He didn't enjoy having his own words thrown back at him, but Roger was right. He'd spent too much time poking through the past the way old men rake leaves, compulsively, out of a sense of duty, continuing even when there's nothing left to do but scratch at the scalp of the lawn.

"So when do we see you again?" Roger said.

"I think it's going to be a while."

"I figured you'd say something vague like that."

They wished each other the best and made the usual promises about keeping in touch. *Au revoir* was what they said at the end, but Philip had to ask himself if an *adieu* wouldn't have been more appropriate. Realistically speaking, would he ever be back? It didn't seem likely. He shook his head as he pondered Roger's solitude, his broken relationships. Still, who was he to judge? One way or another, he figured, we're all broken vessels.

The call he couldn't make was the one to Yvonne. At first he'd planned to phone her after breakfast, then after speaking with Roger, then after packing. Finally he decided they could both do without a long goodbye. This trip had been filled with foolish ideas from start to finish, and it was time for him to disappear.

He ran final errands in town and stopped for lunch at the brasserie. People snuck glances at him, and there were hushed exchanges. They seemed to know he was on the way out. E-mail, telephones and newspapers were all superfluous in Yvetot.

At two-thirty he called the office back in Boston. No, he told Linda, he wouldn't need a day to recover. She should go ahead and fill his schedule. To the brim.

He thought about seeing Edith again. And there was the chess game with Faruk89 to get back to.

Last of all came the purge of documents. The clippings and copies and maps and photos he had accumulated made for quite a collection, and he leafed through them idly. After Édouard Morin's long seclusion in psychiatric facilities, he must have relished being the center of attention for a few days. Probably he had considered the visits a form of recreation. In the end, perhaps Philip had been nothing more than an unwitting actor in a drama he didn't understand.

The transcriptions and photocopies were all records that had been preserved in other locations. He let his copies tumble into the wastebasket. So much for the court files. Goodbye to Monsieur Guérin's handiwork. It was hard to let these papers drop from his fingers, but it also came as a relief.

The original photographs he tucked into his wallet. These he would return to the album behind the books on the bottom shelf of his living room. The little voice recorder he decided to keep. It could be used again.

Last of all came the cornflower-blue diary, with its clumsily sewn binding and cheap dragonfly imprint on the cover. Identical diaries could be found in any stationery shop or supermarket in France, and there was no reason to burden himself with this one. Still, it provided a record of his efforts. The pages told the emerging tale of Édouard Morin, with all his tics and oddities. And there were the tidbits he'd copied from the police reports, the judgment, the newspaper clippings, the affidavits. Interspersed throughout were his own interpretations: the discovery of S M A, the reflections on even and odd, the description of symptoms. Finally there were the extraneous entries—meeting times with Roger, short shopping lists, Yvonne's phone number, notes from his sessions with Melanie.

He couldn't let it go. Not yet.

His plan had been to hole up in his room until the next morning, at which point he'd pay his bill, drive the three hours to the airport, and lounge in the waiting area until his evening flight. But shortly after eight p.m., just after he'd succumbed once again to the temptations of the bottle, there came a knock at his door. When he opened up, it was Yvonne standing before him in a sleeveless blouse and dark skirt, a strand of silver around her neck.

So he'd have to face her after all. "*Madame le professeur*," he said. "What a surprise."

She put her hands on her hips and raised her eyebrows. "So you thought you could sneak away, like a common criminal?" The question could have been barbed, but her tone was light.

"Caught red-handed," he replied.

Then she looked past his shoulder, and her expression soured. The bottle of whiskey stood on his desk.

"What can I say?" he asked, forcing a grin. "Nobody's perfect, you know."

The words produced a reluctant smile on her lips. She took a deep breath. "Well, let's get going. We're already late for our reservation." She intercepted his protest. "Don't start, Philip. You didn't even call to say goodbye, so I took matters into my own hands. We're going to have dinner together."

He didn't need Yvonne's pity. And he'd already complicated things enough.

She rolled her eyes and tapped her watch. "Come along."

He cast about for an excuse. "What will *Hair-vay* say?"

"I couldn't care less what Hervé will say." Her chin was set, the line of her jaw clear. "Hurry up now. They're not going to hold the table forever."

Soon she'd forced him into his sport coat. He managed a knot in the tie he'd brought for Anne-Madeleine's funeral. She straightened his collar and flicked a bit of lint from his sleeve. "Well," she sighed. "I suppose this will have to do." They headed out, and she led him around the square to Chez Pierrot, Yvetot's sole gastronomic outpost, replete with heavy linens, and waiters as formal as fallen aristocrats.

Of all the manifestations of the French language nothing held greater terror for Philip than the menu of an upscale restaurant. They were more intricate than the babble of bureaucracy, more impenetrable than adolescent slang. The regional names and obscure ingredients made every meal a riddle, and more often than not he felt like Champollion in Egypt puzzling over the hiero-glyphs. As in the old days he let Yvonne order for the both of them.

He picked up the wine list. What the hell, he thought. It was his last night. But Yvonne plucked it from his hands and returned it to the waiter. "We won't be needing this," she proclaimed.

Then he understood. She was here to set him right. In the span of two short weeks he had managed to capsize the vessel of his life, fracturing its hull. She aimed to sling him into dry dock and undertake the repairs he'd need before heading back across the Atlantic. It was the old dynamic: he was a project for her. She could fix him up.

"*Salute*," she said in Italian as she raised a glass of mineral water.

He could play the game. "*Salute*," he replied, his Italian accent even worse than his French.

While they ate, he found himself capable of joking, and occasionally Yvonne's teeth flashed with laughter. They allowed themselves tentative remi-niscences, although certain topics—Morin, Hervé—they avoided by tacit agreement, falling back on their old knowledge of each other. After all, Philip realized, a shared history provides a kind of momentum. Or rather, a struc-ture. A comfortable routine. Novelty can be exhausting.

It was after eleven by the time they returned to La Cauchoise. At the front steps, as they said their goodbyes, he leaned in to brush against her cheek, and once there, he paused, lingering against her skin. They stood in this chaste semblance of an embrace for a long moment. What to do? He was leaving the next day, with no plans to return, and he had nothing to lose. Or everything. It was a moment for chances. For risk. For danger.

But he drew back. "I'll be sorry not to see Margaux before I leave," he said. "Give her my best, won't you?" He forced himself to add: "Hervé's a good man, Yvonne."

Her lips cracked with a smirk and she shook her head. "You're such a terrible liar, Philip."

"Well," he chuckled, "I confess that I toyed with the idea of telling him about your encounter with Morin—what you'd been prepared to do. It might give him a whole new respect for you. Just think how many marriages could be saved if only the husband knew how close at hand his wife kept a pair of scissors."

"Yes," she mused. "It would be good for men to realize things like that."

He whispered a hasty goodbye and left her in front of the hotel.

Twenty-Four

As he left the breakfast room the next morning, Monsieur Bécot called to him from the reception desk.

"Monsieur Adler! I did not realize you were in there. I just rang your room." He held out a sheet of paper. "You have had a call. The doctor from Rouen."

He unfolded the page to find Suardet's number, along with the request that he call back. Philip shook his head. His fingers closed on the sheet, crumpling it as he climbed the stairs. In his room he willed his hand to release the ball of paper over the wastebasket.

Then he turned his attention to his packing, assessing his possessions. Those drab, formerly white shirts—were they worth repatriating? The threadbare socks? The trousers with the ratty cuff? He set his suitcase on the seat of the old armchair.

While folding up his clothes, he felt the gaze of the Cyclops eye of wadded paper as it watched him through the mesh of the wastebasket. Who was he kidding? It wasn't in his nature to leave a stone unturned. He retrieved the sheet, and flattened it out on the rickety desk. He closed his eyes, pained. Then he pulled out his phone and dialed Suardet's number.

"Monsieur Adler." Suardet's voice rumbled.

"Doctor. I didn't expect to hear from you again."

"That, I assure you, would have been my preference." He explained he'd called only out of obligation—and, quite frankly, had hoped to be too late.

"I'm afraid I'm still here," Philip said. "What is it?"

"Édouard Morin has asked to meet one more time before you leave."

Philip felt a wave of exhaustion, a hint of dizziness. "Why on earth would I want to do that?"

"Oh, I agree with you entirely. I don't need to tell you that I objected to this request in the strongest possible terms." His voice took an edge. "Nothing you have done has been in my patient's interest, and since your last prank, Édouard has become extremely agitated. But he insisted I make the request and, despite everything, he has his rights. I'll be glad to tell him you have refused."

"What does he want to say?"

"I'm not a mind reader, Monsieur Adler."

"So there's nothing new."

"Not as far as I know." Suardet paused. "He did ask if you had any more information about the word *eyeshot*. That has been a particular preoccupation."

Eyeshot. The old fixation. The word had come up again and again.

He needed to make a decision. One way or the other. There was no middle path.

"My flight departs this evening," he said. "I was to leave Yvetot after lunch."

"I fully understand," Suardet replied. "I'll tell Édouard that you can't possibly—"

Philip cut the older man off. "What I mean is that if we are to meet, it will have to be today. On my way to Paris."

"It's not an obligation. And in fact—"

"I'll do it." He knew too well what it was like to live under the pall of what-ifs.

He wanted to stretch his legs before squeezing back into the little car and inserting himself into a plane for a transatlantic flight, so he headed out for one last wander. At the station on the north edge of downtown the first train of the day came through, depositing no one. The fountain in a small square bubbled. As the air warmed, pigeons began their shuffling and cooing. The bells rang in the campanile of Saint-Pierre. He hiked south, past the cemetery, striding under the shadow of the giant oak, then looped west, eventually arriving back at the main square by way of the skein of side streets. He'd gotten to know this town. He hadn't registered all the names, of course, didn't have Monsieur Bécot's deep sense of the families or Monsieur Guérin's knowledge of the history, but he recognized people on the street, he knew where the stores were, and he no longer got lost.

On the Place des Belges morning activities were in full swing, women moving along the sidewalks, shopping baskets rocking on their wrists or baby strollers rolling under their hands. Children raced along the street.

He stopped in at the *Tord-boyaux*. It was only ten o'clock, but they were all present, the greasy-haired mayor with the driving cap cemented onto his head, the fat man with the baggy trousers, the oversized *patronne*. Even Brigadier Boucher was present, drinking a beer in uniform. Philip nodded his greeting and worked his way to his table, the one tucked in a corner, partially obscured by a pillar.

He downed his coffee in three or four gulps, then called the *patronne* over to pay.

"What do I owe you?"

"Nothing, Monsieur."

"I'm sorry?"

She gestured toward the bar. "It's just been taken care of, Monsieur."

The motley regulars of the *Tord-boyaux* smiled their gap-toothed smiles in his direction, nodding their unkempt heads in a form of greeting. The two who were seated on stools rose to their feet. One of the men raised his beer glass high. "For you. For Raymond Desplanches," he said in heavily accented English.

Philip felt a pulse of warmth, a desire to forgive. Lifting his coffee cup in their direction, he gave them a nod. "*Merci,*" he said.

The others all raised their glasses. "*À la vôtre!*"

On his way out of town Philip passed the Yvetot public library, where he slowed and stopped. Inside, on an ancient computer terminal he hunted through the Internet, scribbling down notes in his diary. Then he headed off again, pointing the Smart Car south, entering the countryside and drinking in sights as he rolled toward Rouen past woods and low-slung farmhouses. The green of Normandy, he'd decided, was different from that of any other countryside, and he sought to commit its hues to memory. A gentle hint of rot hung in the air.

At the bottom of a hill, the road crossed a creek, and a hundred yards up he saw a man in rubber boots stomping along the water's edge with a youngster at his side, each with a fishing pole. They carried their bodies alike, walking in unison, one a miniature version of the other, following in the footsteps of generations before, playing the same trout, untangling the same lines, telling the same stories.

Once, a long time ago, Philip had been the age of that boy. And now, for the first time in a long while he thought of his own father. No, Max hadn't been an outdoorsman. But the décor didn't matter: they'd shared their moments.

It occurred to him that he would miss this country. He had reached that point in life when events are measured in terms of their likely repetition. How many New Years did he have left in him? Twenty? Twenty-five, if he was lucky? How many more visits would he pay to the coast of Maine? Three or four? How many more times would he see Yvetot, Roger, Yvonne, Margaux? Zero.

At the hospital he parked and made his way to Ward C, trudging up the steps one last time. Suardet waited in his office, his hands clasped. The two men exchanged a look, each resigned in his own way.

"For the record," Suardet began, "I'm not in favor of this."

"For the record," Philip replied, "neither am I."

"I don't like what you've done here, Monsieur Adler. Édouard has become nervous and jumpy. He keeps complaining of pains."

"In his tongue?"

Suardet slapped the table with his hand. "There's nothing wrong with him. We even did another scan." He leaned forward. "All in all, he's in much worse shape than before. And I hold *you* responsible."

"I won't be a problem much longer. My flight leaves at eight."

Suardet's mustache twitched over his lip. An evening flight clearly wasn't soon enough for his taste.

A few minutes later he found himself back in the conference room, seated at the table with Suardet at its head. Once more he placed the voice recorder in the middle. He opened up the diary and took out his pen.

When Morin entered, Philip's first impression was that they'd brought in the wrong man. He looked even more pale, subdued, and beleaguered than before. His shirttails were out and his hands were jammed in the pockets of his rumpled trousers. The usually groomed hair was disheveled and his bulging eyes were dull and darkly ringed. He offered no greeting as he took his seat—the same one as always—and he slouched in the chair, staring blankly at the surface of the table.

"Here you are," Suardet announced to the both of them. "For the last time. If there's anything that needs to be said, today is the day to say it."

Philip pressed the button on the recorder. Morin shifted, as if to reach and straighten the device, but then drew himself back, grasping the arm of the chair and squeezing it until his knuckles went white.

What followed was silence. It was the old problem of the opening move, the challenge Philip faced in every session with every patient, in every game with Faruk89. Not just a question of *how* to move, but also one of *whether*. In some ways the first move was always an attack, but there was also a small generosity in going first, a kind of concession. Taking the first step demonstrated a willingness to play. He decided to offer Morin that gift.

"I'm here," he said.

Morin stared back, still not speaking. He shoved his right hand back into his pocket.

"You wanted to see me, Édouard," Philip continued, "and so I've come. On my way out of town."

The other man showed no sign of listening, or even of hearing—as if a barrier of glass separated them, halting the words in midflight. The back of Philip's neck prickled. He hadn't come to be toyed with.

He turned to a page of notes in his diary. "Doctor Suardet told me you wanted an update on the word *eyeshot*," he said. At this statement, Morin glanced up. "You know," Philip continued, "language is an uncanny thing. Take an ordinary word, one you use every day, and if you stare at it long enough, it falls apart before your eyes. It sounds unnatural to your ear, and you begin to wonder if it ever really existed."

Morin nodded slowly.

"And then there's the opposite. A word like *eyeshot* sounds wrong to me, but the more I considered it, the more I thought it was perfectly normal, and that I'd used it all my life. You see what I mean? The familiar becomes strange, but the strange has a way of becoming familiar."

At least he had Morin's attention.

He held the diary in the air, showing the page of notes. "I did a search for that word on the Internet, so I have a little information for you—an answer to your question. It's old-fashioned and infrequent, but the word does crop up. It's used in just the way you thought."

Morin gave a nod halfway between understanding and appreciation.

Irritation nibbled at Philip. He'd made his offering. It was Morin's turn.

"Come now, Édouard," Suardet growled. "You made me arrange this meeting. Doctor Adler has come. It's time to say your piece."

Morin's face was slack, his eyes heavily lidded, his heavy cheeks rough with stubble. There was a sullenness to the way Morin avoided Philip's gaze, a hint of resistance or determination that clashed with the weariness of his slumped posture. Some kind of mismatch was at work: Morin had called for this meeting, but he had nothing to say. He'd made himself physically present, but he remained absent in every other way. His hand mashed the arm of the chair with nervous energy, but the rest of his body seemed unplugged. The whole situation smacked of provocation.

Philip kept his face calm, but underneath the table he clenched and unclenched his fist. Yes, he understood Yvonne's fury, wondered what he would do if he had her scissors now. Time was short. They were in the endgame, and still Philip didn't understand Morin's strategy—didn't even know if there was one.

Only one move seemed possible to him now: a surprise that might force Morin's hand. Not an attack—which would simply trigger greater resistance—but also not a retreat. More along the lines of an offering, like a traveler climbing up on Procrustes' rack of his own accord, inviting the villain to turn the crank.

Reaching into his back pocket, Philip drew out his wallet and retrieved the old photographs of Sophie, worn images of a young girl at play: on her bicycle, gripping the tennis racket, brandishing her arm in the cast . . . One by one he dealt these treasures of his own past out on the table like a deck of cards, ending with the double portrait that formed the Rubin's vase. Morin blinked and grimaced, shrinking from the pictures while eyeing them furtively.

"You know what it's like," Philip said. "You must have pictures of your father. I look at these, and for a little while Sophie is still alive. It's a trick of the mind, of course. A benevolent fraud. One I'm grateful for."

Morin wrested his eyes from the photographs and twisted away, his hands forced in his pockets, the feet of the chair scraping against the tiled floor.

Philip kept his voice calm. "You don't care for it, do you—the fact that she's not where she belongs? Too much play in the system, isn't it? More disorder than you're comfortable with." He took a breath. "I don't mind telling you, I don't care for it either. You once said we weren't so different, the two of us. Maybe that's true. We both appreciate symmetry. You've insisted that everything is already in its place, but you know that's not true. It's not close enough. Not for me, and not for you." He leaned forward. "And in a few moments I'll walk out that door, and it will be too late."

Morin's mouth broadened into a grimace and his brow thickened. It was the expression from the old newspaper clippings, the panicked boy Philip had seen fifteen years ago. He squirmed in his seat.

"Still nothing to say?" Philip continued. "Then let me do the talking." He paused. "You know what I think, Édouard? I think you study your languages and train schedules and maps of France, hoping that if you fill your brain fast enough, it will crowd out everything you don't wish to remember, everything you're trying to forget."

"Monsieur Adler," Doctor Suardet murmured.

But Philip pushed ahead. "The fact is," he said, "you can't forget, can you? The memories keep bubbling up, and you find ways to talk about them. It's like that story of the German blockades. Remember? Sorquainville, Malamare, and Adonville? I understood the connection to Sophie. I figured it out." Now was the time to press on the nerve, and Philip leaned in. "But I'd guess that's not what worries you. What keeps you up at night isn't Sophie, is it? It's your father."

Morin shook his head violently, issuing a grunt.

"That's out of line, Monsieur Adler," Suardet interjected.

"What's the matter, Édouard? Are you ashamed of the life you left him with? Can you imagine what it was like for a father to turn his own son over to the police? And to live forever as a pariah in Yvetot? You knew how it gnawed at him, didn't you? You know that you killed him—every bit as much as the cancer did."

"Monsieur Adler," Suardet snapped.

Morin had cradled his arms over his head, forming a helmet of flesh and bone, trying to fold in on himself. Philip knew he had only moments before Suardet put an end to the meeting. "You don't like to hear these things, do you?" he said. "When I showed up, it set your world in disorder, didn't it? I was a father, returning to the scene. Like your own father. Back to punish you. To punish you the way you wanted."

Morin rose to his feet, glaring at Philip, his eyes slits, and his arms curved with tension.

"Sit down, Édouard," Suardet ordered. "Monsieur Adler, that's enough."

"Isn't that right, Édouard?" Philip pressed, rising to his feet, too. "I under-stand how you've teased me along with your games and riddles. Taunting. Hoping that I'd do what your father should have done fifteen years ago. That's what you want, isn't it? Why don't you just say it, Édouard? Say it now. Go ahead and speak!"

Édouard's hands closed into fists.

"Sit down," Suardet barked at both of them.

"Speak!" Philip commanded.

But instead of speaking, Édouard swatted away the photos of Sophie, send-ing them swirling like leaves. His hand plunged again into his pocket, and it emerged grasping what appeared to be nothing. Then the light caught the jag-ged edge and Philip realized Morin was holding a piece of broken glass.

Now all three of them were standing.

Philip knew he should be afraid. After all, a man stood before him with a weapon. But his breath came easily, his heart felt light. Édouard Morin believed he held a threat in his hands, but to Philip, it looked like a blade of deliverance. He was ready.

"Just *say* it, Édouard," he repeated.

And at the instant Édouard moved, Philip realized his miscalculation. Morin raised the glass edge toward his own face, ignoring Suardet's cries. As he brought the weapon to his chin, Philip foresaw exactly how the flesh of Morin's neck would part, how the blood would surge. But then his arm rose even higher. His other hand was at his mouth, and too late Philip saw him pulling at the tip of his tongue, lengthening this long steak of flesh. Morin locked his eyes on Philip, and he began to saw. Blood flowed immediately.

Édouard Morin was cutting out his own tongue.

Suardet scrambled, bellowing for help. With surprising speed the old doctor rushed to Édouard's side, wrenching his hands away from the bloodied maw, struggling to restrain him. He called again for help while Édouard thrashed, making strange yawing noises. Footsteps clattered in the hallway, and soon the door burst open, two white-coated attendants hurrying in to help Suardet, wrestling Morin's arms down. The glass shard clinked to the floor.

As they dragged Morin from the room, blood dribbling from his face, he turned back to cast a final look at Philip, an indecipherable expression in his eyes.

Twenty-Five

Traffic raced by on the autoroute. The chalk cliffs of Normandy towered in the distance. Philip was at a wayside rest, sitting on a cement bench. On a stretch of grass families circled around blankets, picnicking. By the playground four or five children played tag.

He had seen his share of horrors over the years. He'd known people tortured by their own conscience. He had patients afflicted with unbearable pain. There had been those who, like Melanie, slashed their wrists or put a bullet through their brain. But never once had he seen a man cut out his own tongue.

No, Morin hadn't fully succeeded. An edge of glass wasn't a surgical tool, and Suardet had stopped him before the tongue was completely severed. But that changed little. What mattered was the staging. Morin had prepared himself for the encounter, bringing the props he would need. First he had kept silent, and then he'd underscored this silence in the most physical way possible. It was a performance played for an audience of one.

What did it say, this refusal to speak?

His elbows propped on his knees, he lowered his head into his hands. He couldn't worry about Édouard Morin any longer. All he would do is misunderstand, misread. The way he had fouled everything.

At the playground a knock-kneed girl cornered a boy with short blond hair, trying to tag him. He dodged with monkey-like agility.

Philip turned his thoughts to the coming week. There would be so much catching up. Jonas would want to know everything. Linda would have him scheduled to the gills. And he'd need to go and see Melanie—the sooner the better.

Philip shook his head. He heaved a sigh and dialed a number on his phone. "It's me," he said.

There was a long silence. "*Again?*" said Roger. "Shouldn't you be watching a bad movie right now—and choosing between inedible chicken or pasta?"

"I'm not going."

"It must cost you a fortune every time you fail to board a plane."

"I'm coming back."

"For once you have genuinely surprised me, Philip. I honestly wondered if I would ever hear from you again."

He ran his hand over his beard. "I met with Édouard Morin again, Roger. Today."

There was a creaking sound. Roger was sitting up, his voice alert. "You did what?"

"On my way to the airport. He'd asked to see me."

"What did he have to say?"

"Nothing."

"Nothing useful?"

"No. Nothing at all." Philip paused. "He cut out his tongue, Roger."

"What?"

"Not completely. They stopped him. But enough to make his point."

"Good God. What would make him do such a thing?"

"I'm not sure. But I need to find out." He stood up. "Do you know if Yvonne is still at your mother's old place?"

Roger was pretty sure the house was empty. "But if you're trying to stay out of sight," he said, "it won't help you much. People will find out. It's Yvetot, after all."

It was past midnight by the time the Smart Car rolled up the gravel drive of the Aubert home. Roger had left him the key under a flowerpot. The shutters on the house were still closed, and once inside Philip turned on as few lights as possible. Yvonne and Margaux had cleared out. The dust cover was back on the sofa, and more boxes had been packed. The kitchen, however, was better stocked, and Philip wondered if Yvonne expected to return sometime soon.

In the guest room he lay awake for an hour or more, listening to the familiar aching sounds of the house while he reviewed events. He'd done so much wrong since arriving in Yvetot—misunderstanding, misreading, mishearing, misspeaking. He'd lurched forward in missteps, and yet wasn't that, too, a kind of progress? He'd been wrong to question Roger's motives, but that allowed him now to focus entirely on Morin.

He slept fitfully, and when he woke it was mid-morning. After putting coffee on in the kitchen, he opened the shutters and windows looking onto the backyard. Sunlight and birdsong poured in. He spread his sparse materials on the kitchen table. Most of the documents had ended up in the wastebasket of the hotel room, and all that remained now were the photographs, the voice recorder, and the diary. On the one hand, he regretted having discarded so much. On the other, he could now narrow his focus.

Morin's cutting of his tongue was a testimony to the torment he'd experienced—the very same pain medical tests had been unable to explain. Suardet had claimed the symptoms were psychosomatic, which Philip found entirely plausible. That didn't make them any less real.

Nevertheless, a glossectomy—partial or total excision of the tongue—was a radical solution. In the case of a localized cancer, removal of the tissue was the price one paid for saving the rest of the body. But if the malady were psychological, the goal might be different; resection of the tongue eliminated the very possibility of speech. It was possible that Édouard Morin had wanted to say something he shouldn't, so he found a way to stop himself.

Melanie Patterson's words came to mind: Some people are full of rests.

Philip felt implicated in this act of self-mutilation. Morin had needed him to witness it. The cutting of his tongue annulled the invitation to dialogue, rendering it moot. Or mute.

So many of Morin's tics, his compulsive swallowing, his obsessions with language, his speech, even his humming pronunciation could be reduced to the single image of the tongue. All these tics were forms of expression.

Philip downed his coffee. Through the window he watched a thrush dip in and out of the hedge in the backyard. The grass needed mowing. The garden wall was missing some stones. Yes, there were chores aplenty in this old house.

Now he turned his attention to the wilderness of Morin's words. Carrying the digital recorder with him as he wandered through the rooms of the empty house, he let his attention drift as he listened. He browsed through the books in the study, climbed the stairs to the bedrooms, even ventured up to the third floor. The changes of scenery helped him hear differently. He held on to what he could, whatever felt connected, and the rest he let drain away.

There were the broad preoccupations: the infatuation with language, the problem of indirectness, the anxiety about order. And the quirks: the insistence on *eyeshot*, the references to history, the buzzing accent. Place names ciphered Sophie's initials, but they also alluded to Morin's concern with maps, limits and borders. *Es gibt Grenzen, die man nicht überschreitet.* There are lines one doesn't cross—such as the frontier between languages. Languages, Morin had said, were unfaithful—full of betrayals, like traitors of the fatherland.

Yes, translations were betrayals. But they were also accomplishments. Yvonne used to demonstrate as much. She'd throw up her hands in the middle of a project on Petrarch's verse, complaining that such-and-such a phrase was *untranslatable.* Then she'd take a walk around the block or have a cup of coffee, and sit back down and translate it. Translations were always failures that still somehow worked, achieving something other than what they aspired to. They were mis-accomplishments.

It was Yvonne who understood all about language, about the crossing of borders, the balance between words. He only knew about it from the outside. When he'd started learning French, he'd aspired to the ease and naturalness of a native speaker. But that was never going to happen. Far from it. His French was always a misfire that barely clipped its target. He could manipulate the vocabulary and grammar, but French would always be an appendage, not an internal organ. And as an appendage, it could be separated from him. Like a tongue.

Beneath it all lay Morin's pervasive preoccupation with evenness. Wasn't that somehow the key? Reality is always such a poor match for one's ideals, he had insisted. Nothing is perfectly even.

When he finished the recordings, Philip took the diary out to the back steps and sat in the sunlight by the overgrown lawn. His notes were more selective than the voice recordings, but they were also broader. Some items that Philip had originally marked with bold underlining now seemed unimportant. If he'd written in pencil rather than with Yvonne's black pen, perhaps he would now have erased these passages, reducing their memory to curls of rubber he could sweep away with his hand. Instead, he simply drew a line through them. They survived as a kind of residue.

There were also passages where the opposite had occurred. For example, Morin's first reference to his tongue, noted in passing on page five of the diary, had not initially drawn Philip's attention. Its importance became evident only with the passage of time.

He also wondered about what the diary lacked—the apparently trivial details he had not recorded anywhere, dispatching them to oblivion. Those items might look quite different now. In the haystack of police reports and court records, might there not be a needle he'd failed to recognize, one whose point would prick only when pressed in a particular way? Such traces were now lost and forgotten.

The sun was high in the sky now. A dog barked in the distance.

It occurred to him that this volume also told another story—one about a person never mentioned on a single page, but present everywhere: Philip himself. Like any journal, it reflected the writer's activities—the first meeting with Suardet, which days he met with Roger, where he was to pick up Yvonne. All these items were reported flatly, like a simple chronicle. Although the book in front of him was technically a diary, he'd not actually confided in these pages. Still, he could gauge his mood by the handwriting, which changed from page to page, now calm and upright, now turbulent and misshapen, now restrained but angry. Words were circled, underscored, and scratched out. On one page the letters S M A had three stiff bars of ink stroked beneath them. The corners of some pages were dog-eared, and margins overflowed with interpolated notes and exclamation points. Arrows and numbers linked passages together.

He'd not considered the diary in this light before. It had a main character—Édouard Morin—but it also had a narrator. Both voices spoke of the same subject. *You and I*, Morin had said, *we are not so very different.*

Philip dropped the diary in his lap and stared out over the yard. It was an outlandish notion. And yet, what had Philip done? For fifteen years he had occupied himself as best he could, living in a form of confinement that was no less solitary than Édouard Morin's. He had alienated himself from those he loved, had thrown himself into a profession that exposed him to the intimacy of other people's lives while forbidding him to share his own.

Oh, he could fence with Roger, could even talk around the edge of things with Yvonne. But what most needed to be said wouldn't pass through his lips. The problem wasn't French. It wasn't just language. It wasn't even Édouard Morin. No, the problem was with him.

Words did not mesh with things in Philip's life. Everything was a little off. Everything was always out of whack. It was simply a question of degree. When Morin had insisted at their very first meeting that Sophie's body was not *out of place*, he was undoubtedly right. It all came down to how much leeway you allowed.

Sophie's body. Even that was a dodge, a pretext. At first he'd told himself he owed it to Sophie to recover her. Then he'd wanted to protect Margaux. He'd convinced himself with all manner of noble thoughts. He hadn't needed Roger's slick salesmanship for this; he'd managed to con himself.

In fact, what had kept him in Yvetot was not his daughter. Sophie was gone. Bones or dust, it didn't matter. No, it was not something *missing* that held him there. It was something *found*. It was Roger. Yvonne. Margaux. Bécot. Hell, even Hervé. It was the feeling of belonging, of being tied to something once again. Of walking down the street and sensing that, for better or worse, someone cared. Or at least noticed.

Sophie had been a convenient excuse. But he'd used her as a screen. He'd fudged the truth the same way Morin had fudged geography, pushing the German blockades a little to the left or the right.

If only he could have been more like Yvonne.

The buzz of his phone interrupted the stillness of the garden.

"Hello there," Roger called out the other end. "Say, I just thought you'd want to know: Hervé is on the war path."

Philip closed his eyes and tried to think. "This is no business of his."

"Well, I'll be the last person to side with him. But you did take his wife out for dinner. And someone says you actually embraced her outside the hotel. In the States, I believe such matters are settled with firearms."

"As far as I know, it's not against the law for me to be in Yvetot."

"I suppose not," he drawled. "Not at the moment, anyway."

"What's that supposed to mean?"

"Well," Roger began, "there was the little matter of sneaking in to see Édouard Morin. And then . . . the falsification of documents."

"What are you talking about?"

Roger cleared his throat. Hervé was well connected in Rouen, and he'd managed to lay his hands on the letter they had fabricated for the Bureau of Records in the courthouse.

"It was a simple request," Philip protested. "They could have turned it down."

"Well, it appears he has reported it to the authorities."

Philip heaved out a breath. These tactics exhausted him. He would have been delighted to meet Hervé face to face and have it out once and for all. A duel sounded about right. But as the offended party, the choice of weapon went to Hervé, and he'd already chosen the one he was most skilled at: bureaucracy. Nothing in France was so clumsy and ponderous as the machinery of the administration, yet once put in motion, nothing could be so hard to stop. It wasn't as swift as a blade or a bullet, but it was powerful, inexorable. The complaint would work its way through the chain of command, and someone would come knocking.

"What's going to happen?" Philip asked.

"Well, nothing—right away. I spoke with Francis about it—Brigadier Boucher. He figures they'll send orders to the police station, and he'll be required to bring you in for questioning. He also said he expects to have a great deal of difficulty locating you."

"I'm at your mother's place."

"As I said, Francis thinks it may be hard to track you down." There was a voice in the background. "What?" Roger called out to someone at the other end. "Oh, right." He addressed Philip again. "He says, especially if your car is kept off the road."

He was up in the guest room stuffing clothes in his bag when the phone rang again. From the number he saw it was Yvonne, and he decided to let it ring. A moment later, though, it began anew, and he realized she wasn't going to give up. Maybe she was worried. Maybe, like Roger, she wanted to warn him about Hervé.

"Yvonne—" he began.

"What's going on? Why on earth are you back?" she said, her tone more plaintive than angry.

He sank onto the bed. In fits and starts he told her about his visit with Édouard Morin, about the self-mutilation, about the gagging noises coming from the man's throat. Certainly these were the most proximate causes for his return, but they didn't really address her question, and the very fact of this failure to answer underscored for him the real problem.

From the wall of the bedroom, photographs stared at Philip, a collection of Auberts at different ages in different times—Anne-Madeleine, Roger and Yvonne, Évelyne and Flora, aunts, uncles, cousins, spouses. Even when they weren't blood relatives you could see the resemblance, all part of the same family, community, culture, language. One figure stood out from the others, present only in a few of the shots: a bearded man who was too tall for the group, dressed like a foreigner, carrying his body differently, as though he required more space. The odd one out.

"I understand Édouard Morin," Philip said into the phone. "I know what it's like for him."

Yvonne bristled. "I wouldn't wish that on anyone."

And yet it was true. In a strange way, he felt close to the man. He tried to explain this to Yvonne, the problem of tongues that slipped, tongues that were tied, mother tongues—all those situations in language where he failed to find the right word.

"Don't even think that," she said in a rush. "You're nothing like him."

But he was. He kept putting one thing in front of another, masking how he really felt, expressing everything indirectly, looking for one thing when he should be looking for another.

"You have nothing in common with Édouard Morin," she repeated firmly. "Do you hear me? *Nothing*."

Which is when he surprised himself by saying it.

"I still love you, Yvonne."

The conversation ground to a halt.

He nodded to himself. *That* was why he'd come back. Out of the need to say this. One way or another, he'd had to utter those words. Otherwise he might just as well have cut his own tongue out, for there would have been nothing else worth saying.

When she finally responded, her voice was a whisper. "I know you do."

He lay out in the garden, draped over a chaise longue in the sun. How good it felt to be outdoors, away from Monsieur Bécot's little hotel room! His eyes were closed, and he'd been reliving the life of back then. Why not? Hervé's minions would find him soon enough. There was nowhere to go in the meantime. Besides, since his call with Yvonne, he'd concluded his work in Yvetot. He was at ease. Let them come; he was ready.

In his mind he played the footage of seven-year-old Sophie running across the brand new carpet with muddy shoes. Then there'd been that disastrous—and hilarious—birthday dinner. Next came the images of the Christmas circus they attended when she was nine, when Sophie had watched slack-jawed as the contortionist backed her head through her own legs. Then came the bicycle lessons, followed by the tennis games.

And then there were the other sequences, *after*. The police. The funeral. The court. The arguments. The end.

He shifted on the chair. The sun had gone behind the trees, and there was a chill in the air. He thought about Sophie's tomb. The wilted flowers. The first lines of lichen creeping over the top. The grave. Her name—formed not by the application of ink or paint, but by the presence of a void, by grooves in the stone. Engraving: a form of writing that spoke through absence. Just as Melanie Patterson had said: the rests are as important as the notes.

I can tell you exactly nothing, Morin whispered, *or nothing exactly*.

And then, although he was no longer trying to see anything at all, he opened an eye. Then a second. A moment later he found himself sitting up.

What if saying *exactly nothing* was a way of speaking? What if silence was not the refusal to communicate, but in fact the very vehicle of expression—its voice, its tongue?

A first example of this had occurred when Morin referred to Sophie by way of three French villages: he had named her silently. And this practice had continued as he dipped and swerved into other languages, ceasing to speak in one so that he might shield himself with another. At each transition, everything shifted—everything except, perhaps, for one thing: the buzzing accent that carried through all of Morin's languages, the one that hummed through everything he said.

This accent—if that's what it was—had remained a mystery, and Philip had paid no attention to it, for accents had nothing to do with the meaningfulness of language. Or so he'd thought. But then Roger had lectured him about how much accents matter, what they reveal about the speaker. Yvonne, too, had seconded this: accents were *complicated*, she'd insisted. They were part of language and yet outside of it. Time and again he'd seen firsthand what his own American twang signaled to other people.

He plodded back into the kitchen and pulled out the recorder, listening to a snippet of Morin's words. He repeated the buzzing accent with his own voice, hearing his missteps, correcting them, and trying again. Once he figured it out, it wasn't so hard. Aside from the lilt of French in the background, or the exaggerated burst of British, it consisted simply of the elimination of the sound produced by the letter S. Whenever a word risked hissing, Morin's vocal cords came into action, turning the S into a Z.

He sat down at the kitchen table and reached for the diary. Turning through the pages, he recited phrases that Édouard had uttered, trying to imitate his humming voice. At the end he came to the list of aphorisms pronounced in the library of the hospital. *The kernel of our grief*, he read out loud, and something in the phrase rang odd. He tried another: *I am the boy of my father*. This, too, harbored a kind of strangeness. One by one Philip marched through the six phrases, reading them with Édouard's accent. *The apple fell near the tree. A king gave law by an oak. We each carry a burden. The Calvary, a likely mount.*

What stood out about these sentences was simply that Édouard's humming accent did not affect them, and suddenly Philip understood why. The linguistic contortions that replaced simple words like *son*, *seed*, and *cross* with more unusual forms served one purpose alone: they avoided every single instance of the sound associated with the letter S.

The diary fell from his hands onto the kitchen floor.

Somewhere in Rouen Hervé Legrand was turning the crank of bureaucracy like a monkey at a barrel organ. Perhaps the cogs were already spinning and wheezing. Francis Boucher might be sitting in the Yvetot police station, his feet on the desk, ignoring the e-mails from Rouen as they pinged in his inbox. Philip might still have a little time, but it would be measured in hours, not days. Worse, he wasn't sure where to start. He had a voice recorder, a diary, and the letter S, a squiggle of a sign that meant nothing at all—but that Édouard Morin had gone to great pains not to say.

What does it mean to look for a letter? Most of the time language floats over the surface of the world, but every now and then a connection sprouts between words and things—the way upholstery buttons tether fabric. Philip understood that a connection existed between Édouard Morin's language and the space within which he lived. He just didn't know where to find it.

Cruising through town in the Smart Car, he studied street signs, the curve of walls, the designs in cast-iron fencing. Even the layout of roads in Yvetot felt like a kind of writing, with thoroughfares inscribing shapes on the tablet of the land.

Anyone who found his car would know just how far Philip had gone, so he ditched it in a side street. Not that it would help very much. A six-foot-three foreigner couldn't keep out of sight for long in a French town.

S struck him as the key, as the only possible solution to the problem Morin had presented. But he didn't know where to find the lock that this key would open. It was meaningful only in Morin's intensely personal language, for which there existed no dictionary.

So Philip searched as he walked, circling Saint-Pierre, striding through the commercial district, studying the monuments and fountains. Very quickly he discovered that the problem lay not in detecting the presence of the letter S in Yvetot, but rather in sorting through its superabundance. The town teemed with S's: from the signs of stores to the names of streets, to the words Philip overhead in conversations. Yvetot positively whistled with sibilants. The letter was everywhere, in ways he would never have expected: in the curve of a metal brace in the masonry wall; in the F-holes of the violin displayed in the music store window; in the rippled slide of the playground off the main square; in every instance of the number 2 or the letter Z seen in reverse through the back of shop windows.

And because S was everywhere, it was essentially nowhere. Nothing distinguished one instance from another. No occurrence of the letter brought Philip any closer to the images Morin had carefully clustered in his cryptic phrases: Saint Louis, the cross, the Calvary, the son, the sorrow, the oak. He felt infinitely closer than he had been at Le Mont de l'If, but it was a closeness that left him nowhere. A *non-lieu*.

Soon the sun foundered on the horizon and Yvetot sank into the shadows of dusk, letters becoming harder to read in the dim light. Even with Boucher's obstructions, Hervé would be closing in. Perhaps they would by now have dispatched police straight from Rouen. Night was falling, and he had no option but to interrupt his search, a pause that would in reality mean a full stop. At this point there was nothing left to do but wait. The authorities would escort him back to Paris. They would put him on a plane. Hervé would make sure he couldn't return. In twenty-four hours he would find himself in Boston again, where he'd have to try to lower the lid on his past once more.

The first streetlights flickered on as he passed the entrance to La Cauchoise. What the hell. If Hervé was going to appear at any moment, he might as well finish things right where he'd started, in the lobby of the old hotel. He climbed the steps and pushed through the wooden door. Bécot stood at the reception, as stout as a sea captain.

"Monsieur Adler," he said, greeting him with actual warmth. "I heard you were back in town."

"I see you've followed the news, Monsieur. I'm afraid I'm here for a very short time."

"Oh yes, I heard that, too. It sounds like Monsieur Legrand will find you very soon. That is what they all say."

"Then I suppose he may as well find me here." Philip slumped into one of the armchairs in front of the desk. The old craving was back. As long as he was on his way out, maybe he'd top it off with one last shot. "I don't know if you remember, Monsieur Bécot, but the very first night I arrived in your hotel, you offered me a drink."

"That's right, Monsieur Adler. Of Calvados."

"I'd take a glass of that now, if you're still offering."

"But of course! It will be a much more pleasant way to wait." He disappeared into the back room and reemerged with a bottle and two glasses.

"Would you like some company?" he offered.

Bécot poured the vaporous liqueur, then settled into the armchair opposite Philip. The two men clinked their glasses.

"To S," said Philip.

"What is that?" Bécot asked.

"S marks the spot. The target. The bull's-eye. It's the place I couldn't find. Anyplace. Or no place."

Bécot nodded as if it all made perfect sense. "I have never heard of such a place."

"Neither has anyone else." He rolled the alcohol in his glass, warming the bowl with his hand. He took a swallow, wincing as it burned the back of his throat. "In some ways it will be good to put this behind me. As you said at the very beginning, one should let a sleeping cat lie."

"Yes. I think that's often best."

"I'll let Yvetot take care of itself. You don't need me for that."

Bécot nodded. "As I always say, Yvetot is a dying town."

"A dying town. That's right." Philip could already feel the powerful Calvados seeping into his system. He forced a bitter chuckle. "I thought of that when I saw another tomb from the same year as Sophie's. One family after another. It's as if the people of Yvetot are all lined up, just waiting their turn."

Bécot dipped his head this way and that. Maybe yes, maybe no. He wasn't disagreeing. Then he furrowed his brow. "Who was it?" he asked.

"Who was what?"

"The tomb you have seen, the one from the same year as your little girl? I'm trying to think back. It was 1993, no? Perhaps Josiane Perrin? No, Josiane would have been in '95, I believe." His face lit up. "Perhaps it was old Fenouil?" Then he caught himself. "*Non, non.* I think, he was the year before."

In fact, Philip didn't remember the tomb clearly. It had an arched top with a cross emerging at the peak. Not too far from Sophie's. With the name he'd seen bleeding through on the hardware store sign. The same one that was close to Sophie in Guérin's registry of births and deaths.

"Haus?" he said. Even before Bécot shook his head, he knew that wasn't right. But it had that kind of ring to it, a heavy, German-sounding name with an H. "Hosse?" No, that wasn't it either. Then it came to him. "Hesse," he said.

Bécot stared blankly. "But there is no one by that name." He thought hard, then his eyes brightened. "Wait—I see, Monsieur Adler, it is your accent."

Of course Bécot was right. There he'd gone again, aspirating the H, just as he did each time with *Hair-vay.* He opened his mouth to correct this error, eliminating the initial puff, and the sound that escaped from his lips was simple and short: "S."

"Ah, that's right," the old man was saying, finally recognizing the name. "It is the Hesse family. They lived here for quite a long time. Young Bertrand, he was never . . ."

While Bécot trailed off in reminiscences, an idea began to crystallize in Philip's mind. Hesse. S. He'd separated these words by the thinnest of sounds, the breath of the H, that most vanishing of letters. Édouard Morin's words played back in his ear, every S abuzz, sentence after sentence. But there was static in these recollections, interference from Bécot's voice in the background. The old man was still talking about the family, something about a woman named Gisèle, and then a man called Julien.

"Good Yvetot people, they were," he said.

Bécot had known them, of course. After all, he knew everyone in town, past and present.

But the S of Hesse was too miraculous to be an accident. It called to Philip like a siren's song, an SOS. "Where do they live?" he said, interrupting the old man. "Here in town, or out in the country?"

"Live?" Bécot looked astonished. "Why, they live nowhere, Monsieur Adler. Did you not hear what I said? They are all in Saint-Louis."

Philip narrowed his eyes. Saint Louis was the king who dispensed justice under an oak tree. Guérin had told them where they might find sculptures of him. "What do you mean?" Philip pressed. "That they all moved to America?"

"*Non, non.*" The old man brushed away this idea with both hands, as if shooing a cat. "They are in Saint-Louis," he said, nodding toward the south. "The cemetery. Julien Hesse, he was the last of them. It's what I tell you all the time. Yvetot is dying."

Hesse. Saint-Louis cemetery, the crosses, the Calvary.

"Monsieur Bécot, I need a flashlight."

The old man's mole eyes glimmered at Philip behind his glasses. "Whatever for?"

"I have one more stop to make, if there's time."

Bécot heaved himself out of the chair and trudged behind the reception counter, pulling out a yellow plastic flashlight. He flicked it on and off. "How extraordinary! It works!" he said, handing it to Philip, who was already making for the door.

Across the Place des Belges Philip nearly ran into another man on the walk, one of the regulars from the *Tord-boyaux*. It was the tweed-capped mayor. The man slowed to examine him before tipping the brim of his hat and moving on down the walk. So much for anonymity, even in the dark. He soon followed in the same direction, but as he rounded the corner, there was the mayor again, now standing under a streetlamp, speaking to, of all people, Hervé Legrand. Philip shrank back into the shadows as he watched the two men converse, the man from Yvetot nodding to the one from Rouen, saying *oui, oui*, and then gesturing off into the distance. The mayor was sending Hervé in the wrong direction, and Hervé thanked him enthusiastically for the misinformation.

This small act of charity would buy him a little time. He hurried across the road and headed south. He knew the route. Crossing the main thoroughfare, he curved around behind the church. From there it was a straight shot south, leading to the place he knew all too well. Soon, against the dark sky, the shadow of the giant tree rose before him. Saint-Louis at the foot of an oak.

Under the blackness of the branches Philip could scarcely make out the movement of his own hands. The cemetery gate was locked for the night, but he hoisted himself up on the stone ledge, felt for places to grip, then swung over the metal grating on top, catching his left thigh on a spur of wrought iron. He stifled a cry and let himself drop down. Rising from his crouch on the gravel, he felt the side of his leg. The fabric was torn, the leg tender, gouged.

The cemetery was dark but not black. The moonlight illuminated the sea of stone vessels, crosses listing to the right or left like the masts of sea-tossed ships. He had a rough idea where to look. He had passed it before, had walked on the very spot. Following the path between the rows of tombs, he limped by the war monument, where the flaking statue of the angel of death rose above him in the beam of his flashlight. Further and further back he went, finally turning at the maintenance shed, past the tomb of Anne-Madeleine, all the way to the reddish stone he knew so well. *Sophie Marie Adler, 4 février 1979–2 juillet 1993.*

That was the center. What he sought would be to the side, or a little in front. He didn't remember exactly. One by one he swept the flashlight over the names on stones as he spiraled outward, widening the radius of his search, his leg throbbing.

In the distance came the pulsing wail of a siren. Rouen must have been putting pressure on Boucher.

He checked his thigh in the beam of light. The cloth was saturated, glistening with blood. But he pushed forward, extending the search one more row, and then another beyond that. He fanned out the beam of his light to read the names of the tombs on either side.

And then he found it, a family vault, the one he had seen before, the name *Hesse* chiseled in tall, broad letters at the top. The last name on the list read

Julien Hesse, décédé le 27 mai 1993. This was what had caught his attention days earlier, because of the date, the same year as Sophie's death, just weeks before. And here it was, only twenty yards from her grave.

As he hobbled back to the maintenance shed, beams from headlights splashed over the stone wall at the far end of the cemetery. Brakes squealed to a stop and car doors slammed. That would be Hervé, along with his helpers. The gate rattled.

Philip rifled through the tools in the shed, selecting a hoe. Back at the Hesse tomb he worked to pry the metal edge into the seam between the stone lid and the base. As he leaned into it, the pain seared in his leg and he stopped to clamp his hand over the wound, feeling lightheaded.

He returned to his task, forgetting even the throbbing now. He shoved harder with the hoe, finally thrusting the tip under the edge of stone, working the handle like a lever. With a grunt, he lifted the slab a fraction of an inch and heaved it to the right, leaving it askew. Dropping his tool, he placed his right foot at the corner of the stone, leaned and shoved, trying again, throwing all his weight into it. Finally the slab ground across the surface of the sepulcher, sliding halfway open, enough to reveal the black cavity.

Voices sounded from the far end of the cemetery and lights bobbed in the distance. Dusting his hands on his trousers, he picked Bécot's flashlight up off the ground. He paused for a last moment, looking into the night sky, then tipped the beam of the light down, shining it into the cavity. And he looked.

Whatever else one might think, you had to admire the genius of it. Nothing was out of place, Édouard Morin had insisted. At least, not beyond a certain tolerance.

Because the Hesse grave had already been disturbed for another funeral just weeks before Sophie's death, no one would have noticed the signs of Morin's additional deposit in July of that same year. And because Julien Hesse was the last member of his family, no one was going to disturb this vault again for a very long time.

Morin had hidden Sophie Marie Adler in the one place they would never think to look. He had put her where she belonged. Almost. Just a stone's throw away. Within eyeshot.

Twenty-Six

He woke in the middle of the night in a large and unfamiliar bed. Across the room the wind teased the gauze curtain over an open window. A hint of moonlight glinted on one wall, the corners lost in shadows. It wasn't the room at La Cauchoise. Was he in Boston? Then came a groan of rafters overhead, the creak of a branch rubbing against the house, and he knew. The room was emptier, quieter than it should have been. His leg hurt. He slid his hand toward the right, finding only cold mattress. Where was Yvonne? Perhaps upstairs, checking on Sophie?

The double wrongness of this thought troubled him as he slipped back into sleep.

It was the throbbing of the leg that woke him the next time. Now the room was bright. He recognized the dresser, the shelving, the pictures on the wall. It was the guest bedroom in the Aubert home. Beyond the closed door, from down the hallway, low voices sounded.

He thought to get up, but the deep ache in his thigh put an end to this plan, and he flopped back onto the pillow.

The memory of the previous night returned.

The voices had stopped, and Philip heard footsteps approach. When the door cracked open it was Roger's face that appeared, showing a hint of concern that dissolved into a smirk.

"Aha," he said. "The mummy wakes."

"I'm afraid so." His voice was thick. "What time is it?"

Roger slipped in. "Nearly noon. I'm glad to see you're finally adopting the French work schedule."

"I slept eleven hours?"

"It's the painkillers, don't you think? How's the leg? Do you need another serving?"

At first Philip declined, but as he shifted again, he gasped. It was like a blade plunging into the muscle.

Roger picked up the pillbox from the night table, and rolled a tablet onto his palm. "I thought I might be able to sell you another one."

Philip took it without protest. "Who's out there?" he asked.

"Francis Boucher. And Yvonne. Beauty and the Beast—though not necessarily in that order. Do you feel up to seeing them?"

"I think so."

Roger stopped at the door, paused, and turned back to Philip. "That was a good thing you did, you know. A hell of a good thing."

The brigadier came in first, looking as bashful as always, his cap in his hands. "Good morning, Monsieur Adler. How are you feeling?"

"Better than last night."

"That's the Vicodin," Roger said. "Narcotics are such a wonderful invention."

"What's the news, Francis?" Philip asked.

"Well, we've been busy," Boucher began. "According to the coroner, those are almost certainly your daughter's remains."

Philip nodded. "When I saw the healed break in the bone, I knew what I was looking at."

"They're running some additional tests, just to be sure," Roger added. "It's a waste of time, of course, but it turns out there are protocols for this sort of thing, aren't there, Francis?"

"That's right, Monsieur Aubert. Unfortunately. It's all from Rouen, you know."

Philip raised himself up, and offered his hand to Boucher. "Thank you for your help."

"Oh, I didn't do very much."

"I hope I haven't landed you in hot water with your superiors."

Boucher grinned. "I try not to worry about them, Monsieur Adler. Besides, Monsieur Legrand isn't pressing any charges. How could he, given the circumstances?"

Roger chimed in. "I'd been hoping for a little tarring and feathering, in keeping with that grand American tradition. But it appears I'll be disappointed."

Between the shoulders of the two men, Philip caught sight of Yvonne in the doorway. Roger and Francis went quiet, eyeing each other.

"Say," Roger said to Philip. "How'd you like something to eat? A piece of toast to go with your drugs?" He was already headed out.

"Would you like a hand with that, Monsieur Aubert?" Boucher called as he darted after him.

They spoke for a long time. After the first halting descriptions of the previous night, they turned instead to remembrance. A burden had lifted, and Philip found there was pleasure to be had in conjuring up portions of the past. The memories were still there, preserved under their dust covers. It was possible to peel back a flap from time to time and expose them to light.

Strangely, the discovery of Sophie's remains now seemed unimportant to him. It was at most a kind of tidying up. All the hard work had come before.

And then, for a longer time, after words were exhausted, they sat quietly in the old bedroom. The pill Roger had given him made him drowsy, and he slipped in and out of consciousness. Each time he came to—a minute later? an hour?—Yvonne was still there, sitting on the edge of the bed or in the chair, or standing by the window.

After sleeping much of that day, he grew restless at night. It didn't help that Roger, the self-appointed nurse, was snoring loudly in the next room. Finally he gave up on sleep and limped downstairs, sitting down to drink a cup of tea in the halo of light at the kitchen table. There lay the old voice recorder. And the diary.

So he'd finished the job he'd started fifteen years ago. Not that there was much to show for it. Still, Sophie's remains would be moved twenty yards to the south, to the tomb bearing her name. Her empty grave would finally be occupied. He hoped it would mean something to Margaux for her sister to have been laid to rest. Moreover, he had himself learned a few things. Reforged old connections. For all this he could thank the one other person who had found Sophie's fate as unbearable as he, and with whom he felt an awkward kinship: Édouard Morin.

Philip was familiar with the mechanisms of guilt. Many of his patients struggled with this emotion. Some were paralyzed by it. Others wielded it as a weapon. What differed in Morin's case was this extraordinary delay, the fact that he had kept a lid on his shame for so long, nearly fifteen years. Even when he had begun to reveal the truth, he'd done it indirectly, punishing himself for each revelation.

On his way back to the bedroom he paused before the mantel, where the portrait of Guillaume Aubert looked down. Maybe the old man would have felt more kindly about him now?

As Philip lay in bed, it astonished him to realize that he felt no hatred. In fact, having come to understand Édouard, he could no longer even imagine him as his daughter's killer. His mind could still call up the scene—Sophie twisting on the ground, the dirt and weeds, the thrashing of arms, the muffled cries, the whimper—but try as he might, when he followed the imagined man's hand to the wrist, the wrist to the sleeve, the sleeve to the shoulder, he couldn't make the face resemble Édouard Morin.

They say that understanding is forgiveness, but this didn't even feel like a pardon. It felt like the setting aside of a verdict.

It was sleep that provided the final piece. He woke early in the morning with a feeling of certainty. How had he failed to understand? He needed to return to Rouen, one last time.

By six a.m. he had showered, shaved, and dressed. Roger still snored in the other room, and Philip let him continue. Outside, he backed the car around and pulled onto the road, heading south.

Fog slumbered in the hollows of the countryside. He drove past farms just beginning to stir with the morning. As he slowed in a hamlet, the shutters of a window split open, pushed by a red-haired woman in a nightdress. Finally he curved around the last stand of trees, and the great wheat-colored hospital came into view, the long wings spread across the hilltop.

He arrived at the ward far too early to meet with Suardet, so he haunted the waiting room, fueling himself with espressos from a vending machine in the hall. Shortly after nine o'clock the doctor appeared, his mustache quivering with irritation at the sight of this visitor.

"What are you doing here, Monsieur Adler?" The old doctor sounded bone-tired. "Why won't you leave this poor man alone? You can't think I'd really allow you to see Édouard Morin again?"

But it was with Suardet that Philip wanted to speak.

"Fifteen minutes. That's all I'm asking for. Then you can turn me away."

"I don't have time for this."

"Where can we talk?"

Suardet's shoulders sagged. "You just don't know how to let go, do you, Monsieur Adler?"

"You're exactly right. That's one thing I have never learned."

The doctor shook his head, and with reluctance he pushed open his office door and led him in.

There Philip told Suardet the story as he understood it, pointing out Morin's tics and habits, explaining the indirect communications, the evident desire to speak, the reluctance to reveal, the limits Morin would not cross, the allegiances he bore, the compulsion to even things up, the struggle to accept that which remained asymmetrical.

"I don't need Morin's psychological profile," Suardet interrupted. "You're not telling me anything new."

Philip leaned forward in his chair. "What if I said that Édouard Morin is innocent? That he never killed my daughter?"

Suardet's jaw slackened, and Philip began his explanation. Édouard had tried to tell them this, and in so many different ways. Philip had understood it first in Morin's exaggerated British accent. *I'm nawt at libuhty to discuzz thiz any fawther*, he had said. *No fawther at all.*

"Why this switch?" he asked Suardet. "There was nothing British about what Morin had to say." In fact, he explained, what had mattered was the accent. Morin needed to take advantage of the vanishing R. *Fawther* became a way to utter one word masked as another.

"What are you going on about?" Suardet demanded as he looked at his watch.

"Don't you see? Édouard also referred to French as his father tongue, and he always spoke of the fatherland—which he feared languages might betray."

Suardet frowned, and Philip continued. There was all the wordplay. *Nothing compares to a parent*, Morin had said. *I understand the despair of parents. They aim to repair the irreparable.* "The rhyming word here is *pair*," Philip said. "Which means *even* in French—the very evenness that is so dear to Édouard. And yet it's also *even* with another word, with which it is paired in a very odd way. By sound alone."

"*Père*," breathed the doctor, troubled. He peered at Philip. "But that's madness."

"Precisely. And this is its grammar. *I am the boy of my father.*"

"But Olivier Morin is *dead*, Monsieur Adler."

"Not for everyone. Not for those who live by his law."

Philip explained what he believed to have taken place. Édouard would have been nothing but a substitution, a proxy. A pawn used in a gambit. Sophie had been raped and murdered by the father, by Olivier Morin. Édouard would have surprised him in the act. The father then threatened his own son, swearing him to secrecy. Probably Édouard Morin had moved the body himself, almost certainly without his father's knowledge. He was a smart boy, so he did what he could to make things right, to even them up. Then Olivier Morin made Édouard take the fall for the crime, and the boy accepted his father's law. He revered Olivier, could not break his promise to him, and agreed to be sacrificed in the place of another. To bear that cross. To mount that Calvary. Which meant avoiding, at all costs, mentioning the name of the grave where he had placed the body: *Hesse, S*, and all words containing that sound.

"The secret held as long as the father was alive," Philip continued. "He could maintain control over the boy at the same time that he shielded him from the prying of others. But after Olivier's death, over the months, the father's imperative thinned. Édouard began to look for a way to communicate the truth, but to do so *without saying it*. He wanted to make things right, even to tell us the location—but without breaking the vow of silence he had made to his father."

Suardet gaped. Philip could see him searching for objections, but the weight of conviction was settling upon him.

Finally the doctor spoke. "Even if all this were true," he said, "what do you propose to do about it?"

"That's obvious, isn't it?" Philip said, spreading his palms outward. "Édouard Morin needs to know that his message has been received. The entire case should be reopened. At the very least, his innocence should be recognized. He needs to understand that he no longer has to bear this burden."

Suardet folded his arms over his chest and creaked back in his chair, gazing at the ceiling while he thought. He nodded, paused, nodded again. His eyes thinned, and he looked back at Philip. "But don't you see?" he said. "That's precisely the one thing you must not do."

It was Philip's turn to be taken aback. "What do you mean?"

"Look, Monsieur Adler," the doctor said. "I'm glad you've found what you were looking for. I really am. But think about this clearly. There are two possibilities here, and they both lead to the same place. If you're *wrong* about Édouard, then you have nothing to thank him for, nothing needs to be said, and nothing changes."

Philip nodded. "Yes. But if I'm right . . ."

"If you're *right*, the very last thing you can do is reveal it."

Philip began to protest, but Suardet lifted a hand. "Consider this," the doctor said. "Édouard reads the newspapers. He'll know you have found your daughter, and that's all the news he needs. But if he learns that you understand how she got there, that you have deciphered what he has tried so hard *not* to say, then he'll have broken his oath to his father. That's how he'll feel. You know it is. He'll see it as a betrayal. As you said, this promise means more to him than anything else."

Philip opened his mouth, but words failed him.

"From where I sit," Suardet continued, "it would appear that Édouard Morin has given you a tremendous gift. And the only possible way for you to reciprocate is by not acknowledging it."

Philip searched for the flaw in this logic, but Suardet was right. Either Morin bore the public guilt for a murder he didn't commit, or he suffered a deeper and more private guilt for betraying a man who had never deserved his trust. One guilt would gnaw at him every day of his life, but the other would destroy him. It was a Hobson's choice, and both men knew how it had to go. It wasn't fair. It might not even have been legal. But Philip would have to keep silent about what he thought was the truth. There was no way to even the situation up. His intuition about what had really happened in July of 1993 would have to go unconfirmed. The most generous thanks he could offer Édouard Morin consisted of swallowing hard and not seeking an answer to this lingering question.

The two doctors exchanged handshakes, and Philip took his leave, heading down the hall toward the exit, passing before the observation window looking into the commons area of the ward. The room on the other side of the wired glass teemed with patients, a few seated at tables, playing cards or dominos, others engaged in solitary activities. A woman with auburn hair sat in an armchair chatting vividly with no one Philip could see. A stooped man paced like a bear in a zoo, walking along the back of the room, reaching out and touching the wall with his index finger before turning in the other direction. As two patients moved to the left, they revealed a man hunched over a table, a large volume open before him: Édouard Morin, the man who had been so *eager to help*, who had wanted everything in its place.

Philip turned and headed for the exit.

Twenty-Seven

It took one more day to *complete the arrangements*. In reality there was nothing left to prepare. The grave had been waiting for years, its occupant long overdue. Family didn't have far to travel. Father Cabot had ample time in his schedule.

In short, they were standing on ceremony. The delay allowed Philip and Yvonne the time they needed to steel themselves.

He told Yvonne his suspicions about Édouard Morin's father. She deserved to know. And when he finished his explanation, she was convinced he was right, but she also saw the bind that led to Édouard's purgatory. The one person who should be punished was already dead, she said, and you can't free a man imprisoned within himself. Some things were simply not subject to resolution, like the great tortures described in Antiquity—Sisyphus rolling his stone for all eternity, Ixion spinning on his wheel of fire, Tantalus always reaching, never grasping. Then there were all the scenes from Dante. Yvonne had plenty of examples.

Philip made other preparations, squaring the details of his return with Jonas and Linda back at the office. He placed another call to Melanie Patterson, now home under the fretful supervision of her mother. When he apologized for his delay, she replied with indifference. Her old shield was up, a force field designed to repel human interaction. The fragile bond they'd formed during the last call was barely holding. After hanging up, Philip sighed. Such was the measure of progress in his line of work: two steps forward, one step back—on a good day.

They held no service at Saint-Pierre. That ceremony had occurred fifteen years earlier, a grand performance where the main role had been played by an empty black casket. All they needed now was a simple observance at the cemetery to mark the arrival of Sophie's remains, and to allow those few who still remembered her a chance to lower their eyes.

Philip had the clothes for it. After all, when he'd appeared in Yvetot nearly three weeks earlier it had been for Anne-Madeleine's funeral. Although his coat sleeve missed a button, his shirts were dingy, and his glasses sagged with a blackened Band-Aid, he at least had an appropriately funereal necktie.

On the afternoon of the service, the sky was overcast, the clouds the same color as the stone of the cemetery. Cars rolled into the parking area at the base of the giant oak one by one. Philip arrived first. Then came Roger, in the same car as Élisabeth. They weren't arm in arm, but at least they were together. While she fussed with the bouquet of flowers, Roger strode across the gravel parking area.

"I'm glad to see her here," Philip said, nodding back at the car.

Roger shrugged. "Don't make too much of it. We've been back together before. It's a yo-yo relationship. Still, who knows? I'm going to give it a try." He checked his watch. "Nearly time," he said.

Élisabeth now joined them, the flowers in her arms. She kissed Philip on the cheek.

"Did you hear?" she said. "Évelyne's not coming."

"Really?"

"Says it's too far. Says she'll stop by the grave the next time she's in Yvetot."

Roger looked up at the clouds. "Old cow."

Flora and Pierre arrived. Then came the green Mercedes. Hervé emerged first, going around to open the door for Yvonne. She steadied herself on his arm and glanced a greeting in Philip's direction. Then from the back, out popped Margaux, slender in her sober dress, her black hair clenched in a tiny bun.

Philip kissed Yvonne on the cheek. Hervé extended his hand, and Philip took it.

"No hard feelings?" Hervé asked awkwardly.

"No hard feelings."

Margaux stepped forward. "Hello, Uncle Philip," she said, presenting her cheeks to be kissed.

Philip leaned forward and the two exchanged pecks. He found himself smiling. The touch of those light lips, they made everything worthwhile.

"It's okay if I call you Uncle, isn't it?"

"Certainly. Better than okay."

"Because I had a big conversation with Mother about it. Since there isn't a word for what you are, we decided I could just choose one."

"Does that mean I get to call you my niece?"

Margaux's smooth brow puckered for an instant. "We didn't talk about that." She brightened. "But I guess so."

Hervé pushed open the gate to the cemetery and the group began to move forward. Margaux offered Philip her hand, and he walked with her up the gravel path.

"I think it's a very good thing that you did," Margaux said. "Even though it's kind of creepy."

"Creepy in what way?"

"Well, it's odd having a sister—a half-sister—I never met. I didn't like to think of her being dead, and especially lying somewhere we didn't even know. But it's also kind of weird to be glad to have found her. Do you know what I mean?"

"Oh yes. I know exactly what you mean."

They'd made their way to the far end of Saint-Louis. Father Cabot waited behind the stone of the tomb. He had rubbed up against sepulchers and crosses on his way in, and was now slapping at the dusty smudges on his robe.

Sophie's casket had been lowered into the vacant spot earlier that day, the granite lid already moved back into place. Aside from the wreath set on a metal stand, the tomb appeared the same as before: the same grave with the same stone serving the same purpose. The only difference was the invisible sensation of fullness.

Cabot opened up his Bible and took out a page of jotted notes, squinting at them, then rotating them right side up. The group of five had formed a semi-circle around the end of the slab, heads down, waiting for Cabot to begin.

Behind, in the distance, Philip heard footsteps. Coming up the gravel path was a beefy woman he didn't know. Or rather, that he *did* know, although he wasn't sure how. Her eyes gleamed, and suddenly he realized it was the *patronne* from the *Tord-boyaux*. She halted some twenty feet back from the family, standing with her hands clasped.

The grate at the entrance of the cemetery screeched again, and another person began marching up the gravel path, a tall, balding man with a lanky build. It was Francis Boucher, the Brigadier. He gave Philip a two-fingered salute as he came up even with the *patronne*. Again the gate sounded, and two more entered in the distance, then three more after that, followed by a string of others. There were people of all shapes and sizes, men, women and children, old and young, dressed in everything from farm coveralls to their Sunday best. They congregated two and three rows back, keeping a respectful distance. Soon there were twenty or thirty people, and more were on their way. Men pulled their hats off as they approached. Women smoothed down the fronts of their blouses and clasped their hands. Philip recognized Guérin in the crowd. Monsieur Bécot. The greasy-haired mayor—the tweed driving cap removed, clutched in his hands. The whole crew from the bar. The butcher and his wife. The woman who served him at the bakery. The man from the hardware store. The farmer he'd crossed paths with at Le Mont de l'If. The boys he'd seen playing soccer, along with their parents. And scores of others he didn't recognize, that he wasn't sure he had ever even seen—the owners of all those pairs of eyes he had felt on his back every time he made a move in Yvetot, every time he turned around or took a step or sucked in a breath. They were all there.

Yvonne stood by his side.

Margaux's hand squeezed his fingers.

And then Cabot began to speak, stumbling over the opening remarks and tripping over the names. Soon he moved into the safer territory of a reading, breaking open the book and flipping through the pages. As he warmed up, getting into the rhythm, the priest's voice began to rise and fall in a lilt. It no longer mattered what he had to say. Philip tuned out Cabot's words and listened only to the singsong tones, the voice, the accent, while he looked down at the red-brown slab before him, reviewing everything that had taken place, all the possible futures that had been lost. Behind him was the crowd from Yvetot, standing in silence, turned out for one of their own. And in Philip's right hand lay the lightest of weights, the delicate and almost imperceptible pressure of a young girl's fingers.

There were handshakes and easy conversation in the parking area. Philip worked his way through the crowd, exchanging remarks with Roger, embracing Élisabeth and Margaux, shaking hands with Francis Boucher, Monsieur Bécot, and all the regulars from the *Tord-boyaux*.

Through the crowd he made his way to Yvonne, who stood by the stone wall. He came before her, his hands driven into the pockets of his sport coat.

"Feel better now?" she asked.

"A little. Maybe." He knew enough not to expect miracles. "It's something," he concluded. "What about you?"

"The same."

They hunted for words.

"You need to hit the road, don't you?"

She was right. His flight was at eight. "I'm afraid so."

"Will you come back? To visit?"

He nodded.

A silence stretched between them. He leaned forward and kissed her cheeks. Then he drew his hand from his coat pocket and held out the black pen with the Rouen University logo, the one he'd borrowed the day at the notary. "You lost this," he said.

She frowned at the pen in his hand, then, remembering, smiled. She closed his fingers around it, pushed it back. "A souvenir."

The route to the airport led through Rouen, so he made one last stop in the center, strolling past the medieval half-timbered houses and along the edge of the Old Market. Yvetot could say all it wanted about the big city, but at least Rouen had a strong connection to centuries past. On those stones Henry V of England had walked. Here Joan of Arc had burned. There was the birthplace of Flaubert.

Soon Philip would be back in Boston, working with Jonas, helping Melanie, feeding Edith. Faruk89 would be waiting for his next move. But perhaps he'd add something. A simple tweak. Just a small one, at least to start with. Something new. Something manageable.

Before him rose the great cathedral, at one time the tallest building in the world, its cast-iron spire soaring into the sky. Once again, at the north portal, he found himself before the sculptured panels of the Last Judgment, crowded with demons, damned souls, spits and cauldrons. Mouths gaped in masks of pain, hands rose in protest, flames flickered. And at the bottom, out of view from the guardians of this inferno, the same desperate soul clawed his way upward, striving to clamber up over the edge of hell, tipping back toward the flames. For over five centuries this figure had been frozen in the same pose of imbalance, reaching up while falling back. Still trying.

Acknowledgments

My thanks, first and foremost, to Anne Maple, who believed in this book when I myself was riddled with doubt; then, to Michael Kidd, Greg Johnson, Uli Frick, Laura Goering, John & Kelly Wheaton, Martine Reid, Victoria Skurnick. Another serving of gratitude goes to my son, Paul Carpenter, for photographic help, many useful insights, and general camaraderie. Finally, thanks to Jessica Kristie and the rest of the crew at Winter Goose Publishing for their many contributions.

About the Author

Scott Dominic Carpenter teaches French literature and critical theory at Carleton College (MN), where he has written extensively on the representation of madness in the novel, political allegory, and literary hoaxes. His fiction has appeared in such journals as *Chamber Four, Ducts, Midwestern Gothic, The MacGuffin, Prime Number* and *Spilling Ink*. A Pushcart Prize nominee and a semi-finalist for the MVP competition at New Rivers Press, his first collection of short fiction, *This Jealous Earth* (MG Press) appeared in 2013.